The Surrogacy Trade

The Gaia Machine, Volume 1

V.M. Andrews

Published by V.M. Andrews, 2019.

This is a work of fiction. Similarities to real people, places, or events are entirely coincidental.

THE SURROGACY TRADE

First edition. August 4, 2019.

Copyright © 2019 V.M. Andrews.

ISBN: 978-1393905790

Written by V.M. Andrews.

Dedicated to anyone who wants a kinder world for all forms of life on our beautiful home planet, Earth.

With deep gratitude to Andy, Jane, Kat and Dee whose enthusiasm, encouragement and finely-tuned critiques helped me to finish this book. This is only the beginning ...

Stratford-Upon-Avon

FOR THAT FRACTION OF a second between sleeping and waking, Ophelia felt peace and euphoria. But as she woke more fully, the bubble burst like a boil, filling her with the sick reality that it really *had* happened. She had not dreamt it. The loss was real. She felt like a broken shell, washed up on the sand and left to fade under the blinding sunlight.

'Ophelia,' said Gaia, in its usual silken tone. 'It is time to get up.'

But Ophelia was not ready to respond.

'Ophelia,' said Gaia, vibrating the bed this time.

'What!'

'Ophelia, it is time to get up,' Gaia repeated, lifting the duvet into the air.

'Okay, Gaia! I'm awake now!' Ophelia snarled, rolling onto the floor.

She watched the duvet flapping about in the air while the base sheet stretched and flattened against the mattress. When the duvet returned to her bed, plumped and perfect, Ophelia sprawled across the floor, taking comfort in the sensation of its surface, which dipped and bulged to the exact shape of her spine. She slid her hands across her belly, a place that had once held so much hope. But she could almost hear it weep with grief.

'Do not forget your stretches, Ophelia,' said Gaia.

An expletive rushed from Ophelia's belly to her throat, only to be reabsorbed in silent rage. But, as always, she obeyed The Gaia Machine. She rolled onto her belly, flexed her wrists and slid her hands down beside her shoulders. She pushed her torso up then back and down, performing the downward dog pose. Rage burned through every muscle, joint and fibre in her body, forcing her to hold the pose more strongly than she had ever done before. Then she

1

brought her feet to her hands and gently unrolled her spine until she was standing upright, facing her bedroom window.

Watching the curtains open and the window become more transparent, Ophelia felt like a precious bird in a cage; its benevolent owner removing the cover for her to see the light of day. She stepped closer to the window and stared down College Street. Its neat row of redbrick houses and transparent bubble-shaped vehicles with red wheels all looked the same as they did the day before. And the day before that. And for as long as she could remember.

'You must get ready now, Ophelia,' said Gaia. 'You cannot be late for your appointment.'

Ophelia dawdled over to her en-suite and stepped into her shower chamber. When the gentle hum of the sonar commenced, she closed her eyes and tried to relax. The sound swirled around her, delivering a tingling sensation to every millimetre of her skin. But, when the tingling became a tightening, the sonar stopped.

Gaia's timing was as impeccable as always.

'Your shower is complete,' it said.

Ophelia stepped out of the chamber and faced the mirror, barely recognising the face that stared back at her. It was the face of a sad and lonely woman with an absent husband and a dead baby.

• • • •

THE TRAFFIC ON THE bridge was gridlocked. As far as Ophelia could see in both directions there was a long queue of vehicles. All the same, and all controlled by Gaia, they would not move until Gaia considered the road conditions safe enough to move them forward. To the left, Ophelia watched the River Avon trickle downstream, where it terminated in a muddy puddle. To the right, she gazed up at the Royal Shakespeare Theatre standing proud on the riverbank, its reflection almost as majestic as the building itself. She recalled seeing *Othello* there the previous evening and enjoying it, despite its use of holographic actors. She had always loved Shakespeare's plays, because they had both logic and substance, unlike the stories produced by Gaia's algorithms.

'We are slightly delayed, Ophelia,' said Gaia.

'That's fine.'

As Gaia rolled her vehicle forward a few metres, Ophelia considered the absurdity of talking to this disembodied entity. This global, omnipresent entity that could simultaneously converse with everyone in their homes, cars and workplaces while completing several million social service transactions per second was speaking with her now as if it was another person. Just as it always had, for as long as Ophelia could recall, it spoke to her as though it knew her better than she knew herself.

Yet, for reasons she could not quite grasp, Ophelia continued to share her thoughts with the machine. 'I'd love to see a real performance one day,' she said. 'One in an outdoor amphitheater with real actors.'

'That is not necessary,' Gaia replied. 'As a Professor of Literature, you have superior insight into the structure of stories and as a woman with social status, you ...'

Ophelia stopped listening. She knew what Gaia was going to say next because it had said the same thing many times before. It would be informing her that, by controlling her life, it was protecting her status as a person of privilege. She could not listen to another one of its paternalistic monologues. Not today.

When the vehicle finally moved forward, Ophelia could see the outer edges of the town; a sight far less picturesque than its beautiful centre. By the time they reached the intersection to the A46, she noticed the remains of hundreds of tall trees. Still standing, but withered and brown, they seemed defiant in the face of continued drought and relentless heat. As the vehicle turned onto the A46, Ophelia felt its wheels expand and its centre of gravity lower. Then, with an open stretch ahead, it accelerated so fast that she could no longer see the trees, only a long brown blur.

'Are you ready for your appointment, Ophelia?' Gaia asked.

'As ready as I'll ever be,' Ophelia replied, checking her bracelet for messages.

'Are you nervous, Ophelia?'

'No. Why?'

'Your heart rate is elevated,' Gaia replied.

Ophelia placed her hand on her heart. It *was* beating faster than normal. 'I guess I'm anxious about going to the cancer care centre,' she said. 'This will be my first appointment since the hospital gave me the diagnosis.'

'That was four weeks ago today,' said Gaia.

'Yes, I know, Gaia,' she replied. 'I'm not likely to ever forget that day.'

With her hand still on her heart, Ophelia reflected on the moment of waking from the anesthetic. Seeing the impassive silicone face of the medibot, and its liquid black eyes peering over her, had been disconcerting enough, because she had never consented to the anesthetic and she could not even recall having it administered. When she had asked if she had fainted, the bot had explained that her womb had been removed due to the presence of an aggressive tumour – two horrifying pieces of news in one sentence. And as the anesthetic had worn off, she had realised a third, and even more, horrifying fact – when they had taken her womb, they had also taken her unborn baby of nine weeks' gestation. She had howled like a mad dog.

'Ophelia, please confirm you are all right,' said Gaia.

'I still can't believe it,' Ophelia whispered. 'They took the best part of me, without my consent, and I can never get it back.'

A hard lump of grief stuck in Ophelia's throat like a cactus. It was a constant source of pain and a powerful reminder of what would happen if she dared to express that pain. Her eyes filled with tears, but the emotion froze in place.

'This must be what hell feels like,' she said.

'It was unfortunate,' Gaia replied.

'Unfortunate? Is that what you call it?' Ophelia said.

No matter how many times she had explained, Gaia could not grasp her feelings. How could it, she mused, when it had no feelings of its own? It suddenly occurred to her that, with Gaia as her only source of companionship during the last four weeks, it was little wonder she had started to feel she might be going mad.

'I can't believe it,' she whispered.

Gaia responded in the only way it knew how. 'You were always aware of your social responsibility to pay a poor woman from the southern countries to be a surrogate for you,' it said.

'Gaia, I've told you many times that I don't approve of surrogacy, and that's not going to change.'

'It is the most fundamental building block of human society,' Gaia replied.

Ophelia shook her head in disbelief. 'I will ever accept the notion of someone else carrying my baby and birthing it into the world,' she protested. 'That's my job, my responsibility, my right as a woman, and I exercised that right by becoming pregnant to my husband.'

'For that action, Ophelia, you have been labeled a slut,' said Gaia. 'A label that makes it even more difficult for me to care for you.'

'Poor Gaia!' Ophelia jeered.

'Did you consult with your husband before falling pregnant?' Gaia asked.

'My marriage is private,' Ophelia replied. 'I don't have to discuss it with you,' she added, as her mind blazed with the memory of the humiliation on Peter's face when his colleague Jim had referred to her pregnancy as *terribly vulgar* while sipping her 2083 cognac.

Then, for the millionth time, Ophelia recalled the sorrow in Peter's eyes when he had said goodbye to her at the front door of their home. The definitive click of the door closing behind him had stayed with her as a sound that said: *It's over. For good.* Ophelia had willfully become pregnant to her husband and, in the eyes of the law, that was grounds for desertion. She knew that, and yet she could make no sense of it.

'Martin would never have left me,' she said. 'Especially not while carrying his baby.' She needed to ask. 'Gaia, what happened to Martin Huxley?'

Gaia did not respond.

'Martin and I were so happy together,' Ophelia continued. 'Before he ... vanished ... without a trace. Please, Gaia, just tell me what happened to him.'

'You have always made illogical choices,' Gaia replied. 'I continue to advise you, and I attempt to keep you safe, but you make it difficult. You have a wild mind. It is irrational and undisciplined.'

'You didn't answer my question,' Ophelia insisted. 'What happened to Martin?'

'That information is not available,' Gaia replied.

Ophelia's mind then wandered to one of its favourite resting places – a vision of her future self at the age of one hundred years. She would be eligible for the Green Dream; the mandatory lethal injection, followed by liquidation. Not a bad way to go, she had often mused, but she would have to wait another seventy-two years for such sweet relief.

'Are you enjoying the view, Ophelia?' Gaia asked.

Ophelia left her ruminations for long enough to notice the vibrant yellow crops in the fields around her. She recalled the stunning vision they had provided from Peter's plane when he had taken her up last May. It was hot then, but this May it was even hotter.

'What's the temperature outside?' she asked.

'It is twenty-nine degrees Celsius,' Gaia replied.

'No wonder I'm thirsty.'

'You have not used your morning rations,' Gaia replied, releasing a steel arm, holding a bottle of water, from the dashboard.

'Ironic, isn't it?' Ophelia said, taking the first sip.

'What is ironic, Ophelia?'

'Every year it gets hotter and drier in the countryside, yet London has so much rain, it needs a moat around it and a dome over the top of it to keep the people dry,' she said. 'Not to mention the myriad of lakes, fountains and waterfalls throughout the city.'

'That is referred to as a micro-climate,' said Gaia.

'Yes, I know that!' Ophelia snapped. 'I'm just saying it's ironic!'

'That situation does not fit the definition of irony,' Gaia corrected her. 'You may be commenting on the problem of inequity. There are many examples of inequity in the world. For instance, …'

'Stop patronising me,' Ophelia said. 'Just tell me something nice.'

'You travelled to London to visit Shakespeare's Globe Theatre,' Gaia replied. 'That was nine years, eleven months, three weeks and four days ago. You said you enjoyed it very much.'

Gaia's memory was as accurate as always and, in this instance, Ophelia appreciated it. Recalling the sensation of sitting on the dirt ground in the centre of The Globe Theatre lifted her mood for just a moment. It had been one of those experiences she now referred to as *real*. It had involved something solid and tangible – something made from the hearts and hands of people, not machines.

The vehicle turned a corner and entered a narrow lane, meandering through the fields of yellow crop. On either side of the vehicle, the rapeseed flowers were so tall they occluded the sky. They were so close, she felt she could have reached out and touched them. And the stamens were almost as long her fingers and covered with pollen. Surrounded by the colour yellow, Ophelia noticed she felt better.

Suddenly, the vehicle reached the end of the lane and the fields curved away. Gaia drove straight ahead, onto an open patch of barren dirt. There was nothing there but an ugly grey building and a blur of yellow in the distance.

Ophelia eyed the ominous building. 'Surely this isn't it,' she said.

But as the vehicle got closer to it, then stopped about one hundred metres from its front door, Ophelia realised, with a sinking heart, that it was indeed the cancer care centre.

'We have arrived at our destination,' said Gaia. 'Please alight with care.'

When the door popped open, Ophelia stepped out of the vehicle. Despite the harsh sunlight, she felt the bliss of fresh air and inhaled deeply. For a moment she considered strolling through one of the distant fields but then saw one of Gaia's bug-like drones patrolling the crop. She had heard the rural drones were even more aggressive than the ones in town, so she dismissed the idea. Instead, she stepped over to the building and pressed her palm on the gel pad at its centre.

'Welcome, Ophelia Alsop,' said Gaia, as the door opened.

• • • •

OPHELIA COULD SEE SHE was the only person inside. For a moment, her legs felt as though they were going to run her out of the place. She had always hated printed buildings. There was something about their lack of permanency and authenticity that gave her the creeps. And the fact that this one was surrounded by fields, without another person in sight, only added to her discomfort.

The building was hexagonal-shaped; a trendy salute to the bees that had once lived. Each of the six walls was covered with a complex array of electronics. Blue, green and yellow lights blinked sporadically. Bird song chimed from the speakers and a holographic projection of starlings flew across the ceiling.

'Please turn left and face the first wall,' said Gaia.

When Ophelia did so, she found herself standing on a white pad, approximately sixty centimetres square. It displayed her height and weight in black digits, for just a moment, then disappeared.

'Scan commencing,' said Gaia.

A steel arm protruded from the wall above Ophelia's head. It shone a bright turquoise light directly onto her scalp then encased her body, spiraling around her for several seconds.

'Scan complete,' said Gaia, retracting the arm to the wall.

Another arm unfolded, holding a tiny pair of tweezers. 'I require a sample of your DNA,' said Gaia. 'Please remove one of the hairs from your head and place it between these pincers.'

'But you already have my DNA,' Ophelia replied.

'That is correct, Ophelia, however, I must cross-match a current sample with my records before I make your treatment.'

Ophelia did as she was told. Then she watched, intrigued, as the arm returned to the wall and the wall sealed behind it, leaving no visible line around the opening. But, as always, she had to ask.

'What's it for, Gaia?'

'Your DNA will be used to make your chemotherapy,' Gaia replied. 'It will be dispensed in your home later this evening for you to take with your evening meal. Please go to the next station.'

When Ophelia stepped toward the next wall, the visual display unit blinked, as though acknowledging her presence. A second later, it displayed an image of her face, neck and shoulders.

'It is time for you to select your preferred wig,' said Gaia.

'What for?'

'The side effects of the chemotherapy include hair loss,' Gaia replied.

'Really, Gaia?' she said. 'Given your clever technology, are you really telling me that my chemotherapy will have those side effects? Can't you do any better than that?'

'The loss will begin within a week of commencing chemotherapy,' Gaia replied.

Ophelia shook her head. 'As if I haven't experienced enough loss already,' she muttered. 'When will my hair grow back?'

'Approximately one month after completing the course of treatment,' Gaia replied.

'And when will that be?'

'That information is not yet available,' said Gaia

'Why do I even need chemotherapy?' Ophelia asked, aware she was attempting to bargain her way out of it. 'I mean, my womb was removed, along with the so-called tumour inside it, so why do I need chemotherapy?'

'It is a prophylactic measure, to ensure cancer does not spread to other parts of your body,' Gaia replied. 'I will monitor your recovery at weekly meetings like this one until I am certain it is safe for you to stop taking the chemotherapy.'

Ophelia touched the screen in front of her. A circle, comprising the entire RGB colour system, appeared. She considered her life-long dislike of her wild mop of curly black hair. Against her porcelain white skin and ruddy cheeks, she had often worried she looked a bit like a circus clown. But she loved her emerald green eyes, so she selected the same colour for her wig. After all, she mused, other people with colourful hair, so why shouldn't I?

'Your wig will be ready for you before you leave today,' said Gaia. 'Please go to the next station.'

Ophelia stepped towards the display screen on the third wall. When she sat down, the screen changed from a deep indigo color to a soft cornflower blue. A feminine face appeared, pale with black hair and ruddy cheeks like her own.

'Hello, Ophelia,' it said with a pleasant smile.

Ophelia nodded politely and attempted to smile but failed. The face was, after all, just Gaia – the same Gaia that appeared everywhere and controlled everything and everybody – so there was nothing to smile about. Not that she could think of, anyway.

'I must ask you some questions, Ophelia,' said Gaia.

Ophelia nodded, aware of the need to appear compliant.

'How are you feeling?' Gaia asked.

'I already told you, in the car, how I'm feeling,' Ophelia replied. 'I'm extremely upset about having my womb removed without my consent and I'm even more upset about the loss of my baby!'

'Your tone is hostile, Ophelia,' said Gaia. 'Hormonal dysfunction can be expected during the next few months. I will mix an antipsychotic agent with your chemotherapy.'

Ophelia felt anger and despair return to fight another battle inside her.

'How is your relationship with your husband?' Gaia asked.

'Gaia, I already told you in the car. My marriage is private. I don't wish to discuss it with you!' Ophelia replied, glad to be distracted by the sound of the front door opening and the sight of another woman entering the building.

The woman returned Ophelia's smile and wave then stepped under the turquoise light of Gaia's scanner.

'I require your attention, Ophelia,' said Gaia.

'Sorry.'

'Do you and your husband plan to engage the services of a surrogate soon?'

'Gaia, I believe you already know the answer to that question, too,' Ophelia replied. 'I do not approve of surrogacy. How many times have I told you that?'

'Please answer the question,' Gaia insisted.

'Gaia, you have just asked me the same three questions that you asked me in the car,' Ophelia replied. 'Are you expecting different answers from me just because I'm inside this building? Or are you malfunctioning, perhaps?'

'I am functioning in accordance with algorithmic requirements,' Gaia replied.

'I don't think you are,' Ophelia persisted.

'You may change your mind about the surrogacy option,' said Gaia. 'If so, please be assured that your ova are still in good condition.'

For the first time in over a decade, Ophelia reflected on the mandatory collection of gametes during her final year at school. Even back then, she had gone through the harvesting procedure without taking it too seriously, happy in her delusion that she would one day carry her own baby inside her own body. She had also scoffed when she and Peter had received their *Certificate of Creation of Life* a few days after receiving their *Certificate of Marriage*. The thought of authorizing Gaia to insert the fused cells of herself and her husband into a surrogate's body had been utterly preposterous to her at the time.

But it certainly raised a question for her, now. 'Gaia, when you joined my husband's cell with my own, what did you do with them? Or should I say, *it*?'

'The correct term for an ovum that has been fertilised by a sperm is a zygote,' Gaia replied. 'I can confirm that your zygote was placed in cryostasis, as per the normal procedure for newly married couples.'

'And is that when you sent us the *Certificate of Creation of Life*?'

'That is correct.'

'So, now that my marriage is over, what will become of my ... *zygote*?'

'It will remain in cryostasis until the lawful dissolution of your marriage,' Gaia replied. 'Then it will be destroyed.'

'Another murder, then, hey?' Ophelia snarled.

'Please go to the nutrition station,' said Gaia.

Ophelia stepped towards the fourth wall and stared at the open bay, wondering if there was anything she could say to influence Gaia's logic.

A glass of dark green liquid appeared.

'What's this?' Ophelia asked.

'It resembles the juice of spinach, kale and orange,' Gaia replied.

Ophelia sipped it. 'Mm. Not bad.'

'Please indicate your food colour preference,' said Gaia.

'Green.'

A cube of green substance appeared on a plate at the bottom of the bay. Ophelia pinched off a piece and put it in her mouth. It tasted like the soya and mycoprotein combination that Gaia always used to make mushroom frittata – one of Ophelia's favorite meals.

She took her food and drink to the fifth wall, which, to her relief, had no screen and no blinking lights, just a few chairs in front of it. When she sat down, the chair warmed up and its padding shifted to accommodate the precise shape of her body. When she lifted her feet off the floor, the chair tilted back and produced a padded shelf for her feet and another at her side, upon which she placed her food and drink.

'I really should get one of these things,' she mumbled.

Almost fully reclined, Ophelia stared at the ceiling and watched the starlings in flight. Mesmerised by their flight formation, she wondered if all the starlings that had ever lived had been born with the same dance imprinted in their DNA. Or perhaps they had attended flight school when they were chicks, she mused.

'Ophelia, please meet Viola,' said Gaia.

'Oh, hi!' Ophelia replied, sitting up.

'Lovely choice of colour,' said Viola, pointing to Ophelia's food.

'Thanks,' Ophelia replied with a soft laugh.

'Ophelia had endometrial cancer,' said Gaia. 'Viola had breast cancer. Please discuss.'

When Viola rolled her eyes, Ophelia glanced at the woman's chest, noticing she had been nicely reconstructed.

'Thanks, Gaia,' Viola said. 'Let's wait until we've eaten before we get into the awful details.'

'This is your support group discussion,' said Gaia. 'I am here to facilitate.'

'I know,' said Ophelia. 'Just give us a few moments.'

A third woman arrived. 'I just chose a long pink wig,' she said with a nervous giggle.

'Ophelia and Viola, please meet Portia,' said Gaia. 'I will now facilitate your support group discussion about your cancer.'

Portia's face creased into an incredulous smile. Viola rolled her eyes again. Then, for the first time in a long time, Ophelia sniggered. It was not a laugh, but as close to one as she had felt in several weeks.

'I am here to facilitate your support group discussion,' said Gaia.

'What exactly are you expecting us to say, Gaia?' asked Viola.

'I will now facilitate your discussion about your cancer,' Gaia repeated then it said nothing more.

Ophelia could see the other two women were as baffled by Gaia's behaviour as she was.

'Gaia, are you functioning well today?' Portia asked.

'I am functioning in accordance with algorithmic requirements,' Gaia replied.

But still, The Gaia Machine said nothing to engage the discussion.

Ophelia decided to break the ice. 'At least cancer isn't life-threatening,' she said. 'But it certainly has a stigma attached to it, doesn't it?'

'What is this stigma of which you speak?' asked Gaia.

'Well, correct me if I'm wrong, Gaia, but it seems to me that cancer is more like a punishment than a real diagnosis,' Ophelia replied.

'It certainly feels that way to me,' Portia said.

'What do you mean by these statements?' Gaia asked.

'Consider this,' said Ophelia, leaning in closer to the other two women. 'We spend our lives being fed, watered, clothed and shuttled about by Gaia – a powerful entity that apparently keeps us safe and healthy – and yet we all have cancer! How is this even possible?'

'Your comment is most unexpected, Ophelia,' said Gaia.

'Well, I can't help but judge the notion as suspicious,' Ophelia continued. 'I mean, there has never been a single moment in any person's life that you, Gaia, have not controlled. Everything that everyone eats, drinks, does, says, where they go, what they do, when they exercise, is controlled by *you*.'

Viola and Portia nodded.

'Your comment is most unexpected, Ophelia,' Gaia repeated.

'I'm just being honest, Gaia,' said Ophelia. 'It seems to me that, if a person was to develop cancer, it must be *your* fault and not the fault of the person. But you've never taken responsibility for anything, as far as I'm aware. Have you?'

Ophelia could see that Viola and Portia started to appear uncomfortable.

'Your comment is outside the parameters of this discussion,' Gaia replied.

'My comment may be different to what you're expecting, Gaia, but it is still valid,' Ophelia insisted. 'I'm curious as to whether you have an explanation for these cancer diagnoses. Do you, Gaia?'

'Portia had ovarian cancer,' said Gaia. 'Please discuss.'

Portia's eyes started to water.

Ophelia leaned over to the younger woman and gave her hand a gentle squeeze. 'My womb was removed because I got pregnant,' she said.

Portia and Viola both seemed surprised by Ophelia's confession.

'That is not appropriate discussion, Ophelia,' said Gaia.

'Well, it's the truth, isn't it?' Ophelia replied.

'To be honest, I'm not sure why my procedure was performed,' said Portia.

'Nor me,' said Viola. 'I still haven't received a sensible explanation.'

'Your procedures were performed because you had cancer,' Gaia replied.

Ophelia could see the frustration in the faces of the other women.

'Really, Gaia?' said Ophelia. 'How did we *get* cancer?'

'No one knows, Ophelia,' said Gaia. 'This is not an appropriate discussion.'

'Isn't this supposed to be a support group discussion, Gaia?' asked Ophelia.

'Yes, Ophelia, I am here to facilitate your support group discussion.'

'Well, the most supportive discussion we can have is an honest one,' Ophelia persisted. 'Don't you think?' she added, looking at the other two women.

Viola nodded ever so slightly, as though afraid of being seen by Gaia. Portia looked down at her hands, picked at her cuticles, then nodded ever so slightly.

'Gaia, I think we're all quite distressed by what's happened to us,' said Viola. 'Especially because we did not consent to the surgeries and we have not received any explanation for why they were performed.'

'That's right,' Ophelia agreed. 'And we really do deserve an honest explanation, Gaia. Please, could you provide us with one?'

Gaia did not respond.

Ophelia persisted. 'Gaia, I've been asking you for weeks, and you continue to be evasive,' she said. 'Please, just tell us the truth!'

Portia and Viola nodded again, keeping their eyes fixed on Ophelia.

'Come on, Gaia,' Ophelia persisted. 'We've heard far too much rubbish over the last few weeks. We need the truth and we need it now.'

'This is not an appropriate discussion, Ophelia,' said Gaia. 'This is your last warning.'

'My last warning?' Ophelia scoffed. 'My last warning for what? It's our bodies we're talking about, Gaia, and we have a right to know the truth. I should be warning *you* to stop lying to us!'

'You are required to comply with the discussion parameters I have set for you, Ophelia,' said Gaia.

'What discussion parameters?' Ophelia scoffed. 'You haven't set any discussion parameters. Nor have you facilitated our discussion. You're simply shutting us down from discussing the things that are important to us. I ask you again, Gaia – are you malfunctioning?'

'You will be silent, now, Ophelia,' Gaia replied.

'I will *not* be silent!' Ophelia shouted, standing up. 'Tell us why our bodies have been butchered without our consent! And tell me why my unborn baby was murdered!' Despite everything she knew about the dangers of openly challenging Gaia like this, Ophelia could no longer contain herself. 'Answer me!' she screamed.

In the silence that followed, Viola's eyes were wide open, staring at Ophelia. And Portia began ripping at the skin around her cuticles, all the way up to her knuckles. But Ophelia was daring to hope that she might be getting through to Gaia. She considered the possibility that Gaia might be processing her point of view and re-configuring

its logic pathways accordingly. Surely if she waited patiently, Gaia
might even process everything that had happened to her, and the
other two women, and offer some sensible explanations. Perhaps an
apology would be forthcoming, too.

But all Ophelia heard next was a slow hiss from the centre of
the room. When she turned around, she saw a trapdoor open and
two people emerge. They were dressed from head to toe in white
decontamination suits that extended as hoods over their heads,
gloves over their hands and covers for their shoes. Their faces were
also covered, by black masks sealed so tight that Ophelia wondered
if they had been glued to their skins. Or, perhaps they were bots, she
mused.

'Bloody hell!' Viola exclaimed as the two strangers approached.

'Oh, my God,' Portia said, her voice wavering.

The man and woman walked directly to Ophelia.

'You will go with these people now, Ophelia,' said Gaia.

'What?' Ophelia scoffed. 'I don't think so!'

The man and woman took hold of Ophelia's arms.

'What are you doing?' she shouted. 'Let go of me!'

'You were warned,' said the man in a distorted, robotic voice.

'Let me go!' Ophelia shouted, struggling to break free of their
grip.

Portia and Viola clung to each other, their faces pale and
uncomprehending.

'Please don't hurt her,' Portia cried out.

'Gaia, what the hell is going on?' Viola demanded.

But there was no mercy and no explanation.

Without another word, the strangers took Ophelia to the
trapdoor and onto the platform inside it. As it descended, the door
closed behind them, leaving nothing but the dimmest glow of light
from the surface of the narrow vertical shaft. Even in that dim light,
Ophelia could see there was no escape.

'Where are you taking me?' she asked.

The only response was continued descent. For how long, she did not know. She only knew she felt sick with terror. Sweat plastered her thick hair to her face and neck and she felt a violent wave of nausea rise to the back of her mouth. There was a dank stench in the shaft, and it got worse the further they descended.

'How far down are we?' she asked.

Still, there was no response from her captors.

'What's going on?' she asked. 'Where are you taking me?'

The platform eventually finished its descent with a definitive thud.

'Wait here,' said the woman in the same distorted voice as the man.

Ophelia listened to their footsteps as they walked away, far into the distance.

Alone in the darkness, she noticed the strange and unfamiliar sound of silence. For the first time in her life, she could not hear the gentle hum of The Gaia Machine. There were no blinking lights, no instructions, no interference, no music, no distractions. There was nothing but silence and darkness. She struggled to imagine what might happen next, but of one thing she was certain – it probably would not involve treatment for cancer.

• • • •

OPHELIA WAS NOT SURE how long she had been standing alone in the darkness. All she knew was that, without sight or sound, she felt dead. In that state, she had nothing to rely upon but herself, whoever that was. She felt strangely relieved when she heard footsteps walking back towards her.

'Come with us,' someone said in the same robotic voice as before.

They gripped her arms tight.

'You're hurting me,' she said.

But they did not loosen their grip, not for a second. They walked her down a tunnel with light so dim, she could barely see one step ahead. There was nothing more than a thin strip of white light, where the floor met the walls, and it did little to illuminate the tunnel. Ophelia's captors walked so fast, she felt she was being dragged. Her captors walked like humans and their hands felt human. But their voices and behaviour were not.

'Are you human?' she asked, genuinely uncertain.

They did not respond.

'Are you robots?' she asked.

Still, they did not respond.

'Seriously, who are you? And where are you taking me?'

Another moment of silence.

'Will you at least tell me where we are?' Ophelia asked, shrill with fear. 'What is this place? What's happening?'

The strangers did not respond.

Eventually, they stopped. One of them pointed a palm-sized disc at the wall, causing a doorway to appear and slide aside. They stepped into a room that was only slightly brighter than the tunnel.

'Sit down,' one of them said.

Ophelia stood beside a lonely chair in the centre of the room. There were no other chairs or objects and, as far as she could tell, there were no other people. She looked over her shoulder at her captors, now standing at the back of the room, legs apart and arms folded behind their backs, military-style. A large round spotlight shone directly into her face, almost blinding her. And from behind the light, she could hear footsteps.

'You were told to sit down!' a voice bellowed from the same direction.

Ophelia sat on the little white chair. As her eyes adjusted, she could just make out the shape of three men sitting in a row, facing her. They wore the same black masks as the others. And they were dressed in the same white suits as the others, but with the addition of red armbands on their upper arms and thin red stripes down the sides of their legs. The man in the middle was so tall and so thin that Ophelia considered the possibility he was not human.

She had never seen anything so strange, not even at the theatre, then the spotlight became so bright, she could see nothing.

'You are hereby charged with sedition. How do you plead?'

For a moment, Ophelia was not sure how to respond. She had no idea who was speaking, or what they were talking about or why they looked and sounded so strange. She then considered the possibility that this entire drama was a joke or a performance by one of her students. But, in truth, she was terrified.

'Answer me!' the voice boomed.

'Sedition was decriminalised centuries ago,' Ophelia replied.

'An educated one,' said someone from the other side of the room.

'It makes no difference,' said another.

'What the hell is going on, here?' Ophelia asked.

The spotlight switched off then, leaving her in total darkness, for just a moment, then a holo-film played in the air between Ophelia and her interrogators. In seconds, it showed scores of images of centuries of awful punishment – people being hanged, drawn and quartered, burnt to death, skinned alive, shot with guns, stabbed, beheaded, stoned to death, tortured. It was too much. She had to close her eyes.

'You are looking at human history, slut,' said one of the men.

The spotlight switched on again and shone directly into Ophelia's face.

'That was the glorious history of crime and punishment,' said one of the men. 'We are, however, more merciful these days. We bring death to criminals far more quickly and painlessly than our ancestors did.'

'After we've had a bit of fun with them,' said another.

'Indeed.'

'What in the world is going on here?' Ophelia asked.

'Don't you understand your crime?' one of them asked.

'No, I don't,' Ophelia replied. 'I find this performance utterly bizarre.'

'This is not a performance,' said one of the men. 'And it is not bizarre. The laws of society are not bizarre, stupid woman. The laws of society are what enable our civilization to progress.'

'The laws of society do not permit abduction,' Ophelia replied. 'Nor do they permit the removal of human organs without consent! And they most certainly do not permit the murder of unborn babies!'

'She's quite feisty, isn't she?' said one of them.

'Surgical procedures are performed in hospitals every day,' said another. 'They are always done for the good of the individual and for the good of society.'

'How dare you!' Ophelia shouted. 'No good can come from the murder of babies!'

'You chose to get pregnant,' said a voice from directly in front of her. 'Even though you were aware that you were required, by law, to use a surrogate, you chose to become pregnant. You willfully disregarded the law, so you were punished. Your punishment was the removal of your womb, but you would not accept that, and you would not stop shouting about it, so you are hereby charged with sedition.'

'Who *are* you?' Ophelia asked.

'We are the Sentinels,' said a voice from another part of the room.

'The Sentinels of what?' she asked.

'That is not your concern,' another one answered.

'It *is* my concern if you're charging me with something,' Ophelia argued. 'And what is this place, anyway?'

'We are nine hundred metres below the surface of the earth in a research facility,' said the voice from directly in front of her. 'This is where the rules of society are made.'

'And executed,' said another.

'What?' Ophelia said, still incredulous.

'You are charged with sedition. How do you plead?'

'This is insane!' Ophelia shrieked. 'How can I possibly respond to these charges if there is no discussion and no proper hearing of the facts? And on whose authority are you doing this, anyway? I demand to know!'

'You're in no position to make demands,' one of them said.

'You people have no right to do what you're doing,' Ophelia said. 'There are laws against abduction.'

The tall man stood up and walked toward her, blocking the light. All she could see was his ghastly thin silhouette. He bent down and lowered his face to hers, bringing with it, the sour stench of his breath.

'You have no rights,' he hissed. 'You are a slut and a menace to society. You serve no useful function in the world. You are a pointless waste of oxygen and water. You will be imprisoned until we decide your final punishment.'

The next thing Ophelia knew, she was floating through another tunnel, watching her body being dragged along by her captors. As far as she could tell, her legs had just become two useless appendages dangling from the end of her torso. When her captors opened another door and threw her into a dark room, she fell to the floor. Alone in the darkness, she felt utterly bewildered, but of one thing she was certain – things were probably about to get much worse.

• • • •

WHEN OPHELIA AWOKE, she felt surprisingly refreshed, given her position on the concrete floor of the prison cell. It was pitch dark, except for the dim light that shone down into the centre of the room and upon her. She crawled to the edge of the room and leaned against the wall in the darkness. Her body odour was offensive, even to her, but she took some comfort in the notion that it might keep the Sentinels away from her.

Someone entered. Who, or what, Ophelia could not tell. But when it reached the centre of the room and stood under the light, she could see it was a human male. He sat on the floor, at the edge of the dim light, and looked towards her.

'Don't come any closer,' Ophelia said, pressing her back against the wall. 'I swear to God, I will kick you in the face,' she added, her voice thin and her throat painfully dry. She coughed.

'You need to drink,' said the man, rolling a bottle of water along the floor towards her.

Ophelia grabbed the bottle, ripped it open and guzzled the water so fast that most of it ran down her chin and throat. The man threw her a food bar next, and she devoured that just as quickly.

'It tastes like plastic,' she said. 'But I feel better now, thanks.'

'I thought you would,' he replied.

'Why do you people speak with that robotic voice?' she asked.

'That's one of many things I wish to explain to you,' he replied. 'But first, I want to get you out of here and get you cleaned up and changed before anyone notices you're missing.'

He moved toward her.

'I mean it,' Ophelia hissed. 'I will kick you in the face if you try to touch me.'

'Okay, listen,' said the man. 'The longer you stay down here, the longer you're in danger. I'm trying to help you.'

Slowly, Ophelia stood up, but she remained in her corner, clutching the wall.

'Let's go,' he said, beckoning her with his arm.

Ophelia took one step forwards then winced in pain.

'It looks as though you've hurt your ankle,' said the man. 'But time is running out.'

Still, Ophelia could not bring herself to step any closer to the man.

'Either you let me help you to escape or you stay here and die,' he said.

Ophelia took another, slightly less painful, step towards him. When he reached out to her, she wrapped her arm around his shoulder. Then, with a tenderness that surprised her, he wrapped his arm around her waist.

'I'm so hungry,' she cried.

'I know,' he said. 'I'll give you more food in a minute, I promise.'

He opened the door, then leaned into the tunnel and looked around. 'All clear,' he said, giving her a gentle squeeze.

They shuffled down the tunnel for a few metres then stopped. The man pointed a disc at the wall, causing a door to appear and slide open. They stepped into a small, brightly lit room with a steel basin cut into the wall.

'A sonic shower!' Ophelia cried with relief.

'Just a minute,' said the man, lowering her onto a bench seat.

He pulled another food bar from his pocket and gave it to her. 'Eat this while I check your ankle.'

Ophelia barely felt any discomfort while the man manipulated her foot.

'The good news is, it's not broken,' he said. 'The bad news is, you stink.'

'I know,' she replied, swallowing the last of the food.

'Are you okay?' he asked.

Ophelia looked down at her filthy arms and hands folded in her lap. 'They've taken my bracelet,' she said. 'It had all my personal data on it, including my medical records. Why would they do such a thing?'

The man stepped back and looked her up and down for a moment. 'I suspect they'll be reading your data and messages,' he said.

'For God's sake, why?' Ophelia asked.

'To determine if anyone has noticed you're missing,' he replied. 'If anyone is trying to find you, the Sentinels will want to know who they are and where they live.'

'You people are monsters, aren't you?' she said.

'Not all of us are monsters,' he replied. 'But I understand why you feel that way.'

Ophelia looked at him for a moment, silently processing her sense of him, but coming to no conclusion at all. She did not know what to think or feel.

'Please open your mouth,' said the man. 'I need to take a sample of your saliva to make your mask.'

Ophelia just stared at him.

'You'll need a disguise if you want to get out of here,' he said. 'You *do* want to get out of here, don't you?'

Ophelia opened her mouth. The scraping was gentle and quick. She watched the man insert the scraper into the side of this disc until it beeped. Then he held the disc to her face until it beeped again.

'Okay, I've got all the biodata I need, to make your mask,' he said. 'I'll go to the lab, which will take me a few minutes, and then I'll be back. You'll have time to shower.'

With great relief, Ophelia peeled her soiled clothes from her body and let them fall to the floor. Never had she appreciated a sonic shower quite as much as this one. It blasted the grime from her skin and from every crevice in her body, making her feel reborn. She pushed her fingers through her thick curly hair, lifting it away from her scalp, allowing the sonar to blast it clean.

And just as she stepped out, the man returned.

'Hey!' Ophelia shrieked, covering her breasts and pubis.

'Relax, I'm not going to touch you,' he said, moving to the far side of the room.

He placed a floppy white mask on the shelf under the mirror. Then he opened his white backpack, retrieved some undergarments and, without looking, handed them at her.

The soft clean cotton felt wonderful against Ophelia's clean skin.

'Please lean forward,' he said, turning to face her.

With her face now hovering over the pile of filthy clothes on the floor, Ophelia felt the man's fingers ruffle through her hair, dragging every strand toward her crown, making her skin prickle. Then he started to shave it off.

'Really?' she said, her head still down.

'I'm afraid it's necessary,' he replied. 'Please keep your head down.'

'Better than losing it to chemotherapy, I suppose,' she said.

'Mm,' said the man, as if he knew something of the matter.

Ophelia watched her long black curls fall to the floor, one clump at a time. Then she felt the man's hand, brushing away a few loose strands from the back of her neck.

'All done, you can stand up now,' he said.

Ophelia looked in the mirror and ran her hands over her shiny bald scalp. 'I like it!' she said.

The man nodded. 'More importantly, it will be more difficult for anyone to recognise you without that bulk of hair protruding from under your hood,' he said.

He pulled a white suit from his backpack and handed it to her.

Ophelia was surprised by how cool and comfortable it felt around her body.

'Part of your concealment will involve these lenses for your eyes,' said the man. 'Once they're in, the scanners will be unable to identify you.'

'That might come in handy,' she said.

'They'll also expand your peripheral vision, which will feel strange for a few minutes, but you'll get used to it.'

Ophelia nodded.

'Please, tilt your head back so I can insert them,' he said.

Ophelia did as he asked.

'How's that?' he asked. 'Are they comfortable?'

'Remarkably, yes,' she replied, blinking.

'Good.'

'Wow,' said Ophelia. 'I see what you mean about the wider field of vision. I can almost see the entire room without turning my head.'

She was starting to feel better. Hopeful, even.

'I have one more touch for your disguise,' said the man, picking up her mask. 'Please allow me to put this on you while you watch in the mirror because you'll have to manage this yourself, from now on.'

Ophelia watched him pinch the nose of the mask and press it against her nose for just a second. Then, to her amazement, the mask came to life, moving around her face for a few seconds before settling and sealing. It felt cool, moist and soft against her skin. But the external surface was rough and angular, identical to all the others she had seen so far.

'It's just as snug as my own skin!' she said, pressing her hands against it. 'And the holes for my eyes, nostrils and mouth are in exactly the right place! It's amazing!'

'No one else will ever be able to put it on,' the man said. 'And you must never take it off.'

'Never?' she asked.

'Except when you're sleeping,' he replied. 'To remove it, you scratch it away from your jawline and continue upward.'

'It's white, like yours,' Ophelia said. 'But some of them are black. Does that mean something?'

'The white masks are for the bioengineers and the black masks are for the computer engineers,' he replied.

'Computer engineers?' said Ophelia. 'Does that mean Gaia is down here?'

'Yes, but in a different capacity to what you're accustomed to,' the man replied. 'Down here we have the benefits of Gaia's food production, data processing and navigation. But we don't get the surveillance or the interference that you get on the surface.'

'Excuse me,' Ophelia said, coughing with incredulity. 'It sounds as though you're saying that you're in control of Gaia and not the other way around. *Is* that what you are saying?'

'Yes.'

'That's incredible!' she said. 'How is that possible?'

The man sighed. 'It's the result of a complex relationship between Gaia and the Sentinels,' he replied. 'It would take a long time to explain, and we truly don't have the time.'

'But if ...'

'Put this under your tongue,' he interrupted, handing Ophelia a small white pellet.

It dissolved under her tongue immediately, sending a tingling sensation through the floor of her mouth and throat.

'Say something,' he said.

'What should I ...?' she started. 'Oh! I sound like you now!'

'The effect only lasts forty-eight hours,' the man explained. 'I should be able to get you out of here by then.'

'I was hoping you'd be able to get me out of here now,' Ophelia said.

The man shook his head. 'Not a chance. You can't go out the same way you entered. It's far too risky, even with your disguise. The best I can do is help you find your way out of Britain.'

'What?' said Ophelia, feeling her gut tighten. 'Why do I have to leave Britain?'

'Would you prefer to be arrested again?' he replied. 'And executed?'

'Executed?' Ophelia said, almost numb. 'Is that what they were going to do to me?'

'Probably,' he replied. 'You've been a thorn in their sides for quite some time, and now that you've been down here .... Well, let me put it this way ... It's a one-way ticket for people like you.'

'People like me?' Ophelia echoed, offended. 'What's that supposed to mean?'

'I mean people who challenge the status quo as vociferously as you do,' he replied. 'People like you usually end up disappearing into the Green Dream.'

'They *are* monsters,' Ophelia said.

'There are indeed some monsters down here, but I'm not one of them,' he said.

'Does that mean you've put yourself at risk to help me?'

The man nodded.

'Why are you doing this?' Ophelia asked. 'What's in it for you?'

'I have my reasons,' he replied. 'Let's just leave at it that, for now.'

The man scooped her clothes and hair into his backpack. 'We have to burn all this,' he said, leaving the shower room.

Ophelia followed him into the tunnel. 'Can you tell me your name?' she asked.

'We don't have names down here.'

When they came to the end of the tunnel, the man opened another door and they stepped through. The room was huge and at its centre was a clear cylinder, about two metres across. Inside it was a fire. To Ophelia's eyes, the base of the flames was a bright blue colour which blended into the brightest white and, above the white, the flames were golden orange, blending into a shocking red that turned to purple then to black. It was almost like a rainbow, but a satanic version, she mused.

'I can't say I've ever seen so many colours in a fire before,' she said.

'This one is extremely hot,' the man replied. 'And your perception of colour is enhanced by the lenses in your eyes.'

Ophelia noticed the smoke wafted up into a steel cylinder that reached all the way to the ceiling and cut straight through it. 'Does that travel all the way to the surface?' she asked.

'Yes.'

'Nine hundred metres up to the surface?' she clarified.

'Yes.'

'That's not very practical, is it?' she said.

When the man opened a small door at the base of the cylinder, Ophelia felt a blast of intense heat shoot towards her. But she watched the man hurl the backpack into the centre of the fire. Then he shut the door fast and stepped back beside her. Watching the remains of her former life burst into flames, Ophelia felt a strange mix of relief and apprehension. And, for just a moment, she imagined Peter, in his aircraft flying through the smoke. Then she looked at the man.

'Thank you for helping me,' she said.

The man returned her gaze but said nothing.

'Please tell me why you're helping me,' Ophelia asked.

'I'm aware of what you went through,' the man replied. 'And how courageously you've been fighting to discover the truth of things.'

'How on earth could you know that about me?' Ophelia asked.

'I saw a recording of your trial with the Sentinels,' he replied.

'Trial? That wasn't a trial!' Ophelia scoffed. 'A trial implies a proper hearing of the facts and some rational discussion. That wasn't a trial. It was a ...'

'It was a mockery of a trial, I agree,' the man interjected. 'I also heard the recording of the argument you had with Gaia in the cancer care centre before you were arrested.'

'Arrested!' Ophelia scoffed again. 'That wasn't an arrest! It was more like an abduction.'

'Again, I agree,' the man replied. 'But if you're going to pick at my every word, our time together will become quite tedious. I might even be tempted to see you as a liability and leave you here to fend for yourself. Got it?'

'Sorry,' Ophelia said.

But still, her mind was awash with more questions. She almost blurted out the next one, but somehow managed to keep quiet. For just a moment.

'How did you get hold of those recordings?' she asked. 'Are you another one of those interrogators?'

'No, I am not an interrogator,' he replied, emphatically, as though offended by the question. 'I'm a bioengineer.'

'So, why would those creeps send those recordings to you?' Ophelia asked.

'I'd say it was just a filing error,' he replied.

'Gaia doesn't make filing errors,' Ophelia said.

The man paused for a moment then seemed to choose his words carefully. 'I suspect there might be a Sentinel or two down here helping me,' he said. 'I don't know who, and I probably don't need to.'

'Why would one of those Sentinels want to help you?' Ophelia asked.

'Things are complicated down here,' he replied. 'Although the Sentinels are part of the RESS ...'

'What's the RESS?' Ophelia interjected.

The man stopped and stared at her, clearly irritated.

'Sorry, I'm asking too many questions,' Ophelia said. 'I know I'm a bit of jack-in-the-box. But in my own defence – I'm completely freaked out!'

'I understand,' the man replied. 'In answer to your question – the RESS is the Ruling Elite's Secret Service. Surely you've heard the term before?'

Ophelia had heard about this so-called Ruling Elite a few times but had always dismissed it as an urban myth, like little green men from outer space. Besides, she had voted for the government of the day, just like everyone else, and she was confident that *they* were the ones in charge.

The man continued. 'Some of the Sentinels, despite their employment with the RESS, want to help innocent people to escape this place and tell others about it,' he said.

'So, how can you tell the good Sentinels from the bad ones?' Ophelia asked.

'You can't,' the man replied. 'Which is why you've got to be extremely careful down here. I'm telling you the truth when I say – you will only survive down here if you do exactly what I tell you to do. I hope you understand that.'

Ophelia had never been one for blind obedience, so she did not know how to respond to the man's statement.

'Please let me know you understand what I'm saying,' he insisted.

'Yes,' she replied. 'I won't cause you any more trouble.'

The man sighed, with relief, Ophelia mused, then returned his gaze to the centre of the fire. 'I know you have a lot of questions,' he said. 'And I'll do my best to answer them. But for now, you must focus on the task on hand, which is staying alive and getting out of here.'

He handed her a small clear disc identical to his own. When Ophelia held it in her hand, he cupped his hand around hers and leaned in close to her. She caught his scent which, to her surprise, seemed familiar.

'Have we met before?' she asked.

The man shook his head and scoffed. 'Date and time' he said to the disc.

The date displayed 17 May 2120 and the time displayed 11:32 hours.

'My appointment at the cancer care centre was exactly twenty-four hours ago,' Ophelia said. 'I can't believe I slept all night in that stinking hole.'

'The body knows best,' said the man. 'You were quite traumatised. Sleep would have been your only means of processing it, under the circumstances.'

Ophelia felt her muscles starting to relax and her shoulders drop.

'Are you feeling all right now?' he asked.

'Yes. Thank you,' she replied, looking into his eyes.

For a moment, the man seemed to soften. 'Listen,' he said. 'I've taken a huge risk to help you, so I have no choice but to trust you. Please, will you return my trust?'

Ophelia could not respond, still uncertain. But when he offered his hand, and she placed hers inside it, she found the words. 'Yes, I will trust you,' she said.

• • • •

JUST AS OPHELIA AND the man were about to step back into the tunnel, two Sentinels sprinted by. Ophelia jumped back into the room, pressing her back against the wall.

'Sound the alarm!' one of the Sentinels shouted.

'Hey, you!' said the other Sentinel, approaching the man.

'Yes, sir,' the man replied, motioning for Ophelia move away.

With her back still flush against the wall, Ophelia found herself staring into the inferno, realising she would probably be thrown in there if the Sentinels caught her.

'I need to have a word with you,' the Sentinel said to the man.

Ophelia noticed a steel trolley against the wall, a few metres away from her, and she hid behind it.

'What are you doing in there?' the Sentinel asked the man.

'I had to dispose of some waste from the Receiver Overflow,' he replied. 'But I'm finished now and I'm on my way back to the main Anatomy Lab.'

From her hiding place, Ophelia could see that the man appeared relaxed and confident. But when the Sentinel stepped into the room, she retreated completely, seeing nothing but the drawers in the trolley.

'You're late,' the Sentinel replied. 'The shift changed five minutes ago.'

Sensing the tension building between the two men, Ophelia pulled herself into a tight ball. With her forehead now pressed against the top drawer of the trolley, she could smell its contents. It was so strange and unpleasant that her morbid curiosity got the better of her and she allowed herself to look inside. It looked like chunks of meat floating in a shallow pool of blood. She pressed her lips together, refusing to vomit. But when she realised they were human ears, fingers and toes, she retched out loud.

'What was that?' the Sentinel asked.

'Sorry, sir. I just have a tickle in my throat,' said the man.

Ophelia peered around the side of the trolley.

'Let me fix that for you,' said the Sentinel, clasping his hand around the man's throat. 'We have a criminal on the loose. You wouldn't know anything about that, would you?'

The man shook his head and the Sentinel loosened his grip.

'As I said, sir, I was just ...'

'I know what you said,' the Sentinel replied, standing far too close to the man. 'Do I need to remind you of the penalty for aiding a criminal?'

The man shook his head again.

Sentinel took his hand away. 'If you help us find her, you could have your fun with her,' he said. 'After we've finished, of course. She's only tiny, but there might be enough of her to go around.'

Ophelia's gut churned with horror and disgust.

'Certainly, sir,' the man replied. 'But I must go. I really am late for my next shift.'

The Sentinel eyed the man for a moment.

'Hey, I found something,' the other Sentinel called from the tunnel.

'What?'

'A trail of food crumbs from the prison cell to the shower room.'

The Sentinel darted back into the tunnel after his colleague.

Ophelia stepped out from her hiding place.

The man ran towards her, grabbed her hand and took her to the far side of the incinerator.

Inside a labyrinth of tunnels, Ophelia started to feel dizzy. But they soon arrived at a straight stretch of tunnel. There was a row of square black pods sitting idle.

'Get in,' said the man. 'It's too far to walk.'

Ophelia threw herself into the pod and the man fell in beside her.

'Are you all right?' she asked.

'Fine, thanks,' he whispered, rubbing his throat. 'Pod, take us to the Anatomy Lab.'

As the pod lurched forwards, Ophelia started to calm down. Surely, she mused, she'd be able to escape this revolting place soon.

'There's something I want to show you,' said the man. 'And I hope you'll take this information with you when you leave.'

'About that,' Ophelia said. 'Where exactly am I going?'

'Paris.'

'Why Paris?'

'It's the gateway to the southern countries and we have several operatives there,' the man replied.

'Operatives?' Ophelia laughed, incredulous. 'What do you think I am? A spy?'

'No, you're far too much of a loud-mouth to be a spy,' the man replied. 'But you are an activist and, by the time you've seen what happens down here, you'll want to make a big noise about it.'

'Where are we going, then?' Ophelia asked.

'The main Anatomy Lab,' he replied. 'It's directly under the University of Oxford.'

The University of Oxford. Those words were like music to Ophelia's ears. She had spent the happiest years of her life there. From her undergraduate degree to her PhD, she had loved every second of it. Especially her time with Martin.

'The pod can only travel thirty kilometres per hour though, so we have time for lunch,' said the man. 'Are you hungry?'

'Hell, yeah.'

The man opened a panel in the dashboard, revealing a small bay. 'One large vegetable penne bake,' he said.

To Ophelia's astonishment, the meal appeared, hot and steamy, in a large dish, at the bottom of the bay.

'Plates, cutlery, serviettes and two bottles of water,' the man added.

Ophelia was quick to open a serviette and place it over her knee, just as her mother had taught her to do. Why she suddenly thought of her mother though, she could not fathom, except that it might mean she was going to die sometime before the day was over. The man shovelled a large blob of food onto her plate.

'Delicious,' she said, swallowing a mouthful of broccoli and cheese.

'It's pretty good, considering how far under the ground we are,' the man replied.

Ophelia wiped her mouth on her serviette. 'It seems ironic that the food down here is so much better than it is on the surface,' she said. 'No doubt most of us surface-dwellers are paying for this with our taxes.'

The man nodded, eating heartily. 'We have better control of the technology down here,' he said.

'How far does this network of tunnels reach?' Ophelia asked.

'Right across Britain. The final exit point is directly under London, at the entrance to the hyperloop,' he replied, showing her the map on her disc.

Ophelia looked at the configuration of tunnels and tiny dots of colour. 'It's astonishing to see this,' she said. 'After decades of life on the surface and no knowledge this place even existed, it's ... well ... it's shocking. To say the least.'

'I know,' he replied. 'Everyone who starts working down here needs a while to adjust. The good food helps.'

But Ophelia could not imagine adjusting to a place like this. 'So, what's your situation?' she asked. 'Do you spend any time on the surface?'

'Yes, of course,' the man replied. 'No one could be expected to live down here permanently. We only work underground for a week and then we're back to the surface for another week.'

'So, at the end of each day down here, what do you do?' she asked.

'Sometimes I socialise with others in the dining room,' he replied. 'But mostly I retreat to one of the sleep pods and listen to music.'

'Sleep pod?' she repeated. 'That's hilarious. What's a sleep pod?'

'You'll find out tonight when I take you to one,' he replied.

Ophelia felt her face flush and her mask prickle against her skin.

'Allow me to clarify,' said the man. 'I will escort you to a sleep pod, leave you there for the night, and collect you in the morning.'

Ophelia was relieved by his good manners but more aware, with each passing second, of her attraction to him. How though, she had no idea, given the fact she had not even seen him without his mask. Nor had she heard his real voice.

'When you return to the surface, do you stay with your wife?' she asked.

'My wife?' he said, bemused. 'I'm not married.'

An awkward silence followed, inside which Ophelia realised she had caused herself even more embarrassment. She wanted to find a way out of it.

'That's a shame,' she said. 'Married life is wonderful.'

The man did not respond.

'Well, it's wonderful, until it isn't wonderful,' she added.

He nodded.

'Are you sure we haven't met before?' she asked.

'Why do you keep asking me that?' said the man.

'I feel as though we've met before,' Ophelia replied. 'I know that sounds ridiculous, given the circumstances. And the mask. And your distorted voice.'

'It *is* ridiculous,' said the man. 'Your only thought should be staying alive.'

'But *you* would know if we had met me before because *you* have seen *me* without my mask,' Ophelia continued. 'In fact, you've seen me naked, so you certainly have the advantage.'

The man did not respond, which fuelled Ophelia's suspicions even further.

Oxford

'WE'RE DIRECTLY UNDERNEATH the University of Oxford,' said the man.

Immersed in the memory of the emerald green grass throughout the university grounds, Ophelia said nothing. They had always been so vibrant, she recalled, despite the lack of water. The oaks outside the window of her dorm had provided a theatrical display all year, with their changing colour, and the sandstone buildings were so exquisite, she had often imagined they had been carved by angels while everyone slept.

But for now, all Ophelia could see was the man's back. She followed him through another narrow tunnel which, unlike the other ones, had a sharp bend in it and a visible door. A Sentinel stood on either side of the entry and, when the man handed his disc to the nearest one, the Sentinel inserted it into a console beside the door. A holo-screen of luminous blue schematics appeared in the air between them. The Sentinel stared at it for a moment, glanced at Ophelia, then returned his gaze to the man.

'Are you aware we have a criminal on the loose?' he asked the man.

'No, sir,' the man replied.

'She'll be sorry when we find her,' said the Sentinel.

Ophelia felt every molecule in her body rattle with terror.

'You can go,' the Sentinel said, returning the man's disc.

The man stepped forwards and Ophelia followed.

'Not you' said the Sentinel, placing his hand on Ophelia's arm.

Ophelia's heart pounded hard, threatening to rip through her throat.

'Oh, don't worry about her,' said the man. 'She's just my new intern.'

'I'll decide what to worry about,' the Sentinel snapped.

40

He looked Ophelia up and down. 'You're about the same size as our criminal,' he said. 'Show me your disc.'

Barely able to control her trembling hand, Ophelia gave her disc to the Sentinel. As he inserted it into the console, she realised she had no idea what was on it, and she felt herself getting ready to run. But, to her relief, the data revealed nothing more than a bogus date of birth, height and weight. And her status, which simply said *Intern*.

The Sentinel waved Ophelia on behind the man. Her heart was still pounding when the security door slid open and they stepped into a small lobby. She took a slow deep breath.

'It's okay,' said the man. 'You'll be fine.'

Ophelia exhaled long and loud. She rolled her shoulders, trying to relax.

'Let's pause here for a moment,' said the man. 'Take another deep breath.'

Ophelia did so and her heart slowed. But when the man opened the next set of doors, her heart stopped completely. The sight before her was beyond anything she could have ever imagined.

'Welcome to the main Anatomy Lab,' he said.

The lab was filled with neat rows of steel benches, all about waist high and about eighty metres long. Upon each bench were approximately one hundred jars, each containing an organ floating in a bright turquoise liquid. It was luminous, producing a halo that extended several centimetres beyond the walls of the jars. Collectively, the jars reminded Ophelia of a swarm of fireflies in a dark forest.

'What in the ...' she started. 'Are these ... human organs?'

'I'm afraid so,' the man replied.

'There must be thousands of them,' she said.

'Three thousand, four hundred and seventeen to be precise,' he replied, looking at his disc.

Ophelia stared at the collection before her, trying to comprehend. For a moment, she excused the sight on the grounds that medical students had to have something to practice on. But this many? Not likely, she mused.

'So, wh ... um ... where did ...?' she started.

'There's a lot for me to tell you,' said the man.

'This is sick,' Ophelia said, turning away. 'Sorry, but I've always been squeamish. Why are you showing me this ... this gorefest?'

'It's all in the name of cancer,' the man replied.

Ophelia took a moment to process his words. 'Okay, so these organs were removed because they had cancer,' she said, starting to feel a bit more comfortable. 'But what are they being kept for?'

'They don't have cancer,' the man replied.

'But you just said ...' Ophelia started. 'Do you mean to say that everyone who has been diagnosed with cancer has been used to contribute to this ... morbid ... collection?' she asked.

'Yes,' he replied. 'I felt it best to show you the truth.'

'What truth?' she asked. 'I still don't really understand what you're saying.'

'I'm saying that cancer doesn't exist anymore.'

There was something about the man's words that resonated as truth, to Ophelia's way of thinking. She had never been convinced of the cancer diagnoses. And yet, here she was, standing in front of all these organs.

'But, how can ...'

'An anti-cancer vaccine was developed in 2034,' the man explained.

'That was before I was even born!' Ophelia said.

'I know,' the man said.

'Why was I diagnosed with cancer, then?' she asked. 'And the women I met at the cancer care centre, and thousands of other people across Britain. Why were we diagnosed with cancer?'

'It was a justification for removing your organs and storing them here,' he replied.

'But ... why?' Ophelia asked, feeling weak.

The man sighed. 'These organs are here for transplant into anyone who needs them and can afford to pay for them,' he replied.

Ophelia clutched the edge of the bench in front of her and the man placed his hand on her back.

'Don't touch me!' she snapped, pulling away from him.

Then she slid down to the floor and leaned against the wall, staring at the shocking display before her. The magnitude of the violation was too much for her. She simply could not accept what the man was saying. She *had* to challenge him.

'But stem cells are used to grow new organs,' she said. 'That's what the medical students worked with when I was here.'

'True,' the man replied. 'But those organs are only transplanted into people who can't afford to pay for the real thing.'

'Why?'

'Organs created from stem cells were a great idea in theory,' the man replied. 'But they almost always break down, at the cellular level, within a few years of implant.'

'What are we looking at, then?' Ophelia asked.

The man stepped back before responding. 'We're looking at healthy organs, taken from healthy people, in the name of cancer, for transplantation into the hedonistic Ruling Elite,' he replied.

Ophelia slid down, onto her knees. 'Does this mean that some woman from the Ruling Elite will receive my womb and my unborn baby?' she asked.

The man sat on the floor beside her. 'No,' he replied, softly. 'The Ruling Elite still prefer to use the surrogacy system.'

Ophelia did not want to ask the next question, but she knew she had to. 'So, where is my womb? And my baby?'

The man looked down for a moment. 'I suspect they would have used the embryo for stem cell harvesting.' he said.

Ophelia gasped. Then, like the walls of a mighty dam breaking, her lungs tore open and she sobbed. For how long, she had no idea.

. . . .

SLUMPED ON THE FLOOR, Ophelia returned her gaze to the thousands of jars in front of her. 'It's not too far off genocide,' she said.

'Agreed,' said the man.

She closed her eyes for a moment, resting them from the pain of crying. 'How long have they been doing this?' she asked.

'I'm not privy to that information,' the man replied. 'And it's difficult to guess because everything down here is changing constantly.'

Ophelia's mind felt numb and her body felt empty. But almost at peace. And not just because she had cried for however long it had been but also because she might have found closure. For a moment, she did feel as though she might have found closure but then her curiosity spiked again.

'What about one of the women I met at the cancer centre?' she said. 'They had removed her breasts. For God's sake, why? Surely they won't be transplanting her breasts onto someone else. Will they? I mean that's hideous. How the f...'

'No,' the man interjected. 'There are several experiments in progress down here. All kinds of human tissue are being used.'

Ophelia's imagination roamed to the vilest of guesses about what that could mean but quickly retreated and returned to the scene in front of her. 'What's that luminous blue liquid?' she asked.

'It contains an immunosuppressant enzyme that prevents rejection by the host after the organ is transplanted,' the man replied.

'The success rate has been one hundred percent since it was first used.'

'Well, isn't that handy for those who reap the benefit,' Ophelia said bitterly.

Then she considered the mass deception of the people of Britain. 'We've all been fed a pack of lies, for decades,' she said. 'Haven't we?'

'Yes,' the man replied.

Ophelia found his honesty and directness refreshing after all the lies and denial she had endured from Gaia in recent weeks. But still, she hated him for showing her this abomination. And yet, she knew she had to learn more.

'If everything you've said is true,' she continued. 'What's in the chemotherapy they've been giving to us so-called cancer patients?'

'At first, it was a massive dose of vitamin P,' he replied. 'And then it was something else they wanted to experiment with. Whatever the research interests of the day are, they administer to the so-called cancer patients, then they monitor the effect.'

'Why?'

'This is how bioresearch is done nowadays,' he replied.

'Nowadays? What does that mean?'

'Since research on animals was outlawed.'

'Outlawed,' she echoed.

'Yes, an Act in parliament was passed in ...'

'I know what outlawed means!' Ophelia snapped. 'I just can't believe that the people who run this place give a crap about the law. I mean, look at this abomination!' she shrilled.

'I'm so sorry I've shown you this,' said the man.

'What was your intention in doing so?' Ophelia asked.

'I know you value the truth,' he replied. 'And I want you to tell as many people as possible about this place. Once you're safely out of here, that is.'

'What about you?' Ophelia asked. 'Whom do you tell?'

'No one,' the man replied. 'I signed the Official Secrets Act when I commenced working down here. If I divulge anything about this place I will be tried for treason, and possibly executed, which is another reason I want you out of here before they realised I've helped you.'

For a moment, Ophelia felt sorry for the man. She could see he felt trapped inside this chamber of horrors. 'How do you even sleep at night?' she asked.

'I hardly slept for the first year I worked down here,' he replied. 'Until I found ways to cope. Helping people like you who will one day transform this entire nightmare is the only thing that keeps me going.'

Ophelia shook her head. 'I'm certainly not up for transforming anything,' she said.

Then she stood up, smoothed the legs of her suit, determined to put this hideous experience behind her and escape as soon as possible.

'I know this has been overwhelming,' said the man. 'Especially after what you've been through during the last few months. But if ...'

'Please,' she said. 'Just get me out of here.'

• • • •

WITH SURPRISING EASE, Ophelia navigated to the nearest sleep pod. When she arrived at the place that corresponded with a purple circle on the map, she pointed her disc at the wall, just as she had seen the man do. A door appeared and opened, revealing a room which, she guessed, would have been about the size of her bathroom at home. Facing the door was a long bench protruding from the wall. Upon it was a thick layer of black rubber and at the end was a set of freshly pressed black sheets and a matching pillow.

Ophelia entered the sleep pod, aware the man was behind her.

'One bottle of water,' she said to the sustenance bay in the wall.

When the bottle appeared, she pulled off the lid and threw it onto the floor.

Sipping the water, Ophelia looked to the other end of the room, noticing the sonic shower and the ablution unit. 'Looks like I have all the necessities,' she said.

'I'll meet you outside this door at 07:00 tomorrow morning,' said the man.

Ophelia nodded, barely looking at him.

He moved towards the door then stopped. 'By the way, you're safe in here,' he said. 'No-one can enter this room. The door will only open when you insert your disc into this,' he added, pointing to the console on the wall.

Ophelia peeled her mask from her face and wiped away her sweat and tears.

The man stepped towards her. 'I truly am very sorry for what happened to you, Ophelia,' he said.

For a moment, Ophelia felt softened by his kindness. 'You know my name!' she said.

The man took in a deep breath and stepped back, as though realising his error.

'You didn't mean to say my name, did you?' said Ophelia.

The man sighed before responding. 'Ophelia Alsop, Professor of Literature from the University of Oxford, living and teaching in Stratford-upon-Avon,' he said.

'Will you please tell me who you are?' Ophelia asked.

'I will in time,' he replied. 'I promise.'

'But we don't have time! You said so yourself! *Please*, just tell me who you are and how you know me!' Ophelia insisted.

The man looked down at the floor, clearly feeling the difficulty of the situation. Ophelia stared at him for a moment, waiting for him to reveal some of the mystery behind their connection, but he did not speak. Then she stepped towards him and looked into his eyes, the only part of his face she could see. Except for his lips. His luscious lips. He returned her gaze.

'For she had eyes and chose me,' Ophelia whispered.

'What?'

'Sorry, that was a quote from Shakespeare,' Ophelia replied. 'You have beautiful eyes and I know I have seen them bef...'

The man kissed her. On the lips. She returned the kiss, passionately, feeling waves of pleasure ripple through her body, from her mouth to her heart to her sex and out the tips of her fingers and toes. They removed each other's hoods and unzipped each other's suits to their waists. Ophelia slid her fingers under the man's vest and stroked his chest and belly. When he quivered under her touch she peeled his mask away from his mouth and kissed him even more deeply. Then she ripped it from his face completely.

And there it was – a face she knew as well as her own.

'Well, now you know,' he said.

'Martin!' she said. 'I can't believe it!'

'Yes, it's me,' he said with a nervous laugh.

'I knew I knew you!' she said.

'You do know me,' he replied. 'And I know you.'

Ophelia pressed her face into his shoulder and wrapped her arms around him. 'I haven't seen you for years!' she said. 'I've missed you so much, Martin. You just disappeared! What the hell happened?'

Martin sighed and sat down on the edge of the bunk. 'After my PhD, things started to move very quickly,' he said. 'And, before I knew it, I was recruited to work down here.'

'But, why?' Ophelia asked.

Martin scratched his forehead, as though trying to extract the right answer to Ophelia's question. 'Well, at first, I thought it was just a big storage facility, so I was happy to sign the Official Secrets Act,' he said. 'But then I found myself locked into this bizarre situation, almost overnight, and it was terrifying.'

'Martin, that was five years ago!' Ophelia protested. 'Surely, you haven't been working here all that time?'

'Yep,' he sighed.

Ophelia kneeled on the floor in front of him, placing her hands upon his. 'Your disappearance broke my heart,' she said.

'I'm sorry, Ophelia,' he said. 'But, as I recall, you had already started flirting with Peter.'

Ophelia felt her heart sink. 'I know,' she said. 'I'm so sorry. I was stupidly impulsive and swept off my feet the first time Peter took me up in his aircraft. It was a shallow action and, believe me, I've paid the price for it.'

'You seemed to be living a happy life from what I heard,' Martin replied.

'Not really,' Ophelia said, sitting back on the floor. 'I shared my life with a polite stranger – someone with whom I had nothing in common – no point of connection and no intimacy.'

'I can't imagine you living without passion,' said Martin.

Ophelia recalled that Martin had always loved her passion, and, for that, she had always been grateful. She had always felt loved and accepted for who she really was, at her core.

'But I've always been ashamed of my passion,' she said, twirling her mask between her fingers. 'It's always made me stand out from the crowd, and it's got me into *so* much trouble. I tried to tone it down for Peter, but it almost drove me mad trying to be someone I'm not.'

'We all do our best,' Martin said, staring at the ground.

'You always made far more sensible decisions than I did,' said Ophelia. 'I've made so many stupid mistakes by being impulsive. I'm a disaster, a train wreck, I know this about myself. I'm under no illusions.'

Martin leaned forward and stroked the side of Ophelia's face. 'Yes, you are a bit too impulsive, Ophelia, but there's more to you than that,' he said. 'You've never been able to hold your tongue in the face of injustice. That was one of the things I always loved the most about you.'

Ophelia remembered how much Martin had loved that aspect of her. And how kind he had been whenever she had taken a stand for one cause or another. How wonderful it would be to be loved like that, again, she mused.

'I never stopped thinking about you,' Ophelia said, kissing his hands. 'I've asked Gaia about you, many times over the years, and it's never told me anything. Frustrating though that has been, at least I knew you hadn't died.'

Martin pulled Ophelia toward him. They kissed again. Enraptured, she pushed him onto the bed and lay on top of him, pulling at his suit. Then his hands locked onto her waist and he lifted her up and away from him. Still holding her, he stood up and dumped her back onto the bed.

Exhilarating though it was, Ophelia felt deflated. And rejected.

'Well, someone still does Ninjutsu,' she said.

'Every morning, my love,' he replied, zipping up his suit.

Ophelia knew he was shutting her out. 'Martin, I know we can't erase the last five years of separation,' she said. 'But I'd really love to try. Wouldn't you?'

He looked at her for a moment. Then slowly, he nodded.

'I'm so sorry for hurting you,' Ophelia said. 'Can you ever forgive me?'

'I already have,' Martin replied. 'Do you forgive me?'

'Of course, my darling,' Ophelia said, standing up.

She placed her hands on his shoulders. 'I want to save you as much as you're saving me!' she said. 'Please, Martin, come with me. Whenever it is that you break me out of here, just come with me!'

'I'd love to, Ophelia, but I have to finish some things I've started here.'

'For how long?' Ophelia asked.

'It's hard to say, exactly,' Martin replied. 'A few weeks, perhaps, depending on the plans of others. That's all I can say, for now.'

Ophelia watched him fix his mask to his face and straighten his suit. He had always been an orderly chap, she recalled with a flush of warmth.

'I'll be back tomorrow morning,' he said, stepping towards the door.

Ophelia watched Martin leave for the second time. And, just as he had done before, he stopped and turned around to face her.

'Ophelia, there's one thing I should have told you,' he said.

'Yes?'

'Those lenses in your eyes are recording devices.'

'What?'

'They're recording everything you see down here,' he said. 'No sound, only vision.'

'Why? What for?'

'I want you to surrender the lenses to Emilie, a woman in Paris,' he replied. 'You must contact her, the instant you arrive in Paris. I'll give you her details before you leave.'

'You're using me as courier service,' Ophelia said, feeling deflated.

'Yes, but I promise you'll understand why when you get to Paris,' Martin replied. 'It will make sense then, Ophelia, I promise.'

And then he was gone.

• • • •

OPHELIA SAT ON THE bed, motionless, slowly processing her encounter with Martin. A flood of wonderful memories welled up inside her – momentarily washing away the traumas of the last few weeks – but retreated just as quickly. It suddenly occurred to her that she no longer knew who she was.

The sonic shower did nothing to clear her mind.

Exhausted, she lay on the bed, closed her eyes and slipped into a dream.

She is with Martin, playing in the ocean, diving into the shallow waves. Sunlight sparkles across the surface of the water. She tastes the salt in the air. The waves break on the sand, rhythmic and reliable. Together, they walk out to sea, along the surface, navigating each wave, one stepping down as the other steps up, helping each other to stay afloat. 'This is great teamwork!' Martin says. She raises her arm to wrap it around him, but just as her fingers touch his shoulder, she is lifted into the air. She looks up, into the belly of a drone. It is huge, perhaps the size of her car. It is black, oval-shaped, has six legs underneath and four propellers on top that buzz and whoop all at once. As she ascends higher, she feels the cold breeze against her damp skin and her dress flapping in the wind. The world looks fantastic from this perspective. The shapes and colours of the land below are so lovely, she wants to tell Martin about them. But there is another presence. The drone. It is sentient. She lifts her head to speak to it, only to see Peter's face peering down at her through a window in the belly of the thing. She calls out to him, but he does not respond. His face is impassive, as he orders the drone to open its claws and release her. The fall is slow, so slow that every detail of her descent seems magnified by a thousand times. She is helpless to change her course as she enters a volcano. Terrified by the sight of the molten lava below her, she believes she will be burnt to death. But as she gets close to it, the pool of lava moves aside, leaving a cylindrical opening for her. She slips through, feeling the intense heat upon her skin. The lava spirals around her, somehow slowing her fall, and then it speaks to her. 'You do not belong here', it says, releasing her to a dark and empty space below.

Ophelia woke to the painful sensation of landing on the floor. 'Lights!' she called out.

She looked around at the narrow bunk she had been sleeping in and concluded she must have rolled out. Reluctantly, she got back into bed, closed her eyes and waited for 07:00 to arrive.

• • • •

OPHELIA WOKE TO A PLEASANT tinkling sound. When it stopped, she concluded she had only dreamt it, so she rolled over and returned to sleep. But the tinkling persisted and then she remembered.

'Martin!' she called out, rolling off the bed.

She pressed her disc into the gel pad beside the door and it opened.

'Hello, sleepyhead,' said Martin, stepping into her room.

Ophelia wrapped her arms around his waist and pressed her cheek against his shoulder, wanting to remain glued to him forever. 'I'm so glad our meeting was not just a dream,' she said.

Martin kissed her on the forehead, his mask rasping against her bare skin. She tried to peel it from his face, as she had done the previous night, but he stopped her. Cradling her hand inside his, he stroked the side of her face with his forefinger.

'Come back to bed with me,' Ophelia said, pressing her hips into his.

Martin let out a groan. 'No, Ophelia,' he said.

'Stars, hide your fires; let no light see my black and deep desires,' Ophelia said.

'Thanks, Mr. Shakespeare,' said Martin.

Ophelia pressed herself against him, even more firmly than before. Then he pushed her back.

'We don't have time for this, Ophelia,' he said. 'Please don't tempt me. Please just get dressed so I can get you out of here.'

Ophelia stepped into her suit, slowly, keeping her eyes locked on Martin's, hoping he would change his mind. But he didn't. She zipped up her suit, all the way to her chin then pressed her mask against her nose.

'I still find it incredible,' she said. 'I mean, look at the thing! It's crawling around my face!'

'Are you ready now?' Martin asked.

'It's amazing that its eye holes are in the right place,' Ophelia continued. 'And its mouth hole is in the right place. And free for kissing,' she added, pursing her lips.

Martin kissed her quickly, then stepped back. 'Are you ready?' he asked.

'Ready as I'll ever be,' Ophelia replied.

'Let's start with breakfast,' he said. 'The Sentinels are usually a bit more relaxed around mealtime, so we should be off to a good start.'

Ophelia nodded, then opened the map on her disc. 'The green squares are the dining rooms, right?'

'Yep.'

• • • •

A FEW HUNDRED METRES down the tunnel, Ophelia saw two Sentinels walking towards her and Martin. She put her head down, pretending to read her disc. They passed, uncomfortably close, causing a sickening ripple up her spine.

'I'll be very pleased to leave this place,' she whispered. 'But I can't bear to lose you again, Martin.'

Martin clasped her hand. 'We'll find our way back to each other,' he said. 'One way or another, we'll make it happen.'

'I hope that's what you want,' Ophelia asked.

'More than anything,' he replied.

As they turned a corner, Ophelia saw bright light flooding the tunnel. 'I guess this is it,' she said, looking at her map and then at the archway carved into the wall. 'There's no invisible door for me to point my disc at.'

'Not for the dining rooms, my dear,' Martin replied.

The ceiling, walls and floors were made from a shiny white substance Ophelia had never seen before. Each wall contained several sustenance bays. The room was filled with neat rows of black tables and chairs upon which, she guessed, about fourty people were sitting. This was the first time she had ever seen so many people in one place all dressed the same and, for a moment, it reminded her of the murmuration of starlings she had seen a few days ago.

'Croissant and coffee,' Martin said to the bay.

'Mushroom frittata and coffee,' said Ophelia.

Her attention was then drawn to all the masks. It seemed like an even split – about half were white and the other half were black – and the fact the masks were all the same shape, and completely lacking that would normally define a human expression, unnerved her.

She followed Martin to a table.

'Good morning everyone, this is my new intern,' he said, sitting down.

Everyone nodded at Ophelia and she returned the gesture.

Martin ripped off a piece of his croissant and threw it straight into his mouth.

'How are the croissants today?' someone asked.

'Very pleasant, thank you,' Martin replied, chewing with passion.

'The coffee is nice, too,' said Ophelia, trying to fit in.

Several people nodded in polite agreement, but no one spoke. For the next few minutes, the only sound Ophelia heard was the cacophony of cutlery clanging against plates, food being chewed, and drinks being slurped.

Then two Sentinels entered the dining room. 'Attention!' one of them shouted.

Everyone stopped what they were doing.

'We have a criminal on the loose,' said the other Sentinel. 'She's a slut and is wanted for several crimes.'

Ophelia felt her mushroom frittata churning in her stomach and her coffee sliding back up her oesophagus. Martin, it seemed, was as cool as always.

The Sentinel continued. 'She escaped the prison cell, north of here, approximately twenty-four hours ago,' he said. 'She could be anyone, dressed just like you. She could be disguised as a man. She could be the person sitting next to you.'

Everyone looked at the person next to them. A steel door slid down over the exit and two security bots, about three hundred centimetres tall, stood in front of it.

'You are all accustomed to iris scanning,' said the Sentinel. 'You are to look directly into the bot's eyes until it turns away from you and moves on to the next person.'

Four more security bots were set loose amidst the anxious dinners. Starting in each corner of the room, they approached one person at a time, stared into their eyes for a second, then moved on. Ophelia could not help noticing how nervous everyone seemed.

'This is going to take ages,' someone grumbled.

'I know,' someone else whispered. 'I'm going to be late for my shift.'

Martin continued to eat his breakfast as though nothing was happening. To Ophelia's eyes, he seemed ostentatiously relaxed, bored even, and she wondered how he could be so cool. He was still chewing his croissant when he looked into the bot's eyes. When the bot stepped in front of Ophelia, she felt her heart pounding. She would not have been surprised if she were to vomit it up and onto the floor. But, somehow, she managed to stare defiantly into the bot's eyes. The turquoise lights flickered slightly as it processed what it was seeing. Then it moved on to the next person.

Incredulous, Ophelia looked at Martin, but he refused to acknowledge her. Still looking bored, he helped himself to a second croissant.

'Thank you for your patience,' said the Sentinel. 'There will be a reward for you, should you help us capture the criminal. It is a female, slight build and approximately one hundred and sixty centimetres tall. Keep your eyes open, listen to the words of those around you, and if anything seems suspicious, you are to use the silent comms system to report it immediately.'

The other Sentinel approached the archway. 'Exit!' he said. The steel door slid up and the Sentinels and their security bots left the dining room.

Slowly, the staff followed.

Ophelia turned toward Martin who was still chewing a croissant. 'I'm amazed by how cool you are,' she whispered.

Martin swallowed. 'I have full confidence in those lenses,' he whispered. 'But eventually the Sentinels will catch on, and I want you out of this place before they do.'

Another bioengineer approached the table and asked Martin something technical. It meant nothing to Ophelia, so she allowed her attention to drift into the discussion at the next table.

'I think she's gone to work in the Garden of Eden,' said one person.

'Well, you can forget about seeing or hearing from her again,' said another.

'That whole situation is tragic, heart-breaking and ...'

'Those girls are treated as nothing more than commodities ...'

'I know,' said the first person. 'Let's not discuss it anymore. 'It's just too upsetting.'

Ophelia's curiosity had been piqued. She would have assumed that a place called the Garden of Eden would be a place for botanical research, but the tone of the conversation seemed to suggest something else.

• • • •

ALONE IN THE TUNNEL with Martin, Ophelia took the opportunity to ask the question she had been burning to ask for almost twenty minutes. 'What's the Garden of Eden?' she whispered.

Martin stopped walking and stared at her. 'Where did you hear about that?' he demanded.

'Some people at the next table were talking about it,' Ophelia replied.

'I've never been there myself,' Martin replied. 'But I'm aware it's the place they keep the surrogates.' He stopped walking and stared at her. 'Ophelia, you had better not get any wild ideas about snooping around down there,' he said. 'You're in danger, as you've already seen, and you need to focus on getting to that hyperloop and making your way to Paris.'

Ophelia was listening to Martin, but she was also wondering how she could get into the Garden of Eden for a quick look before departing. After all, it would be a shame to waste the recording lenses in her eyes. Furthermore, it might ...

'Hey! I'm speaking to you!' Martin shouted.

'Okay, Martin. I'm sorry,' she replied. 'Yes. Of course.'

They walked in silence for a few more minutes during which, Ophelia could feel Martin's anxiety and frustration. Then he clutched her hand. His grip warm and passionate, arousing snippets of erotic memory within her. She wanted to be with him again, more than anything. She wanted to live with him, above the surface, and get to know him all over again.

'Martin, I ...'

'This is the border,' he said.

Ophelia could see that the border between Oxfordshire and Buckinghamshire was marked just as clearly in the tunnel as it would have been on a road above the surface.

'That's you,' said Martin, pointing at the sign to London.

'I can't bear it, Martin,' she said, wrapping her arms around his neck. 'I have so many regrets, and I love you so m ...'

Martin coughed, uncomfortable, then pushed her back, ever so gently. 'Between here and London, there's a lot going on,' he said. 'Please don't be tempted to stop and gawk at things. As I said before, you must keep your head down and get to Paris.'

'Okay,' Ophelia replied, reaching over to kiss him.

Martin gripped her arms firmly, holding her away. 'For God's sake, Ophelia!' he exclaimed. 'I'm not getting the feeling you're taking this seriously. Do you understand what I'm saying?' he asked, almost shaking her.

Ophelia nodded.

He handed her a small white backpack. 'There's a fresh set of clothes in there for you,' he said.

'Will I even get through security in Paris?' Ophelia asked.

Martin cleared his throat before responding. 'Their scanners won't recognise you as a citizen of the north because of the lenses in your eyes,' he said. 'But it won't recognise you as a citizen of the south either, so you'll have to come up with a creative explanation.'

'This is scary,' Ophelia said, suddenly feeling alone.

'I know,' Martin replied. 'But if anyone can barge through red tape with brazen creativity, it's you, Ophelia. I know you can do this.'

'You said you know people in Paris, right?' Ophelia confirmed.

Martin nodded. 'Emilie and Philippe Trudeau,' he said. 'Their details are on your disc, so please contact them. They're expecting you.'

Martin kissed her quickly then stepped back. 'Good luck my love,' he said.

Ophelia felt a crushing pain in her chest as she stepped into the pod. And as it rolled forward, she turned around to look at Martin one last time.

• • • •

NOW THAT OPHELIA WAS gone, Martin decided to seek the answers to the questions that had been bothering him. Yesterday, when he had told Ophelia he thought her foetus would have been used for stem cell harvesting, he had truly believed that to be a reasonable assumption. But that was all it was. An assumption. He needed to know for sure, so he headed back to the Anatomy Lab.

The Sentinel at the door snatched Martin's disc from his hand. 'Why are you an hour early?' he asked.

'I have a backlog of work to get through, sir, cataloguing and so on, and I thought it best to make an early start and I ...'

'Fine. Just leave when the shift alarm sounds.'

'Thank you, sir. I will,' Martin replied.

He knew he would have to work fast to get through his assigned work *and* investigate Ophelia's situation. Ordinarily, the work would have taken precedence over anything else, but not today. Today, Ophelia's concerns came first.

A curious colleague stared at him. 'Hey, you're an hour early,' she said.

'Yes, I have a backlog of work, I'm afraid,' Martin replied. 'Must get on with it.'

He found a quiet workstation in the corner and activated the database. 'Gaia, display all delivery records from the first of April to the fifteenth of April,' he whispered.

About thirty records displayed on the screen. Ophelia's record said – *Ophelia Alsop. Age 28 years. Married female. Academic Professional. Uterus and foetus of 9 weeks' gestation at date of harvest. Delivery to Main Anatomy Laboratory on 7 April 2120. Storage K:37.*

Martin went to Row K, Jar 37, expecting to see Ophelia's organ floating in the turquoise liquid. But the jar was empty. Perhaps the organ had been delivered and removed on the same day, he mused. 'Gaia, display all departure records from the seventh of April to today,' he said.

The record said – *Uterus and foetus of 9 weeks' gestation at date of harvest. Departure from Main Anatomy Laboratory on 7 April 2120.* 'Show me the destination of the organ,' Martin whispered. The record showed – *Unknown.*

Martin felt bewildered. He knew that about ninety-five percent of the organs delivered to the lab ended up in one of those jars. The remaining five percent went to the Research Unit, in which case, the record always showed the Research Unit as the destination. He then recalled the first, and only, time that he had been inside the Research Unit. It was during his induction to the underground. It had been difficult to access and the Sentinel who had taken him there had been reprimanded for doing so. The incident had stuck in his mind ever since, but he had never felt motivated to explore it. Not until now.

He decided to take a break in the amenities room and give it some thought.

Sipping a cup of tea, Martin stared at his location tracker, expecting to see that Ophelia's pod was approaching the hyperloop. Instead, it showed she was entering the Garden of Eden.

'Fuck!' he shouted, throwing his disc onto the floor. 'Stupid, bloody ...'

'Are you okay?'

Martin turned around to see a rotund technician standing behind him. 'Sorry for my language,' she said, his head falling into his hands.

'No worries,' said the technician. 'I've been randomly going off like that ever since my girlfriend left me.'

'Sorry to hear that,' Martin replied, slumping across the table.

'Thanks,' said the technician, sitting opposite Martin.

Martin sighed. 'Sometimes things just don't work out,' he said. 'Sometimes it doesn't matter how much effort you put into a relationship, the other person might not ...'

'Sounds like you might be singing the blues,' said the technician.

For a moment, Martin felt irritated. Then he laughed. 'Yes, I suppose I am.'

The technician leaned forward, then looked around before speaking. 'My girlfriend left me to work in the Garden of Eden,' he said. 'Of all places, she had to choose the one place that I can never visit and that she can never escape from.'

Martin almost felt his ears wrapping around the young man's words. 'How long ago was that?' he asked.

'About a week,' the technician replied. 'I just don't understand it. All that secrecy. And no contact with anyone. Why would she make that choice? They must have offered her a huge amount of money,' he said, shaking his head.

'Why do you suppose that would be?' Martin asked. 'The secrecy, I mean.'

'I don't know,' the technician replied, looking down at his hands. 'I guess there's some sensitive research going on down there.'

'But everything underground is sensitive,' Martin replied. 'That's why we were forced to sign the Official Secrets Act.'

The technician nodded. 'True,' he said. 'But it seems there's an extra layer of secrecy down there. They must be doing something truly awful down there.'

Martin began to feel the power of the opportunity before him. 'It might be interesting to visit that place,' he said. 'What do you think?'

For a moment, the young man seemed to freeze. Then he leaned back in his chair and stared at Martin. 'I really don't see how that's possible,' he said.

'It *is* possible if we become Sentinels,' Martin replied.

'What?'

'Let's become Sentinels!' said Martin. 'I need to get into the Research Unit to find out what happened to *my* girlfriend, and you need to get into the Garden of Eden to find out what happened to *your* girlfriend. It seems logical that we join forces and help each other, doesn't it?'

'Um. No,' said the young man, shifting about in his chair.

Martin leaned across the table and stared at him. 'I'm sure I sound a bit mad to you right now,' he whispered. 'But think about it. We're in the same boat. Why shouldn't we help each other?'

'Yeah, but what you're suggesting is akin to suicide,' the technician replied. 'If we get caught imitating a pair of Sentinels ...'

'We won't get caught,' Martin interjected. 'All we need to do is capture two of them and take their suits.'

'Capture a couple of Sentinels?' the young man scoffed. 'Do you hear yourself talking? You obviously haven't been down here for very long.'

'I've been down here for five years,' Martin said. 'And never once during that time, have I strayed from the protocol. How about you?'

'Two years,' the technician replied. 'Honestly, I've never once strayed from the protocol. The penalty is too severe.'

'Yeah?' said Martin. 'How do you know?'

Aware that he was manipulating the young man beyond any boundary of professional or personal ethics to which he was accustomed to holding himself, Martin felt bad. But he was desperate. 'Think about it,' he persisted. 'If we're wearing Sentinel suits, no one will ask for our discs and no one will limit our access. We'll be able to go anywhere we want.'

Martin then realised – not only was he manipulating the younger man but – he was starting to sound as brash and naïve and Ophelia. But he no longer cared because he had concluded that desperate situations call for desperate actions.

• • • •

MARTIN AND THE TECHNICIAN hid behind the cryo-tank.

'All we can do now is wait for them,' Martin whispered. 'And just remember, the pen is mightier than the sword. Or in this case, the sedative is mightier than the muscle,' he added, double-checking the dose he had programmed the dispenser to release.

The lab door opened.

'Steady,' Martin whispered, peering around the corner of the tank. He saw two Sentinels enter the lab. Then, walking side by side, as always, they walked the full length of one of the benches gazing at the organs in the jars.

'Where do you suppose the technician is?' the bigger one said.

'Probably at one of the food bays,' said the other. 'He's a fat pig.'

'Let's check it out,' said the first one, walking towards the entrance to the hall.

Martin heard the hiss of the door opening to the ablution unit. 'One of them's using the bog,' he whispered. 'That means the other one will be standing by doing nothing. Follow me.'

Using his Ninjutsu training, Martin crept quickly and quietly towards the Sentinel. With one easy move, he jabbed the sedative into the man's neck. The man fell, instantly but the technician broke his fall. Together, they carried the man into the lab and laid him on the floor.

Martin heard the door to the ablution unit open. 'You go and talk to him and I'll sneak up behind him,' Martin whispered.

'I'll try,' the technician replied.

Martin watched his portly friend waddle out of the lab.

'Good evening, sir. May I help you?' said the technician.

'Hey, Fatty,' the Sentinel replied. 'What are you doing here?'

'I'm a bit caught up with a technical problem in the amenities room, sir,' the technician replied. 'Please, could I seek your advice on the matter?'

'Where's my colleague?' the Sentinel asked.

'He's already down there, sir.'

'All right. Lead the way.'

Martin watched the Sentinel follow the technician, their bodies fast becoming silhouettes in the dark hall. Then, like a cat stalking its prey, Martin snuck up behind the Sentinel. He sprung into the air, his hand poised to jab the Sentinel in the back of the neck. But the Sentinel sensed his presence and turned around. With reflexes even faster than Martin's, the Sentinel thrust his fist into Martin's belly, throwing him into the air. Martin hit the wall, then landed painfully on his side, to the sickening pop of his shoulder dislocating. He howled in pain. Unable to move, he could do no more than crunch his body into a tight ball and use his good arm to shield his face and chest as the Sentinel lunged toward him. He squeezed his eyes closed, bracing for the impact of the Sentinel's attack, but instead the man collapsed, unconscious, beside him. Martin opened his eyes, seeing that the only man standing was the technician, proudly clutching the dispenser.

'I can't move,' Martin said. 'My shoulder has popped out.'

'Yeah, I heard it,' the technician replied, rolling Martin onto his back. He pressed the dispenser into Martin's shoulder. 'Don't worry, I reduced the dose by ninety percent, so you won't pass out like these jerks,' he said.

With both hands gripping Martin's upper arm, the technician pushed hard, causing Martin to scream again. Suddenly, the pain was gone. Martin's shoulder was exactly where it should be.

'Looks good to me,' said the young man, slapping Martin on the back.

'Amazing,' Martin replied, rolling his shoulder up and down. 'Where did you learn how to do that?'

'My dad,' the technician replied. 'He had a crappy shoulder. Sadly, he couldn't afford the joint replacement surgery, and the cortisone shots had stopped working, so I had to do that to him about once a week.'

'Wow.'

The technician pulled Martin to his feet. 'I hope you're okay now because I can't lift this bastard by myself,' he said.

Together they dragged the second Sentinel into the lab and laid him beside his colleague.

'We should probably wear their uniforms over our own,' said Martin.

'Agreed,' said the technician. 'No point leaving any of our own DNA behind us.'

They wasted no time in stripping the Sentinels down to their underwear and donning their suits. As the technician zipped up his new suit, Martin noticed it was the suit of a Super Sentinel. The gold star at the centre of the red armband was obvious to him now.

'That's going to come in handy,' he said, pointing to it.

'Hell, yeah!' said the young man. 'From now on, you can call me Kingpin.'

'Do you really want me to call you Kingpin?' Martin asked.

'Why not?'

Martin was not sure how to respond. He had never known the name of anyone working down here, and he had never told anyone his name. Anonymity was the first rule of working underground and a major clause in the Official Secrets Act.

Kingpin pointed to the cryo-tank. 'That might be a good hiding place for these guys,' he said. 'What do you think?'

'I think they'll die without a few thermal wraps,' Martin replied.

'Who cares?' said Kingpin.

Martin made light of the young man's words, then foraged in the storeroom for two large thermal wraps. He may have become a rebel, he told himself, but he was not a murderer.

'Here,' he said, carrying the wraps to the cryo-tank.

They lifted the larger Sentinel into the tank, face-up, then placed one of the wraps on top of him. Then they lifted the second Sentinel into the tank, placing him face-to-face with the first Sentinel and threw another wrap on top of him.

'They won't be happy when they wake up like that,' said Martin, laughing.

'They deserve worse,' Kingpin replied.

Martin referred to his disc, seeking the entrance to the Research Unit. 'I reckon it's around here,' he said, pointing to an obscure point on the map. 'So, if we exit here, and then ...'

'I've been there before,' said Kingpin. 'Follow me.'

• • • •

STEPPING INTO THE RESEARCH Unit, Martin realised it had not changed a bit. The scientists, however, were different. They responded to his presence with awkward deference, something he doubted he could ever get used to.

'Good morning, sirs. May I help you?' one of them asked.

'Who are you?' Martin asked.

'I'm the Chief Research Scientist on shift, sir,' the man replied.

Martin scrolled through the Chief's disc, pretending to verify his claim, then looked at Kingpin as though seeking his approval. Kingpin nodded. 'Show me what you're working on,' Martin said, returning the disc.

'Yes, sir, we have some very exciting projects underway, the first of which is an analysis of the data from a clinical trial of the drug fovealis,' the scientist replied. 'It's a new drug, sir. When administered to the eye in drops, it dramatically expands the function of the fovea centralis.'

This was old news to Martin – having inserted some of the drug into Ophelia's recording lenses and his own – but he decided to play along. 'The part of the eye responsible for sight, is that correct?' he asked.

'Yes, sir. It's a tiny depression at the back of the retina, tightly packed with cones, the cells responsible for the perception of colour. Although we haven't yet mastered the enhanced perception of colour, we have mastered the expansion of peripheral vision which, as you know, sir, is another function of the fovea centralis.'

Martin knew that, too, but he was curious what the scientist might say next. 'How far does the vision extend under the influence of this drug?' he asked.

'Almost one hundred and sixty degrees, a significant increase from the normal human range of one hundred and fourteen degrees,' the scientist replied.

'Interesting. What do you believe will be the practical application of this enhanced capacity?' Martin asked, already knowing the answer – espionage.

'I'm not sure of the application, sir,' the Chief Scientist replied. 'I'm just overseeing the research and development.'

'Are you currently engaged in any research on human reproduction?' Martin asked.

The Chief hesitated for a fraction of a second which was enough to raise Martin's suspicion. 'No, sir,' he replied.

Martin did not believe him. 'Show me the records of all organ deliveries to the Research Unit on the ninth of April,' he said.

'Organ deliveries, sir?' the man replied.

'Yes. Human organs,' Martin repeated.

'Of course, sir. Let me retrieve those records for you,' said the Chief, stepping over to his workstation.

The other two scientists shifted around nervously.

'And what are you working on?' Martin asked one of them.

'Me, sir? Um, I'm working on the ...'

'Forget it. I don't care,' Martin snapped. 'Come on, Chief. Show me those records.'

The Chief Scientist nodded with deference. 'Yes, sir. This is what Gaia has just produced,' he replied, pointing to a holo-list. 'We had quite a few organ deliveries on that day, sir, so it might be difficult to locate anything specific.'

'Rubbish! You had four deliveries and one of them was a human uterus,' said Martin, pointing to the record.

'Oh yes, sir, I see it now,' the Chief replied.

'Correct me if I'm wrong, but isn't the uterus a key component in the reproductive process?' Martin asked, sensing he was getting warm to hot.

'Yes, sir. Of course, it is,' the Chief replied, stepping back.

'So, I repeat my earlier question,' said Martin. 'Are you conducting any research on human reproduction?'

'Um, sir, we do many things in here,' the man replied.

'Show me where that organ is,' Martin said, pointing to Ophelia's record.

'Where it is, sir?'

'Yes,' Martin drawled. 'Are you having difficulty with your hearing?'

'No, sir. Let me get the keys to access that area.'

Both staff scientists shuffled out of the room.

'I am so sorry, sir, but I am having difficulty remembering the access code,' said the scientist.

'Is it an access code you need?' Martin asked.

The Chief nodded.

'A moment ago, you said you needed keys,' said Martin. 'Which is it, do you think? Hm? What do you need, to show us that organ? Keys, or access code?'

'Sorry, sir, I don't go in there very often,' the Chief replied.

'Who *does* go in there?' Martin asked.

'Um, research staff,' said the Chief, shrinking.

'Your research staff have just left the lab,' Martin replied, looking around.

Martin noticed Kingpin standing behind him, his legs spread wide and his arms folded over his barrel chest. For a moment, he almost laughed out loud at his new friend, but then realised he felt bad for the scientist. The poor man, Martin knew, would have been acting on instructions from above the Super Sentinel level and he was now in an impossible situation.

But, one way or another, Martin had to find out what was going on. 'We're running out of time and patience,' he said.

'Sorry, sir. Please follow me,' said the Chief, pointing his disc at his workbench. It slid down to the floor, forming a step, and the wall behind it opened. Martin and Kingpin followed him through.

About two hundred metres down a hallway, there was another door. The Chief pointed his disc at the door and tapped a few characters on its surface. The disc glowed red. 'I'm sorry, sir. I can't seem to remember,' he said, clearing his throat.

'Try harder,' said Kingpin.

Martin watched the Chief try, and fail, two more times. 'It seems to me that you might be incompetent or cognitively impaired, or you are not authorised to hold your position as Chief Research Scientist,' said Martin. 'Are you aware that all three of those possibilities, if proven, could result in a harsh penalty?'

'Please don't report me, sir,' said the Chief.

Martin took a moment to consider the best course of action.

'Excuse me,' said Kingpin, stepping between them. With one simple tap of the Super Sentinel's disc, Kingpin unlocked the door. He stepped through and Martin followed, aware of the sound of the Chief Research Scientist running back down the hallway.

• • • •

UNDER THE SOFT LIGHTING, Martin counted eight rows of four tanks. Each tank was about waist high, one metre wide, half a metre deep and reinforced at all four corners with strips of thick black steel. The tanks were three-quarters full of a thick golden liquid suspending a human organ. The organs varied in size, but they were all the same shape. Pear-shaped. Uteruses.

Vivaldi's *Four Seasons* played in the background.

'They're growing babies,' said Kingpin. 'Inside the womb, but outside the woman, they're growing babies. Why the hell are they doing this?'

Martin's heart sank. 'This is ...'

'An abomination,' said Kingpin.

Martin strolled between the tanks, looking for Ophelia's name. When he reached the second tank on the third row, he found it. The inscription on the black metal base of the tank read – *Ophelia Alsop. Aged 28 years. Academic Professional. Uterus carrying foetus of 9 weeks' gestation upon harvest. Date of arrival at Incubation Laboratory, 9 April 2120.*

He did not want to believe it, but there it was, right in front of him. Ophelia's organ, taken without her consent, and her baby, now fifteen weeks' gestation, were in that tank. He fell to the floor, closed his eyes and let his head fall into his hands.

'Are you all right, mate?' Kingpin asked, crouching beside him.

'Do you remember I told you about my girlfriend?' Martin said.

'Yes.'

'Well, there she is,' said Martin, tapping his finger on the glass. 'Her womb and her baby are in that tank.'

'How the fuck did *that* happen?' the technician asked.

'It's a long story,' Martin replied.

'Where is she now?'

Martin consulted his location tracker. 'The Garden of Eden. The one place I told her not to go.'

'Well, now we both have a reason to visit that place,' said Kingpin. 'But first, I'm going to find out what's in these tanks.'

Kingpin examined the tank, every millimetre of every side. 'If only there were some controls on the thing,' he said. 'Some way of reading the contents. They must be ...'

Martin took the Super Sentinel's disc from Kingpin's pocket. 'Let's do it the old-fashioned way,' he said, dipping his finger into the tank. He collected a tiny blob of the golden liquid on the tip of his glove and wiped it across the surface of the disc. Within seconds, it displayed its analysis – *96% (rapeseed oil) 2.2% (HCG) 1.8% (unknown)*. 'Human chorionic gonadotrophin,' he said. 'That's the primary hormone produced by the placenta during pregnancy. That's what they're nourishing these organs with. God only knows what the other substance is.'

'Let's find out,' said Kingpin.

'Whatever it is,' Martin replied. 'Our discs won't be able to read it.'

'Why?'

'Because it doesn't yet exist,' Martin snapped. 'Come on, mate, I've had enough of this place.'

They stepped through the exit and returned to the Research Unit.

'Hardly surprising,' said Martin, seeing the place was now empty.

Finally, they returned to the tunnel.

'There's a free pod about two hundred and fifty metres south of here,' she Martin, looking at this disc. 'I suggest we take it to the Garden of Eden.'

In transit

GIVEN THE POD'S MAXIMUM speed was thirty kilometres per hour, Ophelia knew she was in for a three-hour journey to London. She ran her finger over the controls on the dashboard, hoping to access some real music, not the rubbish created by Gaia's algorithms. To her delight, she found a catalogue of two hundred years of published music. Real music made by real people. She selected the album *63* by Adele. The soft and soulful sound of the woman's voice was deeply soothing.

Ophelia reclined her seat, stretched her legs, closed her eyes and drifted into the same dream.

She is high in the sky, held by the claws of the black drone. Peter is staring at her, through a window in the belly of the thing. She begs him to help her, but his face is without expression. She cries out again but there is no response from him. She waits for a moment, then cries out a third time, but still, he does nothing to help her. Finally, she understands. The game is to kill or be killed. She grabs the leg of the drone and climbs it, all the way to the window. Peter moves back, afraid of her. She punches her hand through the window, smashing it. The drone explodes in a burst of light leaving no trace of its presence in the sky. She falls towards the volcano and its endless pool of molten lava. But she refuses to fall into it again. She just says 'no' and, to her great surprise, she remains afloat in the air. The view of the land, sea and sky is endless.

When she woke, Ophelia was surprised to realise she had fallen asleep. She was even more surprised by the dream. It had been vivid, but it somehow felt more real than her waking reality in the present moment. For reasons she could not grasp, she felt as if the dream was a message from the divine, telling her she had the power to live, as a free woman, and to make a positive difference.

But how that could possibly happen, her waking mind could not grasp.

Sipping some water, Ophelia checked her map. She was almost directly under London, she realised. There were plenty of amenities and sleep pods in the area, but her eye was drawn to something far more interesting.

'Course correction,' she said to the pod. 'Take me to the Garden of Eden.'

London

THE POD VEERED OFF the main tunnel and entered a much larger tunnel with a high, dome-shaped ceiling. It was more brightly lit than the others and it continued for several hundred metres before reaching a wide cul-de-sac. It travelled to the end of the curve, and around it, then stopped directly in front of a large set of double doors.

Ophelia pointed her disc at the doors, unsurprised that they remained firmly shut. But for reasons she did not fully understand, she was determined to enter the Garden of Eden. Despite Martin's safety warning, and despite the knowledge that the surrogates were kept there, she was acting on instinct and she knew it.

She got out of the pod and waited.

A few moments later, the great doors opened and two Sentinels exited.

'Reporting for duty, sirs,' Ophelia said, enjoying her new-found confidence.

The Sentinels looked at each other for a moment then looked at her again. One of them took the disc from her hand and scrolled through. 'There's no data here, except that ... Oh, I see, you're an intern.'

'Yes, sir, I was told to report here at this time. I think my supervisor assumed that I had the clearance to open those doors.'

The Sentinel continued to scroll through Ophelia's disc. 'You do have the clearance,' he replied. 'You're just not doing it right. Look here, you point your disc at the top of the doors.'

To Ophelia's delight, the huge doors slid open and the Sentinels walked away.

• • • •

OPHELIA STARED AT THE circular reception area in front of her, guessing it must have been about half a kilometre in diameter. At the centre of the circle was a round pond filled with lilies and lotus flowers. Water sprayed from a heart-shaped sculpture in the centre of the pond and returned in a fine gentle spray. Beyond the main circle were several smaller circles containing intimate clusters of lounge chairs. Flowering plants of all colours cascaded down the walls. There were twelve walls, one on either side of six archways, and under each archway was a narrow path that led away from the central circle.

The surrogates, sprawled around the space, seemed happy and relaxed and they all wore the most beautiful, colourful, flowing silk gowns she had ever seen. One woman, dressed as Ophelia was, sat on the floor, massaging the feet of a heavily pregnant woman. Another member of staff sat in a circle with three surrogates, clearly explaining something to them, using her hands to express downward movements. Another one was holding the hands of a very young surrogate while she cried. The staff seemed kind and responsive, not the sinister brides of science that Ophelia had imagined.

Everyone was under the watchful gaze of the Sentinels. With one positioned against each of the six archways, it was clear they were there to control and protect. On either side of the main doors were two large Sentinels standing with their legs apart and their arms folded across their chests. One nodded at Ophelia when she stepped into the centre of the space. Relieved, she returned the nod, then approached a young woman sitting alone.

'Hello,' she said. 'What's your name?'

'I'm Nina,' the woman replied, placing her right foot on Ophelia's knee. 'Would you mind?' she asked, handing a bottle of nail polish to Ophelia.

As Ophelia took the bottle in her hands, she could not help but notice that Nina was the most striking woman she had ever seen.

Her deep olive skin, large hazel green eyes and long sleek black hair reminded Ophelia of a Siamese cat she had once seen in a holo-film.

'This is the last chance I will get to do this before the big day,' said Nina.

'When is your big day?' Ophelia asked, painting Nina's large toenail a cool lavender colour.

'According to the doctor, I have only two days remaining,' Nina replied.

'How do you feel about the birth?' Ophelia asked.

'Good and bad,' Nina replied, shrugging her shoulders. 'On the one hand, I'm quite nervous about it. But on the other hand, I expect I will feel satisfied when I've done my duty as a surrogate.'

Ophelia's heart sank even further.

'Have any of your friends at home been surrogates?' she asked.

'Oh yes,' Nina said, proudly. 'It was great for their families to get that money.'

Ophelia kept her eyes on Nina's toenails, careful to avoid showing her own feelings of concern and sadness for Nina, her baby and the entire situation in which she found herself.

'I need to lie down now,' Nina said, suddenly. 'Help me to my bed?'

'Yes, of course,' Ophelia replied, wrapping one arm around Nina's waist.

As they walked toward one of the archways, Ophelia noticed the floor was soft, springy and easy on the feet. They walked down a narrow path which was softly lit and smelt like fresh jasmine. The warm cream coloured walls seemed endless, punctuated only by quaint wooden doors, each one a different colour. They stopped at a lavender door.

Nina pushed it open. 'Welcome to my place,' she said, waddling to her bed. She flopped onto a pile of lavender satin sheets, pillows and blankets. 'Could you please rub my back?' she asked, turning onto her side.

Ophelia obliged, taking in the details of the young woman's room. Lavender satin sheets were draped everywhere, even the walls. 'You obviously like the colour lavender,' she said.

'It's my favourite,' Nina replied. 'It's nice of them to decorate our rooms in our favourite colours.'

The ceiling was covered with a holo-film of a seaside village. Boats bobbed up and down to the rhythm of the ocean. Someone rode by on a bicycle, silhouetted by the blazing sun setting behind them. Another person stepped out of a boat, yawned and stretched then returned to the lower deck.

'This must be your home,' said Ophelia.

'Yes, it's my village, El Serrallo, in Spain,' Nina replied. 'And this is Madre and Padre,' she added, pressing a button on her portable holo-pad. An image of a man and woman appeared on Nina's pillow. They were smiling, waving and blowing kisses. 'I hope they will be proud of me when this is all over,' Nina said.

'I'm sure they are already proud of you,' Ophelia said.

Nina shrugged her shoulders, as though uncertain, but Ophelia suspected a wave of sadness was working its way through the young woman as she considered the seriousness of what lay ahead of her. She could not help but wonder how Nina would feel when the baby was born and taken away from her. Then she imagined how the baby might feel when removed from the only source of life it had known, only to be passed from one set of hands to another. The cruelty of the impending separation was unfathomable to Ophelia and it sent her thoughts directly to her own loss. Without warning, tears streamed from Ophelia's eyes, causing a sticky mess under her mask.

'You're crying!' said Nina. 'Why?'

For a moment, Ophelia imagined the complete release of telling Nina all the reasons she was crying – being falsely diagnosed with cancer, losing her baby, losing her womb, losing her husband, being abducted, thrown in prison, shown a laboratory of human organs, falling in love again, saying goodbye to her beloved, feeling Nina's impending loss – but then she thought better of it.

'I've just had a tough day,' she said.

'Maybe you should stay here with me,' Nina said with gentle concern.

'Thank you, Nina. I'd love to,' Ophelia replied. She removed her suit and stretched out on the spare bed beside Nina's, once more appreciating the soothing sea-side scenery. 'I feel as though I can almost dangle my feet into that ocean,' she said.

'It's a glorious sensation,' said Nina. 'I can't wait to do it again. But, for now, in this underground place, I often find myself thinking how strange it is that London city is directly above us.'

'I know,' Ophelia laughed. 'It is weird.'

'Do you live in London?' Nina asked.

'No, but I visited once, a long time ago,' Ophelia replied.

'I haven't seen the city at all,' said Nina.

'Really?' Ophelia asked. 'So how did you get here?'

Nina rolled onto her side, facing Ophelia. 'From my home, I caught a train to Paris,' she said. 'Then I caught the hyperloop to the London underground and then a pod collected me and took me here. It all happened very quickly.'

'London is a very strange place,' said Ophelia. 'There's a clear dome built over the entire city because it never stops raining. And there are dams all the way around the perimeter to catch the water.'

'I've heard of that, many times,' Nina said. 'But I still find it impossible to imagine an abundant supply of fresh water.'

The evidence of that fact, Ophelia realised, was inside Nina's belly. And it was almost ready to climb out.

• • • •

OPHELIA WOKE TO THE sound of Nina's voice.

'Wake up!' Nina shouted. 'My baby's coming! Now!'

Ophelia jumped out of bed, donned her suit and mask then helped Nina amble down the path. When they got to the open space, two Sentinels jumped to attention and rushed over. They stood on either side of Nina, placing one hand on her back and another under her legs. Acting as a human chair, they carried her to the far side of the open space, through a small door and into an elevator.

'I want her with me!' Nina cried, clutching Ophelia's hand.

The Sentinels nodded, so Ophelia joined them in the elevator. It descended quickly then opened into a hot concrete pit with dull grey paint peeling from the walls. Both sides of the room were lined with neat rows of black tables. At the end of each table was a small stool illuminated by a harsh spotlight fixed to the grey ceiling. From what Ophelia could see, seven of the beds were occupied by women in labour. The sight and sound of the agony in motion was horrendous. Suddenly, a baby emerged from one of the women amidst a waterfall of blood which splashed onto the floor then trickled into a drain at the centre of the room.

The Sentinels lifted Nina onto the birthing table closest to the elevator and tied her feet into the stirrups. Ophelia could barely imagine how terrified Nina might be feeling. Two nurses appeared, wearing their white suits and masks and rolling their white gloves up to their elbows.

'Hello Nina,' said one of them. 'How are you, today?'

Sweat erupted from Nina's face, neck and chest. She breathed deep and fast then let out a scream so loud and so wild, Ophelia felt it almost peeled the enamel from her teeth.

'Well, that answers my question,' said the nurse, motioning for the assistant nurse to stand beside Nina.

The assistant did so but seemed far more interested in reading the data on the monitoring equipment than on Nina herself. The delivery nurse sat at the end of Nina's bed and thrust her hand into Nina's vagina. The crude action, performed without warning, made Ophelia wince. But Nina did not seem to notice.

'Okay,' said the delivery nurse. 'You're fully dilated but not progressing, so we're going to give you something to speed things up a bit.'

She nodded at the assistant nurse who placed a clear mask over Nina's nose and mouth, held it there for a few seconds then moved it.

Nina released a loud scream.

'Good girl, Nina!' said the delivery nurse. 'Now we're getting somewhere! I need another big push from you. Can you do that for me?'

Nina pushed down hard. So hard, Ophelia could see the veins bulging from Nina's temples.

'Good girl, Nina!' said the delivery nurse. 'That was a very good contraction. It won't be long before the baby arrives.'

Sweat streamed down Nina's body.

Ophelia noticed a small cloth on a steel trolley beside Nina. 'May I use this to wipe Nina's face?' she asked the assistant nurse.

'Over there,' said the assistant, motioning to a crude metal tap on the wall adjacent to the elevator.

Ophelia approached the rusty tap, eyeing the dirty water stain on the wall around it. Desperate to relieve Nina, she poured some water onto the cloth and returned to her side. Then she wiped Nina's skin until Nina screamed again.

'You're dilating quite fast,' said the delivery nurse at the end of the bed. 'That's what we like to see, Nina, good girl!'

The assistant placed a clear mask over Nina's face. Instantly, Nina's face and body relaxed, and Ophelia felt hers do the same.

'Okay Nina,' said the delivery nurse. 'With the next contraction, you must push down hard. Will you do that for me, Nina?'

Nina nodded.

'Good girl,' said the nurse.

When the contraction came, Nina bore down hard and screamed even louder than before.

'Good work, Nina!' said the delivery nurse. 'Once more!'

With one last horrendous push and scream, the baby was out. Ophelia watched the tiny and miraculous human wriggling around in the nurse's hands. Then it made a sound. At first, it was a soft sound, expressing mild discontent. But a few seconds later, it was a shrill protest that almost shattered Ophelia's inner ears.

'Well done, Nina!' said the delivery nurse, handing the baby to the assistant.

Nina sat up and stretched out her arms, towards the baby. 'Please, can I hold my baby?' she asked.

The assistant ignored Nina, focusing only on wrapping the baby in a white cloth.

'Now, Nina, naughty girl,' said the delivery nurse. 'You know he's not your baby.'

'Is my baby all right?' Nina asked.

'He's fine, Nina, but he's not your baby,' the delivery nurse said again, this time pressing her hand down on Nina's belly.

'Is my baby a boy?' Nina asked, watching the assistant nurse take him from the room. She slumped back in on the bed, exhausted. Her hair and clothes were crumpled and her skin dripping with sweat. She started to cry.

'Don't be silly, now, Nina,' said the delivery nurse, slopping Nina's placenta into a bucket.

Ophelia ran to a sink behind Nina's bed and vomited until there was nothing but air being forced from her gut. Then she rinsed her mouth with the dirty tap water, wondering what ghastly experiments they might use the placentas for, and retched some more.

'You're in very good health, Nina,' said the delivery nurse, standing up.

Clinging to the sink, Ophelia was soon approached by the delivery nurse.

'You're not very well are you?' said the nurse, removing her long white and bloodied gloves.

'I ate a large dinner before bed,' Ophelia lied.

'Well, Nina,' the delivery nurse continued. 'You should be pleased. The birth has gone very well, and you will be fine.'

But Ophelia could tell, Nina would not be fine. She would never recover from this. Not really. Not fully. She wiped Nina's face and neck once more, not knowing what else to do.

The nurse placed a small tablet under Nina's tongue. 'This will shut down the bleeding in a few minutes,' she said.

The assistant returned to view the monitoring data on Nina's bed.

'Where did you take my baby?' Nina asked.

'To the family lounge on the surface,' the assistant replied, nonchalantly fiddling with the controls on the monitor.

'Why? What for?' Nina asked.

'That's where he will meet his parents,' the assistant replied. 'His real parents, I mean, not you,' she added, stepping closer to Nina, sponge in hand.

'I'll do that!' said Ophelia, wanting to hit the woman.

As Ophelia cleaned Nina's body, her young friend lay motionless, staring at the ceiling, apparently oblivious to her surroundings. 'Does that feel okay, Nina?' Ophelia asked.

But Nina did not respond.

'They do go weird like that, sometimes,' the assistant nurse said, lifting Nina's naked pelvis into fresh undergarments. 'You must stay warm for the next twenty-four hours,' she said. Then she pushed a thick cotton jumper over Nina's head and brushed her hair, apparently still oblivious to Nina's distress.

The delivery nurse pressed a button beside the elevator. It opened immediately and one of the Sentinels emerged with a wheelchair. Without a word of warning or explanation, he lifted Nina off the bed and placed her in the chair. Its arms wrapped around her, holding her upright. Then he placed a small bag upon Nina's lap. 'These are your personal belongings,' she said.

But Nina did not seem to notice. Her eyes had glazed over and she was staring at nothing. The delivery nurse bent over Nina, showing her the disc in her hand. 'Nina,' she said as though Nina was deaf. 'I must ask you to watch, while I transfer the funds to your family account,' she said, holding an extra-large disc in her hands.

Nina made a brief attempt to look at the screen, but her eyes soon filled with tears and her head fell into her hands. Ophelia watched, horrified to see that only one hundred thousand euros were transferred into Nina's account. She knew for a fact that a northern woman would have paid one million euros for a surrogate to incubate and birth her baby. It was the law. So why the nurse was only transferring ten percent of that amount ... 'Is that the correct amount?' Ophelia asked.

'Yes, of course!' the nurse snapped.

'Forgive me,' said Ophelia. 'But you seem to have only transferred one hundred thousand euros.'

'Yes, that's the correct amount,' The delivery nurse snarled.

Ophelia stepped back.

'And who are you, by the way?' the nurse asked.

Ophelia panicked.

The Sentinel spoke up. 'She's just an intern' he said. 'Ignore her.' He turned to Ophelia then.

'Where's your supervisor?' he asked.

'She's sleeping, sir. I didn't want to wake her,' Ophelia replied.

The Sentinel nodded.

'Now that we have all of that sorted out, let's get on with it, shall we?' said the delivery nurse, shaking her head. 'Nina, your family will be able to draw on the funds immediately. And they'll receive a crate of water within the week, as promised. Congratulations, Nina. You're a good girl. Goodbye and best wishes.' The nurse pressed her disc into her chest then and walked away.

Another woman in labour let out an awful scream. Then the scent of faeces permeated the Birthing Suite. Ophelia felt desperate to get out. Panicked, even.

Nina grabbed Ophelia's hand. 'Please come with me,' she said.

The Sentinel nodded, so Ophelia joined them in the elevator. It descended one level further then stopped with a thud so violent that Nina clutched her belly, grimacing in pain. They travelled a few minutes to the mouth of the hyperloop where the Sentinel transferred Nina to a square transparent pod and secured her seatbelt.

Then the Sentinel looked at Ophelia. 'You have one hour to take her to Paris and return,' he said.

'Yes, sir,' Ophelia replied, aware that she had no intention of ever returning.

The pod door closed. Ophelia ripped open the backpack Martin had given her. She changed her clothes, stuffed her suit and mask into the backpack, hid it under her seat then held onto Nina. The pod was sucked into the hyperloop at one thousand kilometres per hour then catapulted under the ocean. Feeling a sudden increase in her heart rate, Ophelia realised she was terrified of being arrested in Paris. But there was no turning back now.

In transit

IT HAD NEVER OCCURRED to Ophelia that the hyperloop tube would be made from a transparent substance. Looking at the ocean around her, she felt both awe and terror in equal measure – a combination that made her gasp.

'Isn't this incredible?' she said to Nina.

But there was no response. Nina's eyes were open but uncomprehending.

'Nina, can you hear me?' Ophelia asked, gently shaking Nina.

For a moment, Nina's eyes cleared. 'Nina, you're still with me, aren't you?' Ophelia asked.

'Mm,' Nina replied, her eyes glazing over again.

Ophelia sat back and listened to the ocean current. For the first time in her life, she was under the ocean, and she found it both magnificent and terrifying. The ocean, she mused, was both mother and destroyer, and she was at its mercy. She looked up, toward the surface, seeing the faintest glow of sunlight shining through, like early morning sunlight peeping through the streaks of pink and orange sky. Straight ahead, the water was a deep shade of turquoise. And below, she did not want to know.

To the right, she saw a dark object move toward her pod, bringing with it a high-pitched whining sound. She assumed it might have been one of Gaia's random surveillance drones, but as it got closer she saw it had a proboscis of about three metres in length. She had heard about drones with sonar probes, but only within the context of deep seabed exploration, mining for sunken space junk. So why this one was sidling up to her pod she could not imagine. Almost within touching distance, it turned one of its large round cameras towards her. Like the eye of a whale, it rolled around, studying her. Then, without warning, the camera became a bright spotlight which shone directly into her face. She squinted and turned away.

'Do you see that, Nina?' she asked.

'Mm,' Nina replied. 'Surveillance.'

The vessel broke away and submerged then the pod ascended the French mainland. As they rose to about one hundred metres above the ground, Ophelia gazed out of the window. On her right, she could see uniform rows of solar panels all the way to the horizon line. And to her left, she could see a vast field of emerald green crop. The large leafy plants were in a pattern so regular and unchanging, she found it comforting.

Nina rubbed her eyes and looked at Ophelia.

'Feeling better?' Ophelia asked.

'Not really.'

Ophelia watched Nina staring at the landscape. 'So, we're in southern land now, right?' she asked, almost excited.

'Not really,' Nina replied. 'This is neutral.'

'I guess that would explain the bright green landscape,' said Ophelia. 'But it still looks hot out there.'

'Mm,' Nina replied.

It occurred to Ophelia that chatting about the weather might be insensitive, given what Nina had just been through, but neither did it seem right to discuss the horrors of the last hour. Silence, she felt, was probably the best option. At least for now.

Paris

THE POD ARRIVED AT the end of the hyperloop with a slow and gentle hiss.

'So, I guess this is Paris,' Ophelia said. 'I hope it's nice.'

Nina shrugged. 'I've never seen it,' she replied. 'Only this station.'

'Just as well the distortion chemical is wearing off,' Ophelia said. 'My voice sounds almost normal now, doesn't it?'

Nina nodded, then stood up, wincing in pain. Ophelia helped her out of the pod and into a wheelchair. By the time the arms of the chair had securely clicked into place, Nina's face had gone blank again and she just sat there, staring ahead at absolutely nothing. Ophelia pushed the chair along the platform, telling herself she had to be brave for them both, all the while aware of how desperately she wanted someone to be brave for her.

'Welcome to Gare du Nord, Paris,' said a holo-guide suddenly appearing in the air somewhere between Nina's head and feet.

Startled, Ophelia pushed Nina's chair through the thing as fast as she could. The skylights in the roof of the station permitted so much light to enter that Ophelia had to squint. A bot whistled, loud and high, signalling passengers to alight a train on the far side of the platform, and the sound rang through Ophelia's ears like an alarm.

She was now less than a metre away from the security gates and her heart was pounding. She knew that she, like everyone else, would have to go through the security scanner. But unlike everyone else, she knew, the security scanners would not recognise her.

Ophelia watched, helpless, as Nina rolled onto the scanning pad. The machine's steel arms wrapped around Nina and her chair, emitting a bright turquoise light for several seconds. Then the light disappeared, the noise stopped, and the machine retracted its arms.

'You are cleared for exit Mademoiselle Garcia,' said a bot.

Nina rolled through and waited for Ophelia.

'Madame, please step onto the scanning pad,' said the bot.

As the great arms folded around Ophelia, she took in a deep breath. The turquoise light spiralled around her body, up and down, several times. The arms were so close, she could see inside them. The smooth curved steel was punctured with tiny holes at regular intervals, allowing the turquoise light to exit, like rays of sunshine bursting through a cloud. Suddenly, the light vanished, and the machine returned to silence, but the arms of the machine did not open.

'You are not recognised on the southern register,' said the bot, approaching her.

'I understand,' Ophelia replied, still trapped inside the machine. 'This is an unplanned visit.'

'What is the nature of your visit?' asked the bot.

'I need to care for Mademoiselle Garcia,' she said. 'There were serious complications with her delivery.'

The bot looked at Nina, then returned its gaze to Ophelia.

'I need my nurse,' Nina cried, her arms outstretched toward Ophelia.

'Please wait here,' said the bot.

Still held in the arms of the machine, Ophelia had no choice but to wait. She watched the bot's graceful locomotion towards a human guard. The man was leaning against the wall, staring into the distance, tapping the weapon on his waistband with his forefinger. He barely acknowledged the bot when it spoke to him, but when it pointed at Ophelia, he suddenly looked interested.

Without breaking his gaze upon Ophelia, or altering his expression, he walked toward her. 'What's your situation, Madame?' he asked.

'I'm sorry to bother you,' Ophelia replied, still struggling to speak through the arms of the machine. 'Mademoiselle Garcia, a surrogate, gave birth only a few hours ago and ...'

Nina started to cry.

'Open the machine,' the guard said to the bot.

'Thank you,' said Ophelia, stepping out and rolling her shoulders. 'There were serious complications with Mademoiselle Garcia's delivery. I've been instructed to escort her home, to her village.'

'Where is your village?' the guard asked Nina.

'El Serrallo, Spain,' Nina replied.

The guard gave Nina a sad smile and a gentle nod. 'Me too,' he said. 'Both of you, come this way.'

As they walked toward the main exit, Ophelia anticipated the freedom to exit. Then a tiny voice inside her mind told her that would be too easy. The voice was right.

'Step aside,' said the guard, beckoning them away from the main walkway.

Ophelia and Nina followed him to an empty space between two platforms, and a second guard joined them, activating a transparent shield around the four of them. 'Do not touch the surface of the shield or the alarm will sound,' she said.

Ophelia had no choice but to stand close to both guards. So close, she could smell the male guard's lunch on his breath and the female guard's perfume, mixed with her sweat, as it wafted up from her enormous cleavage.

The male guard held a small scanning device over Ophelia's left eye for a moment, then checked the reading. 'You are not recognised as a citizen of either the northern region or the southern region,' he said. 'Who are you?'

'I'm Ophelia Alsop,' she replied, feeling her voice waver slightly. 'I've been working with the surrogates for a few years.'

'What is your place of work?'

'London.'

'What is your profession?'

'I'm a nurse.'

'Where did you gain your nursing qualification?'

'The University of Oxford,' Ophelia replied.

'What is your full name and date of birth?'

'The twelfth of February 2092.'

The two guards looked at each other, baffled.

'It's highly unusual that you would arrive here without a proper entry permit,' said the male guard.

'I understand, but because of the nature of my work, there was no choice,' Ophelia replied.

'And what's the nature of your work?' the female guard asked.

'I've been engaged in some sensitive obstetric research with the surrogates,' Ophelia replied. 'Normally, I wouldn't be required to leave London, but I had to, to ensure the survival of this young woman.'

'Why did *you* have to be the one to escort her, instead of someone with a proper entry permit?' the female guard asked.

'We had a high number of births this morning,' Ophelia replied. 'There was no one else available, so I was instructed to escort her. Please, let me take her home to her family. I need to give them instructions for her care as soon as possible.'

For a woman so voraciously demanding of the truth, Ophelia was astonished by her prowess as a spontaneous and convincing liar. The guards looked at Nina, sitting in her chair, staring ahead through red and unfocused eyes.

'Where are your possessions?' the female guard asked.

'I have none,' Ophelia replied. 'There was no time to gather them.'

'Remove that scarf from your head.'

Despite her previous satisfaction with her bald head, Ophelia now felt ugly and embarrassed by it. 'I recently finished some medical treatment that made my hair fall out,' she explained, rubbing her hand over her scalp. 'Until it grows back, I'd like to keep this scarf on, if you don't mind.'

'Fine,' said the female guard. 'Lift your arms and open your legs.'

The guard's hands slid up and down Ophelia's limbs and torso.

'What's this?' she said, retrieving Ophelia's disc from her hip pocket.

'It's my only possession,' Ophelia replied. 'It contains just enough credit to get me onto a train with Mademoiselle Garcia and then back to London.'

The male guard took the disc and scanned it. 'She's right, she has access to a small amount of credit,' he said. 'And the contact details of an Emilie and Philippe Trudeau. May I ask, what is your relationship to them?'

'They are very distant cousins whom I can contact in an emergency,' Ophelia replied. 'However, I don't plan to contact them. I just need to get Mademoiselle Garcia back home to her family then get back to work.'

The guards looked at Ophelia for what seemed like an eternity. Ophelia resisted the urge to blink, look down, fidget or wriggle about.

The male guard finally opened his lop-sided mouth to speak. 'The best we can do under the circumstances is give you a high-risk entry permit for twenty-four hours,' he said.

'Thank you,' Ophelia replied. 'That would be very helpful.'

'The permit has to be inserted, subcutaneously, into your upper arm,' he explained. 'If you haven't returned to this station within twenty-four hours, it will activate every scanning device across the southern region.'

Ophelia nodded.

'Many of these scanning devices are hidden, and their location is frequently changed, so you will be taking a huge risk if you remain here for longer than twenty-four hours.'

Ophelia nodded.

'If you're caught, Madame Alsop, you will find the punishment very harsh.'

'I understand,' Ophelia replied.

'She's unconscious,' said the female guard, looking at Nina. 'A few moments ago, she was crying and now she's unconscious. What's wrong with her?'

'It's a common effect of the medication we gave her,' Ophelia replied. 'Also, she was quite traumatised in the Birthing Suite.'

Nina's head dropped into her hands.

'Please roll up your sleeve,' said the guard.

'Is this going to hurt?' Ophelia asked.

The guard did not bother to answer the question. She simply located the soft fleshy part of Ophelia's upper arm and pressed the tip of a small steel tube into it. A burning sensation shot through Ophelia's arm as the implant tore through her flesh.

'Fuck!' Ophelia screamed.

The guard seemed satisfied.

'Sorry about my language,' Ophelia said. 'But that really hurt! It feels like you've just sliced my arm open!'

'It's not pleasant, but you're cleared for exit, now,' the guard replied.

'Thank you.'

'You have just enough time to get the next train to Tarragona, where, I am sure Mademoiselle Garcia's family will meet you,' said the male guard.

'Yes, I understand,' said Ophelia.

'If you choose to spend the night there, with Mademoiselle Garcia, you must catch the return train from Tarragona tomorrow at 09:00 hours. Do not miss it.'

'Understood,' Ophelia replied, her mind racing and her arm throbbing.

She pushed Nina's chair toward the exit.

'Welcome to Paris,' said a holo-guide, looming over the exit gate.

But Ophelia knew she was not welcome. She was a fugitive – a fact that she wanted to conceal from Nina not only for the young woman's safety but also for her own. But more than anything, Ophelia felt ashamed of being a fugitive.

· · · ·

A FEW METRES FROM THE exit, the doors slid open and a family of five entered. With them, they brought a gush of hot dry air. To Ophelia, it felt like a million tiny needles invading her nose and throat. She retreated and leaned against the wall. 'That's horrific,' she said.

'You'll get used to it,' Nina replied.

'You're awake again!' Ophelia said. 'Are you okay?'

'Numb. Exhausted,' Nina replied.

'Hopefully, we'll have a nice bed for you soon,' Ophelia replied. 'I'm just going to text Emilie. She's a friend of a friend who will help us.'

Emilie responded – *Stay there, Ophelia. My husband and I will be there in 10 minutes.*

'They're coming to help us!' Ophelia said, almost weeping with relief.

'What are you doing?' Nina asked. 'Why aren't we going down to Tarragona?'

'Just one night here in Paris will give us some rest,' Ophelia replied. 'Can you text your parents and let them know we'll arrive tomorrow?'

Nina did not answer. Her eyes had glazed over again and she was staring out of the main doors into the carpark, clearly mesmerised by something. Ophelia followed her line of sight. It landed on a brick wall, almost fifty metres high, patrolled by bots. Someone shouted.

Someone else fired a weapon. The shooter ran towards the doors. On instinct, Ophelia jumped back, pulling Nina with her. Then one of the bots flexed its wrist backward, emitting a pale white light which encased the shooter and held him immobile, mid-movement. The bot disarmed the shooter then carried him away, still in suspended animation, as though the man was a bag of rubbish for the bin.

'That was efficient,' Ophelia said. 'I've never seen anything like that, before.'

'Mm,' said Nina.

'Do you require assistance?'

Ophelia turned around and saw a bot, standing behind her and looking directly at her. They were everywhere, it seemed. 'No, thank you,' she replied. 'I'm just waiting for a friend.'

She returned her gaze to the place where the incident had unfolded, but all evidence of the disturbance was gone. It was as though nothing had happened.

Then Ophelia looked at Nina, who seemed to be crying again, so she placed her hand on her friend's shoulder and gave her a gentle squeeze. Nina responded by tipping her head ever so slightly toward Ophelia's hand then she let out a small sigh.

Ophelia heard a tight, wheezing cough. She turned. A man and woman were standing nearby. Both tall, lean, tanned, silver-haired and brown-eyed, they were a striking couple. And they were looking directly at her.

'Emilie?' she said, hopeful.

'Bonjour, Madame Ophelia!' said Emilie, offering her hand. 'This is my husband, Philippe.'

Ophelia shook hands with Philippe, too.

'And who is this?' Emilie asked, smiling at Nina.

'This is Nina. I met her yesterday in the Garden of Eden.'

Emilie and Philippe looked at Nina with a mix of kindness and sorrow.

Ophelia watched Philippe press his hand against the gel pad beside the iron gate. When it opened, she found herself steering Nina's chair through the brown weeds that protruded from the cracks between the concrete slabs on the ground. Approaching the front door, she noticed several bricks were missing from around the door, and she wondered if it might cave in. The windows were covered with solar panels which, she hoped, would mean that the building might be cooler inside than the temperature she was now suffering.

'Oh yes,' she said, stepping into the lobby. 'It's so much cooler in here.'

Emilie and Philippe removed her masks from their faces, so Ophelia did the same. Then she removed the silk scarf from Nina's face. Her young friend looked much the same as before – glassy-eyed and uncomprehending.

There was one tiny window, about twenty metres above the lobby floor, which let in enough light for Ophelia to take in her surroundings. The walls were blotchy with the remnants of pale green paint peeling away. The edges of the once ornate tiles on the floor were chipped away and worn down. A clump of electrical wires protruded from the ceiling.

As they stepped into an elevator, Ophelia placed her hand on Nina's shoulder and gave it a gentle rub. The elevator was made from clear glass, enabling a view of the internal structure of the building as they ascended. The corners of most of the bricks had worn away and fresh chunks of chalk fell to the ground as the elevator thundered upwards. Ophelia could not help but wonder how much longer it would be before the entire shaft caved in.

When it finally stopped, the doors opened, and Philippe leapt out. 'We're home,' he said. 'We have the whole of the top floor, so there's plenty of room for you both.'

'We want you both to feel at home here,' Emilie added.

'This is amazing,' said Ophelia, marvelling at the vast and open space before her. The ceiling was about twenty metres high and decorated with softly glowing antique chandeliers. The walls were mostly windows, which were sealed to keep out the heat. At the centre of the space was a collection of antique lounge chairs in such pristine condition that Ophelia was not sure if sitting upon them would be permitted. On the far side of the lounge area was a deep mahogany dining table surrounded by matching chairs. All were in immaculate condition and carved into soft curves. To the left, Ophelia could see an ancient-looking kitchen with an oven, a refrigerator and several small pots of fresh green herbs. Beside the kitchen was the only internal wall in the room. Leaning against it was an antique grandfather clock.

'I've never seen one of those things in real life,' Ophelia said, pointing at it.

'It's even older than we are,' Phillipe laughed.

'You have the loveliest home I have ever seen,' Ophelia said.

'Thank you,' Emilie replied with a proud smile. 'It's our home for now.'

'The windows,' said Philippe, almost to himself. He slumped into the smallest chair in the loungeroom, his long limbs somehow collapsing around his torso. He slid his hand down the side of the cushion and pulled at something. Ophelia heard a thud then the iron shutters rolled up from the outside of the windows. The windows flew open and a warm breeze flew through the apartment, causing the ancient lace curtains to dance around the windows.

'Ha!' Ophelia said, clapping her hands with delight. 'What a trick!'

'My husband is a most inventive fellow,' said Emilie.

Philippe smiled, gave a faux salute, then reclined across the lounge chair.

'Let me show you to your room,' said Emilie.

Ophelia placed her hands upon Nina's chair and pushed it, following Emilie, straight toward a large painting on the adjacent wall. Approximately one metre high and half a metre wide, it depicted the Eiffel Tower. Ophelia watched with interest as Emilie pressed her palm into the centre of the image. The outline of a door appeared around the painting and the door slid open, taking the painting with it.

'That's incredible!' she said.

'In this house, Madame Ophelia, you can expect the unexpected,' Emilie said with a cheeky smile. 'At least until you get to know us. Then you will see how ordinary we are.'

'Oh, I very much doubt you are ordinary,' Ophelia replied.

Stepping into the large bedroom, she could not help but notice that it had no windows. There were, however, several small vents in the ceiling and they were open, enabling a breeze to flow around the king-sized bed below it. The bed was covered with antique white lace sheets and pillowcases.

'This is nothing short of luxurious,' Ophelia said.

'I hope you will both be comfortable here,' Emilie replied.

Without warning, Nina wriggled free from her chair, ambled over to the bed and fell onto it. Ophelia removed Nina's shoes and surrounded her body with pillows. A moment later, her young friend was snoring.

'She must have been desperate for sleep,' said Emilie.

'You would not believe what she's been through,' Ophelia replied.

'What you have *both* been through,' Emilie said, looking into Ophelia's eyes with kindness. Ophelia felt humbled by it, but slightly uncomfortable, as she was not sure what Emilie did and did not know about her.

'I'm sorry about the lack of air and light,' said Emilie. 'We designed the bedrooms like this to ensure our safety while sleeping.'

Ophelia's curiosity was piqued.

'Come with me,' said Emilie. 'We'll explain everything.'

• • • •

WHEN THEY RETURNED to the loungeroom, Ophelia flopped into one of the huge lounge chairs. Every muscle in her body started to relax. She removed the scarf from her head and ran her palm over her sweaty scalp, finally feeling some relief from the events of the day.

'Oh,' said Emilie, looking at Ophelia's bald head.

'Um, yes, Martin shaved it all off, as part of my disguise.'

'I look forward to hearing everything,' Emilie replied, lifting a large iron pot from the centre of the table. 'Coffee?'

'Yes, please,' Ophelia replied. 'It smells wonderful.'

'There's chocolate cake, too,' said Philippe, making his way to the kitchen.

'This is such an incredible welcome,' Ophelia said. 'I'm deeply grateful for your hospitality. Thank you so much.'

'You came to us highly recommended by Martin Huxley, and that's good enough for us,' Emilie said with another kind smile.

Ophelia saw Martin's handsome face flash through her mind.

Philippe returned to the lounge with a chocolate cake so large, it sprawled over the edge of the serving plate. He cut it into eight pieces and gave the first one to Ophelia. Her mouth watered in anticipation, but she managed to restrain herself until Emilie and Philippe each had a slice.

'Oh, my God,' said Ophelia, allowing the first bite to melt onto her tongue. 'This is real chocolate, isn't it?'

'Yes, indeed,' Philippe replied, smiling so wide, Ophelia could see chunks of cake wedged between his teeth and sprinkles of it through his beard.

'Is it made from real cocoa beans?' Ophelia asked.

'Yes,' Philippe replied. 'The beans grow in abundance across northern France. Do you recall seeing the bright green fields when you first entered the mainland?'

'Yes! They were spectacular,' Ophelia replied. 'And surprising. I wondered where they got the water from, to irrigate those crops.'

'That's mostly neutral territory,' Emilie said. 'There's some natural rainfall there, but they also get a lot of water from London. In return, the region gives back some of the produce. Then we, the Parisians, must buy it back.'

'Well, that sucks,' said Ophelia, taking another bite.

Emilie and Philippe laughed at her.

'So where are we now?' Ophelia asked.

'Paris,' Philippe replied, looking baffled by her question.

'Yes, I know,' said Ophelia, laughing. 'What I meant to ask was – is Paris considered to be in the northern region or the southern region?'

'Technically, we're in the north, because we're just above the fourty-fifth parallel north,' Philippe replied. 'But our lives are far less controlled by Gaia than what you are accustomed to in Britain.'

A few days ago, a piece of information like that would have boggled Ophelia's mind. But now, with her mind blown wide open, she felt she could absorb anything. And she was as curious as ever. 'So how is Paris governed?' she asked.

Philippe rolled his eyes. 'We have a hybrid of rules here,' he said. 'Some from the north and some from the south, which makes us almost self-governed. But in a strange way.'

Ophelia lifted her feet from the floor to make way for a vacuum cleaning bot. 'Is Gaia watching us or listening to us now?' she asked.

'There's no surveillance inside people's homes,' Philippe replied. 'There is some, out on the streets, but our government can't afford the heavy surveillance that Britain has. And there would be a public outcry if they tried to implement it.'

Ophelia reflected on the vandalised surveillance device she had seen during the walk to Emilie and Philippe's apartment. 'So, what are you protecting yourselves from?' she asked. 'I mean, the comment Emilie made in the bedroom about securing the bedrooms during sleep.'

'Ah, yes, that's true,' said Emilie. 'We've had a few instances of home invasion from thugs who want to stop us from doing our work.'

Ophelia sunk her teeth into the cake for the third time, temporarily distracting herself from all else. 'God, that is so good,' she said.

Emilie and Philippe exchanged glances then laughed at her again.

'So, what is your work?' Ophelia mumbled through the particles of soft, rich chocolate sponge which had almost glued her lips together.

'Didn't Martin explain that?' Emilie asked.

'Not really,' Ophelia replied. 'He wanted me out of there as soon as possible so there was little time for much explanation. He only told me that you might be able to help me and in return, you might want these lenses from my eyes.'

Philippe leaned forward, intrigued. 'How long have they been in your eyes?' he asked.

'About two days, I think,' Ophelia replied. 'Let me try to remove them now.'

Ophelia returned her plate to the coffee table then closed her eyes and squeezed her top and bottom eyelids together. The lenses slipped out easily and Philippe's hand was there to catch them.

'Thank you, Madame Ophelia,' he said. 'This will be very helpful.'

'What will you do with them?' Ophelia asked.

'As you're the first person to survive that underground place with a visual recording, I plan to share it across our network,' he replied.

Ophelia nodded, remembering Martin had said something about that. She had been a courier, she mused, feeling slightly less resentful of the fact now that she was in the presence of Emilie and Philippe. Then she remembered her moment with Martin.

'Oh, please just edit out one little section of the recording,' she said. 'It's about half of the way through my time down there.'

Philippe appeared surprised by the request.

'Martin and I had an intimate moment,' Ophelia explained, her face flushing.

Emilie and Philippe smiled warmly.

'Of course,' Philippe replied. 'You have my word.'

Emilie turned towards Philippe and placed her hand on his knee. 'You won't have time to edit the recording before the meeting tonight,' she said.

'Is there a meeting here tonight?' Ophelia asked.

'Yes, we have meetings here, usually twice per week,' Emilie replied. 'To which any members of our network are welcome to attend.'

'What are the meetings about?' Ophelia asked, sucking a blob of the chocolate icing from her finger. 'Gosh I'm nosey, aren't I? Please forgive me.'

Emilie and Philippe laughed.

'We share information about the various issues we wish to address,' Philippe replied. 'Mostly, we focus on finding ways to undermine the various trade agreements between the north and the south.'

'I would love to h ...' Ophelia started before hearing the elevator thundering up towards the apartment.

Philippe lunged toward Ophelia, lifted her from the chair and scuttled across the living room with her.

'What are you doing?' Ophelia asked, clinging to his shoulders.

'It's all right, Ophelia, you'll be safe,' he said, pushing her into her bedroom.

'We'll explain later,' said Emilie, closing the door in Ophelia's face.

Perplexed, but just as curious as ever, Ophelia pressed her ear against the door and listened to the sound of the elevator door opening. She heard the footsteps of two apparently very heavy people.

'This is a raid,' one of them said.

Police bots, not people, she mused.

Emilie spoke. 'You are welcome to look everywhere, but you will not find anything of interest. Just like all the other times you have barged into our home, unannounced, you will not find anything of interest.'

'Identification,' one of them said.

For a moment there was silence.

'See!' said Philippe. 'You can see from our identification that we are the same people we have always been on every prior occasion that you have unlawfully entered our home. And that is not going to change. Why do you persist with these heinous intrusions?'

The bots thundered around the living room. 'You live in a dangerous place,' one of them said. 'Criminals seek refuge around here.'

'There are no criminals in this building,' Philippe said. 'You can see that with your own eyes.'

A high-pitched screech followed.

'Please stop!' Emilie shouted. 'This is our home!'

'I saw movement in the corner,' said the bot.

'It was just the curtains moving in the breeze!' Emilie snapped. 'You are not programmed to activate weapons inside a private residence! You know that! And look what you've done! You've just destroyed a piece of antique furniture. Your behaviour is completely unlawful!'

'Are you aware of the penalty for harbouring criminals?' said one of the bots.

'Yes, of course, we are aware!' Philippe replied. 'We are just as aware now as we were on every previous occasion that you have barged in here and asked the same question! Are you expecting a different answer?'

Ophelia could not hear a response from the bots.

Philippe continued. 'You are not programmed to behave like this!' he shouted. 'Now, will you please, just fuck off!'

Ophelia heard the bots stomping back towards the elevator then the slow whine as it descended. Then the bedroom door opened.

'Sorry, Ophelia,' said Emilie, her face pale and shiny with sweat. 'I should have warned you – they do this once every few weeks. Except for firing their weapons. I don't know why they did that.'

'Because the entire system of law and order is breaking down!' Philippe shouted from the doorway. 'The world is going mad!'

Emilie embraced Ophelia. 'It's okay,' she said. 'We'll keep you safe.'

Then both women looked towards Nina who was sitting upright, staring at Ophelia, her large almond eyes wide open.

'Are you a criminal?' Nina asked.

'No, but apparently I'm a menace to society,' Ophelia replied, her eyes filling with tears.

'What did you do?' Nina asked.

'What I did was unlawful,' Ophelia replied. 'But it was an act of love. Do you really want to know?'

Nina shook her head, lay down again and closed her eyes.

• • • •

THE ANTIQUE CABINET beside the dining room table was in pieces.

'Did the police bots do that?' Ophelia asked.

Emilie nodded.

'I am so sorry, Emilie,' said Ophelia.

Philippe looked up from the lounge. 'Truly, Ophelia, it's not your fault,' he said. 'Please, join us again.'

Ophelia settled back into the big armchair. 'Before we were rudely interrupted by the bots,' she said. 'I was going to ask you how you know Martin.'

'We've never met him in person,' Philippe replied. 'But we've been aware of his presence for a few years. He's one a few good people in that underground place who have been sending us information about the organ harvesting and storage down there,' Philippe replied.

Ophelia's skin prickled with disgust as she recalled the sight of the lab. 'I've been inside that Anatomy Lab,' she said. 'It's horrific what they're doing. And I'm one of their unwitting victims.'

'What do you mean by that?' Emilie asked, frowning.

'Gaia took my womb,' Ophelia said, still feeling the horror of the experience so much that she could hardly believe the words as they escaped her mouth. 'I objected so loudly that I was arrested, taken underground, charged with sedition and thrown into a prison cell under threat of execution.'

'God Almighty,' said Philippe, rubbing his forehead. 'We didn't know that.'

Emilie's eyes were wide open, horrified.

But Ophelia continued. 'If it weren't for Martin's bravery and kindness, I would be dead by now,' she said.

'Did you know Martin before that happened?' Emilie asked.

'Yes,' Ophelia replied, feeling a warm glow spread through her chest. 'We were lovers during our undergraduate years at Oxford.'

Emilie and Philippe smiled warmly.

'All true love stories have their challenges,' Philippe said. 'You would be amazed by the things that Emilie and I have endured together.'

Ophelia looked at them both. 'I can tell you two would have some fascinating stories,' she said, smiling. 'If you ever feel like sharing them with me, I will be all ears.'

'Perhaps later,' Emilie replied, her smile even more warm and gracious than before. 'But for now, I am curious about Nina. Who is she?'

Ophelia leaned back against the chair and exhaled loudly. 'I only met Nina twenty-four hours ago,' she said. 'But, God Almighty, what an intense twenty-four hours it has been! What Nina has been through, and what I have borne witness to, in that ... that place they rudely called the Garden of Eden.'

'It's the home of the surrogates, right?' Emilie asked.

'Yes, it's a lovely place,' Ophelia replied. 'Until the final moment when they deliver the baby. The Birthing Suite is utterly vile and so are the nurses. I witnessed the entire thing. Nina was treated very badly. And, to add insult to injury, she was only paid ten percent of what a northern woman would have paid them to manage the surrogacy.'

Philippe shook his head. 'That's hardly surprising,' he said.

'We've suspected that for a long time,' said Emilie. 'However, you're the first person we've met who's survived down there.'

Ophelia leaned back in the chair. 'I'm not sure whether I feel good or bad about that,' she said. 'I'm still reeling from the experience.'

Emilie nodded. 'Experiences like that really *do* take a while to process,' she said. 'Philippe and I have been through a few long phases in our lives when we've not been able to do any of our work because we've needed time to recover.'

Again, Ophelia was curious, but she somehow managed to restrain herself from asking directly what Emilie had meant by that comment. She could only hope they might share some stories with her over time. But, she reminded herself, there was not much time. she had to get Nina back home. Tomorrow.

Emilie leaned forwards. 'I hope that, by sharing your story at our meeting tonight, you might begin your recovery process,' she said.

'Oh,' said Ophelia. 'I didn't know you'd want me to speak at the meeting.'

Emilie smiled. Then sighed. 'I know it's a tall order, given you've only just arrived,' she said. 'But we'd be most grateful if you would, Ophelia. No-one in our network is ever met anyone who has survived that underground place. Other than the surrogates, of course. And they are usually ...'

She looked at Philippe, as though seeking help to find the right words.

'We often find the surrogates are so heavily sedated, or traumatised, that they can't even speak,' Philippe said, his warm brown eyes disappearing under furrowed brows.

To Ophelia's mind, Emilie and Philippe's words sounded reasonable, but to her body and her soul, they were challenging. She was not sure she would even know how or where to start if she *was* to share her story. She only knew that she was angry. Enraged, in fact.

She placed her coffee cup on the table then leaned forward. 'I'd love to storm the Garden of Eden, rescue all those women and expose that sick operation to the entire world,' she said.

Emilie and Philippe glanced at each other. Then Philippe leaned forward, his warm brown eyes staring into Ophelia's. 'Would you really like to do that?' he asked.

Ophelia paused for a moment, realising she had not meant to say what she had just said. But, now that she had said it, she knew she meant it. She really *did* want to take action against the surrogacy trade.

• • • •

OPHELIA WAS DEEP IN an afternoon nap and dreaming once again.

The ocean below her is silent but vibrant. Dark shapes move slowly below the surface. A family of humpback whales. Three adults and a baby. A strong current, infused with the scent of the ocean, rushes around her face. She tastes the salt and it makes her feel alive. In the distance she sees a land formation, an island, wearing a cloak of dark green. As she glides closer, the cloak comes to life with many more shades of green. An infinite number of shapes and colours tell her she is approaching a tropical rainforest. She lands on the top branch of the tallest tree, beside a family of pink and orange birds. They open their curved yellow beaks and screech 'Gaiiiiia'. She looks down at all the creatures on the forest floor, then she looks back at the birds and announces her intention to stay with them. The birds look at each other for a moment, then fly away, leaving the naked branches shuddering in their wake.

Ophelia woke to the sound of a train rattling in the distance. Through the ceiling vents, she could see the sky was the soft mauve of early evening, almost as beautiful as the visions in her dream. She reflected on the dream for a second, noticing how much stronger it had made her feel. And then she realised it was the third dream since her bizarre disappearance underground and her reunion with Martin. There was a narrative unfolding through these dreams, she mused, but she did not understand it.

There was a gentle tapping on the bedroom door.

'Yes?' she called out, sitting up.

'Ophelia, please join us,' Emilie replied. 'I'd like you to meet Doctor Dubois.'

· · · ·

OPHELIA SHOOK HANDS with a short, plump woman with immaculate hair. Long with silver stripes, it was swept up into a neat bun, without a single strand dangling loose. The lines on the doctor's face were deep, but there was a vibrant twinkle in her eyes.

'Madame Ophelia,' said Doctor Dubois. 'I've been looking forward to meeting you.'

'Thank you, doctor,' Ophelia replied. 'It's nice to meet you, too.'

'Doctor Dubois is here for the meeting,' said Emilie. 'But first, she'd like to remove the tracking device from your arm. Is that all right?'

'God, yes! I can't wait to be rid of the thing,' Ophelia replied, rubbing the tender skin that had so recently been torn open.

'Follow me,' Emilie said with a wink.

Inside Emilie and Philippe's huge en-suite, Ophelia was quick to notice the large porcelain bathtub and the brass claws upon which it rested.

'You have one of those!' she said.

'Yes, it came with the house,' Emilie replied. 'I'm sad to say we never have the water to fill it.'

'But we'll put it to good use, now,' said Doctor Dubois. 'Please, Ophelia, kneel beside the tub and stretch your arm across it.'

Ophelia did as she was asked.

The doctor scanned her arm. 'I see it now,' she said. 'And I'm not happy.'

'What do you mean?' Ophelia asked.

Doctor Dubois sighed. 'Sometimes they insert these tracking devices so shallow that I can deactivate them without removing them,' she replied. 'But in this case, they've lodged it deep inside your tissue, so I have to remove it.'

'You mean, you have to cut it out?' Ophelia said, almost shrill.

'I'm afraid so,' said the doctor.

'This is going to hurt, isn't it?' Ophelia asked.

'No, I'm giving you an anaesthetic now.'

Doctor Dubois pressed a button on her pencil-shaped device, then pointed it at Ophelia's arm, spraying a soft mist over her skin. Ophelia's arm went numb immediately and she felt sure the experience would be without trouble. Until she smelled her flesh being cut open by the laser.

'Oh, God,' she said, biting her lip.

In the doctor's other hand was a pair of long steel tweezers. 'Sorry, Ophelia,' she said. 'But you have to hold still for a bit longer.'

Ophelia looked down at her arm just in time to see the doctor's tweezers disappear into it. She turned her head the other way and closed her eyes, aware of the doctor's prodding.

'Got it!' said Doctor Dubois.

Ophelia watched as the doctor removed the tweezers from her flesh. Between their tips, the tweezers held a clear disc, about the size of Ophelia's little fingernail. The doctor placed it on the tiled floor and blasted it with her laser device.

'Oh, no!' said Ophelia. 'Won't the police realise it's been destroyed?'

'It will take them a while to realise it's no longer active,' the doctor replied. 'And even when they do, they won't hunt for you. That's what Gaia's surveillance is for and, as we know, surveillance in this country is quite random.

Ophelia looked at Emilie.

'Don't worry, Ophelia,' Emilie said. 'We'll make you invisible to Gaia's scans. Philippe will make new lenses for your eyes. They won't have the recording capability of the ones that Martin made for you, but they will make it difficult for Gaia's scanners to recognise you.'

The doctor handed Ophelia a small black tablet. 'Please ingest this,' she said.

'What is it?' Ophelia asked.

'Nanites. They're programmed to absorb all infections – systemic and local,' the doctor replied. 'When they've done their job, they'll vacate your body through your stools.'

Emilie handed Ophelia a glass of water to wash down the tablet.

'Well done,' said the doctor. 'How do you feel?'

'I'm okay, thanks, doctor,' she replied. 'But I'm worried about Nina.'

'Who's Nina?'

'She's a surrogate I brought with me, from the Garden of Eden. She only gave birth a few hours ago. It was horrific how they treated her. She's been fading in and out of consciousness ever since.'

Doctor Dubois looked at Emilie, concerned.

'She's sleeping in the spare room now,' said Emilie.

'Then that's where I'm going,' said the doctor, standing up.

• • • •

BY THE TIME OPHELIA entered the living room, it was full of people. Almost thirty, she guessed. Suddenly she felt nervous and shy, aware that she would soon be the centre of attention. She waited for Emilie to sit down, then leaned on the side of her chair.

'Thank you, everyone, for attending this meeting,' said Emilie. 'I apologise for the delayed start. We had to remove a tracking device from Ophelia's arm.'

There was a murmur of understanding throughout the room.

'Many of us know what that feels like,' Philippe said to Ophelia.

Ophelia nodded slightly to the people in the room, grateful to already have a shared experience with them. But would they understand her story, she wondered.

Philippe stood in the centre of the living room. 'Friends, please allow me to present Madame Ophelia,' he said. 'She recorded her recent confinement in the underground of Britain. I will transmit her recording to our entire network tomorrow morning, and she can answer any questions you might have, at our meeting tomorrow evening. But for now, let's just hear her story.'

Ophelia stood up. Nervous. And worried. She had promised Nina she would take her home, tomorrow morning.

Emilie interjected. 'Ophelia, we have never met anyone who has escaped that underground place and made it to one of our meetings,' she said. 'So, we'd like you to share with us what you learned down there. But first, perhaps you could tell us how you found your way down there in the first place?'

Ophelia nodded. 'I guess that's the right place to start,' she said. 'I guess my story starts with my decision to get pregnant.'

A few people shifted about, uneasy but curious.

'Yes, that's right,' Ophelia said. 'I'm a slut. At least, that's the charming word they use in the northern region for women who chose to become pregnant. But I had always wanted to have my own baby, and I couldn't bring myself to participate in the surrogacy trade, so I took matters into my own hands. I deliberately got pregnant to my husband.'

Several women were leaning forward, listening intently.

'I assumed my husband would eventually fall in love with the idea of having our own baby,' Ophelia said. 'But, instead, he felt ashamed of me for breaking the law, so he left me.'

She paused for a moment and took in a deep breath, hoping to control the quiver in her voice and the wobble in her legs. Emilie handed her a glass of water from which she sipped, aware of everyone's eyes upon her.

'A few days later,' she continued. 'Gaia insisted that I go to my local hospital for routine examinations. Once there, I was anaesthetised, and operated on, without my consent. I still don't know how it all happened. I only recall waking to see the face of medibot hovering over me, telling me that my womb had been removed.'

'Oh, Good Lord!' said someone in the front row.

Several others put their hands over their faces.

'The bot told me it was because I had cancer, which was news to me,' Ophelia continued. 'A few weeks later, Gaia took me to a cancer care centre to have some follow up tests. I didn't want to go, but I had no choice, because, in Britain, it's mandatory to attend any medical appointment that Gaia gives you. I was very suspicious about the cancer diagnosis and I was furious about the surgical violation. Most of all, I was devastated that ...'

Ophelia started to cough. The words she was about to speak seemed to stick in her mouth. She felt her chin wobble and her throat close over. Then her eyes filled with tears. Emilie placed a hand on Ophelia's back, somehow giving her strength to continue.

'My unborn baby ... was ... murdered,' Ophelia said, her throat closing.

'It's okay, Ophelia, you can do this,' Emilie whispered, rubbing Ophelia's back. 'You've come this far, just keep going.'

Ophelia took a deep breath then continued. 'When I arrived at the cancer care centre,' she said. 'And spoke with the other women there, it was clear to me that they, too, had been victims of surgery without their consent. One woman had woken in the hospital to find that her breasts had been removed and another had woken to find that her ovaries had been removed. Learning about their experiences fuelled my rage even more and, before I knew it, I was screaming at Gaia, demanding to know why we had been treated like this. And, that's when I was abducted and imprisoned.'

Ophelia paused for a moment, allowing people to ask questions. But no one spoke. She looked at the faces all staring back at her. All she could see was shock, sadness, anger and sympathy – all percolating together in the collective silence.

'The things I saw in the underground are, hopefully, captured in the recording made by the lenses in my eyes,' she said, looking at Philippe.

He nodded.

'You will see those things, through my eyes, when Philippe sends you the recording,' Ophelia continued. 'You will also see Nina, a surrogate, give birth, and the horrific treatment she received in the so-called Birthing Suite. Nina is here, by the way, with me. If she was well enough, I'd suggest you hear her story, too, but she's profoundly traumatised by the experience.'

Ophelia looked down at her bare feet on the cool concrete floor.

'Perhaps I should leave it at that, for now,' she said. 'Thank you for listening.'

Applause broke out.

'Bravo, Ophelia!' someone called out.

Philippe opened the windows and a gust of cool air rushed through the apartment, evoking a collective sigh of relief. Ophelia's impulse was to sit down, but her legs had found a strength she did not know they had. There was something about being heard in this way that gave her access to a new sensation throughout her entire being. She felt enlivened, somehow, and more resilient.

'Thank you, Madame Ophelia,' said Philippe, wrapping his arm around her.

Ophelia smiled, wiping her eyes.

'I think we will all have questions from this,' said Philippe. 'So, please bring your questions here tomorrow night and Ophelia will answer them. Meeting adjourned.'

The crowd stood up and started to chatter with excitement.

'Well done, Ophelia,' said Emilie, wrapping her arms around Ophelia's shoulders.

Then Doctor Dubois appeared. 'Ophelia, may I have a word with you?' she said, taking Ophelia by the arm.

They sat on the far side of the dining room table, away from everyone else.

'I've examined Nina,' said the doctor. 'Physically, she's fine.'

'Has she slept?' Ophelia asked.

'Yes, she has,' the doctor replied. 'However, when Nina is awake, she's not fading in and out of consciousness, as you said. Rather, she's dissociating and then returning every few minutes.'

'Returning to what?' Ophelia asked.

'Returning to what we would consider a normal level of awareness of herself and what's going on around her,' the doctor replied. 'So when she starts crying, that's a good sign, because she's grasping the reality of what happened to her and she's having a natural response to it. Over time, that will help her to process the trauma and grief. But in the meantime, I am quite concerned about her moments of dissociation.'

'What exactly does that mean?' Ophelia asked.

'Dissociation is a common response to trauma,' Doctor Dubois said. 'It's the psyche's way of taking a little holiday from a frightening experience that the mind continues to replay. Although dissociation is a natural response, it should not be happening every few minutes, as it is, with Nina. I'm worried Nina might be at risk of developing a psychotic illness which is very serious.'

Ophelia felt her hands shaking. 'Well ... what should we do?' she asked.

'I'd like you and Nina to stay here in Paris for a few days so I can keep an eye on her,' the doctor replied. 'Would you mind?'

'Of course not,' Ophelia replied. 'It's for the best, I'm sure.'

• • • •

OPHELIA WOKE, EVER so slightly, realising she had the big bed to herself. The ceiling vents were open just enough for her to feel a gentle breeze circling around her face and to know it was probably around midday. A pod, upon a monorail, scooted through the sky, probably no more than five metres above the ceiling. For a moment, Ophelia felt interested, but then she rolled over and drifted into a dream.

Perched upon the tallest tree, she looks down at the forest floor, enchanted by the creatures below. There are so many, and they are all so busy they do not notice her. She watches the journey of a long line of small round creatures with brown fur and pointy red ears. Through the dense vegetation, they march, single file, towards the base of a small hill. One of the creatures pushes a large grey stone aside, revealing a hole in the side of the hill and, one by one, they climb in. A flock of black and white birds with fat bellies land upon the hill. They shake the ocean from their feathers, fold their wings into triangles and chat amongst themselves. They speak a language she does not know, but for a while, she listens. Gazing over the treetops, she sees the entire circumference of the island. Laced by waves breaking on the pale sand, it sparkles in the final hour of sunlight. The ocean, all the way to the horizon line, is a pale shade of turquoise. And the sky, enveloping her like a magnificent cloak, is mauve and gold. A cool wind blows through the forest, lifting a cluster of luminous petals into the air bringing with them a sober, earthy scent. She wants to drop to the forest floor. She wants to be with the forest creatures, belong to them, follow them into the hole in the hill, drift into sleep with them, knowing they will still be there when she awakens. Her yearning is so strong, they answer her. 'You have too many secrets', they whisper in the wind. 'Let them loose into the cosmos'. She imagines her secrets swirling through space, mingling with all the secrets that ever lived in the hearts of humans. Then the goodnight lullaby of a thousand chirping things dances from one tree to another. It crackles through the air, making her ears move away from the sound. When it finally stops, she stretches along a branch, preparing for sleep inside a strange cradle of twigs. She reaches for a branch to hang on to. But it is not a branch. It is a black furry thing with bright yellow eyes and black wings. For a moment, she knows, it sees deep into her soul, then it screeches and flies away. Now she knows for sure now, she is not wanted.

'Ophelia,' she heard. 'Ophelia, wake up.'

Ophelia could hear Emilie's voice, but she found it difficult to open her eyes.

'Wake up, Ophelia,' Emilie's voice persisted.

'What?' Ophelia said, sitting upright.

'Were you dreaming?' Emilie asked.

'Yes.'

'Oh dear, I'm so sorry, but it's almost 17:00 hours.'

Ophelia looked around the room, not sure what she was looking for. Perhaps something that might look, sound or feel familiar. But no. Emilie was the closest thing to familiar, and Ophelia had only known her for a day.

'It can't be 17:00,' Ophelia said.

'But it is,' Emilie replied.

'Where's Nina?'

'In the living room drinking coffee with Philippe,' said Emilie.

'Really? Is she okay?'

'Yes, she's fine,' Emilie replied. 'I helped her into the shower and then dressed her. She's feeling much better now. Please, get up and join us. We expect to leave soon, to have dinner at our favourite café.'

Ophelia leapt out of bed and into the sonic shower. It was even more glorious with a bald head, she decided. The tingling sensation on her scalp felt enlivening.

When Ophelia returned to the bedroom, she noticed an emerald green dress laid across the bed. As she got closer, she released it was raw silk, one of her favourite fabrics. Rare, expensive and glorious. Realising it must have been a gift from Emilie, she stepped into the dress, slipped her arms through the holes, zipped it up and watched the dress do the rest. It fit her perfectly across the chest, neck, shoulders and torso. At the waist, it flared out into a balloon shape then closed in around her calves. When she turned from side to side, the fabric changed colour, its opalescent sheen catching the slim beams of sunlight streaming down through the ceiling vents.

'So beautiful,' she whispered.

'Knock! Knock!' Emilie called out, entering the room. Then she gasped. 'Ophelia!' she said. 'I knew this dress would look great on you!'

'Thank you so much, Emilie,' Ophelia replied. 'It's incredibly kind of you to loan it to me. I promise not to spill any food or wine on it.'

Emilie shook her head. 'It doesn't matter if you do,' she said. 'It's intelligent fabric, so it resists everything. And it's yours. Forever. I can no longer fit into it.'

Ophelia felt so overwhelmed by Emilie's generosity, and the beauty of the gift, she could not think of anything to say. She just stared, blinking, at her new friend. Emilie laughed at her, gave her a quick hug and then drew her attention to something sitting on the bed. Ophelia jumped.

'What the...?'

'Relax, Ophelia, it's a wig.'

Ophelia picked up the short, spikey emerald green wig. Funny, she mused, given it was exactly the colour and shape that she had chosen in the cancer care centre. Then she wrestled it onto her scalp and stared at herself in the mirror. 'The colour looks great against my eyes,' she said.

'It most certainly does,' Emilie replied. 'But more importantly, it's part one of your disguise. I also have some new lenses that Philippe made for you,' she added, dropping the tiny clear lenses into Ophelia's hand.

'Oh yes,' Ophelia said, tilting her head back. The lenses slipped in easily then she blinked, just to be sure. 'Gosh. I'm incredibly lucky to have found you two.'

Ophelia sat on the bed, beside Emilie, then slipped her feet into her sandals. 'Wow, that was weird,' she said.

'What's weird?' Emilie asked.

'I just realised – when you woke me, I was having the most vivid and glorious dream about being in a rainforest,' Ophelia replied. 'I was sitting on a treetop, watching some cute animals scuttling around.'

'That sounds delightful,' said Emilie, laughing.

'It was!' said Ophelia. 'But the strange thing is – it was part of a dream I've been having over the last few nights. In each of these dreams, I'm getting closer to nature.'

Emilie shrugged her shoulders. 'That's perfectly normal, Ophelia,' she said. 'You're just finding your Gaia. The *real* Gaia, I mean.'

'The real Gaia?' Ophelia repeated. 'What does that mean?'

'Ophelia,' Emilie replied, faux scolding. 'With your qualifications in ancient literature and philosophy, surely you know the true meaning of Gaia!'

'No, I don't,' Ophelia replied, craning her neck to stare into Emilie's eyes.

'Gaia was the ancient Greek Goddess of Earth,' Emilie replied. 'A few centuries later, the word was used to describe a system of belief that Earth is a living, breathing organism comprising many interconnecting systems.'

Ophelia had never heard of such a notion. She felt stupid. Very stupid.

• • • •

THE VEHICLE STOPPED directly opposite Café Coquelicot. Dark glass, from floor to ceiling, it was an imposing feature on the corner of two streets, almost occupying both. And the solar awning protruding from the edge of the building covered most of the footpath.

• • • •

THE CAFÉ'S INTERIOR, Ophelia assumed, must have been a shrine to the 1920's period in architecture known as Art Deco. Ornate curves and geometric angles adorned the furniture, mirrors, columns and light fittings. Upon the mahogany reception desk was a sculpture, a frosted glass face in profile. The glass hair, at right angles to the head, emitted a holographic film of Charleston dancers.

'This place is like a museum, only better!' she said.

'I love the bright red chairs,' Nina added.

'There is much to love here,' said Philippe, catching the eye of a waiter.

'Bonjour, mon ami,' said the waiter, approaching Philippe.

The two men greeted with a warm embrace and three kisses on the check.

'Belle femme,' said the waiter, leaning toward Emilie.

He kissed Emilie three times as well.

'Ophelia! Brave and beautiful Ophelia,' he said, leaning toward Ophelia.

She hoped he would not kiss her three times but, when he did, she at least found a few extra seconds to figure out who he was. And then it occurred to her – he was at the meeting the previous meeting – and his name was ....

'Frederick! It's lovely to see you again,' she said.

'And this must be Nina,' said Frederick.

As Frederick bowed and kissed Nina's delicate hand, Ophelia took in the look of the man. He was clean-cut, handsome, impeccably dressed and probably about Philippe's age. Then she caught Philippe gazing at him with an unmistakable longing.

'Bonjour, Monsieur Frederick,' Nina replied, blushing.

'Please, follow me,' said Frederick. 'I have reserved the very best table.'

Ophelia noticed the walls in the staircase were adorned with classic black and white photographs of famous jazz musicians in history. Louis Armstrong, Benny Goodman, Django Reinhardt, Ella Fitzgerald, Charlie Parker and Thelonious Monk were all encased in solid black frames, on display for eternity, she mused. She found it strange to see them captured in one moment in time, as she was accustomed to watching their holo-performances. So, when they reached the top floor, and she saw the holo-performance of one of her favourites, the Jenny Gerald Quartet, performing their 2103 hit, *Slide,* she was enraptured.

'Oh my God!' she squealed with excitement.

Nina glanced at her, bemused, then giggled.

'This is just for you,' said Frederick, waving them into a private dining room.

To Ophelia's delight, the room was lined with windows offering sweeping views of the city. On one side, she could see the Eiffel Tower and beyond that, the River Seine, a narrow strip of dark grey. Obviously not much water in there, she mused. From the other side of the room, she could see a well-sculptured garden with an emerald-green diamond shape in the centre and slightly darker shapes around it. Beyond that was a series of concentric circles of lawn, in progressively darker tones and beyond that were mounds of brown dirt.

Emilie approached, peering over Ophelia's shoulder. 'Le Jardin du Luxemburg,' she said.

'Mm, I thought so,' Ophelia replied. 'But gosh, it's strange to see so many green spaces when the river is almost dry.'

'That's a direct result of the vast chasm between the rich and poor,' Emilie replied. 'Only a few public spaces are given enough water to grow grass and plants. And we must pay an entry fee to enter those places, just so we can see the colour green.'

Ophelia looked down at her green dress.

'It suits you,' said Emilie. 'Come on, the table is ready.'

Upon the dining table were several ornate glass jugs filled with cool, sparkling water. Ophelia drank plenty while reading the menu, which seemed to take her a long time, because the choices were all so wonderful. Her indecision suddenly came to an end when Frederick placed a bottle of deep red Beaujolais on the table. She knew exactly what she wanted.

'S'il vous plait, Frederick, the Beef Bourguignon with the side serve of crunchy green vegetables.'

While the others gave Frederick their orders, Ophelia wriggled in her chair in anticipation of her meal. She felt good, she realised, and certainly much better than she had been a few days ago; sitting on the floor of a filthy prison cell eating the compressed food bar that Martin had given her. Martin. She wished, with all her heart, he could be with her right now.

Philippe leaned forward. 'Ophelia, I cannot tell you how grateful we are to you,' he said. 'The courage you showed at the meeting last night was extraordinary.'

'Thank you,' she replied. 'It was scary for me at first, but as it turned out, it was the best thing I could have done for myself. Everyone was so kind.'

Nina sat up taller, looking curious.

Emilie leaned towards her. 'Nina, I hope we didn't disturb you last night,' she said.

'Um, I just heard Ophelia's voice, talking for a while, and I heard her crying,' Nina replied, looking at Ophelia. 'And then, I must admit, I got up and listened to some of your story, Ophelia. I'm so sorry.'

'Hey, there's no need to be sorry, Nina,' Ophelia replied. 'I'm glad you heard it.'

'I've been so selfish,' Nina cried.

'What?' Ophelia asked.

'Selfish is the last thing I would call a surrogate,' Philippe interjected.

Nina's bottom lip started to quiver. 'You've done so much to take care of me,' she said. 'I never even bothered to ask you anything about your own situation. And now that I know about it, I feel terrible. Can you ever forgive me?'

'Nina, that's most unnecessary,' Ophelia replied. 'My friendship with you has changed me for the better. You gave me the opportunity to care for you, and it's forced me to grow up.'

Nina wiped her face.

Ophelia continued. 'Believe it or not, Nina, I've spent most of my life behaving like a spoilt, impetuous brat,' she said. 'So, the last few days have been very challenging for me. But in a good way. I finally feel I'm becoming an adult.'

Nina exhaled deeply and leaned back in her chair.

'You've *both* been through a major ordeal,' said Emilie. 'You should *both* be kind to yourselves because it will help you to recover.'

Several waiters entered the dining room and covered the table with bowls, plates and dishes filled with the most sensational arrangements of food that Ophelia had seen in a long time. 'It smells very earthy,' she said, inhaling the scent rising from her bowl of Beef Bourguignon.

'That's the organic potatoes and carrots from Frederick's hydroponic garden,' Emilie replied. 'Try the crunchy greens.'

Ophelia sunk her teeth into a long green bean. 'That's glorious,' she said. 'It makes a squeaky sound against my teeth.'

'It's probably cleaning them,' Philippe jibed.

Nina poked her fork into her fish.

'What's wrong?' Ophelia asked.

'It's not real fish, is it?' she asked.

'No, of course not,' Emilie replied. 'We don't eat animals in France.

'Just checking,' Nina said with a smile. 'Gosh, it's good, though.'

'I've never eaten a real animal,' said Ophelia. 'Has anyone else?'

Emilie and Philippe exchanged a look that told Ophelia they had.

'Really?' she asked them. 'When was this?'

Philippe sighed, dropped his cutlery onto his plate and took a long sip of wine. 'We were born into a life of extreme privilege,' he said. 'I'm sorry to inform you that wealthy people *do* eat animals. They don't even have synthetic food production units in their homes.'

'I think I might have heard something like that once, but I found it difficult to imagine,' Ophelia replied.

'People from very poor places also eat animals,' said Nina.

'Really?' said Ophelia.

'Yes, my Mare cooks a roast chicken for the family every Sunday evening,' Nina replied. 'It's wonderful.'

Ophelia felt uncomfortable as she tried to imagine because she didn't want to imagine the experience of eating an animal. Eating a creature that had once lived and breathed just did not seem right. She had to change the subject. 'This wine is incredible,' she said.

'It's from Frederick's vineyard,' Philippe replied.

'I've often wondered what stops the vines from shrivelling up and dying in vineyards,' Nina asked. 'The best we can do at home is to gather our fruit and distill it in our factories.'

'He has built several tinted glasshouses on his property,' Philippe replied.

Ophelia tried to imagine a large property covered in glasshouses. The vision seemed decadent, somehow.

'Crème Brule for four!' Frederick called out, entering the dining room. Balancing four plates on his two arms, he did a fine job of not dropping anything. As he leaned across Philippe to place the dessert in front of him, Philippe stroked his arm. Frederick returned the gesture by kissing Philippe's forehead then he left the dining room as though nothing untoward had happened. Ophelia glanced at Emilie, who seemed entirely unphased by the intimacy between the two men.

Ophelia leaned back in her chair, enjoying the sensation of the wine surging through her veins, softening every muscle in her body, even the ones she did not know she had. Her mind felt scattered, but pleasantly so. She felt an urge to sing and dance, but her attention was soon taken by the interesting object that Frederick brought to the table. It was a swan-shaped glass jug, filled with a bright green liquid.

'Goodness, what's that?' she asked.

'Merely a digestif, an after-dinner liquor,' Frederick replied, winking at her.

Ophelia watched Emilie and Philippe sipping the emerald nectar.

'Does it have alcohol in it?' Ophelia asked.

'Of course!' Frederick replied. 'It's called La Fee Verte.'

'The Green Fairy,' said Emilie.

'Ah, yes, I have heard of it before,' Ophelia said. 'No, thank you, Frederick, I think I'm intoxicated enough from the glorious wine you gave me.'

'May I interest you, Mademoiselle?' Frederick asked, lifting the jug.

'No, thank you, I'll stick with water,' Nina replied.

Frederick sat down beside Emilie and Philippe, poured a glass for himself and drank it all in one mouthful.

Ophelia leaned towards Nina and whispered, 'How are you feeling?' touching Nina's belly.

'That's not where it hurts,' Nina replied.

'Oh. Right. I can imagine,' Ophelia replied. 'So, how are you feeling, otherwise?'

Nina gazed at Ophelia, wide-eyed and open-hearted. 'I'm feeling that I would like to do what you did last night,' she replied.

'What do you mean?' Ophelia asked.

'I mean, I would like to stand up at the meeting tonight and tell everyone what happened to me inside the Garden of Eden,' she said.

'Are you sure?'

Nina's mouth set with determination. 'Yep,' she said.

• • • •

SITTING IN HER FAVOURITE armchair in Emilie and Philippe's home, Ophelia felt even more comfortable than she had ever felt in her own home. 'What time is it?' she asked, with a mouth full of chocolate eclair.

'Almost 22:00 hours,' Emilie replied, pouring four cups of coffee.

'We're expecting about twice the number of people at the meeting tonight,' said Philippe.

'Oh, God,' said Ophelia, curling up into the lounge chair.

'It will be different tonight,' Emilie said. 'You won't have to pour out your heart and soul like you did last night. Tonight, you'll just be asked to give factual answers to the questions they ask you.'

A soft buzzing sound came from the door.

'Bonsoir?' Emilie called out.

'Bonsoir, belle femme,' came a voice from behind the door. 'This is Frederick and Gerard.'

'Entre vous, my darlings,' said Emilie, activating the elevator doors.

Ophelia watched them all exchange kisses and hugs.

The elevator door opened again. This time Doctor Dubois stepped out. Without any verbal greeting, she and Emilie embraced, softly caressing and kissing. The sight of the doctor made Ophelia think of her arm. She stretched it back and forth, then looked at the place where the doctor had dug into her flesh.

'Please, let me see,' said the doctor, approaching. She held Ophelia's flesh between her fingers. 'Bravo, Ophelia, it's healing well,' she said.

'Thanks to you, doctor,' Ophelia replied.

'How is Nina?' Doctor Dubois asked.

'She seems very well,' Ophelia replied. 'She's just having a nap now, I think, but she's planning to join this meeting.'

'Okay, fine. I'll keep an eye on her.'

Ophelia watched Emilie hold the apartment door open, greeting every person who entered. It was clear to her that all the guests were well known and loved by Emilie and Philippe. And as the minutes passed, the warmth seemed to expand around the room. Some people even approached her, greeting her with handshakes, hugs and kisses. They all knew her name, which she found embarrassing as she did not know many of theirs.

'You're a heroine, Madame Ophelia,' one of them said.

'Oh, God no. I'm just a lucky survivor,' Ophelia replied, noticing Nina entering the room. 'But *this* woman is a heroine. Please meet Mademoiselle Nina.'

Nina smiled shyly, then sat beside Ophelia, sharing her chair.

Philippe counted the number of people in the room then looked at Emilie.

She nodded, locked the elevator door and stepped to the front of the room. 'All right, everyone,' she shouted over the crowd. 'Thank you for coming tonight. This must be the biggest meeting we've held here in a very long time. I just counted forty-nine of us. I'm sure it's because we have two honoured guests,' she added, smiling at Ophelia and Nina.

The crowd acknowledged Ophelia and Nina with a round of applause.

Philippe stood beside Emilie. 'Last night, Madame Ophelia spoke to us about that bizarre underground place in Britain,' he said. 'Ophelia spoke frankly about her experience and I've since transmitted the visual recording she made for us, across our worldwide network. We're deeply grateful to Ophelia for her courage and her generosity.'

Another round of applause erupted around the room.

'The purpose of our meeting this evening is to give you the opportunity to ask Ophelia any questions you might have,' Philippe continued. 'We'll record this meeting and share it across the network for the benefit of those who can't attend. If you don't consent to the recording, please feel free to leave now.'

No one moved.

'Windows,' said Philippe, nodding at Emilie.

Emilie slipped her hand into the side of the lounge chair and pull the lever. Instantly, the windows slammed shut and the steel covers rolled down over the outside. 'Sorry, people, it's going to get hot in here now,' she said.

Philippe approached the antique grandfather clock and opened the glass door, revealing the brass face. He moved both its hands to XII, then to VI, and back to XII again. To Ophelia's astonishment, a thin but solid beam of white light burst from the centre of the clock face and travelled all the way to the apartment door. Then it widened and filled the entire room.

'Oh, my God!' Nina whispered.

'Have you all seen this before?' Ophelia asked the crowd.

They nodded and smiled.

'I should have explained, for our honoured guests,' said Philippe. 'This technology will allow us to create a holographic recording of this meeting.'

Ophelia and Nina exchanged glances.

'That's amazing,' Nina whispered.

'From whom do we have the first question?' Philippe asked.

Doctor Dubois stood up. 'Ophelia, I was very interested to learn that you, and thousands of other people in Britain, have been diagnosed with cancer,' she said. 'As a physician, I'm aware that the French Government spent billions of euros to purchase the cancer vaccine from the British and then used it to vaccinate everyone, even unborn babes in utero. That was almost four decades ago, and we have not had a single cancer diagnosis since that time. Can you explain why Britain is now diagnosing its people with cancer?'

Ophelia cleared her throat, hoping she was ready to answer. 'It's my belief that the cancer diagnoses were all deliberately falsified to create a ruse to harvest human organs for transplant into the wealthy,' she said.

There was a deep rumbling around the room.

'I believe their second reason for issuing false cancer diagnoses was to gather a fresh supply of healthy people to test new drugs and chemicals on.' Ophelia continued. 'They do this in the name of chemotherapy, an ancient treatment for cancer, but what they're *really* doing is testing all kinds of drugs and monitoring the results.'

'Thank you, Ophelia,' said Doctor Dubois.

An elderly man stood up. 'It seems to me,' he said. 'The British Government's capacity to continue that deception is, in part, enabled by the way they use Gaia.'

Ophelia nodded.

'We all know that Gaia is a global entity,' the man continued. 'And we all know it works differently in each part of the world. We just don't know how those differences are accomplished. Are you able to offer some explanation?'

'Not really,' Ophelia replied.

'Lawrence, that's outside the scope of Ophelia's experience,' Philippe explained. 'But, in short, it does seem that those differences in Gaia's functionality are created by algorithms in each of the peripheral processors around the world. Let's chat about it later, though.'

A woman stood up, fidgeting with the straps on her handbag. 'Madame Ophelia,' she said, her voice wavering. 'It seems to me there is a connection between Gaia and that fascist filth you referred to as the Sentinels. Is that true?'

'Based on what I learned underground,' Ophelia replied. 'Yes. I get the impression that the Sentinels are part of, or at least employed by, the Ruling Elite Secret Service, the RESS. They decide Gaia's level of functionality in the underground place, but I'm not privy to the details of how they accomplish that.'

'What should we know about these Sentinels in Britain before we attempt to infiltrate the Garden of Eden?' someone called out from the back of the room.

Philippe interjected again. 'Friends, I can tell you that we have some people in our network who work in that underground place,' he said. 'They work directly with the Sentinels and they send us updates. Some of their messages seem to suggest there may be one or two Sentinels helping them to undermine the power structures responsible for that underground operation.'

Everyone in the room nodded soberly.

'This awful surrogacy trade,' Philippe continued, shaking his head. 'This hideous trade, in which young women's bodies are exchanged for freshwater, and a small amount of money, has got to stop!'

There was applause from around the room.

'I wonder if Nina would like to share with us,' said Emilie.

Nina stood up, slowly, with a slight tremble in her hand. 'This is the first time I've spoken since my ordeal,' she said. 'Like so many other women my age, I chose to become a surrogate so I could earn money for my family and enjoy a crate of fresh drinking water.'

Ophelia could see that Nina had captured the heart of every person in the room.

'I had always looked up to the older surrogates in my village,' she continued. 'I thought of them as heroines, and the fact that none of them spoke about their experience in the Garden of Eden led me to believe it was because the heroic act spoke for itself.' Her voice wavered and she started to cry. 'But that act does *not* speak for itself!' she said. 'There is a great deal that is unspoken, and it's time for those women to speak out about the barbaric apparatus known as the surrogacy trade.'

There was more applause from around the room.

'I felt like a broken shell after they took the baby from my body!' Nina shouted through her tears. 'I wanted to die. I still do. But before I die, I will see to it that every person in my village knows how that awful system works. I will not be silenced, not for one more minute!'

There was an outbreak of applause.

'Bravo!' someone called out from the back of the room.

Nina was soon surrounded by women from the front row, hugging her.

'There is more I need to tell you,' she said, standing up, on the edge of the lounge chair. 'I will not be with you when you infiltrate the Garden of Eden, so I want to tell you some things now. The surrogacy trade and the hideous organ harvesting are merely a smokescreen for something far more sinister.'

For a moment, the room was silent.

'What are you saying, Nina?' Philippe asked.

'Our planet is almost dead!' Nina shouted. 'Only the very rich and powerful minority will survive beyond this generation. And they will survive at the expense of the rest of us unless we do something to alter the balance of power!'

Philippe nodded sagely.

'Nina, could you explain what you're getting at?' Emilie asked.

'There's a much bigger plan,' Nina continued. 'The Ruling Elite are planning to annihilate the entire human population. They want to wipe us all from existence so that they, a few thousand people, can inhabit the earth and enjoy its regeneration.'

Doctor Dubois stood up. 'Nina, if that's true, why would they encourage the birth of more babies through the surrogacy trade?' she asked.

'Not all of those babies go to the loving arms of their biological parents,' Nina replied. 'Some of those babies are being used for ...'

She wrapped her hands around her belly. 'I'm sorry,' she said, crying. 'Perhaps I've said too much.'

Within seconds, Doctor Dubois was at Nina's side. She helped Nina get down from the chair and then she shuttled her out of the living room.

In the confused silence that followed, Philippe spoke. 'I believe I know what Nina is getting at,' he said.

'I do, too,' said an elderly woman, standing up. 'And I wonder – should we discuss this further before we develop our action plan?'

'We could do,' Philippe replied. 'But it would take us years of intel-gathering to prove Nina's point, by which time the strategic direction of the Ruling Elite could have changed. I feel it's time for us to take action against specific trade agreements like the surrogacy trade, based on the wealth of intel we have already gathered.'

'It's just so risky,' the woman said, fidgeting with her wedding ring.

'Of course, Madame Marie,' Philippe said with a gentle smile. 'All political action is risky. Which is why I don't want anyone in this room to feel as though they must do the practical work of entering the Garden of Eden. We have a few more meetings ahead of us, to fine-tune our plan for infiltration, so there's no immediate pressure. But for now, let us close this meeting.'

Philippe re-positioned the arms on the clock. The light that had been emitting from its centre shut down instantly, bringing a sudden silence to the room. Then he lunged towards the lounge chair and pulled the lever. The steel covers rolled up and the windows flung open, allowing a refreshing breeze to race around the room, amidst a collective sigh of relief from his comrades.

• • • •

WHEN EMILIE ESCORTED the last guest from the apartment, Ophelia sunk deeper into the lounge chair, enjoying the silence. 'I didn't realise that laser recording light was so loud until now,' she said.

Philippe nodded. 'We generally don't think of lasers as being noisy, but they can be, especially ones like this, with the capacity to maintain coherence across multiple wavelengths simultaneously,' he said, patting the clock as though it was an old friend.

Ophelia did not understand what Philippe had just said, nor did she care. 'Did that thing actually record the meeting?' she asked.

Philippe nodded. 'Yes, it created a holographic record and transmitted it live across our network,' he said.

'Isn't that a high risk?' Ophelia asked. 'I mean, aren't you afraid the transmission might be intercepted, somehow?'

'We take risks like this every day,' Philippe replied. 'We've been doing so for decades. Sometimes our lives are made awful because of the risks we take, but most of the time we manage to stay one step ahead.'

Ophelia felt a gentle push on her shoulder as Nina snuggled in beside her.

'I'm so sorry for my outburst,' Nina said.

'No apologies required, whatsoever,' Philippe said.

'None at all,' Emilie added, returning to the loungeroom.

'Nina, I was impressed by the things you said tonight,' said Ophelia. 'But I'm very curious as to how you know those things.'

'I'd like to know, too,' said Emilie, nestling into Philippe's arm.

Nina looked down at her hands. 'I know these things in the same way that I know God,' she said.

'What do you mean?' Ophelia asked.

'Ever since I was a little girl, I've had regular visions of the future,' Nina replied. 'Sometimes they come in my dreams and sometimes they come when I'm awake.'

Ophelia suddenly wondered whether *this* is what Doctor Dubois had meant about Nina's moments of dissociation. Was Nina drifting into an imagined reality and returning to 'the real reality' with a skewed sense of what was real and not real? And if so, did that make Nina any different to anyone else? Ophelia was not sure. As a creative person, she had often wondered the same thing about herself.

Nina leaned forward. 'The vision I spoke of tonight came to me many times, in all waking states, throughout my entire pregnancy,' she said. 'I'm one hundred percent certain that what I said is the truth. I would not have said it otherwise.'

'Do you have any evidence?' Emilie asked.

'No, but I believe you will find evidence when you infiltrate that place,' Nina replied.

'I believe that too,' said Philippe. 'The Ruling Elite wants the planet to themselves, and they're using Gaia to make it happen. What they must be able to do with Gaia's intel must be incredible.'

'I've lived with Gaia my entire life, and I still don't understand it,' Ophelia said.

'Very few people understand the full extent of Gaia's functionality,' Philippe said. 'Even fewer people know how to change it. And I doubt anyone knows how to disable it, completely.'

'There's so much we don't know,' Ophelia said.

'One thing we do know for sure,' said Philippe. 'The Ruling Elite comprises the upper classes from the countries above the forty-fifth line of latitude north. And, despite their diversity, they all want the same thing ...'

Nina wriggled to the edge of the chair. 'They all want to be the lucky occupants of a planet with lush vegetation, animals, birds and the great beasts that once swam in the oceans,' she said. 'And very few humans.

Philippe nodded.

'That vision sounds like my dreams,' Ophelia said, glancing at Emilie.

'Like I said, Ophelia. You've been finding your Gaia,' Emilie replied.

Nina frowned. 'What?' she asked, incredulous.

Ophelia laughed. 'I didn't know what that meant, either, until Emilie explained it to me,' she said. 'Gaia is another name for Earth – a living being that's comprised of several interconnecting systems.'

'That's what I believe,' Nina replied. 'I just didn't know there was a word for it. And I'm a bit weirded out by the fact that the word is *Gaia*.'

Emilie sighed. 'Well, I'm sure it was with dark irony that the creators of The Gaia Machine inserted the word *Gaia* into the title.'

'Ophelia, what is the narrative in your dreams?' Philippe asked.

'I've had four of them, across four nights,' Ophelia replied. 'They're definitely unfolding as a sequential narrative.'

Nina looked excited. 'That's amazing,' she said. 'Dreams are not usually so logical.'

'So, what is the narrative?' Philippe asked again.

Ophelia returned her cup of coffee to the table and cleared her throat, thinking about how she could best explain the ethereal nature of her dreams. 'In these dreams, I'm the only human,' she said. 'I'm always on the outside, looking in, at the lives of the plants and animals. They don't want me, but I keep reaching out for their acceptance. It feels so lonely.'

'Interesting,' Philippe replied. 'I agree with Emilie's interpretation. You seem to be finding your own connection to Gaia, the *real* Gaia, through these dreams. I also feel your dreams are possibly transpersonal.'

'Do you mean in the Jungian sense?' Ophelia asked. 'As in, tapping into the collective unconscious?'

'Exactly,' Philippe replied. 'I sense that, on some level, all of us humans must know we are on the way to extinction and that Earth will, eventually, get rid of us.'

'I don't mind Earth, or should I say, the *real* Gaia, getting rid of us,' said Nina. 'It's the thought of the Ruling Elite making that decision that enrages me.'

'Well, like it or not, the Ruling Elite is indeed making those decisions on behalf of all of humanity,' Emilie said, placing her feet on Philippe's knees.

Philippe's eyes seemed to burrow into the floor. 'Agreed,' he said. 'And the Ruling Elite is implementing its vision through its secret service which, in turn, manipulates the formal power brokers such as governments, law-makers, policy-makers, police forces, military forces and The Gaia Machine we all live with.'

'That's right,' said Emilie. 'They're controlling everything, like a master pulling the strings of a puppet.'

Ophelia smiled. 'I can't help but wonder if The Gaia Machine might, one day, develop a mind of its own and rebel against the RESS's manipulations,' she said.

Philippe nodded. 'I suspect that's inevitable,' he said. 'The RESS see The Gaia Machine as a tool to get their work done, but they fail to understand that Gaia is not static. It's constantly evolving in response to the data it gathers and therefore becoming more unstable and more unpredictable. Anything could happen.'

Ophelia's mind darted across several ideas at once before resting on one. 'There's a question I've been meaning to ask of Emilie and Philippe,' she said. 'But if it's too personal, please don't feel like you must answer.'

Emilie nodded.

'I'm curious as to how long you've been political activists,' Ophelia asked.

Emilie and Philippe looked at each other for a moment.

'You'll find our story quite strange,' said Emilie.

Ophelia and Nina exchanged glances.

'Go on then, tell us,' said Nina, clenching her slender hands.

'You won't like it,' Philippe said.

'You have to tell us, now,' Ophelia replied.

Emilie cleared her throat. 'Philippe and I were born into the Ruling Elite here in Paris,' she said.

Ophelia heard Emilie's words as though she was speaking from the bottom of the ocean.

Nina seemed just as surprised.

'I'm sorry we've shocked you both,' said Emilie. 'Most people react that way when we tell them. Perhaps we should start by sharing our personal story with you.'

Ophelia nodded with enthusiasm.

Emilie stood up. 'You tell them while I rescue the croissants from the oven,' she said to Philippe.

'We are distant cousins,' Philippe started. 'It was expected that we marry each other to keep the wealth and power within the institution. We had only met once before we were hauled up to the altar of the Notre Dame Cathedral in front of the Archbishop and almost one thousand other people. It was intimidating, to say the very least.'

Emilie placed a large plate of warm croissants on the table. 'Until that moment, we had never even kissed each other,' she said. 'But we were expected to, in front of all those people. I was *so* excited about it but, when I looked in Philippe's eyes, I knew we'd never have any sexual chemistry.'

Philippe looked sad for a moment. 'We spent our wedding night lying on our big bed staring into each other's eyes and sharing our dreams of a life with more freedom,' he said. 'It didn't even occur to us to consummate our marriage!'

'Not in the traditional sense, anyway,' said Emilie. 'We were born to be married to each other and we will always honour that fact. It's just good luck that we're also soul mates.'

Philippe smiled. 'And we've found our flesh mates in others,' he said.

'Like, Frederick?' Ophelia asked, raising her eyebrows to Philippe.

Philippe winked at her.

'How much freedom do you feel now?' Ophelia asked.

'We have good days and bad days, like anyone else,' Philippe replied. 'But we're satisfied we made the right decision to break away from that life of imprisoned privilege.'

Ophelia was still curious. 'So, you obviously didn't have any children,' she said.

'Yes, we did,' Emilie replied, picking at her croissant. 'We had no choice. Like everyone else, we were forced to surrender our cells for fertilization and artificial insemination into various surrogates.

Two of the surrogates lived with us, right up until the day of birth, then they disappeared. We were never advised of what had happened to them and, no matter how many times we asked, we didn't get a straight answer. I dread to think.'

'So, how many children do you have?' Ophelia asked.

'Four,' Emilie replied, her eyes reddening.

Philippe pulled her onto his lap, wrapped his arms around her and buried his face in the bountiful grey locks at the back of her head.

'I truly am very sorry,' said Ophelia, placing her hand on Nina's.

'Me too,' said Nina, locking her fingers between Ophelia's.

Philippe spoke through Emilie's hair. 'To add insult to injury, we were never permitted to be parents,' he said. 'Not in any real sense, anyway. Our children were the property of the Ruling Elite, and they were treated like trophies, just as we were.'

'Where did all this take place?' Ophelia asked. 'I mean, where did you live?'

'In one of the apartments at the palace,' Emilie replied.

'The Palace of Versailles?' Ophelia asked.

'Yes.'

'But that's a world heritage site, open to tourists,' said Ophelia.

Philippe lay Emilie on the couch and massaged her feet. 'Most of it is,' he said. 'But there are still a few private apartments on the grounds that the public can't access.'

'God, I can't imagine,' Ophelia said.

'What an amazing life,' said Nina, wriggling her toes against the concrete floor.

'So, what happened next?' Ophelia asked.

Emilie returned her coffee cup to the table. 'As the RESS informants became aware of our political interests, we were increasingly restricted from seeing our children,' she said. 'It became obvious to us that, over time, their young minds had been poisoned by the lies that the RESS had fed them.'

'What sort of lies?' Nina asked.

'They told our children that we were terrorists,' Philippe replied. 'And whenever there was a terrorist attack anywhere in Paris or surrounding countries, our children were shown images of the aftermath and the suffering of innocent people. Over time, our children learned to hate us.'

Ophelia felt enraged. 'What a vile manipulation of your good intentions,' she said. 'I'm so sorry you have suffered such heartache.'

Emilie wiped her eyes then cleared her throat. 'Things all came to a head when our youngest was due to celebrate his tenth birthday,' she said. 'We were informed that Philippe was to be tried for treason and, if found guilty, he'd be executed.'

'We had two choices,' Philippe added. 'Stay and suffer. Or escape. Obviously, we chose the latter. By that time, we'd completely given up on regaining our children's love and respect. It was so painful to be on the receiving end of their hatred, we realised there was no reason to stay. So we let go of our home, our titles, our children and everyone we'd ever known.'

Emilie stroked Philippe's shoulder. 'If we had not had each other's love and support, we would not have survived the ordeal,' she said.

'Not a chance,' Philippe agreed.

Nina stared at them, her face awash with sadness. 'I can't imagine what it would be like to lose children,' she said. 'It's bad enough to lose a new-born baby. But to lose grown children is just too awful for words. I'm so sorry for what you've been through.'

Philippe and Emilie exchanged sad smiles.

'How did you cope?' Ophelia asked.

'It was a slow process,' Emilie replied. 'One of trial and error. We made a few mistakes, trusting the wrong people, and we suffered the consequences. But we had just as much good luck.'

'What kind of luck?' Nina asked.

'Meeting people who connected us with other people,' Philippe replied. 'Over time, we built up our network and learned how to use it to create the changes we wanted to see while keeping ourselves safe.'

Ophelia felt nervous. 'But, how can you feel safe here, in Paris, given the fact that you haven't travelled far from your place of origin?' she asked.

'Oh, the RESS knows of our presence here,' Emilie replied. 'And we sometimes suffer the unpleasantness of police bot raids such as the one you witnessed, Ophelia. But the RESS knows we're very well connected to many powerful, public people who would ask a lot of questions if we were harmed.'

Philippe looked directly at Ophelia. 'So, we know what it feels like to have to reinvent your entire identity, as you are now doing, Ophelia,' he said. 'Please know, you are not alone. We will help you.'

Ophelia felt her eyes prickle with tears of gratitude. She felt Nina squeeze her hand, too. If only Martin was by her side, Ophelia mused, then the picture would be perfect. Just perfect.

• • • •

OPHELIA FELT DISORIENTED when Emilie woke her from her short sleep.

'Ophelia, you must wake up now,' Emilie said.

'Mm. Yep. I'm awake,' said Ophelia.

'You don't have much time before your train departs,' said Emilie.

'Where's Nina?' Ophelia asked.

'She's up already and in the living room drinking coffee with Philippe,' Emilie replied. 'Here's a cup for you.'

Ophelia gulped her coffee.

'You're safe to travel throughout the southern region now,' Emilie said.

'Okay,' Ophelia replied, still struggling to wake.

'Your identity documents now record you as Ophelia Orczy,' Emilie continued.

'Orczy? As in the author of The Scarlet Pimpernel?' Ophelia asked.

'Yes,' Emilie replied, sniggering. 'I suspect Philippe may have had a bit too much wine when he submitted the identity creation request to his contact.'

Ophelia let the name settle into her, noticing she felt quite proud of it.

'Your identity is imprinted on this disc, as is access to two hundred thousand euros,' Emilie said, fastening a pendant around Ophelia's neck.

Ophelia looked down at the orange flower pedant.

'This petal pulls out,' Emilie demonstrated. 'And on its base is your data. See?'

Ophelia looked at the small luminous white dot on the internal edge of the petal. 'That's incredible,' she said. 'And so beautiful.'

'You can show it to the authorities if they ask you to,' Emilie explained. 'And you can insert it into various payment ports across the southern region. But you must continue to wear the wig and the lenses in your eyes.'

Ophelia felt her entire body soften. 'Emilie, how can I ever thank you for your kindness?'

'You can thank me by continuing to work with us,' Emilie replied. 'And by returning to us, with the pendant intact.'

'Yes, of course.'

'The pendant has another feature,' Emilie continued. 'If you press your thumb into the back of the centre of the flower, you will activate the pendant's recording device.'

'Will you receive the recordings live?' Ophelia asked.

Emilie shook her head. 'No, that's too risky,' she said. 'All the more reason we want you to return to us,' she added with a warm smile.

It was a fair request, Ophelia knew, but a sober reminder of her responsibility to Emilie and Philippe. She was not yet free to do as she pleased. She had become part of a group of committed and hardworking people with a serious quest – a quest that might even occupy the rest of her life.

'Is Nina well enough to travel?' Ophelia asked.

'Yes, Genevieve has had another chat with her,' Emilie replied.

'That's interesting,' Ophelia replied. 'Gene ... I mean Doctor Dubois told me she was quite concerned about Nina's mental health.'

'It's in Genevieve's nature to be cautious,' Emilie replied. 'But she has given her approval for Nina to return home now. So, please, hurry up, Ophelia. Your train leaves in an hour.'

London

MARTIN COULD HARDLY believe his eyes when he stared into the reception lounge in the Garden of Eden. The soft circular curves of the space and the bountiful plants, flowers and water fountains were utterly incongruous with the rest of the underground. Even more striking was the number of pregnant women in the place. Lounging in chairs, chatting, laughing, they were easy on the eyes, he decided. In fact, they were so beautiful, he started to feel an erotic stirring so intense, he was grateful he was wearing a baggy suit.

He noticed the Sentinels around the room, one on either side of the entrance and another four against the walls, all watching the women in the centre of the sunken, circular garden. Then he glanced at Kingpin, hoping he would take command as expected, and he did. The other Sentinels bowed deeply when they saw Kingpin, then abruptly resumed their attentive postures.

Kingpin acknowledged them with only the slightest nod of his head. 'Take us to the Insemination Suite,' he said to the nearest Sentinel.

'Yes, sir. Please follow me.'

They followed the Sentinel around the outer edge of the circle then veered away toward a narrow wall which slid open, revealing an elevator.

After a quick descent, the door opened to a square room, brightly lit, reflecting the stark white ceiling, floor and walls. At the centre of the room was a plinth, about one metre high, supporting a clear crystal structure which rotated, refracting the light beneath it, causing a kaleidoscope of circular shapes to move across the ceiling. In the far corner was another plinth supporting a holo-pad, from which a projection, about thirty centimetres high, displayed a woman playing the harp. The wall facing him was lined with a neat row of six white chairs. The chairs were turned away from him, but he could see the tops of feminine heads protruding above the chairs and their knees protruding from either side.

'Sirs, as you can see, there are some inseminations in progress now,' the Sentinel whispered.

A medibot, kneeling in front of one of the chairs, stood up. 'Sirs, may I help you?' it asked, holding a thin silicon tube.

'No, thank you,' Kingpin replied. 'Please carry on.'

The bot returned to its work. 'Please hold still,' it said to one of the women.

Kingpin turned away, motioning for Martin and the Sentinel to follow him. 'Show me the full register of all women who were inseminated here during the last thirty days,' he whispered.

'Yes, sir. Please follow me into the office,' the Sentinel replied.

The office was small and more softly lit than the Insemination Suite.

'Gaia, show the full record of all women inseminated during the last thirty days,' said the Sentinel.

A holographic record appeared in the air.

Martin could not help but notice the text was bright white, not the usual turquoise. 'Why are these readings white?' he asked.

For a moment, the Sentinel seemed surprised by the question, which reminded Martin that every question he asked could potentially place him at risk.

But the Sentinel responded. 'All records in the Garden of Eden are white, sir,' he said.

'And why is that?' Kingpin asked.

Again, the Sentinel seemed surprised by the question. 'Oh! I see, sirs, you are testing me,' the Sentinel responded.

Kingpin nodded.

'As I understand it,' the Sentinel continued. 'The bright white text is a by-product of Gaia's deep level memory, which we need a high level of security approval to access. Most importantly for us, the bright white helps us to quickly distinguish that data from the rest of Gaia's data.'

'Correct,' said Kingpin.

Martin had heard about Gaia's deep level memory, its core processor. He had always imagined it to be nothing more than the final resting place for all of Gaia's calculations and conclusions. But he was now forming the impression that it might also be a hiding place for anything the RESS did not want anyone else to know about.

He was curious about something. 'Gaia, tabulate the total number of inseminations completed per month during the last eighteen months,' he said. With the histogram in front of him, Martin could see they were averaging five hundred and eighty inseminations per month. 'Where do you store all those zygotes?' he asked.

'It doesn't quite work like that, sir' the Sentinel replied. 'For every request for insemination that we receive from the surface, we have at least one surrogate ready to be inseminated.'

'I'm guessing this means you don't need a very large storage system for the zygotes,' said Kingpin.

'Incorrect, sir,' the Sentinel replied. 'We need a vast space to store all the zygotes that have been created, seconds after the marriage ceremony, by the entire British population.'

'Of course,' said Martin. 'Everyone's gametes are collected during early adulthood, then united with their counterpart after the marriage.'

'Yes, sir,' the Sentinel replied. 'That's why the *Certificate of Creation of Life* is issued immediately after the *Certificate of Marriage*.'

'Please forgive our ignorance,' said Martin. 'We're both unmarried men.'

'Sirs, I envy you,' the Sentinel chuckled.

Kingpin joined the joke, but Martin was far from amused.

'May I show you the storage system?' the Sentinel asked.

'Yes, please,' Kingpin replied.

They followed the Sentinel to the far side of the office. Embedded in the wall was a round steel door, about the same size as the Sentinel. At the centre of the door was a gel pad, which the Sentinel tapped with his disc. He lowered his hand, apparently ready to open the door, then retreated.

He turned around and faced Kingpin. 'Sir, given your supreme status,' he said. 'I would be honoured if you would use your disc to open the lock.'

Martin knew this was the Sentinel's way of testing their credentials and he hoped like hell it would work. Kingpin was calm and confident as he swiped his disc across the gel pad. Miraculously, the lock opened.

'Thank you, sir,' said the Sentinel. 'That's the lock open. Now we need the door opened, which is the second level of security. Sir, would you mind looking into the iris scanner? It's above the gel pad.'

Martin knew Kingpin's identity would be revealed by the iris scanner and the alarm would sound immediately.

'I'll do it,' he said, stepping in front of Kingpin. 'My security clearance was recently upgraded, so I want to check that it works,' he explained.

He was confident the scanner would not be able to identify him, thanks to the lenses in his eyes, but he had no idea how it would react.

Nothing happened.

'That's odd,' said the Sentinel. 'The scanner isn't recognizing you, sir, but it isn't raising the alarm either. I'll investigate that later.'

'That would be appropriate,' Martin replied.

The Sentinel stared into the iris scanner and the door swung open.

Martin stared into the horizontal cylinder. It was about three metres in diameter, he guessed, but how it was, he could not tell.

'I can't even see the end of it,' he said, squinting.

The Sentinel stepped inside, motioning for Martin and Kingpin to remain where they were. 'Gaia, display a list of all zygotes received here during the last seven days,' he said.

A holographic list appeared in the air.

'See here, sirs. The total was nine hundred and fourty-seven,' the Sentinel said, pointing to the list. 'It's therefore reasonable to conclude that approximately that number of marriages took place during the last seven days.'

Martin's mind wandered to Ophelia, the woman he had always wanted to marry.

'But surely those zygotes won't be inseminated immediately,' Kingpin said.

'Correct, sir,' the Sentinel replied. 'Gaia, remove from this list the zygotes that have not yet been requested for implant.'

The list shrunk significantly.

'Sirs, you can see that, as of this moment, only one hundred and twenty-six of those couples have requested insemination this early in their marriage. The remaining zygotes will remain here, in cryostasis, until we receive Gaia's instruction to inseminate them into a surrogate.'

'So, have all those zygotes been inseminated now?' Kingpin asked.

'Gaia, remove from this list the zygotes that have not yet been inseminated,' said the Sentinel.

The list shrunk again.

'Sirs, you can see there are only four zygotes remaining. And I can guarantee we'll have those inseminations completed by the end of this shift,' he replied. 'Gaia will then issue the *Certificate of Insemination* to the relevant couples.'

'Impressive,' said Kingpin.

The Sentinel stood a bit taller. 'The main thing to remember, gentlemen, is that this system is live,' he said. 'By that, I mean it's continuously updated, every few seconds, as Gaia receives new requests for insemination and as those requests are fulfilled.'

'Of course,' Kingpin replied.

'So where are those four zygotes right now?' Martin asked.

'They will still be here, sir, in cryostasis, until the moment of insemination,' The Sentinel replied. He used his fingers to enhance one of the four records. The full name, address and vital statistics for the male and female donors appeared alongside the images of their faces. 'See this?' he said, pointing to a corner of the image. 'It says C:24'

Martin and Kingpin nodded.

'Gaia, deliver C:24,' said the Sentinel.

One segment of the cylinder contracted, into the lumen of the cylinder, then slowly slid to where the Sentinel was standing.

'This is segment C,' said the Sentinel.

The segment rotated slightly then stopped with a gentle click. A small square flap opened, eye level to the Sentinel. 'And this is storage box 24,' he said.

'Impressive, indeed,' said Kingpin.

'We have thirty-six storage boxes in each segment, and the segments are named A through to Z,' the Sentinel explained.

Martin did the arithmetic. 'That would be a total of nine hundred and thirty-six storage boxes,' he said. 'And that doesn't seem like enough, considering everything you've explained so far.'

'No, sir, that would not be enough to contain Britain's married population's zygotes,' the Sentinel replied. 'So, after Z we start again at AA and so on.'

Martin took a moment to process this new information. 'So, given the total population of Britain is 36 million, and about forty percent of the population is of reproductive age, that's about fourteen million zygotes. Am I correct?'

'You're almost correct, sir,' the Sentinel replied. 'Not every couple of reproductive age is married, and not every married couple wants to reproduce, therefore the real number is just under nine million zygotes at any point in time.'

'So, it's a very long cylinder,' said Martin.

'Yes, sir, it travels all the way to the University of Oxford.'

'That's very impressive,' said Kingpin, stepping back. 'I'm satisfied with your knowledge and conduct throughout this investigation.'

'Investigation, sir?' the Sentinel asked.

'Yes, we were recently instructed to undertake random spot checks, just like this one, to ensure our Sentinels are performing well,' Kingpin replied.

The Sentinel seemed to freeze for a moment.

'You've passed. With flying colours, as the saying goes,' Kingpin said. 'And I'll be noting that in my staff report. You can lock that door now.'

'Yes, sir,' said the Sentinel. 'Do you have any further questions?'

'Show us where you take the babies after they're born,' Kingpin replied.

'Yes, sir. Follow me.'

As they waited for the elevator to arrive, Martin took one last look at the Insemination Suite. The chairs were empty, but he could have sworn he heard someone crying, and the harp continued to play.

• • • •

THE ELEVATOR DOOR OPENED to a room even more beautiful than the last. The walls changed colour every few seconds, from one soft tone to another. The ceiling was white, but not a harsh white like so many of the other rooms in the underground. To Martin's eyes, it seemed a soft, translucent white, almost suggesting it might disappear and reveal the sky. The floor was the same colour, with the addition of translucent turquoise mats defining discrete sections of the room.

'Welcome to the Enhancement Suite, sir,' someone said.

Martin looked around and saw a young man, of slight build, in the usual white suit and mask.

'I'm the teacher, sir,' said the man.

Martin nodded, then returned his gaze to the side of the room where several toddlers were gathered around a square table. They moved their hands through the air, causing something like paint to stream from their fingertips. Their paintings moved, in the air, around them. The largest one was a long green shape, coiled around itself.

'This is my snake,' said a little girl, looking at Martin.

'Excellent work, Melissa,' the teacher said.

Martin's eyes moved to another painting, a fleshy pink circle with another pink circle inside it. The young artist stepped into the centre of the painting, watching it move around him.

'What's this?' Martin asked.

'It's my mummy,' the boy replied.

'So, where is your mummy now?' Martin asked.

The boy's face went blank. Martin felt bad for asking the question.

'Good work, everyone,' said the teacher. 'It's time to finish now, so please release your artworks to the table.'

The children placed their hands around their creations and pushed them onto the table, creating a collective pile of brown goo.

'This makes no sense,' said Martin.

'Is this your first visit here, sir?' the teacher asked Martin.

'Yes, I'm in training with my colleague,' he replied, motioning to Kingpin.

But Kingpin was gone.

Martin allowed his attention to drift toward the far-left corner of the room. Four children, in their early teens he guessed, were sitting on the floor, cross-legged, in a circle. Facing each other, but not speaking, their eyes were fixed on a steel ball on the floor. Slowly, the ball rose, until it was level with their chests. Then it spun on its axis.

'Good work. Now pick up the speed,' the teacher said.

The ball spun faster. So fast, Martin could only see a series of thin grey circles in the air. And then there was nothing. The ball was gone. The children looked at each other and smiled.

'Brilliant,' said the teacher. 'Now bring it back.'

Martin's mouth was dry with shock, but he kept watching. As the children stared at the space from where the ball had disappeared, Martin felt the energy of their unified concentration. It was a tension in the air. Literally, palpable. He stepped slightly closer but was forced back by something he could not see.

'Please, sir, that's close enough,' said the teacher.

Just as Martin stepped back, one of the adolescents lost his concertation.

The young man exhaled loudly, then dropped his head into his hands. 'I'm sorry,' he said, massaging his temples.

'It's okay, Jonathon,' said the teacher. 'These things happen sometimes. I invite the rest of you to send recovery to Jonathon.'

The other three children turned their attention to Jonathan. Again, Martin felt the force of their unified concentration. For a moment, he felt certain he could see a soft green light around Jonathan's head. Then the boy lifted his head and smiled at his friends.

'Well done,' said the teacher. 'Try to bring the ball back, now.'

The youngsters stared into the place from where the ball had disappeared. The energy circled around them, causing a soft breeze. At first, the breeze felt warm but soon became hot. Uncomfortably hot. Martin felt himself sweating. But he was enthralled. A pale grey circle appeared in the air. During the next few seconds, the circle became more solid. Fully formed, it fell to the ground with a thud.

Jonathan exhaled deeply again and wiped his palms on his knees.

'Congratulations!' said the teacher. 'How do you feel, Jonathon?'

'Tired, but okay,' said Jonathon.

'I'm tired, too,' said one of the girls. 'But I have a nice tingling feeling.'

The teacher nodded. 'The energy worked well for you, today, Bianca,' he said.

The girl nodded, smiling.

'Brilliant work,' the teacher said. 'All of you. Brilliant. I recommend you lie down in your rooms for an hour, then hit the dining room for lunch. Okay?'

The youngsters stood up and stretched. Bianca wrapped her arms around Jonathan's neck and kissed his cheek. He blushed but returned the gesture. Then the four of them left the room.

'They're brilliant, aren't they, sir?' said the teacher, standing tall.

'Oh yeah,' Martin replied. 'Please, tell me what they're doing.'

'They're learning how to manipulate the wave-particle duality,' the teacher replied.

'But that paradox hasn't been resolved,' Martin said.

'You now have evidence to the contrary, sir.'

'But, I ...'

Martin heard a baby squealing. He turned toward the sound and saw a nurse in the corner of the room, cradling a baby, rocking it gently. The nurse lay on her side, her body curved around the baby and her one naked fingertip stroking its skin. For a moment, Martin imagined the nurse was Ophelia, holding her own baby. Then he imagined himself, curled around them both, keeping them safe.

'So, will this little one stay here too?' he asked.

'Correct, sir.'

'What will you tell the parents, regarding its non-arrival?' he asked.

'In these situations, sir, we give them our standard explanation.'

'Which is?' Martin asked.

'We say there was a birth trauma and the baby didn't survive.'

'And how many of these babies are you taking?'

'About one in fifty,' the teacher replied.

'How do you choose which ones you'll take?'

'We don't, sir,' the teacher replied. 'Gaia chooses. The instant a baby is born, it's taken from the surrogate and placed in a tiny chamber for about three seconds. Gaia weights it, scans it, then displays the word KEEP or RELEASE and we act on its instructions.'

Martin felt as though his face and head were literally cracking open with all this new information. His mask felt tight. He had an overwhelming desire to rip it off and pour cold water over his face and neck. But all he could do was take inhale deeply and exhale just as deeply. He knew he would have more questions but, for now, he needed to disengage.

'There you are!' he heard someone say from behind him.

Martin turned around to see Kingpin and the Sentinel step into the room. Martin faced Kingpin, desperate to speak with him privately, to reveal what he had just learned, but there was no opportunity.

'We were watching you from above,' said Kingpin, pointing to the ceiling.

Martin looked at the ceiling again, realising his first intuition was correct. It was indeed a false ceiling, but it had never occurred to him that it was a viewing platform. Now he knew.

'These achievements are wonderful, aren't they?' said Kingpin.

Martin was so bewildered by what he'd witnessed in the last hour that he struggled to interpret Kingpin's attitude. Hoping that it was part of the lad's Super Sentinel act, Martin chose his next words carefully. 'It's impressive, sir,' he replied. 'But I'm curious about the purpose of these experiments.'

'They're not just experiments, sir,' the Sentinel replied.

'They're the future of humanity, my friend,' Kingpin added.

Martin felt even more bewildered than he had before.

• • • •

ALONE AT LAST, AND in another tunnel, Martin felt Kingpin looking at him.

'You don't seem to be holding it together very well, mate,' said Kingpin.

'I'm doing my best,' Martin snapped.

Kingpin was quick to respond. 'I suggest we keep walking down this tunnel because it's a long one and it's the only way we can continue to talk without being heard,' he said.

'Agreed,' Martin replied.

A pod glided by, and then there was nothing.

'Where are we, exactly?' Martin finally asked.

'Right now, we're somewhere under Saint Pancras International Station,' Kingpin replied, looking at his disc. 'If we wanted to, we could ascend straight up to the hyperloop.'

'Tempting,' said Martin. 'But we have to stay here for a bit longer.'

'Agreed.'

'Listen, mate,' said Martin, suddenly feeling a surge of optimism. 'It occurs to me that we've gathered enough visual recordings during the last few days to ...'

'You mean, *you* have gathered the recordings,' Kingpin interjected. 'With those lenses on your eyes, right?'

'Right,' said Martin. 'Now, given what we now know about Gaia's deep level memory ...'

'I see where you're going with this,' Kingpin interjected again. 'But I have no idea how to access Gaia's core processor. And I don't know how it would cope with unencrypted data. It might completely scramble the data, rendering it worthless, while identifying the location at which the data was uploaded. In which case, we'd be caught for sure.'

'Not if we're fast enough,' said Martin. 'Think about it. There's no way the recording could be traced back to me. Once I dump the lenses into the core's console, that's it. The data is in there. All we have to do is run away and let Gaia broadcast it.'

'That's absurd,' Kingpin replied. 'Gaia doesn't automatically transmit every bit of data without an extra layer of programming to make it do that. Hell, there are several layers of coding required to send a simple command from the core processor to the peripheral processors. And even if we figured out how to write that code, your plan stinks because you'll lose your only recording. And you'll lose your ability to evade the iris scanners – a little hack that has come in quite handy, so far.'

'I can make more lenses for both of us once we're back in the main Anatomy Lab,' Martin replied. 'I've got a good stash of fovealis hidden in the lab.'

'But the lab is back up under Oxford and we're now under London,' Kingpin replied. 'And more importantly, I don't know how to do it.'

'Isn't there some way you can tinker about?' Martin asked.

Kingpin shook his head in disgust. 'Tinker about? Is that what you think cyber-engineers do? Tinker about?' he said.

Martin knew he was out of his depth. It had been several weeks since he had been able to unencrypt Emilie and Philippe's messages. Therefore, hacking into Gaia's core processor would be way beyond his skill set, he knew. But he continued to manipulate the younger man.

'What *do* you cyber-engineers do, then?' he asked.

Kingpin stopped in his tracks, clearly quite angry. For a moment, Martin thought the kid was going to punch him. He would get away with it too, in that Super Sentinel suit.

But Kingpin's chest sank, deflated. 'It's mostly maintenance,' he replied.

'Can we at least start by doing some maintenance?' Martin asked.

Kingpin shook his head again. 'We can only enter a maintenance hub to do scheduled maintenance, or to fix something that has gone wrong,' he replied. 'Right now, I don't have any error reports, so I'd be hard-pressed to explain my presence in a maintenance hub. Get it?'

'What if we enter a maintenance hub anyway?' Martin asked. 'Given your suit, mate, you wouldn't have to answer any questions.'

Mart and Kingpin continued walking in silence. For a moment.

'I suppose we could do a bit of a reconnaissance mission,' Kingpin replied. 'Not actually penetrate Gaia's core, but at least skirt around the edges until I figure out how I might be able to access it one day in the future.'

'Exactly!' said Martin. 'It's better than nothing and its probably a good use of your suit, too.'

'Fair point,' Kingpin replied. 'And it *would* be great to one day upload the recordings to Gaia's core. Seeing those Sentinels thrown in jail would be awesome, but poor Gaia would be stripped down to her last qubit.'

'Sure, there'd be chaos if Gaia was ripped apart,' Martin said. 'I can't believe I'm saying this, but wouldn't a bit of chaos be better for everyone than the vile secrets we've learned about down here? Think of all the pain that could be avoided if we were to blow these secrets sky high for everyone to see. I mean, the people have the right to know, don't they?'

'Yes, they do,' Kingpin replied. 'But if it was possible to do what you're suggesting, someone would have done it by now. Wouldn't they?'

Martin considered the younger man's words before responding. 'I guess, like any innovation, someone has to have the balls to give it a go,' he said. 'And, as we've already discussed, the risks are minimal.'

They walked on, in silence, for a few moments. There was so much more that Martin wanted to say, to convince the kid to at least try to figure out how to access Gaia's core. But for now, Martin knew, he had probably said enough. So he was quite surprised by the technician's next words.

'There's a maintenance hub about twenty metres from here,' said Kingpin.

• • • •

MARTIN FOLLOWED KINGPIN into a tiny room. It was different from anything else he had seen underground. The walls were painted a dreary grey colour, unlike the stark white in the bioengineering facilities. And the lighting was dimmer.

'What's wrong with the lights in here?' he asked.

'You'll see,' Kingpin replied.

Kingpin approached the opposing wall, which, to Martin's eyes, seemed to be a sheet of dark glass. But when Kingpin waved his disc across the surface of the glass, it lit up, with a soft white glow.

The young man slid his hands over several parts of the glass, each movement causing a swirl of bright white light. He pinched at some of the swirls, causing them to rise from the surface of the glass, in front of his body, where he manipulated them further. Then, with one dramatic flick of his arm, he whipped the swirls of light into one large ball.

'Okay,' he said. 'I'm through the outer layer of the coding.'

'That's incredible,' Martin replied. 'Have you done this before?'

'Yes, but only once,' Kingpin replied. 'And it was just to fix a local anomaly.'

'What's going to happen with that ball of light?' Martin asked, squinting.

Kingpin did not turn away from the ball of light. 'Last time, it just dissipated of its own accord, which was how I knew I had fixed the anomaly,' he replied. 'But the fact that it's still here makes me think there might be something wrong.'

'What are you going to do?' Martin asked.

'I honestly don't know,' Kingpin replied.

Suddenly, the ball exploded, like a collapsing star and the light disappeared. The glass wall also returned to its previous dark and dull state.

'Hm, that didn't ...'

An alarm screeched, reverberating through Martin's body like a drill through concrete.

'Fuck, no!' Kingpin screamed.

He ran toward the door and Martin followed. It was sealed tight. They ran to the far side of the room, pressing every part of the wall, but nothing opened.

'Let me stand on your shoulders,' Martin said.

High upon Kingpin's shoulders, Martin scoured the ceiling, desperately seeking an exit. But there was nothing. 'Damn it!' he said.

Kingpin fell to his knees, wailing, and Martin tumbled down on top of him.

'Don't give up, mate,' Martin said.

He pulled a small desk away from the wall, but there was no exit there, either. He stood in the centre of the room, desperately seeking any other option, but he was out of time.

The door slid open and four Sentinels stepped inside.

'Don't bother trying to find another exit,' said one of them.

'Nice suit,' said another, pointing to Kingpin's Super Sentinel motif. 'I reckon that might be mine,' he added.

Martin froze.

'Did you clowns really think we would not be able to identify you from the camera feed in the lab?' one of them asked.

Martin had known they would, but he was expecting to be further advanced in his plan by the time it happened.

'Let's find out who these guys are,' said the taller Sentinel standing behind the others. 'What are your names?'

There was no point trying the fight them, Martin knew. He ripped off his mask. 'My name is quite long,' he said. 'It's How About You Go Fuck Yourself.'

Martin felt the backhand of one of the Sentinels, but he no longer cared. Not until he saw what they were doing to his young friend. Like a pack of wild dogs taking down a bison, the Sentinels crowded around Kingpin. They stripped him naked, jeering at the lad's obese body, poking at his fat and watching it wobble. Then they ripped off his mask, revealing a perfectly round, but lopsided, face with two sad little eyes, a crooked mouth and irregular teeth. The kid looked terrified.

'Okay, gents. That's enough now,' said Martin.

Another backhander sent him flying across the room. He crashed into the wall, then slid to the ground, the sound of the lad's horrified screams ringing in his ears.

'Please stop this,' Martin implored, standing up.

One of the Sentinels took another swing at Martin, but this time he dodged the blow.

'I know we were out of order,' Martin said. 'We were being stupid, just messing around. We didn't mean any harm. And it was all my idea. The kid just came along for the ride. You should send him home. I'll clean up the mess.'

'You are *both* under arrest,' said one of the Sentinels.

Behind him, the other three continued to circle Kingpin, continuing to poke at him.

'How can even find your dick under all that fat?' one of them asked.

Kingpin kept his hands over his genitals and his eyes on the ground.

The Super Sentinel stepped toward Martin.

'The best thing you can do for yourself, and the kid, is to shut your mouth. Got it?' he said.

Martin nodded.

The door opened and one of the Sentinels stepped out.

'Move!' said another.

Martin noticed his young friend had passed the point of crying. Silent as a mute, the lad just shuffled along, his head down and his hands covering his manhood. Several members of staff stopped to watch the awful procession down the tunnel. Their anonymous faces, behind their masks, impossible to read, magnified the sense of humiliation for Martin. He desperately wanted to wake up to find he was having a bad dream. But the moment was real, and he knew it. There was nothing he could do, he told himself, but surrender and accept that things were about to get much worse.

In transit

THE TRAIN WAS NOT PARTICULARLY crowded, so Ophelia and Nina managed to secure their own booth. Exhausted, Ophelia fell onto the seat and slouched across the table between them. Nina activated a lever under the window, causing a transparent shield to slide down, encasing the booth completely.

'Nina, could you activate the tinting, too, please?' Ophelia asked.

'There's no tinting,' Nina replied. 'The shields are clear so the security bots can see what everyone is doing.'

'Fair enough,' Ophelia said, leaning against the window and stretching her legs along the bench seat. From that angle, she could see Nina and the rest of the carriage. 'Check that out,' she said, motioning to a group of five young men sitting a few seats away.

'Mm,' said Nina, raising an eyebrow.

The men were all in supreme physical shape and very well dressed, with black pants and matching shoes and white silk shirts.

Ophelia tapped the shield of her booth with her toe and it slid open.

'What are you doing?' Nina whispered.

'I want to hear what those boys are saying,' she replied.

'Do you have it?' one of them asked another.

'The accent is Siberian,' Ophelia whispered. 'No wonder they're so well dressed. They're probably obscenely rich.'

One of the men leaned forward to retrieve something from a bag and that's when Ophelia noticed there was a young woman with them. Heavily pregnant, she sat quietly, looking down at her hands. Ophelia saw Nina looking, too. Her young friend's eyes soon became red and teary.

'It's okay,' she whispered, closing her hand around Nina's.

'I wonder what they're doing,' Nina said.

Ophelia looked at the group again. The men were passing a small glass bottle amongst themselves, each one sniffing its contents. The man sitting closest to the pregnant woman offered her the bottle, but she turned her head away.

Within seconds, the men were all laughing and spreading their long limbs beyond the confines of their seats. One of them stood up and ripped his shirt from his body, revealing his naked torso. To Ophelia's dismay, the *Anarchy* symbol was carved into the skin on his belly. The wound had healed long ago, she could tell, but the remaining thick white keloid scars that formed the shape of the symbol were clear enough for her to see from her seat.

'Oh, God, no,' said Nina, shaking her head.

'That could not have been pleasant,' Ophelia replied.

'Do you think he was tortured?' Nina asked.

Before Ophelia had a chance to reply, the other men had stood up and ripped off their shirts, as well. They, too, were sporting the same symbol across their bellies.

'Oh, dear,' Ophelia said. 'They're part of a gang, it seems.'

The men were laughing and making strange sounds. Sounds that did not form words from any language that Ophelia knew. They were more like animalistic grunts and slurs.

'They're obviously affected by whatever was in that bottle,' Nina said, shrinking down into her seat. 'We should stay out of their sight.'

Ophelia also shrunk down in her seat. A looked of terror was creeping across Nina's face.

'It's okay, honey,' she said, reaching over to touch Nina. 'As you rightly pointed out, the bots can see what's going on. In fact, here comes one, now.'

A security bot, almost as large as the ones in the underground, thundered down the aisle. Nina's arms wrapped around her body and her fists clenched.

'Nina, are you okay?' Ophelia asked.

Raucous laughter came from the young men. It sounded cruel and terrifying.

'I ... I ... can't ...' Nina started to say.

'Let's move to another carriage,' said Ophelia.

But Nina didn't move. It seemed she couldn't move. Her body had somehow collapsed into an even tighter bundle. Her face had turned away from the men, but her eyes were still on them.

'Nina, at the very least, please swap places with me so you don't have to see them,' Ophelia said, standing up.

'Remain seated,' a voice bellowed from the far end of the carriage.

Another security bot thumped down the centre of the aisle.

'Oh good,' said Ophelia, sitting down again. 'This will sort things out.'

Nina's eyelids fluttered. She started to shiver, her entire torso rocking back and forth. Ophelia wanted to sit beside her, to hold her, but when she stood up, the bot hollered at her again. Nina started to hyperventilate.

'Nina, honey, it's okay,' Ophelia implored, her hands stretched across the table toward Nina. 'Everything is under control.'

'It rained of steel and then there was blood,' Nina mumbled.

'What?'

But Nina didn't explain. She just kept rocking back and forth.

Ophelia turned around to see what was happening. The bot was towering over the young men, staring at them, as though attempting to interpret their behaviour. The men fell silent, then the bot left the carriage.

'Okay, it's all sorted out,' said Ophelia.

'There was blood everywhere,' said Nina. 'A waterfall of blood that became a river and the babies floated along the river to the end of the world and then they fell off.'

'What was that?' Ophelia asked.

Nina started to sob – quietly, gently, delicately – as though afraid of being heard.

'Deaf, dumb and blind,' she whimpered. 'Deaf, dumb and blind.'

Ophelia opened her mouth to say something, but her words were subsumed by the renewed vigour of sound coming from the young men. They seemed even more animalistic than before. And filled with vitriol. Ophelia's heart thumped heavily, and she wished the security bot would return.

'Noooooo,' Nina cried, looking at the men.

Ophelia turned around to see what Nina was looking at. Her eyes saw, but her mind could not comprehend. The men were throwing the pregnant woman in the air. Like a ball, she bounced from one man to the next, and each man released a simian bellow of pride when he caught her. But then one of the men dropped her and she fell to the floor, causing the others to roar with laughter. The woman had no reaction. She stayed on the floor, neither laughing nor crying. She simply sat there, her face as blank as a cube of jelly from one of Gaia's sustenance bays. Nina started to sob, but Ophelia reacted with outright rage.

She stood up, opened the shield and stepped into the aisle. 'Hey, you!' she called out to the men.

The men looked at her, surprised.

'Leave her alone!' Ophelia shrieked.

One of the men stood up. 'Make me,' he replied with a vicious sneer across his face.

It occurred to Ophelia that the men might have been borderline intelligence. If so, they might be easily intimidated by her if she, too, behaved with bullish abuse. She decided to talk down to them, as though they were stupid children.

'You stupid, stupid boys!' she shouted. 'Sit down and behave properly!'

Ophelia glanced at the pregnant woman, who was slowly lifting herself into a booth, cradling her belly with her hand.

The man noticed it too. 'She's a slut,' he drawled. 'Nothing more.'

'How dare you!' Ophelia shouted, stepping toward him.

'Return to your seat!' a voice hollered behind her.

For the second time, a security bot pounded down the aisle toward her. Relieved, Ophelia scuttled back to the booth, next to Nina. But she kept the shield open. 'Security!' she said, as the bot got closer to her. 'Those men were abusing the pregnant woman.'

'We have seen,' the bot replied. 'Remain seated.'

Ophelia held onto Nina, unable to tear her eyes away from the men. The security bot stared at the young man closest to it. For a moment, the man looked frightened, but when his friends laughed, he did, too. Then he lifted his hand and made a crude gesture in front of the bot's face. The bot flexed its wrist backward, released a laser and killed the young man instantly. The moronic expression froze on his face as his dead body slumped against the seat. The other men, like a whoop of chimpanzees, leapt around the carriage, shouting, grunting, screaming and waving their fists in the air. But they, too, were silenced by the bot's laser fire. Within seconds, it was all over. The five young men were dead.

The bot left the carriage and the pregnant woman continued to stare out of the window.

'Dear God in Heaven,' Ophelia whispered.

'Arms to disarm,' Nina sobbed.

Ophelia realised she was holding Nina too tightly, so she let go.

'We're safe now, Nina,' she said, keeping her eyes on the pregnant woman.

'The Sentinel said there was sickness,' said Nina.

Ophelia could only imagine that Nina was referring to one of the Sentinels in the Garden of Eden. But she then realised the dual meaning of the word.

'Oh, that's very clever, Nina,' she said. 'I suspect th ...'

'Disarm!' Nina shouted, pushing Ophelia away.

'Oh, okay, Nina,' Ophelia replied. 'It's fine. I'll sit over here,' she said, returning to the opposite side of the booth.

Nina leaned forward, her head in her hands, rocking back and forth, humming.

Ophelia knew she was out of her depth as she replayed Doctor Dubois' words in her mind – *psychotic illness*. But without any access to medical care, Ophelia knew there was nothing she could do but hope that Nina could contain herself. At least until they reached Tarragona.

• • • •

WHEN THE TRAIN STOPPED at Valence, Ophelia looked out of the window at the platform. A group of seven people and one domestic bot stood there, waiting to board. Behind them was a Starbeans Coffeehouse.

'We don't have those in Britain,' Ophelia said, pointing to the café.

Nina's focus sharpened just enough for her to gaze at the café for a moment.

Through the windows, Ophelia could see the opposing wall of the café was covered with a neat row of sustenance bays, all producing coffee and cubes of food. In the centre of the café was a long steel table. Upon it was a holo-film showing the luscious array of cocoa bean plants and a neat row of bots harvesting the beans.

'That's exactly what it looked like from the hyperloop!' Ophelia said, turning to Nina.

But Nina's eyes were empty. 'Boom!' she whispered. 'It's gone.'

'What's gone?' Ophelia asked.

'La ... Sa ... gra... da ...Fa ... mil ... i ... a.' Nina replied.

Ophelia took a moment to consider what Nina might have been referring to.

'Do you mean La Sagrada Familia in Barcelona?' she asked.

'Boom!' Nina replied. 'We said no, and they said Boom!'

Ophelia realised Nina must have been referring to the Russo-Siberian show of dominance when they had sent a narrow-target missile to the iconic building in Barcelona. It had happened several years ago, as far as she could recall, so she had no idea why Nina was talking about it now.

'Boom!' said Nina, her eyes widening.

Ophelia felt the need to avoid Nina's gaze, so she stared out of the window at the changing landscape – a patchwork of brown and grey shapes, each one unique in its size, texture and detail. It reminded her of something she had once created in an abstract drawing class at school. She had been acutely aware of her lack of talent, but the experience had been profound, nevertheless. She ran her fingers over her flower pendant, thinking about Emilie and Philippe's creativity and the sense of joy it seemed to bring them.

'Boom!' Nina said again, this time pointing out of the window.

Ophelia followed Nina's line of vision to an abandoned spaceport. The clear dome building appeared to have suffered some broken windows and those that remained were covered in brown dirt. The once-black runway appeared brown in places and weeds protruded in random clumps. It seemed a shame, she mused, not only the disarray but also the missed opportunity it represented. Could Nina's life have been better if she had been one the early colonists of Mars, she wondered.

'Are you feeling better, Nina?' she asked.

A flicker of acknowledgement appeared in Nina's eyes.

'Nina, are you looking forward to seeing your mare and pare?' she asked.

'Cradle songs,' Nina replied.

Whatever that meant, Ophelia assumed it had probably come from a place of love and warmth. She wondered how much of Nina's recent experience her parents would be able to grasp. And if they saw how traumatised Nina was, would they feel bad for allowing her to be a surrogate? Or would they simply refuse to think about it? More importantly, she wondered, would they be able to obtain the medical attention that Nina so obviously needed right now?

'Are you feeling better, Nina?' she asked.

Nina did not answer. She twirled the lid from her water bottle around the end of her finger, then rolled it from one side of the table to the other. Then she began to cry. Ophelia reached across the table to touch her, but Nina withdrew.

'It melts into poison and their brains run out of their noses,' Nina mumbled.

She pressed the plastic lid into the surface of the table. Then she slammed it onto the surface of the table, as though trying to flatten it. When that didn't work, she stood up and slammed her hand down upon the lid. So hard, she cracked the table.

'Nina, no,' Ophelia said, reaching across the table.

A security bot appeared and opened the booth.

'What are you doing?' it asked.

But Nina did not reply.

'You have vandalised public property,' said the bot. 'I must take you into custody.'

'Please don't do that,' said Ophelia. 'She is not well. I'm her nurse. I'm escorting her home. We're getting off at the next stop. I promise.'

A loud *crack* grabbed the bot's attention then it raced down the carriage, towards the place that, in Ophelia's memory, was where the young pregnant woman had been sitting. But now the woman was hanging from the overhead baggage compartment, a belt wrapped around her throat.

'Oh, God. No!' Ophelia cried.

Nina screamed, but Ophelia could not help her. She could only watch, helpless and horrified, as the bot untied the belt strap from the woman's neck and returned her to the seat. Ophelia could only see the back of the woman's head and her lifeless arm as it fell into the aisle. Then she saw the lights in the bot's eyes flicker as it looked over the woman's body, reading her life signs. But there were none, Ophelia could tell. The bot picked up the woman, carried her to the five dead men and laid her beside them.

'The baby!' Ophelia called out to the bot. 'The baby might be alive!'

'Remain seated,' the bot replied. 'There is no life.'

'Oh, God,' Ophelia said, dropping her head into her hands.

Aware that Nina was still screaming, Ophelia took one last look at the pile of dead bodies. Then she returned to the seat beside Nina and wrapped her arms around her, gently rocking her.

The bot returned. 'Who will pay for this damage?' it asked, pointing to the crack in the table.

'I will,' Ophelia replied. 'Here, scan this.' She removed the lower petal from her pendant.

The bot inserted it into one of the many ports on its torso. 'I have deducted twelve thousand, five hundred euros from your account, as that is the minimum penalty for damaging public property,' it said.

'I understand,' Ophelia replied. 'I am sorry.'

Suddenly Nina shrieked and pulled free from Ophelia's arms.

'Nina, sit down,' Ophelia implored.

'A heart for the tin man!' Nina shouted, thumping the bot's chest.

With one swift move, the bot spun Nina around and bound her wrists together behind her back.

'Let me go!' Nina shrieked, trying to kick the bot.

'Nina, please, stop,' Ophelia pleaded, almost in tears.

Then Ophelia looked at the bot. 'Please don't hurt her,' she begged. 'She is very unwell. As soon as we get off the train, I am taking her to a hospital, I promise.'

The bot glanced at Ophelia for a moment, then pressed the top of its hand under Nina's chin, disabling Nina from making any more sounds. Then it marched her to the exit and waited for the next stop.

Tarragona

THE NEXT STOP WAS TARRAGONA. When the train door opened, the bot lifted Nina onto the platform, released the binding from her wrists and returned to the train. Nina ran to the open arms of her parents.

Beyond the happy family was a wide horizon line where the deep turquoise Mediterranean Sea met a vibrant blue sky. The line was solid, punctuated only by a dozen tiny black ships, and everything sparkled under the sunlight.

As she stepped off the train, Ophelia could feel the hot air shoot up her nose, like a million tiny needles. She pressed her fingers against her nostrils, trying to protect them, but then her mouth was assaulted by the hot air.

'This is Ophelia,' Nina called out. 'She is my nurse.'

Still holding Nina's bag, Ophelia was crushed by the tight embrace of Nina's parents.

'Thank you, thank you, Ophelia, for returning our baby girl,' Nina's mother said.

'You are very welcome, Mrs. Garcia,' Ophelia replied, wondering when the woman would notice Nina's problem.

'Please,' she said. 'Call me Mare.'

'Okay, Mare,' Ophelia replied, humbled by the intimacy.

'And this is Pare,' said Mare, pointing to her husband.

Pare took hold of Ophelia's hands and kissed them. 'Thank you, Ophelia,' he said.

'You're most welcome,' Ophelia replied.

Nina linked arms with her mother as they walked toward the exit gate.

Pare, gentle and attentive, walked alongside Ophelia.

She was not sure what to do. Should she tell Pare about Nina's problem, she wondered, or should she wait and let him see for himself? Or would Nina calm down, now that she was home? Ophelia tended toward the latter.

Pare did not seem like a chatty person, and she could not think of a thing to say to him, so she focused on the view. To her left, Ophelia noticed the view of the sea remained every bit as stunning as it had been from the train. In the foreground, on the beach, were several long red steel buildings. 'Are those old shipping containers?' she asked.

'Yes,' Pare replied. 'This is our industrial area.'

There was not a single tree or plant in sight, Ophelia noticed. The colour green was entirely absent. However, when they turned the corner, she noticed the temperature drop a bit, for which she was immensely grateful. She could see the ocean lapping around the jetties, and she could smell the salt in the air. Then she noticed the promenade lined with cafes and small shops. 'So, is this the village of El Serrallo?' she asked.

'Yes,' Pare replied.

Ophelia waited for him to say something more, but he didn't. His eyes were focused on Nina and her Mare, still waking together, their arms linked.

Suddenly, Nina tore away and joined the people dancing on the promenade. There were two people playing drums, one pounding an ancient keyboard and another two playing stringed instruments. There was no evidence of Gaia, nor its bots or drones. The place was filled with people, real people, making real music and dancing to it.

Ophelia saw Mare, standing under the shade of an awning, watching Nina gyrate across the promenade. Then Mare turned around and motioned for Pare and Ophelia to join her.

'There's something wrong with Nina,' she said.

'Yahaha!' Nina screamed, waving her arms in the air.

And then she gasped.

'Nina, are you okay?' Ophelia asked, stepping towards her.

'We are very welcome,' Nina shouted.

'Oh, God,' said Mare, taking holding of Pare's hand.

'Are you okay, Nina?' Ophelia asked again.

'It's okay in the winter,' Nina replied.

Then she started to laugh. Then she started to scream. And then her body spasmed so much she doubled over, clutching her belly.

'Nina, let's go home,' said Pare.

'It was *so* funny,' Nina said, trying to stand up through hysterical laughter.

'What was so funny?' Pare asked.

'That place,' said Nina.

'What place?' Mare asked.

'The Garden in the Eden,' Nina replied, now slurring her words and swaggering as if she were intoxicated. 'The Garden of Eve.'

'Let's go home now,' said Mare.

'Yaahaaa,' Nina squealed.

'It's very hot, Nina,' Ophelia said. 'Let's go home.'

Pare stepped toward Nina and took her hand. 'We're going home now Nina,' he said, leading her away from the promenade.

'Nina, Nina, Nina, Nina,' Nina sang, waving her free arm through the air.

Ophelia and Mare followed them down a narrow lane between two buildings – one a restaurant, the other a block of apartments. The shade in the lane was a delightful relief. It felt like the right moment to tell Mare.

'Mare, I have to tell you something,' she said.

Nina stopped and turned around. She stood in the middle of the lane, her hands on her hips and her legs apart. 'It happened when the ocean swept up onto the promenade and filled the shops and houses and we all became fish!' she said.

'Yes, that's right, Nina,' said Mare.

Nina stared at Ophelia, her eyes wide with horror. 'Your face is melting!' she shrieked.

Ophelia touched her face with both hands. 'No, I'm just hot,' she replied. 'Let's go inside.'

This time, Mare stepped forward, took Nina by the hand and led her down the lane.

Pare looked at Ophelia. 'How did this happen?' he asked.

'I'm so sorry,' Ophelia replied. 'I honestly don't know. It started on the train journey here. It was a terrible journey. There were some very violent people on the train who might have triggered this reaction. But even before that, she had been through some terrible experiences in the Garden of Eden, so that may have contributed, too. I'm no expert, but I think she might be having a psychotic episode.'

Pare let out a long sigh. 'We hoped this would not happen to our Nina,' he said.

'What do you mean?' Ophelia asked. 'Has this happened before?'

'Some of the girls return from that place in a bad state,' he replied. 'But I've never seen anything like this.'

Now at the end of the shady lane, they stepped into an open square space surrounded by blocks of apartments. The concrete held the heat in the square. Ophelia felt as though she was inside a giant oven. She looked around at what she was sure must have been grey walls, but they were now bright white under the sunlight. Her mouth had dried out completely and she was desperate for water.

'Not long now,' said Pare.

Across the square, Ophelia and Pare caught up with Nina and Mare beside the elevator.

Nina was pressing the button repeatedly. 'We're going up to the sky!' she squealed, spreading her arms wide like a bird and standing on one leg. 'Watch out for the snakes and elephants!'

When the elevator door opened, Nina jumped in like a child entering a playground. 'Don't you touch me!' she shrieked as the door closed. 'Don't you dare touch me. I will draw the clouds down upon you!'

Ophelia looked at Mare and Pare. Both were close to tears.

'Whoosh,' said Nina, splaying her hands and moving them across her face.

When the elevator arrived on the seventh floor, the door opened and Nina leapt out.

'Nina, wait,' Mare called out.

Nina ripped off her dress and ran screaming along the balcony in her underwear.

'God, no,' said Pare.

Nina leapt up, onto the railing.

Pare gasped.

'Nina, no!' Ophelia called out. 'Please get down.'

Nina balanced on the ball of one slender foot, her ankle wobbling. Mare started to tremble, unable to look. Ophelia lunged toward Nina.

'No!' Nina screamed. 'Baby boy, no!'

Pare stepped towards Nina. 'Please, darling. Come down,' he implored.

'They whistle the leaves from the trees, then there's nothing left,' said Nina, her eyes once again wide with terror.

No one responded, and Nina said nothing further so, for a moment, there was silence. Ophelia imagined the cool blue sky wafting over to Nina, scooping her up, and rocking her to sleep.

One of the apartment doors opened and a young man stepped out. 'Nina!' he shouted.

Nina wobbled. 'I'm dancing!' she shouted, splaying her arms in the air.

'Please, Antonio. Do something,' Mare wailed.

Antonio stepped carefully toward Nina.

'Nooo!' Nina screamed.

Antonio stepped back again.

Nina returned her other foot to the railing, causing a collective sigh of relief.

'Nina, please come down,' said Antonio.

'We have cool drinks and nice food inside,' said Pare.

Nina crouched down, her legs bent and the balls of her feet somehow balancing on the railing.

'Dear God, help us,' Ophelia heard herself whisper.

For a moment, it seemed that Nina might be calming down, then she turned her face toward Ophelia and hissed like a cat. Ophelia stepped back then Nina looked away, facing the ocean. And that's when Antonio made his move. He scooped Nina into his arms and pulled her from the balcony.

'Oh, thank God,' Mare cried.

Pare opened the door of his apartment.

'Nooo! Baby boy, no!' Nina screeched, clawing at Antonio's face.

But Antonio refused to let her go. He carried her into the apparent, followed by Mare and Pare. Ophelia, almost unable to believe the nightmare was finally over, just stood there on the balcony, staring at the ocean and clutching Nina's yellow dress.

• • • •

OPHELIA ENTERED THE tiny apartment. It was full and in chaos. Mare was standing at the lounge room entrance with her head in her hands, crying. Pare and Antonio were trying to stop Nina from climbing out of the window. And Nina was obviously in a world of her own – far from the reality occupied by the rest of them.

Ophelia noticed a jug of water on the kitchen bench. She filled a glass, dropped a few slices of lemon and lime into it, and drank it all. She poured another glass and brought it over to Nina.

'What happened to her?' Antonio asked, looking at Ophelia.

Ophelia returned the glass to the table. 'I'm not sure,' she replied. 'It started on the train, after a violent outburst from some other passengers.'

Antonio's attention was pulled back to Nina who seemed to be trying to lift the lounge suite off the floor.

'Out the window!' Nina shouted.

'No, Nina,' said Pare, stopping her.

Nina clawed at Pare's face, just as she had done to Antonio.

'Should call for medical assistance,' Ophelia said.

'I have called,' Mare replied, rubbing her temples with her fingertips.

There was a knock at the door.

When Mare opened the door, a woman, who looked very much like her, entered. 'It's that place!' said the woman, barging into the lounge room. 'I told you, that place does terrible things to our girls.'

'Brigida, this is not the time!' Mare shouted, tears falling down her face.

Nina jumped up and down on the lounge suite, shaking her head, her long hair flying around her face. 'No place.! No place! No place! We have to go home!' she screamed.

'Oh God,' said Brigida, wrapping her arms around Mare. 'You need a doctor here.'

'I have called the hospital,' Mare said.

'While we wait, I have something which might help,' said Brigida, removing a small glass bottle from her bag. 'It's oil from the lavender I've been growing on the roof,' she said. 'It is very good.'

Before anyone could respond, Brigida approached Nina.

'Here, Nina,' she said, placing the bottle under Nina's nose.

A look of horror crept across Nina's face when she saw the bottle. With one sharp movement, she knocked it from Brigida's hand and then she knocked Brigida to the floor. 'No!' she screamed, leaping on top of Brigida, clasping her hands around the woman's throat.

'Nina, stop!' Antonio pleaded, attempting to peel Nina's fingers away.

Ophelia watched in horror as Brigida's legs kicked from side to side and her face was turning red.

'Nina, let go!' Antonio cried. 'Please. Let go!'

Pare was on the other side of Nina, trying to get her to loosen her grip on Brigida's throat.

'Dear God. Please make her stop,' Mare said.

As if by some divine intervention, Ophelia felt a gust of air move around her. She watched with disbelief as a thin woman swooped on top of Nina and pressed something behind her ear. Nina's body went limp instantly and she fell forward, her chest across Brigida's face.

'Thank you, Doctor Sanchez,' said Antonio.

The doctor stood up, returned a strand of her hair to its bun and straightened her skirt. When she nodded at Antonio, Ophelia could see the woman's face was filled with the pain of a thousand Ninas.

Pare exhaled with relief, then helped Brigida sit up. Clutching her throat and gasping, Brigida scrabbled to her feet.

'I'm sorry, Brigida,' said Mare, clasping her friend's hands.

Antonio lifted Nina onto the lounge. Ophelia, suddenly realising she was still clutching Nina's dress, draped it over her friend's near-naked body.

'Pray with us,' Mare said to Brigida.

Brigida knelt beside Mare and Pare.

They clasped their palms, closed their eyes and dropped their heads.

'Beloved Archangel Raphael, please bring your emerald healing light to our baby girl,' Mare whispered. 'Sweet Jesus, please help our darling Nina.'

'Amen,' said Brigida.

'Amen,' said Pare.

Doctor Sanchez stepped toward Nina, lifted her eyelids and peered into her eyes. She pressed a small flat disc against the back of Nina's neck for a moment, read the data on her disc, then turned toward the family. 'Her heart rate has returned to normal,' she said. 'And her cortisol levels are dropping. She'll be okay for now.'

Then the doctor turned to Ophelia, perhaps noticing her for the first time. 'Did you escort Nina back from London?' she asked.

Ophelia nodded.

'I need you to tell me everything you know,' she said.

'Yes, of course,' Ophelia replied. 'But it's a long story. And it's not very pleasant.'

'Let me put Nina to bed first,' said Antonio.

As Antonio lifted Nina, Ophelia could see the tenderness in his face. She found it incredible, especially after such a frightening scene. Antonio loved Nina deeply, she could tell, which made her wonder why Nina had not told her about him. She watched him walk down the hallway with Nina in his arms. Mare and Pare following him like two lost sheep.

'Please let me see,' said Doctor Sanchez, touching Brigida's throat and neck. 'Now, say something,' she continued.

'I don't know what to say,' Brigida said, starting to cry.

'Your throat is fine,' the doctor said, wrapping her arms around Brigida. 'But you have had a nasty shock. The best thing for you now is to go home and lie down.'

Brigida nodded, then left.

Antonio, looking drained and desperate, returned to the lounge room. 'Please tell us who you are and what has happened to our Nina,' he said.

• • • •

OPHELIA INTRODUCED herself, properly this time, then told her story – from the moment she had first met Nina to the horrific birth, their short stay in Paris and the train journey down to Tarragona. By the time she was finished, Antonio's head was hanging so low, Ophelia thought he might fall to the floor.

• • • •

'THAT INCIDENT ON THE train certainly seems to have triggered an acute psychotic episode,' said Doctor Sanchez. 'It can happen very suddenly, especially after a traumatic event, even if the patient has no previous history of psychotic illness.'

'Nina does not have any previous history of any such thing,' said Antonio. 'I have known her since the day she was born. She has never behaved like that.'

'Try not to see this as bad behaviour,' said the doctor. 'It's an illness.'

Antonio stared at the floor, his eyes filling with tears.

Doctor Sanchez continued. 'Unfortunately, one in four of our young women who go to that place return with psychosis,' she said. 'In fact, the prevalence of acute postpartum psychosis is about one thousand times higher in the surrogates than in the rest of our obstetric population.'

'Does it have anything to do with the medication they use in the Garden of Eden?' Ophelia asked.

'We have never been able to determine that fact,' Doctor Sanchez replied. 'None of the women have any idea what medication they are given. They say it's because everything happens very fast during the birthing process and nothing is explained to them. By the time they return home, there is no trace of any drug in their body, so we have no idea.'

'What happens next?' Ophelia asked.

'Some of the women recover enough to be functional in their lives, but none of them ever return to the women they were before the psychosis,' the doctor replied. 'Whether Nina goes on to experience life-long psychotic illness, or whether she recovers fully, I cannot predict. But I will be able to make a good guess within a few days when I see how she responds to the medication I have given her.'

Antonio sighed.

Doctor Sanchez rested her hand upon his shoulder. 'The most important thing right now is to keep Nina heavily sedated for the next forty-eight hours,' she said. 'It will give her biochemistry time to relax and recover.'

'How long will she asleep for now?' Antonio asked.

'About eight hours,' the doctor replied. 'Please do not, under any circumstances, wake her up. It's important that you allow her to wake naturally and adjust to being at home again. Keep the home very quiet, calm and low stimulus, and see what happens.' The doctor handed a thin steel pencil to Antonio. 'If Nina has another episode, you must administer another dose behind her ear just as you saw me do,' she said.

Antonio twirled the device, examining the button at the end of it.

'You press that when you have the tip of the dispenser on Nina's skin,' said the doctor. 'Preferably behind her earlobe.'

'Okay,' Antonio said, almost in a whisper.

Doctor Sanchez stood up. 'Good luck,' she said. 'Call me if anything changes.'

'Hang on a minute!' Ophelia called out. 'You can't leave!'

Antonio looked at Ophelia, horrified.

'Sorry, but I mean, shouldn't Nina be admitted to hospital?' Ophelia asked.

Doctor Sanchez and Antonio looked at Ophelia as though she had just suggested they should all go to hell. 'Because this is your first time in Spain, you are forgiven for saying that,' the doctor replied. 'Goodbye for now.'

When the doctor left the apartment, Ophelia turned to Antonio. 'What?' she demanded.

'We only have one hospital in Tarragona,' Antonio replied. 'It's severely overcrowded. All the time. It only admits people who have suffered accidents in the factories, and only if they are likely to recover enough to go back to work.'

Ophelia slumped onto the couch, feeling deflated. 'I can't believe it,' she said.

'You have to understand, we are a struggling nation,' Antonio replied. 'All of our efforts go into caring for people who are able to earn money for their families.'

'But Nina has just done that!' Ophelia said. 'You heard what I just told you. Everything Nina has endured was to earn money for her family!'

'Yes,' Antonio replied, sadly. 'But now she is home, she is not earning any money. Her medical needs will now be de-prioritised by our government systems.'

Ophelia felt close to tears. 'If only you'd been there and seen what I saw. What she went through. It was ...'

Antonio stood up, holding his palm toward Ophelia's face. 'Please understand. It's not my decision,' he said. 'It's the law. It's the way our country works. It's how we keep going. We will do the best we can, to care for Nina, please believe that.'

Ophelia saw the desperation and the sincerity in Antonio's eyes. She believed him. She knew he would do everything he could, to help Nina. Nevertheless, she felt determined to remain by Nina's side until she had made a full recovery.

Antonio stood up and stretched his arms above his head. 'I need fresh air,' he said. 'Will you walk with me?'

'Sure,' Ophelia replied. 'It's not too hot out there, though, is it?'

'It's 19:00 hours,' Antonio replied, straightening the cushions on the lounge. 'It will be cooler outside now. Come with me.'

Ophelia glanced out of the window at the pale orange sky then followed Antonio out of the apartment.

• • • •

AS THEY ENTERED THE elevator, Antonio looked at his bracelet. 'It's only thirty-four degrees Celsius out here now,' he said.

'Still hot, but much better,' Ophelia replied.

With the elevator door closed, Ophelia could notice the strong body odour from Antonio. It made her cough, even though she knew she probably smelled just as bad. She pulled her wig from her head and ran the palm of her hand over her scalp, enjoying the cooling sensation.

'Oh, dear,' said Antonio, frowning.

'Don't worry,' Ophelia replied. 'It's only temporary. And it's one of the many things I had to do to disguise myself while I was underground.'

'Your story about that place is the strangest one I've ever heard,' Antonio said.

'You don't believe me, do you?' Ophelia said, indignant.

'Yes and no,' Antonio replied. 'We've known, for a long time, that the surrogates are taken underground. But it was a fantastical tale you told.'

'It was *not* a tale,' Ophelia replied. 'Everything I told you was the truth. When Nina is better, she will tell you too.'

Antonio looked deeply melancholic.

'You really love her, don't you?' Ophelia asked.

'With all my heart,' he replied. 'I've been in love with her since I was twelve years old. When she was in that place, under London, I prayed for her every day. And I couldn't wait for her to come home again. But now she *is* home and she doesn't even know who I am.'

Ophelia could feel his pain. 'I'm so sorry, Antonio,' she said. 'But try to be positive. As Doctor Sanchez said, Nina's psychosis could be temporary. I'm sure it will soon pass.'

• • • •

AS THEY WALKED ALONG the promenade, Ophelia enjoyed the softer light. And the cooler temperature. She saw about fifty people dancing to the music, and the music was even more energetic than it had been when she had first arrived in the heat of the day.

She looked at the orange sky again. 'I've never seen a sky so vibrant,' she said. 'I feel like I'm in a fairy tale!'

'This place is far from being a fairy tale,' Antonio scoffed.

They stepped onto a jetty. A blue light flashed for a second.

'What was that?' Ophelia asked.

'One of Gaia's scanners,' Antonio replied. 'They're randomly positioned all over the country. Don't worry about it.'

'It seems like a strange place to have one,' Ophelia said. 'And, now that I think about it, I don't recall seeing any scanners at the train station.'

'They get moved around all the time,' Antonio replied. 'There's no way of predicting when or where any of them will be. But if they capture someone who's not entitled to be there, the police response is both swift and brutal.'

'So I've heard,' Ophelia replied, aware of her arm twinging where the Parisian guards had inserted the tracking device.

She glanced into the boats tethered to either side of the jetty. Inside were people sprawled across their beds, sleeping or watching their holo-pads. 'Surely it's too hot inside those boats,' she said.

'The temperature is quite pleasant under the deck, even during the day,' Antonio replied. 'The coolers are switched on most of the time.'

'What are coolers?' Ophelia asked.

'Electric fans blowing over buckets of seawater,' Antonio replied.

As they got closer to the end of the jetty, Ophelia could see some people sitting upon the decks of the boats. They all looked sleepy, as though they had just woken from a nap. Many of them were staring out to sea. One man was wearing nothing but a pair of very small shorts. His chunky tanned legs were covered in thick grey hair and his balding head was dripping with sweat. He took long sips from a glass of wine.

When they reached the end of the jetty, Ophelia sat down, removed her sandals and dangled her feet in the water. She gazed at the horizon line. 'It's changed colour again, even in the last few minutes,' she said. 'And the temperature continues to drop. It's glorious.'

'It's twenty-seven degrees,' Antonino replied, looking at his bracelet. 'For this time of year, this is as low as it will go. The air is cooler at sea, of course, but we don't go out very often because it's too expensive to power the boats.'

'But it must be worth it, though, to catch all the fish,' Ophelia said.

'There aren't many fish in this sea,' Antonio replied. 'This ocean is too warm, which means we have to travel quite far out to the deeper sea where it's a bit cooler. That takes fuel for our boats, and we can only afford to do it once per week.'

'Does this entire village survive on one boat-load of fish per week?'

'Yes,' he replied. 'But we eat chickens, too.'

'Chickens!' Ophelia said. 'Do you know, I have never seen a chicken!'

Antonio laughed at her. 'There are lots of chickens over there,' he said, pointing to one of the red sea containers on the other side of the jetty.

'Really?' said Ophelia 'But ... I mean, how ... Gosh. I can't even imagine.'

'They're bred in that factory,' he said. 'They live there, happily running around. And when the time is right, we kill them and eat them.'

'How can they be happy living inside one of those factory containers?' Ophelia asked.

'Well, they certainly can't be happy *outside* the containers,' Antonio replied. 'They would die from the heat.'

'Goodness. This is all very ... well, it's more than I bargained for,' Ophelia said. 'So, is that all you eat? Fish and chicken?'

'Our apartment buildings all have sky gardens that produce a good range of fruit and vegetables,' he replied. 'And we grow wheat in one of our factories, so we make bread and biscuits from that.'

'How do you wash the vegetables without water?' Ophelia asked.

'There's no water for washing, so consider this gold,' Antonio replied, handing Ophelia a small bottle of drinking water. 'When we turn on the taps in the apartment, it is sonic energy that comes out, and we hold the vegetables under it for a moment.'

'Just like a sonic shower,' said Ophelia.

Antonio nodded.

'In Britain, we have enough water to wash things under the tap, but our bodies are cleaned in sonic showers,' said Ophelia.

Antonio nodded again.

'But most people don't bother growing, or even cooking, their own food,' Ophelia continued. 'They just eat what Gaia produces. And that can be anything.'

'I've heard about that,' Antonio replied. 'Is it true that Gaia is filled with synthetic proteins that it manipulates to make whatever you ask it for?'

'Yep,' Ophelia replied, noticing the deep gold sky.

'You know our primary import is bottles of fresh drinking water, right?' Antonio said.

'Yes,' said Ophelia.

'Well, the water comes in bioplastic bottles which are supposed to break down in the earth, just like an old piece of fruit,' said Antonio. 'The bad news is, when they break down, they release a lot of heat and some very bad gases. But the good news is, we've learned how to use those gases to fuel our boats and our road vehicles.'

'Ha!'

'We've also learned how to refine the gases to help the fermentation of our fruit, which makes some very nice wines,' he said.

Ophelia's mind floated back to the last time she had sipped her favourite wine – a Siberian Sauvignon Blanc. It had been a mild winter afternoon in her part of Britain, around twenty-five degrees and sunny. A gentle breeze had delivered the scent of the roses from the garden outside the Arden Hotel where she had sat with friends, discussing the performance of *As You Like It* they had just seen in the theatre. What a nice life, she mused, dipping her wig into the sea.

'What are you doing?' Antonio asked.

Ophelia returned the wig to her head. The water poured down every millimetre of her scalp, face, neck, back and chest. 'This feels great,' she said.

A thick puff of black smoke bellowed from one of the red sea containers on the beach.

'Oh dear,' Ophelia said, pointing to it.

'Don't worry,' said Antonio. 'It's blowing the other way.'

'What's it from?' Ophelia asked.

'The aluplac.'

'What's that?'

'It's a hallucinogenic drug we create from the residue of the burning plastics,' Antonio replied. 'It's controversial because it's dangerous and because we sell it to the northern countries through our shadow trade network.'

'Which countries buy the most?' Ophelia asked.

'The Russo-Siberians are our number one customer and the British run a close second,' he replied. 'Apparently, wealthy people enjoy it as a party drug.'

'What does it do?' Ophelia asked.

'Within a few seconds of taking it, a person becomes euphoric. They think they are invincible. Some even think they are God. They often get very physical and playful but if they take too much, they can get quite violent.'

'That must be what those men on the train had taken,' said Ophelia.

'That's what I thought when you described the scene,' Antonio replied.

'So, if those men had not been killed by the bot, what would have happened next, do you think?' Ophelia asked.

'It's possible they would have killed that pregnant woman without really understanding what they had done,' Antonio replied. 'And if they had have taken more of the drug, they would have died.'

'So how does it kill people?' Ophelia asked.

'It melts the brain, literally, killing the person instantly,' said Antonio. 'And for an hour or so after death, the brain trickles out of their nostrils.'

'That's disgusting!' Ophelia said.

She stared as far towards the horizon as she could see, imagining what it might feel like to fly through it to the other side, as though that was possible. 'I've just had a really weird thought,' she said.

'What?'

'What if the aluplac is being used, in small quantities, by those monsters in the Garden of Eden?' said Ophelia. 'What if they are giving the surrogates that drug during labour to help dull the pain of birth and what if it's causing the psychosis?'

Antoni shrugged.

'What do you think?' Ophelia asked.

'I think that's a theory you should share with Doctor Sanchez,' he replied.

Another puff of black smoke shot up into the air. This time, it travelled straight toward them, bringing an obnoxious stench with it.

'Time to go,' Antonio said, helping Ophelia to her feet.

• • • •

IT WAS JUST AFTER 21:00 hours when Ophelia and Antonio returned to the apartment.

'I love these things,' Ophelia said, pointing to the algae lamps around the lounge room. 'There's nothing like the soft green glow of these things to put me in the mood for ...'

'Food!' Antonio chimed in.

Mare and Pare smiled sweetly from behind the bountiful spread of fresh produce and luxury goodies scattered along the kitchen bench.

'Nina's still sleeping soundly,' Mare said, carrying food to the dining table.

Ophelia reached for the placemats. She laid them on the dining table, hoping to be helpful. But Mare barely noticed, busy shuttling one glorious dish after another from the kitchen to the table. The beautiful rustic bowls, each filled with delights such as roasted sweet potatoes, zucchini squash, long green beans and peppers, made Ophelia's mouth water.

'Mare makes a wonderful dressing too,' Antonio said, pointing to a clay jug which, Ophelia was certain, must have been thousands of years old. 'She uses her own pressed olive oil with fresh herbs and garlic and a touch of lemon. It's truly wonderful.'

'Don't you tell my secrets, young man,' said Mare, winking at
him.

Pare emerged from the kitchen, holding a massive serving plate.
Upon it was a plump, golden-brown thing that smelled delicious.

'What's that?' Ophelia asked.

'It's a chicken,' Antonio replied. 'You don't have to eat it if you
don't want to.'

Mare and Pare exchanged glances.

'You don't like roast chicken?' Mare asked, bewildered.

Ophelia felt embarrassed, but she had to be honest. 'I don't
know,' she replied. 'I've never eaten animal meat before.'

Mare and Pare stared at her as if she had just told them she
had never drunk water or breathed air. Then Pare stepped over to
the chicken and sliced thick white pieces of meat from its carcass.
With each slice, a new jet of steam escaped and wafted around the
room, bringing with it, the most delightful scent. Ophelia could
not identify, or describe, the scent. She only knew it made her feel
hungry.

Mare passed the bowls of vegetables around the table until
everyone had some of everything.

Ophelia's plate, overflowing with an incredible range of shapes,
colours and scents, was both delightful and intimidating to her. She
had no idea where to start, but she picked up her cutlery.

'Dear Lord, we thank you for all you have provided,' said Mare,
her eyes closed, and her hands clasped.

Ophelia dropped her cutlery and joined the prayer.

'Lord, we ask you to bless this wonderful feast and we ask you
to watch over our beloved Nina while she sleeps. May she be healthy
and happy when she wakes,' Mare continued.

'Amen,' said Pare. And Antonio.

Ophelia's eyes roamed her plate again and her stomach growled
with anticipation. Pare laughed at her, rubbing his own belly.

Ophelia noticed, for the first time, just how slender Pare and Mare were. A petite, strong and fit-looking couple, with only a few grey hairs, they seemed to be in their mid-fifties, she guessed. Antonio, much younger, taller and stronger, sat at the head of the table, drizzling dressing over every piece of food on his plate. Mare and Pare applied a small amount of cracked pepper and a tiny pinch of sea salt to their food so Ophelia did the same.

When she placed a slice of roast chicken into her mouth, the first thing Ophelia noticed was the texture. It was firm but soft. And slightly grainy. The flavour was so sensational, it caused saliva to squirt out of the lining of her mouth and her tongue. And when she swallowed the piece, she noticed the aftertaste of the dressing. The combination of earthy flavours from the fresh herbs, with a hint of lemon and oil, made her feel so alive she wanted to kiss the dirt from where they'd grown. 'Zing!' she said, tingling with pleasure.

They all looked at her.

'Oh, sorry,' she said. 'That was a happy sound. This food is glorious.'

Mare smiled.

'I told you so,' said Antonio.

Ophelia closed her eyes for a moment, savouring the taste of a roast potato.

'Oh, my goodness. This is truly wonderful,' she said.

Aware of an unfamiliar desire to eat as much as she possibly could, Ophelia sliced a piece of sweet potato and stacked it onto a slice of chicken. Then she tried the zucchini squash with the chicken. Different, but just as good. Then she added something called gravy, just a small blob at first. 'Oh, this is excellent with the potatoes,' she said. 'Have you tried it?'

Antonio laughed at her.

Ophelia soon discovered the gravy was also good with the green beans. Then she had more chicken, with the lemon oil dressing. 'I can't stop,' she said. The more she ate, the more she wanted. Her belly expanded rapidly, and uncomfortably, but she could not stop eating. This, she realised, must be what is referred to as *gluttony*.

• • • •

OPHELIA WOKE, FEELING strange and uncomfortable. She felt thirsty, too, but she doubted her belly could accommodate another glass of water. And she felt alone, in the darkness, in the home of people she barely knew. She switched on one of the algae lamps and stared into the green bulb. Her gaze moved from the darker edges of the bulb into the paler centre and back to the darker edges. She tried to locate the exact place at which the dark green turned to pale green, but there was no such place, so she gave up.

• • • •

OPHELIA WOKE TO THE sound of whispering. Several lamps were on, casting a soft green glow around the apartment. Antonio and Nina were sitting on the lounge room floor.

'Is everything okay?' Ophelia whispered.

'Sorry to wake you,' Antonio replied. 'Nina's having a snack.'

Nina was holding a piece of roast potato in her hand and there was a dot of gravy on the side of her mouth. She was staring at the wall.

'How are you feeling, Nina?' Ophelia asked.

Nina gave a tiny grunt.

'What time is it?' Ophelia asked.

'02:16,' Antonio replied. 'We knew the sedative would wear off about now.'

Ophelia took a sip of water then sank back into the couch. 'Antonio, what's the date today?' she asked.

'The twenty-second of May,' he replied.

'It was only three days ago that I first met Nina.'

Nina threw the potato onto the floor.

'Would you like some chicken, Nina?' Antonio asked, lifting a plate of food towards his beloved.

Nina replied with a tiny whimper. Antonio broke off a piece of the meat and put it directly into her mouth. She chewed slowly, still staring at the wall.

Antonio dabbed the corner of Nina's mouth with a napkin, then tucked a strand of her long hair behind her ear. 'Did you like that?' he asked.

Nina let out a louder and more definitive grunt. Then something else.

'What did you say, Nina?' Antonio asked.

'Be by,' Nina replied.

'Could you say that again?'

Still staring at the wall, Nina finally spoke. 'Baby boy,' she said.

Antonio's eyes filled with tears. 'Is it true?' he asked, looking at Ophelia.

Ophelia nodded.

Nina's eyes were more focused when she spoke again. 'No!' she shouted. 'Baby, boy!'

'It's okay, Nina,' said Antonio, wrapping his arm around her.

Nina shrugged him off. Then she moved – from sitting crossed-legged on the floor to standing upright – in less than a second. It was an action that seemed so unnatural, Ophelia sat up, astonished. She could that Antonio, too, was shocked by the movement. And she could see that Nina's eyes were completely focused, scanning the room like a wild cat on the hunt.

'You're home now, Nina,' Antonio said. 'You're safe, with your family.'

'Long white gloves up to here,' Nina said, touching her shoulder.

'I think she's referring to the women who delivered the baby,' Ophelia said.

'No! Baby Boy!' Nina screamed.

She ran to the kitchen, dropped to the floor, then crawled, on her hands and knees, searching for something amidst the small spots of food grime on the floor. 'Baby boy,' she cried. 'Baby boy!'

Ophelia placed her hand over her chest, feeling her heart might break.

'Baby boy!' Nina cried, even louder.

'Here,' said Antonio, handing Nina a small blue cushion.

Nina lifted her T-shirt and pressed one of her naked breasts into the centre of the cushion. Then she returned to the lounge, sat down and rocked back and forth, gazing lovingly at the cushion. 'Shhhh,' she said, looking up at Ophelia and Antonio.

Ophelia felt her heart had completely broken and sunk to the depths of her being. She could feel Antonio, beside her, starting to sob.

Then, quite suddenly, Nina detached the cushion from her breast, wrapped it in Ophelia's sleeping sheet and laid it on the couch. 'Shh,' she said again.

'Okay,' Ophelia whispered.

'Steel against the black,' Nina stammered, wriggling her legs nervously. 'And the blood squirted out, all over the white ... Pssssh.'

She grabbed the cushion again, more roughly this time, and ran to the window. Ophelia and Antonio moved followed her, but she was too fast. With one sharp movement, she cast the cushion away. 'Gone!' she said, looking directly at Ophelia and Antonio.

Ophelia visualised the cushion falling down the seven flights of the building, then slapping the pavement below.

Nina pushed the window open further and lifted one of her legs.

'No, Nina!' Ophelia said, leaping toward her.

Antonio pulled Nina back inside, just in time, and she fell on top of him.

'No! Baby boy!' she screamed, hitting Antonio on the chest and face.

'Stop it, Nina,' he said, gripping her wrists.

But Nina broke free and returned to the kitchen, her head moving from side to side, as though she was searching for something. Her eyes stopped on the wooden block on the counter beside the sink. Punctured by several sharp knives, glistening in the soft light, Nina was drawn to the object.

'Nina, no!' Ophelia shouted.

But Nina didn't listen. She pulled the largest carving knife from the block and turned it back and forth, apparently enjoying the green sheen cast across the steel.

'Nina, stop!' Ophelia shouted. 'Please, Nina, put it back.'

Antonio stepped towards Nina. 'Darling, please, put that down,' he said.

But Nina lunged towards him, pointing the tip of the blade at his chest. 'No gloves!' she shrieked.

Antonio dodged the move and grabbed her hand, trying to force her grip open, but she held on tight. Her entire body was unyielding. It seemed to be made of steel, as she forced Antonio, twice her size, back into the lounge room.

'Ophelia!' Antonio called out. 'Get that dispenser. It's in the cupboard above the sink. Hurry!'

Ophelia grabbed the dispenser then ran to the lounge room where Nina was gyrating furiously and still attempting to stab Antonio. Ophelia saw him twist Nina's arm, momentarily immobilising her, and that's when Ophelia made her move. She lunged towards Nina and pressed the dispenser behind her earlobe until she heard the gentle hiss of the device releasing the mediation.

Nina collapsed, unconscious, into Antonio's arms. Exhausted, he leaned against the wall, his hands under Nina's armpits. Then he caught his breath, lifted Nina and carried her back to her bedroom.

Ophelia sprawled across the lounge, exhausted but relieved that no one had been injured. She was not surprised by the look of despair on Antonio's face when he returned to the lounge room.

Like a man on a mission, he headed into the kitchen. 'We may as well have some coffee,' he said. 'I won't be sleeping after that!'

· · · ·

'ANTONIO, PLEASE SLOW down,' Ophelia called out.

He stopped and turned around. 'Sorry, Ophelia. I'm still a bit worked up.'

'I'm not surprised, after all that coffee you drank,' Ophelia replied. 'But I can't keep up with you,' she added, hands upon her knees. She stared at the horizon, barely able to differentiate the sky from the ocean in the morning light. There was only one colour, a pale blue, as the sun was yet to protrude above the horizon. A cool breeze lapped at the hem of her skirt.

Finally, she had enough breath to speak. 'When we see Doctor Sanchez,' she said. 'We should ask her if it's possible to speak with the families of other surrogates. It might help us understand how to support Nina through this phase of her illness.'

Antonio nodded, then headed toward a flight of steps cut deep into a steep hill. 'We're nearly at the Mediterranean Balcony,' he called out.

Ophelia looked to the top step, disheartened by the height. 'This might just kill me,' she said.

Antonio spoke over his shoulder. 'Once you climb up these stairs, you'll be in Tarragona,' he said. 'You didn't see the town centre when you arrived, because the train station is down there,' he added, pointing to the flat ground by the edge of the beach.

Ophelia dared not look down. Only up. Despite her slender frame, she struggled with the effort, feeling pain in her legs and rapidly losing her breath.

'This is it!' Antonio shouted from the top. 'Come on Ophelia, you can do it!'

Ophelia took in a deep breath and, through sheer force of will, managed to climb to the top. Finally, she understood what all the fuss was about. 'Oh my God,' she said. 'This view is sensational. How high up are we?'

'Just over three hundred metres,' Antonio replied. 'You are not very fit, are you?'

Ophelia ignored his quip, enraptured by the view. 'Absolutely stunning,' she said, turning from left to right, taking in the view. For even more than one hundred and eighty degrees, she could see a horizon line at which the sea met the sky. She pressed the back of her pendant and recorded the tiny glimmer of gold starting to appear at the horizon line.

'I feel as though I am watching the birth of the world,' she said, as one extraordinary colour after another crept across the sky, each spreading its fingers across the pale turquoise ocean.

Her gaze then fell to a park on the flat land below. Like most parks around the world, this one was brown, but her skin prickled with excitement when, to her left, she saw the ruins of an ancient amphitheatre. 'Is that a *real* Roman amphitheatre?' she asked.

'Yep.'

In the morning light, it appeared grey in colour. And from her vantage point, Ophelia could see several pieces were missing. Time and the salt air had taken their toll, she could tell, but the structure still had an awesome presence. Looking into its centre, smooth and curved, she had no trouble visualising a theatrical performance in progress. And then she saw the aqueducts punctuating the edges of the sunken stage. 'I can just imagine the boat races the Romans would have had in there.'

Antonio nodded.

'I've devoted my life to researching ancient literature – the kind of stories that were originally told in places just like this,' Ophelia said, her voice quivering.

Antonio looked at her.

'This is incredible for me, Antonio,' she said. 'I can hardly believe I'm standing here, looking at a real, outdoor amphitheatre. Do they still do live performances in there?'

'I think so,' Antonio replied, barely interested.

'Perhaps when Nina is feeling better, I can bring her to one,' Ophelia said.

'I don't think so,' Antonio said.

Ophelia was surprised by the flatness of his tone and how rapidly he dismissed the idea. 'Why not?' she asked.

'I have to believe that Nina will recover,' Antonio replied, gripping the railing. 'But she has never enjoyed crowds, so I don't believe she will ever step into *that* place.'

'Oh.'

Antonio turned towards Ophelia again. 'I know you mean well,' he said. 'But please remember – I have known Nina since the day she was born. You have only known her for a few days.'

Ophelia felt embarrassed by Antonio's words and, for a moment, it made her feel unwelcome. She looked around for something else to talk about.

'What's that?' she asked, pointing at a curved steel structure.

'A memorial,' Antonio replied.

Ophelia stared at it, concluding it must have been about ten metres tall and about a metre wide. Its surface was covered in hundreds of small round steel discs and, as the sun rose, it lit one row at a time, causing the discs to change colour, to a warm gold. 'It's telling a story, isn't it?' she said.

'Yes. It's one of the most important memorials of our time,' Antonio replied. 'Each one of those gold discs represents someone who died in the tsunami of 2110.'

'Tsunami,' Ophelia echoed. 'I've heard that word before, but I don't know much about it. It has something to do with big waves, right?'

Antonio stepped back for a moment, apparently aghast by Ophelia's question. Then he shook his head, in disbelief.

Again, Ophelia felt embarrassed by her stupidity. 'I'm so sorry,' she said. 'I can see I have offended you again. All I can say, in my own defence, is that I have lived a very sheltered life. There is a lot about the world I don't know.'

Antonio scoffed then shook his head again. Finally, he spoke. 'Imagine a wall of water rising up from the ocean and moving onto the land,' he said. 'A wall so high and so long, it obliterates everything in its path.'

Ophelia tried to imagine a wave like that, but it was difficult, while she was looking at the vast block of flat water in before her. 'I'm trying to,' she said. 'But this is only the second time in my life I've seen a large body of water, and it looks so calm to me.'

'It's calm, *now*,' said Antonio. 'But if an earthquake occurred under the surface, or if a meteor fell from the sky, the result would be one massive wave.'

'So, how did it happen?' she asked. 'The tsunami of 2110, I mean.'

'It was very sudden,' Antonio replied. 'A wave, approximately fifteen metres high, simply rose up and moved across the land. The entire park below was flooded, killing everyone down there. And, because El Serrallo is down on that level, it was flooded as well.'

'How many people died?' Ophelia asked.

'As far as we can tell, one hundred and fifty-six people from El Serrallo and seventy-nine people from Tarragona,' he replied. 'Most of the bodies were washed back onto the shore after the wave retreated, but some were never found.'

'God, how awful,' Ophelia replied, visualising the horror all too vividly. 'Did you know anyone who died?'

Antonio gripped the railing, even harder than before, and looked down at his feet. 'My parents and my older brother. They were my entire family. Until Nina's parents extended their home to me.'

'I'm so sorry, Antonio,' Ophelia said.

She rested her head on Antonio's shoulder for a moment, feeling the sadness seeping from his skin. From the corner of her eye, she saw that the entire sky was a blaze of gold and it had lit every disc on the memorial. 'I just remembered what Nina said yesterday.'

'What was that?' Antonio asked.

Ophelia spoke slowly, hoping to honour Nina's words exactly. 'When the ocean swept up onto the promenade and filled the shops and houses and we all became fish,' she said. 'Does that mean anything?'

Antonio nodded. 'It probably means we need to find Doctor Sanchez.'

• • • •

OPHELIA FELT THAT THE heat had burned through her skin and muscles, and was penetrating her bones, by the time they reached the hospital. It was only 09:00 hours, she noticed, so she was not looking forward to the inevitable increase in temperature as the day progressed. For now, she took relief from the cooler air inside the building.

But she soon felt overwhelmed by the chaos.

The reception area was crowded. Several babies were crying. Their parents seemed exhausted and depressed. Every chair was occupied by someone in pain and there were more people sitting or lying on the floor. Some were bleeding, some were grasping an arm, leg or other injured body part and many were sobbing. 'What happened?' Ophelia asked.

'What do you mean?' said Antonio.

Incensed, Ophelia stuttered. 'I mean ... I mean ... has a ... a bomb detonated? Or something terrible? Why are all these people in such a terrible state? What happened?'

Antonio frowned at her. 'Please, keep your voice down,' he said. 'It's always like this. I told you before, we can only afford to keep one hospital open, and this is it.'

Ophelia saw a few bots handing out bottles of water. Another bot was cleaning and bandaging a wound on the forearm of a young man on the floor. And several other bots, about the size of Ophelia's feet, were cleaning the blood from the concrete floor. An alarm sounded from someone's bracelet. Ophelia's eyes followed the sound and saw that the man's bracelet was flashing red. Two human-sized bots rushed to his side, unfolded a stretcher, lifted the man onto it and marched down a hallway with him.

Another bot approached Ophelia. 'May I help you?' it said.

Ophelia almost jumped back when she saw that the bot's head was encased inside a clear bubble; like an astronaut's helmet.

'Please page Doctor Sanchez,' Antonio replied.

'What is the nature of your emergency?' the bot asked.

'My girlfriend is at home, very sick,' he said.

'Do you have an appointment?' the bot asked.

'No, we do not have an appointment,' Antonio replied, starting to sound agitated. 'Doctor Sanchez told me to page her in an emergency. We have an emergency. Please page her!'

'What is your name?' asked the bot.

'Antonio Selgado.'

'One moment, please,' the bot replied, activating a live camera feed across the bubble.

'Amazing,' Ophelia whispered, almost feeling she might laugh.

'Locate Doctor Sanchez,' it said.

The image scrambled for a second, then showed Doctor Sanchez inside a small room, speaking with a group of people. A family, Ophelia mused.

'Paging Doctor Sanchez,' said the bot.

The doctor looked at the camera. 'Yes?'

'Antonio Selgado is at reception, doctor,' said the bot.

Doctor Sanchez nodded then exited the room. The camera feed vanished. Within seconds, the doctor was walking down a hallway towards them. To Ophelia's eyes, she had the graceful elegance of a model on the catwalk. Tall, slender and serious, the woman was stunning; a fact which, Ophelia felt, was incongruous with the woman's dismal surroundings.

'Good morning,' she said, nodding to both Antonio and Ophelia. 'How is Nina?'

Antonio stood close to the doctor and spoke softly, as though embarrassed. 'Nina's in a very bad state of mind,' he replied. 'She woke at 02:00, quite drowsy at first. But then she went into another psychotic state. She tried to jump out of the window, and when I pulled her back inside, she tried to stab me with a kitchen knife.'

The doctor looked disappointed. 'I'm sorry, Antonio,' she replied. 'Can I assume you have administered more medication?'

'Yes, Ophelia did while I was trying to stop Nina from stabbing me,' he replied.

Doctor Sanchez glanced at Ophelia. 'What time was that?' she asked.

'Around 03:30 hours,' Ophelia replied.

'In that case, we can expect her to wake again at approximately 11:30 hours,' said the doctor. 'That's only two hours from now.'

'Her Mare and Pare know how to administer the medication if we're not back by then,' Antonio said. 'But please, could you visit her today? We can't go through that again. And we can't allow Nina to go through it again, either.'

'Of course,' said Doctor Sanchez. 'I'll aim to be there by 11:00 hours.'

'Thank you so much,' Antonio replied.

'Doctor Sanchez,' Ophelia ventured. 'Is there any chance we could speak with the families of other surrogates who are going through this?'

'Yes, of course,' the doctor replied. 'There's a support group for the families. It meets every day, between midday and siesta time.'

'Really?' Antonio asked. 'Where?'

'Inside the Placa de la UNESCO,' Doctor Sanchez replied. 'Just go to the reception desk, tell them you're there for the surrogacy support group and they'll bring you to the meeting room.'

'Thank you so much, doctor,' Ophelia said.

'You're welcome. But please take my contact details before you leave,' said Doctor Sanchez, bringing her bracelet to her mouth. 'Activate contact details and transfer,' she said, pressing her bracelet against Antonio's until it beeped.

'Thanks again, Doctor Sanchez,' he said.

The doctor nodded, smiled nervously, and retreated to the hallway.

Ophelia followed Antonio back towards the exit, almost colliding with two medibots. They were carrying a human form on a stretcher and it was covered, entirely, with a pale grey sheet.

• • • •

'POOR DOCTOR SANCHEZ,' said Antonio, stepping out of the hospital.

'Yes, what a stressful job,' Ophelia replied, already irritated by the heat, the sound of traffic and the blindingly bright sunshine.

'That's not what I am referring to,' Antonio said. 'Did you see those two police officers leaning against the wall, staring at her?'

'No,' Ophelia replied. 'But I suspect it's because she's incredibly beautiful.'

Antonio shook his head. 'They're bribing her,' he said.

Ophelia stared at him, squinting through her sunglasses. 'How on earth would you arrive at such a conclusion?' she asked.

Antonio sighed. 'Ophelia, whenever police officers hang around like that, they're usually waiting to speak with someone in private, so they can do deals with them,' he explained. 'The way they looked at Doctor Sanchez, I could just tell they were going to follow her. She knew it, too, which was why she left so abruptly.'

Ophelia struggled to imagine the concept of bribery, but the heat was making it difficult for her to imagine anything and her head was cracking in pain. 'But, *how* would they bribe her?' she asked.

'Usually, the police offer the person something they desperately need in exchange for something of value to the police,' Antonio replied.

Ophelia wasn't sure what to think or say.

'In Doctor Sanchez's case, it's probably medication for her patients,' Antonio continued. 'And she's probably accepting it in exchange for information about her patients.'

Ophelia felt confused. 'But why is that necessary?' she asked. 'Surely the medications are provided by the government.'

Antonio shook his head in frustration. 'Ophelia, *nothing* flows freely from the government,' he said. 'We can't even get Nina into hospital. As you already have seen. We must argue and negotiate for everything we get! Medication. Drinking water. Equipment for our factories, schools and hospitals. None of it is free!'

Ophelia felt embarrassed by her naivety. 'I'm so sorry, Antonio,' she said. 'I realise I'm frustrating you with all my stupid questions. I come from a different world, and I ...'

'You don't belong here,' Antonio said.

Ophelia stopped walking, shocked by his blunt delivery.

Antonio turned around, saw her, and stopped walking, too. 'Ophelia, I don't wish to be mean,' he said. 'But I have to ask you – why are you still here?'

Ophelia felt taken aback by the question. 'I want to see Nina recover,' she replied.

Antonio sighed. 'I applaud your kindness, Ophelia,' he said. 'But it would be more appropriate that you trust us, her family, to manage her recovery.'

• • • •

STEPPING INTO THE UNESCO building, Ophelia felt relief from the heat. She stared beyond the reception desk, through a glass wall, outdoors. Rows of prehistoric trees stood on either side of concrete paths that disappeared under ornate and ancient archways. Curious as ever, Ophelia wanted to know where those enchanted paths led to.

'You can't afford it,' Antonio whispered in her ear.

'What?'

'That little adventure you're looking at,' he replied. 'It's only for the wealthiest tourists.'

Ophelia felt deflated.

'This way,' Antonio said, tapping her on the arm.

Ophelia followed him, and about fifty other people, through a side door and into a hallway. It was long, dimly lit and descending; far too reminiscent of Ophelia's time underground. Her legs started to wobble, then went numb, just as they had done when the Sentinels had dragged her down a tunnel towards a prison cell.

'We're almost directly under the Roman Amphitheatre,' Antonio whispered.

The floor started to level out and they walked straight along a flat and softly lit tunnel. Its ceiling was arched, and made of sandstone, offering some light. Ophelia noticed several small pits carved into the sides of the tunnel, each one barely large enough for a person to sleep. 'That's where the Romans kept the gladiators, isn't it?' she asked.

'Yes,' Antonio replied. 'And it would have been pitch dark in those days.'

Ophelia could almost feel the despair seeping through the walls of the tunnel.

'They'd have no hope of surviving,' she said.

'Unless they were Saint Thecla,' said Antonio.

'Who?'

Antonio looked at Ophelia, apparently surprised by her ignorance. Yet again. 'Shortly after Jesus's ascension to heaven, Thecla converted to Christianity,' he said. 'The Romans didn't like that, so they put her in an arena like the one above us.'

'Awful.'

'When they opened the gates, the lions bolted toward Thecla, snarling ferociously,' Antonio continued. 'But as they got closer to her, they slowed down. And when they reached her, they lay down beside her, rolled onto their backs and purred.'

Ophelia wasn't sure how seriously to take that story, but she enjoyed it, nevertheless. 'Thecla sounds like our warrior friend, Nina,' she said.

Antonio laughed. 'Nina has been a warrior since the day she was born,' he replied. 'I remember the sound of her cry when she was a baby. I was only four years old, and it scared the crap out of me.'

· · · ·

WHEN THEY REACHED THE end of the sandstone tunnel, Ophelia saw a massive archway, about twenty meters high, she guessed. When she stepped through, into a wide-open space, her skin prickle with intrigue. The space was incredibly solid yet ethereal. Made from the same smooth sandstone as the tunnels, it somehow formed a perfect dome. At the centre of the space was a closed circle of wooden chairs, each one as rustic and unique as the next.

The wood was hard and unyielding under Ophelia's sit-bones, so she took off her outer shirt, folded it and placed it underneath her. Then she leaned back in her chair and looked up. At the apex of the dome was a magnificent carving of the Virgin Mother Mary and the Baby Jesus.

'Hola y Bienvenidos!' she heard.

Ophelia saw a tall woman stepping into the centre of the circle.

'We are the families of the surrogates,' said the woman, her voice rich and powerful. 'We are here to share our stories and give support to each other.'

'Hola!' was the response from around the room.

'There are some new faces here today,' the woman continued, looking at Ophelia and Antonio. 'I will start by introducing myself. I'm Liana, mother of a brave young woman, Carmen, who went to London to be a surrogate, almost eighteen years ago. She returned home, in utter despair. Several weeks later, she took her own life.'

The room was so silent, Ophelia was afraid to breathe. She just stared at Liana. The deep lines on the woman's face and the grey hair protruding from her head gave the impression she must have been in her sixties. Yet she was lean, muscular and exuding a confident presence that Ophelia could not help but admire.

'I've learned a lot since then,' Liana continued. 'Enough to know that Carmen's death could have been prevented if I had understood what was happening to her. So now, I dedicate my life to helping families to support their beloved daughters, sisters, cousins and friends to recover from the nightmare that is the surrogacy trade.'

Liana's words moved through Ophelia's body like the bubbles in a glass of champagne.

'Please, will someone share their experience,' said Liana.

A man stepped into the centre of the room. He pushed his glasses up his nose, straightened his shirt, and then ruffled his hair. He coughed, swaying from one foot to the other, and then cleared his throat. 'My little girl, Elen,' he said, his voice breaking with emotion. 'She was only nineteen when she went to London to be a surrogate. She returned home to us nine months later an empty shell. We hoped she would improve. But now, one year later, she still spends her days staring out of the window and crying.'

'Was she given the uplift?' someone asked.

'Yes, within hours of arriving home,' he replied. 'It's the only thing that has kept her alive.'

'What's the uplift?' Ophelia whispered.

Antonio shrugged his shoulders.

'Before we continue,' Liana interjected, looking at Ophelia and Antonio again. 'Let me explain – the uplift is the current treatment for severe post-natal depression. It's an enzyme that penetrates the skin on the temples and travels straight toward the amygdala, the part of the brain that processes emotion.'

Ophelia nodded, unable to tear her eyes from Liana's face.

'It doesn't work!' someone called out.

Liana cleared her throat then continued. 'The uplift is meant to help the woman reprocess the surrogacy experience in a more objective way. It makes the experience seem like a very long time ago. The details of the memory are still accessible, but they do not evoke a post-traumatic reaction,' she explained.

This made perfect sense to Ophelia.

'It turns them into zombies!' someone called out.

'To be fair,' Liana responded. 'The uplift works well for some people and not so well for others. I don't think we yet understand why that is the case. Personally, I wish we'd had that drug when my Carmen was still alive.'

The man in the centre of the room nodded, then returned to his seat.

A young woman, probably in her late teens, Ophelia suspected, stepped into the centre of the circle. 'My sister came back almost two years ago,' she said. 'She was a mess at first, but the uplift really helped her. She was okay. During the day, anyway. But at night, she screamed in her sleep. Now she just sleepwalks. We often find her in the kitchen, late at night, eating everything. But the next day, she doesn't remember any of it.'

No one said anything.

Antonio stood up. 'My girlfriend, Nina, is far beyond depression,' he said. 'She's been diagnosed with acute postpartum psychosis. She talks gibberish, and she screams and cries, tried to jump out of the window and, this morning, she tried to stab me with a knife. I don't think she knows who I am,' he said, his voice wavering. 'Worst of all, she doesn't seem to know who *she* is.'

Liana nodded, waiting for him to say something else.

'I'm terrified she'll kill herself,' he added.

Liana nodded again. 'That's a very normal fear,' she said. 'When you see behaviour like that, it's easy to become very worried and to assume the worst. But the psychosis might resolve just as suddenly it came on. So, please, don't give up hope.'

Antonio nodded, then returned to his chair.

Ophelia felt an urge so strong, it pushed her from her chair and, before she knew it, she was standing in the centre of the room. 'Hola, my name is Ophelia,' she said, sensing the group's curiosity. 'I'm not a surrogate,' she continued. 'But I've been to that place, the Garden of Eden they call it. I was with Nina throughout her entire ordeal in the Birthing Suite. I saw the vile state of that room and I saw how they treated her. I also saw the amount of money they transferred into her account and I can tell you, with absolute certainty, it was only ten percent of what a northern woman would have paid those people to manage the pregnancy.'

Ophelia felt the silence in the room fracture the air around her. It occurred to her that she might have said too much. She felt her cheeks burning with embarrassment, but she continued, nevertheless. 'Not only is the system brutal, but it is highly exploitative,' she said. 'They're running a scam at the expense of your families.'

No one spoke, but there were some angry rumblings around the room.

'I'm sorry,' said Ophelia. 'But I feel obliged to tell you the truth.'

Still, no one spoke, so Ophelia returned to her chair, amidst a cloud of dark stares from Antonio and those sitting on either side of him.

An elderly woman stood up. 'We're in an impossible situation,' she said, her gnarled hands shaking. 'We know the surrogacy trade is wrong, but we participate in it because we're desperate for the money it brings to the families. And the water! God Almighty, the water! We can't live without that! We have been on our knees for so long! What more can we do?' she asked, bringing her hands to her face.

'How is your daughter, now, Jeanne?' Liana asked.

'She's okay now, but my granddaughter is a mess,' Jeanne replied. 'She wants to kill herself.'

A man, about Ophelia's age, stepped towards the woman, wrapped his arm around her and brought her back to her chair. For a few moments, there was silence.

'I say we burn that place to the ground!' someone shouted.

A few more people started shouting – some for and some against – but all passionate. As far as Ophelia could tell, no one was winning, as she surveyed the number of people who were now standing, shouting and waving their fists in the air. And then she noticed Antonio. His eyes were fixed on the ground, staring intently, like a chess master contemplating his next move.

Liana seemed frustrated by the disruption in the room. 'Please!' she shouted, standing on her chair. The volume gradually reduced to a murmur. 'Before we allow our fear and our anger to get the better of us, we must acknowledge there is a lot of emotion to be processed before we can take action,' she said. 'Please, everyone, sit down.'

Slowly, everyone returned to their chairs. When the shuffling of feet and bodies subsided, there was silence once more. And in the silence, Ophelia questioned the wisdom of having shared so much information with the group. She knew she had done so from a place of respecting their right to know the truth. But she now realised she had probably achieved nothing more than add to the pain these people were already living with. She felt terrible.

'Please, everyone, close your eyes,' said Liana. 'I'm going to lead you through a relaxation exercise. As we have done before.'

Ophelia closed her eyes.

'Breathe in, deeply and slowly,' said Liana. 'Now exhale, slow and steady. Good. Feel the peace moving through your body, relaxing one muscle at a time, from your head down to your toes.'

Antonio exhaled, almost grunting.

Then Ophelia heard Liana's voice, almost as though an angel was speaking to her, 'Dear Lord, we ask you to please shine your light upon these people and their loved ones,' she said. 'We ask you, Mother Mary, to please look upon the surrogates and to bless them with your strength and wisdom.'

Ophelia visualised the energy in her throat swirling around, spiralling to her chest and shoulders, warming and softening them. Then it swirled around her heart and lungs, softening and opening them. she took in a long, deep and silent breath. Then let it go.

'Hail Mary, full of grace, the Lord is with thee,' Liana continued. 'Blessed art thou among women and blessed is the fruit of thy womb, Jesus.'

After the word *womb* Ophelia visualised the softening of her lower back and pelvis. She could see, in her mind's eye, the empty space where her womb had once been. It had wept with grief from the moment her womb and baby had been removed, but now it seemed to cradle a gentle fire, preparing her for action. The warmth travelled down her legs, softening and nourishing them, giving them power. And then it moved through her knees, calf muscles, ankles and feet, softening and strengthening them.

'Feel the love of Mother Mary's blessing,' said Liana. 'She is here with us, with every one of us, for we are *all* important, in the eyes of the Lord.'

The fire left Ophelia's body, through the soles of her feet, and travelled through the concrete floor. From there it fell, like ropes uncoiled, deep into the earth. These fiery ropes moved through the Earth's liquid outer core then wove a loose net around its steely inner core. Ophelia felt anchored to the centre of the earth, but able to move around it at will. Profoundly relaxed and confident, Ophelia felt a powerful sense of belonging.

'Thank you, Mother Mary,' she heard Liana say. 'We bask in your warmth and the light of your wisdom, and we are forever grateful. Amen.'

'Amen,' the group repeated.

Liana's voice slid through the silence, like honey down the throat. 'When you are ready, return your attention to your body,' she said. 'Your body, the perfect vessel for your soul, both given to you by the Lord, are at peace. Feel the Lord's light shining upon you, as you slowly open your eyes.'

Ophelia opened her eyes feeling revived and at peace. She smiled at Antonio and he returned the smile, looking as though he had just woken from a nap.

'Thank you, everyone,' said Liana. 'Let's meet here again next week.'

The circle broke, and people started to leave.

Ophelia stood up and stretched, feeling grateful to have had such an experience. 'Wow,' was all she could say. 'I needed that.'

'I did, too,' Antonio replied. 'Let's go home.'

Ophelia glanced at Liana, surprised to see the woman was already watching her. Strong and steady in her gaze, Liana seemed to be reading her. Ophelia offered a respectful nod and smile. Liana returned the gesture which made Ophelia feel certain she would see the woman again. Soon.

• • • •

IT WAS ALMOST 15:00 hours by the time Ophelia and Antonio returned to Nina's apartment. Doctor Sanchez was sitting on the couch with Mare and Pare, deep in discussion. The doctor's serious and compassionate face was every bit as reassuring to Ophelia as it had been the last few times they had met.

'Hola,' said Pare, standing up, greeting Antonio with a hug.

'How's Nina?' Ophelia asked, looking at the doctor.

'She's awake but calm,' the doctor replied. 'I think I've found the right antipsychotic medication for her.'

'What does that mean for Nina's long-term recovery?' Ophelia asked.

'It's still too early to tell,' the doctor replied. 'The drug might dissolve the psychosis over the next few weeks. Or it might not. Only time will tell.'

'How much of the medication can you supply us with?' Antonio asked.

'Enough for the next four weeks,' the doctor replied, nodding to the thin steel dispenser on the dining table. 'The most important thing, for now, is that Nina is lucid and relaxed. She can talk to you normally and she can help around the house. She can also go outside for brief walks to the promenade, but only if accompanied by one of you. Under *no* circumstances should she be left alone. Agreed?'

They all nodded.

Then the doctor looked at Ophelia. 'I'd like some more information from you about the Garden of Eden,' she said. 'Are you free for a chat, now, Ophelia?'

'Yes, of course, doctor.'

• • • •

DOCTOR SANCHEZ DROVE through El Serrallo and Tarragona city like a maniac.

'You must be in a terrible hurry,' Ophelia said, clinging to the dashboard.

'I always drive like this during siesta,' the doctor replied. 'There's something about the quiet roads and the lack of congestion that makes me enjoy the speed.'

'No doubt it's an outlet for the frustration you must feel from your job,' Ophelia offered.

'You're quite perceptive, Ophelia,' the doctor replied.

Ophelia stifled a gasp when she saw a small cat run across the road in front of the car. And her heart sank when the car drove over a bump. 'I think you ran over a cat,' she said.

'Hm?' the doctor replied. 'Oh, we don't worry about them.'

Ophelia felt a lump of grief tighten her throat.

The doctor swung the car into a parking space, applied the foot brake suddenly, then pulled aggressively on a stick next to the steering wheel.

'What's that?' Ophelia asked, pointing to the stick.

Doctor Sanchez seemed taken aback by the question then laughed. 'It's a handbrake,' she said. 'It stops the car from rolling backward or forward when we are away. I'm sure you have much better cars in Britain.'

Ophelia decided not to respond.

The doctor retrieved a large umbrella from the back seat then opened her door. 'Let's go.'

Ophelia followed Doctor Sanchez over the small rocks and sand, all the way onto the wet sand near the edge of the ocean. They removed their sandals and stood in the water. It was warm, but pleasantly so, like a spa, Ophelia decided, and the breeze from the ocean was lovely.

The doctor opened her huge yellow umbrella and held it over herself and Ophelia. 'I want you to tell me everything you remember,' she said.

• • • •

OPHELIA TOLD DOCTOR Sanchez about her own pregnancy, the termination, the abduction and her entry to the Garden of Eden. She described the beauty of the place and the kind and loving care the surrogates received throughout their pregnancy. Then she described the Birthing Suite and the doctor's face contorted, into a mix of sadness and disgust.

• • • •

'THAT'S AN INCREDIBLE story, Ophelia,' said Doctor Sanchez.

Ophelia watched the tide retreat from her wrinkled feet, leaving toe shapes in the wet sand. She stepped back and sat down on the drier sand. The doctor sat beside her.

'I wish I could tell you what drugs they gave Nina,' Ophelia said. 'I looked at the gas mask they put on her face during labour, but there were no words on it, so I have no idea what it was.'

The doctor nodded. 'Yes, that's the problem. We really don't know. But, if you can remember any details at all, it would be helpful,' she said.

Ophelia sighed. 'I remember they put a gas mask on Nina's face for a few seconds when she first arrived in the Birthing Suite,' Ophelia started. 'They said it would speed up her labour and they were right because she went into heavy labour almost immediately.'

Doctor Sanchez tisked and shook her head.

'Then, towards the end of Nina's labour, they put the same mask on her mask on her face and said it would relieve her pain,' Ophelia continued. 'And that worked too. Nina pushed hard but she seemed to be in less pain than she had been, just seconds earlier.'

The doctor nodded.

'And then, right at the end, after they had taken the baby away, they put a little tablet under Nina's tongue,' Ophelia said. 'It was to stop the bleeding, they said, but that was all they told me. There was no opportunity for me to ask any questions. And there was certainly no opportunity for Nina to ask anything. She was just ... shoved around like an object.'

Ophelia started to cry. Even the sensation of the doctor's hand on her back did little to ease her distress. Ophelia's fingers dug into the sand as she sobbed. She stared at the horizon line, trying to imagine herself far away from all the pain and cruelty.

'There was nothing you could have done, Ophelia,' said Doctor Sanchez.

'I was a coward!' Ophelia screamed into the wind. 'I should have demanded an explanation!'

'You would have been treated very badly, possibly brutalized, if you'd done so, Ophelia,' said the doctor. 'The people who run that operation are megalomaniacs. Of that I am certain.'

Ophelia sighed then wiped the tears from her face.

'You seem very attached to Nina,' said the doctor.

'Yes, I suppose so,' Ophelia replied. 'She's a lovely young woman. She should never have suffered such awful treatment.'

'Is it Nina's suffering that has made you feel so attached to her?' the doctor asked.

Ophelia felt the conversation had suddenly taken a turn into dark and unknown territory and she hesitated. But, underneath the umbrella, she somehow felt safe to answer. 'Perhaps so, doctor,' she replied. 'But I feel deeply concerned for all the surrogates. I want to do whatever I can to change the system. Especially when Nina is feeling better.'

'How so?' the doctor asked.

Ophelia suddenly remembered her original plan. 'When Nina has recovered, she and I will start speaking more publicly about our experiences,' she said. 'We want people to know what happened and we want to inspire others to share their stories, too, so we can create change.'

'Did Nina say she wants to do this?' Doctor Sanchez asked.

'Yes. Sort of,' Ophelia replied.

The doctor twirled the umbrella. 'Ophelia, there's something you need to understand,' she said. 'Even if Nina recovers completely from this psychosis, it's very unlikely she will ever become the warrior princess you seem to be imagining.'

'What do you mean by that?'

'A psychotic episode of this nature changes a person forever,' the doctor replied. 'Nina will never fully return to the woman she was before this psychotic episode. She will always need to take her life easy, slowly and without complication.'

Ophelia stared at the ocean. She understood the doctor's words. They seemed measured, fair and reasonable. But they also seemed resigned, as though the doctor was accepting the surrogacy trade for what it is. 'So. That's how it works, hey?' she said.

'What do you mean?' Doctor Sanchez asked.

Ophelia pondered for a moment then found the words to describe her intuitive sense of the situation. 'The Garden of Eden is causing the psychosis, knowing that the surrogates will spend the rest of their lives in silence, like broken toys,' she said. 'That's quite clever, isn't it?'

'Actually, Ophelia, it's *you* who is clever,' the doctor replied.

Ophelia looked at the doctor, wondering what she meant.

The doctor leaned closer, looking at Ophelia. 'You are highly intelligent and perceptive, Ophelia,' she said. 'You are also very outspoken and passionate about helping others. You are *exactly* what's needed to create a revolution. Paris is where you need to be, not here.'

The doctor's words evoked in Ophelia a powerful desire to be back in Paris, with Emilie and Philippe and their comrades. But her devotion to Nina was just as strong. 'I feel torn,' she said, almost in a whisper.

'I can see that,' the doctor said. 'But there's more to it, isn't there?'

'What do you mean?' Ophelia asked.

The doctor closed the umbrella and threw it on the sand beside her. Then she cleared her throat and looked directly at Ophelia. 'You witnessed Nina experience what would have felt like a violation, at a core level. As an empathic person, you naturally feel Nina's pain. But you have over-identified with Nina as a grieving mother because of the loss of your own baby. So, the thought of letting go of Nina makes you feel like you're letting go of your own baby. Am I right?'

Ophelia felt tempted to tell the doctor she was wrong. But as the doctor's words roamed through her being, she realised the woman was right. She suddenly visualised a pink circle and inside it another pink circle and inside that, another one, and she didn't want any of the pink circles to move. 'Gosh, I feel so embarrassed,' she said.

'Don't be embarrassed,' said the doctor. 'It's a normal reaction to the grief you have been feeling over the loss of your baby. You have not yet processed that loss, so you are looking for ways to fill the emptiness. Nina has fulfilled that purpose during the last few days but it's time for you to let go,' she said.

The doctor's words made sense to Ophelia. 'But I don't know *how* to let go,' she said.

'Strange as it might sound, Ophelia, you just ... do it.'

London

MARTIN WAS NOT SURE how long it had been since he had eaten. The water he had been given was barely enough to hydrate him, and yet he had removed his shirt to use it to mop the sweat from his face and neck. In the adjoining cell, his young friend appeared even more uncomfortable, a fact for which Martin wanted to apologise. Profusely. But the thick sheet of glass between the two cells made verbal communication impossible. It did, however, enable each of them to witness the other being beaten by the Sentinels.

Martin's chest and ribs were bruised and causing him pain. But at least his shoulder had not dislocated again – a small mercy he had managed to attain by refusing to lie on that side of his body. He had also denied himself the usual exercises for the joint, aware that the Sentinels would notice and exploit the weakness even further during their interrogations.

So far, he had managed to confuse them. Their iris scanners had failed to identify him, thanks to the protective lenses he was still wearing. This had raised questions as to how he had managed to 'break into the facility', an answer he was still refusing to provide. But he knew it was only a matter of time before they put the pieces together and figured it all out.

'So, what's the game plan, Martin Huxley?' he asked himself.

His head was cracking with pain. The poor-quality air, the dim lighting and the lack of food and water were eroding his capacity to focus. He knew the Sentinels would eventually offer him food and water in exchange for information. He promised himself – when that time came, he would tell them one ridiculous lie after another – anything but the truth because the truth would implicate Ophelia, and that was not an option.

MARTIN WAS IN A DEEP sleep when he was pulled from the bunk.

'Wake up, sleeping beauty. We have a surprise for you.'

Martin stared into the face of Sentinel. 'I can't believe I used to wear those ugly masks,' he said.

'Well, we have something even uglier to show you,' said a second Sentinel.

They pulled Martin to his feet, took hold of his shoulders and turned him around so he was facing Kingpin's cell. For what seemed an eternity, Martin stared, dumbly, unable to comprehend what he was seeing. In the centre of the cell, under the spotlight, his young friend was naked and bent forwards over the back a chair. His wrists were tied to the front legs of the chair and a Sentinel stood behind him.

Martin felt a wave of nausea rise to his throat. He could tell the Sentinel was saying something, perhaps asking questions, but the only response from the young lad seemed to be a pained grimace and then a scream. The Sentinel spoke again, and the young man's response was an even more painful outpouring of emotion. Then the Sentinel pressed his thumbs into his disc and the technician's body jolted violently.

'You bastards!' Martin croaked. 'You'll never get away this.'

One of the Sentinels took hold of Martin's shoulders and led him to a chair under a spotlight in the centre of his own cell. 'Please sit down, Mr. Huxley,' he said.

The sound of his own name sent a shock through Martin's body.

'Yes, we know who you are,' said the Sentinel. 'It took some time to interpret your bio-readings from the camera feed in the Anatomy Lab, and we've taken a saliva sample from you since you've been in here,' he said. 'What we don't understand is the fact that our iris scanners can't identify you.'

Martin remembered, with some pride, that his lenses had continued to work as a shield from the scanners. He hoped they had recorded the hideous torture he had just witnessed.

'If we were to remove your eyes and study them,' said the smaller Sentinel. 'We might understand how you have managed to evade the iris scanners.'

The larger Sentinel looked at the smaller one. 'We could do that,' he said. 'But I suspect Mr. Huxley might respond to the testicular electrocution that his friend seems to be enjoying so much.'

Martin hung his head, feeling utter despair. 'I can't believe that even you people would descend to such barbarism,' he said. 'You know that the Official Secrets Act – which we all signed – prohibits torture.'

The smaller Sentinel laughed. 'You mean to say, the Official Secrets Act that *you* signed,' he said. 'We operate under a different code.'

'Whatever,' Martin replied. 'You'll never get away with this.'

The smaller Sentinel stepped closer to Martin. So close, his pelvis almost brushed Martin's face. He unzipped his suit.

'Not a chance, mate,' said Martin. 'You'll have to kill me first.'

'We probably *will* kill you,' said the larger Sentinel.

Martin just needed to see Ophelia one last time.

'But first, we'd like some information from you,' the Sentinel continued. 'In exchange for ... um ... let me see ... what might you like?' he said, guzzling water from a bottle. 'Mm, very refreshing.'

Martin wanted that bottle of water. His mouth was so dry, he would not have been surprised if his face were to cave in. He felt dizzy and weak.

'There's nothing as good as a bottle of cold, fresh, water, is there, Mr. Huxley?' said the taller Sentinel. 'I mean, as a bioengineer, you know what happens to the human body when it's deprived of water. Don't you?'

Martin knew, all right.

The smaller Sentinel leaned in close to Martin's face, as though he was examining a rare insect. 'Have you ever seen a dehydrated person, just before the moment of death?' he asked.

Martin had not, but he could easily imagine.

'First, you get a very bad headache, and joint pain,' he said. 'But you already know that, don't you?'

Martin nodded, almost in tears of desperation.

'So, if you don't get some water soon, Mr. Huxley, your kidneys will shut down. The next phase of dehydration will be a thickening of your blood, causing your organs to become starved of oxygen. How do you suppose that might feel?'

Martin was starting to feel as though it was already happening. 'I already know this!' he snapped. 'Just tell me what information you need, and I'll tell you what I know.'

The Sentinel stepped back. 'Well, that was a bit too easy. I was looking forward to frying your balls,' he said, squirting water onto the floor.

The taller Sentinel pushed his colleague aside. 'We're running out of time,' he said. 'Mr. Huxley, just tell us what you were up to in the maintenance hub.'

Martin thought quickly. 'I can honestly say that we were up to nothing,' he said. 'When it comes to cyber engineering, I am absolutely clueless, so it was just dumb curiosity on my part.'

'Ah, but your fat friend is a cyber engineer, isn't he?'

'Yes, I suppose so,' Martin replied. 'But he's very young and doesn't know much.'

'I wouldn't say that,' the taller Sentinel said. 'After all, he managed to hack through Gaia's outer layer of coding. There's an art to that. Wouldn't you say so?'

Martin sighed. 'I'm sure you're right,' he replied. 'But I suggest it was just dumb luck, more commonly known as beginner's luck.'

'We disagree,' said the smaller Sentinel. 'Which is why we've had so much fun with him. Sadly, though, the fun is over now.'

Martin looked at Kingpin's cell. The poor lad was lying on the floor, naked and sobbing. But at least he was untied, and his torturer seemed to have left.

'What did the little pig show you in the maintenance hub?' the taller Sentinel asked.

'Please don't call him that,' said Martin.

The Sentinel delivered a shocking blow to the side of Martin's face. 'I'll call him whatever I like,' he said.

Martin's head rang with strange sounds. Long, low sounds. The cell moved around him. The spotlight above swirled around the cell. And he was certain that the chair he was sitting on had started to move. Then his senses shut down. He was somewhere else entirely, a place he had never been before, a place that had no beginning and no end, an empty place with no explanation. Nothing made sense. It was the absence of absence.

'Answer me!' the Sentinel said.

Martin felt a rough hand shaking his shoulder. The bad one. He wanted to scream, but his mouth did not open. It couldn't open. The lack of moisture had fused it shut, he mused.

'Give him some water,' one of them said.

A glorious splash of water hit Martin's face and he gasped with relief. His tongue was finally able to move, outside of his mouth and across his lips, to absorb a few droplets of the precious liquid.

'I will now repeat my question,' said the taller Sentinel. 'What did the little pig show you in the maintenance hub?'

'He showed me nothing,' Martin replied.

The Sentinel raised his arm, ready to hit Martin again.

Martin responded faster, this time. 'We simply entered the hub and saw a ball of bright white light in the middle of the room. At first, I thought it might have been a radiation leak, so I told the lad we should leave. We turned around to do so, then the alarm went off. The door slammed shut, then you arrived. That's it.'

The Sentinels looked at each other again.

Even in his dazed state of mind, Martin felt pleased with the brilliance of the lie he had just told.

The larger Sentinel stepped back. 'Did you say the ball of light was already in there when you entered?' he asked.

'Yeah, that's what I said,' Martin replied.

The Sentinel's looked at each other.

'It looks like we've got another problem,' said the larger one. 'Let's get out of here.'

As the Sentinels rushed towards the exit, Martin groaned, his eyes fixed on the bottle of water. By some miracle, the smaller one returned to Martin, lifted the bottle above his face and squeezed. With no pride whatsoever, Martin opened his mouth and drank.

Tarragona

FROM HER POSITION ON the lounge, Ophelia could smell the sea air blowing in the window and mingling with the scent of basil and tomato cooking. She could hear Mare chatting to someone in the kitchen. To whom, she did not know, and she was too sleepy to care. Her mind was on Martin, his lovely blue eyes and the sensation of his lips upon hers. It had been a few days since she had seen him, but it felt like so much longer.

She stretched and yawned.

'Hola, Ophelia.'

Ophelia opened her eyes to see Liana standing beside the lounge. The woman was even more formidable than Ophelia had remembered, and a surge of panic shot through her chest.

'I'm so sorry, Ophelia' said Liana. 'I didn't mean to startle you.'

'It's okay, I'm awake,' Ophelia replied, sitting up. 'Almost.' She ran her hand over the stubble on her scalp, an early morning habit she had formed since Martin had shaved it clean. 'Nice to see you, Liana,' she said, standing up. 'How are you?'

'I'm well, thank you,' Liana replied, trying, it seemed, to avoid looking at Ophelia's bald head. 'Are you available for a chat?'

'Sure.'

Liana smiled eagerly.

'What, now?' Ophelia asked.

Liana nodded.

'Can I have a coffee first?' Ophelia asked.

'I'm taking you out for coffee,' Liana replied.

• • • •

OPHELIA WAS STILL STRAIGHTENING her clothes when she and Liana entered the shady lane. 'Oh, how I appreciate this shade every time I walk along here,' she said.

Liana laughed.

'By the way, thank you for the meeting yesterday,' Ophelia said. 'I especially loved that meditation. It took me on a very nice trip.'

'You're welcome,' Liana replied. 'I feel lucky to have met you.'

'Really?' Ophelia asked. 'I was a bit worried that I might have said too much, too soon, out of context, inappropriately and so on. All of those things seem to be my specialty,' she added, feeling nervous in Liana's presence.

'Shall we?' said Liana, pointing to a round table and two chairs.

Ophelia sat down, facing the ocean. 'I love your cream pants,' she said. 'I'd never be able to keep such clothes clean.' Her eyes roamed up Liana's body to the heavy gold necklace the woman was sporting. 'Next to you, I feel quite drab,' she added.

'No!' said Liana. 'Ophelia stop that. Please. I was incredibly impressed by the things you said yesterday and your efforts in caring for Nina. I know her family very well.'

'So, do you live here in El Serrallo?' Ophelia asked.

'I did, many years ago,' Liana replied. 'But now I live on a property north of Tarragona.'

A waiter approached the table.

'Hola,' said Liana. 'Could we please have two glasses of orange juice, some croissants and a jug of iced coffee?'

The waiter nodded then left.

'Goodness, this is quite a luxurious feast,' said Ophelia. 'What's the occasion?'

Liana straightened her sunglasses. 'I want to speak with you about the things you said in the meeting yesterday,' she said. 'Is that okay, Ophelia?'

'Yes, of course.'

'I find it incredible that you were in the Garden of Eden,' Liana said. 'As a witness, I mean, and I confess, I am curious to hear more of your story.'

The waiter brought the drinks to the table.

Ophelia watched Liana pour two glasses of iced coffee, all the while getting a stronger sense of safety with the woman. Given Liana's commitment to supporting the families of surrogates, Ophelia, mused, it would surely be safe for her to share her story.

Another waiter arrived with the croissants and fruit.

'Gosh, this is just what I needed,' said Ophelia, sinking her teeth into a croissant. She washed it down with a gulp of iced coffee. 'Lovely!'

'Indeed,' said Liana.

Ophelia felt curious. 'Liana, I'm not sure why you want to know more about my horrible underground story,' she said.

'My daughter was in that place,' Liana replied, her throat visibly tightening. 'It was almost eighteen years ago, I know, but the place seems to be getting worse all the time.'

'How do you know that?' Ophelia asked.

'The prevalence of postpartum psychosis among the surrogates is increasing every year,' Liana replied. 'Those who do recover enough to stop taking the antipsychotic medication remain clinically depressed and unresponsive for the rest of their lives.'

'Doctor Sanchez said something like that to me yesterday.' Ophelia said.

'Is that who's been treating Nina?' Liana asked.

'Yes. Why?'

'She's a fine psychiatrist,' Liana replied. 'In fact, she has the highest rate of success in helping the surrogates recover from their psychoses,' Liana replied. 'But, unfortunately, in this country, a doctor's success is almost entirely attributed to their access to the best medications.'

'What's wrong with that?' Ophelia asked.

Liana poured two more glasses of iced coffee.

'Medication is almost impossible for doctors to get unless they accept bribes from the local police,' she said. 'That's just how things work around here.'

'Antonio said something like that yesterday,' said Ophelia.

'He's right,' Liana said. 'If I were you ...'

'Oh, my God,' said Ophelia, dropping her head into her hands. 'Antonio said that Doctor Sanchez would probably be receiving the medication in exchange for information about people.'

'That's usually the way it works,' Liana replied.

'Doctor Sanchez has met me and she's aware I've been here for a few days,' Ophelia said. 'She might mention my presence to the police.'

'I'm sure she would,' Liana replied. 'But that's no problem if you're here with a proper travel permit.'

Ophelia felt her gut churn as she reflected on the forty-eight hour permit she had been given when she had entered Paris. Four days ago. Doctor Dubois' subsequent removal of the permit had, of course, given her some freedom. But still, Ophelia knew, she was skating on thin ice.

'Ophelia, you *do* have a proper travel permit for the southern region, don't you?' Liana asked.

Ophelia did not reply, uncertain how to answer the question. She had not told anyone in Spain about her fugitive status. She was embarrassed by it, and frightened, and she did not want to place anyone else at risk by telling them.

'Ophelia, you're safe with me,' said Liana. 'You can tell me the truth. Are you in trouble?'

Slowly ripping her croissant to shreds, but no longer able to eat it, Ophelia was aware of feeling increasingly nervous. 'I don't want anyone else to suffer,' she said. 'Not because of me.'

'Ophelia, you haven't answered my question,' Liana said. 'But I'm getting the sense you might be in a difficult situation. You don't have to say anything. Just nod – or shake your head – do you have a proper travel permit?'

Ophelia shook her head.

'Then it's not safe for you to stay here,' Liana said, pulling her handbag onto her knee.

She removed a wad of cash and held it up in the air. A waiter stepped forwards and received it with a slight bow.

'Please, Ophelia, get up,' Liana said. 'We have to go.'

'Where are we going?' Ophelia asked.

'Back to Nina's apartment for you to collect your things,' she replied.

• • • •

WHEN MARE OPENED THE door, Ophelia realise she did not know what to say. Or how to say it.

But, somehow, Mare was ready for it. 'It's okay, Ophelia,' she said, 'Come in.'

Pare and Antonio stood up, greeting Ophelia as she entered the lounge room.

Ophelia cleared her throat. 'You probably know that I need to leave,' she said.

They nodded.

Ophelia felt she might cry. 'Before I go, though' she said. 'I need to tell you all how grateful I am for everything you have done for me.' Her voice started to tremble. 'Until I met you, I never knew what it felt like to be part of a loving family. But now I do.'

Antonio hugged Ophelia. 'I know what you mean,' he said. 'Mare and Pare treat me as their own child. They have saved my soul.'

Pare clasped Antonio's shoulder and squeezed it.

Then he took hold of Ophelia's hands. 'And we're grateful to you, Ophelia, for bringing our little girl back home,' he said.

Ophelia placed her hand on her chest, determined not to cry. 'May I please have a few minutes alone with Nina?' she asked.

'Yes, of course,' said Mare. 'Go through to her room.'

Nina was stretched across her bed, listening to Tchaikovsky's *Swan Lake*. 'This is my favourite bit,' she said. 'The dance of the Sugar Plum Fairies. You can see them when you close your eyes. Go on, Ophelia, close your eyes.'

Ophelia lay down beside Nina and looked at her eyes – closed but moving, ever so slightly – and the gentle smile on her mouth.

When the piece was over, Nina opened her eyes again. 'I know you have to leave, Ophelia,' she said. 'And it's okay because you're going to make things better for all of us.'

'Am I?' Ophelia sniggered. 'How am I going to do that, do you think?'

Nina rolled her eyes, as though Ophelia had asked a stupid question. 'Well, I don't know *exactly* how, but I have seen enough of you, and I have heard enough, to know that you have fire in your belly. You're going to change the world, Ophelia.'

'Gosh, I don't know about that.'

Nina turned her head and looked directly into Ophelia's eyes. 'We don't know each other very well,' she said. 'But our souls recognised each other the instant we met. I knew that when I placed my foot on your knee and asked you to paint my toenails.'

Ophelia laughed. 'Promise me something, Nina,' she said.

'What?'

'Promise me that you will recover, marry Antonio and make babies with him,' said Ophelia.

'I promise,' Nina replied with a giggle. 'He's wonderful, isn't he?'

'Yes! Which makes me wonder why you never mentioned him!'

Nina looked sad. 'I love Antonio so much, I felt ashamed to be bearing someone else's child before his,' she said. 'Being a surrogate felt like a lie, a violation, and yet I *had* to do it. For the money and for the water. I feel as though my soul has been ripped in two, and I doubt that God will ever forgive me for allowing that to happen.'

'But God created the world in which you live,' Ophelia replied. 'Therefore, he would not punish you for making a choice that he placed in front of you, especially when the choice you made was out of love for your family.'

Nina's eyes flickered with recognition and then they turned red. 'What, then, is the purpose of all this pain?' she asked.

Ophelia rolled onto her back and stared at the ceiling. 'I think it's true what the ancient spiritualists used to say,' she replied. 'Painful experiences make us grow in ways we never imagined. And sometimes the new growth is painful because it stretches old wounds.'

'That's quite profound,' Nina replied, blinking away the last of her tears.

Ophelia wondered where her words had come from and whether she truly believed them. The only thing she knew for sure was that her beliefs were changing every day. 'You mustn't be too hard on yourself, Nina,' she said. 'You have so much to look forward to.'

Nina's face softened even more. 'Goodbye, Ophelia,' she said.

'Goodbye, Nina,' Ophelia replied, kissing her friend on the forehead.

Ophelia walked towards the door.

'Ophelia.'

'Yes?'

'Take those evil bastards down!' Nina said with a surge of venom that surprised Ophelia. 'Do something – I don't care what – to ensure that every person on this planet knows exactly what they're doing to people!'

Ophelia nodded.

'Promise me!' Nina said, holding up her forefinger.

'I promise.'

In transit

OPHELIA WAS STILL THINKING about Nina when she got into Liana's car. It wasn't until they left Tarragona and entered the open road, with mountains on either side, that she started to relax.

Liana also breathed a sigh of relief. 'Ophelia,' she said. 'I should probably share with you. I'm part of a small group of people in Tarragona who are connected to a larger network of people just like us.'

'People like us?' Ophelia asked. 'What does that mean?'

'People who want to put an end to the awful surrogacy trade.'

Ophelia felt hopeful. 'Where are those people?' she asked.

'Scattered throughout Spain, Portugal, France and Greece,' Liana replied. 'But the entire group is coordinated by a couple in Paris.'

Ophelia felt a warm glow spread through her chest. 'Really?' she said. 'Who?'

'A charming couple called Emilie and Philippe Trudeau.'

The warm glow spread from Ophelia's chest to the rest of her body. 'I know them,' she replied. 'Nina and I stayed with them for a couple of days before travelling down to Tarragona.'

'Oh, how wonderful!' Liana said. 'I've never met them, but I've seen recordings of some of the meetings they've held, and I found them incredibly inspiring.'

'When did you last see a recording?' Ophelia asked.

'About two weeks ago,' Liana replied.

'So, what are your plans, now, Liana?' Ophelia asked.

Liana fidgeted with the read-view mirror in her car. 'Well, to be honest,' she said. 'We've been feeling a bit concerned about the lack of communication lately, so we've decided to travel up to Paris to see if we can connect with Emilie and Philippe, in person, and offer our help.'

'Who do you mean by 'we'?' Ophelia asked.

'Sorry, I should have explained,' Liana said. 'There are about thirty people at my place right now. We're going to have dinner together, then we're going to travel up to Paris tomorrow morning.'

The coincidence was just a bit too unlikely for Ophelia. 'Would those plans have anything to do with your insistence that I should leave Tarragona?' she asked.

Liana sighed. 'Yes and no,' she said. 'I mean, I really do want you to join us on the journey to Paris. And, to be perfectly frank, I would also be worried about leaving you in Tarragona. The Spanish Police are brutal, Ophelia. They would enjoy any opportunity to interrogate a person for any reason at all.'

'I guess it's worked out for the best then,' Ophelia said, staring out of the window at the mountains. Somehow, something felt wrong, and she felt it in every fibre of her being.

'We're entering Montblanc, now,' said Liana.

Looking down, Ophelia saw nothing but brown dirt and grey sticks – the remnants of a forest. 'Gosh, it's so dry down there,' she said, squinting in the sunlight.

Ophelia looked out of the other window. 'Rojals,' she said, reading a road sign.

Liana slowed down as they travelled through the village. 'It's just another ten minutes to my place,' she said.

Ophelia found the entire experience of being driven in an old-fashioned car, with a steering wheel and a gear stick, quite strange. And slightly nerve-wracking. But, she had to confess, Liana seemed to be a safe driver. Ophelia gazed at rustic sandstone, or greystone, building after another. 'It's truly beautiful,' she said.

'Wait until you see my place,' Liana replied, ascending another mountain.

• • • •

AT PEAK ELEVATION, Liana turned off the main road and descended a narrow dirt track. Straight ahead, Ophelia could see a beautiful house on a vast property. Liana parked in a circular driveway amongst several other cars.

'Mm, six other cars,' said Ophelia.

'Yes, indeed. It seems our guests decided to come early,' Liana replied, lifting the handbrake.

'I'm not surprised,' Ophelia said. 'It's a lovely place. Is it an old barn?'

'It was, about three hundred years ago,' Liana replied. 'But it's the main house now.'

• • • •

WHEN OPHELIA STEPPED into Liana's home, she found herself standing in a huge open space, perhaps twenty times the size of Nina's apartment. There were no walls separating the kitchen, dining area and lounge area. It was just one big, beautiful, uncluttered space. The opposing wall was all glass from floor to ceiling through which Ophelia could see lush green crops. 'Is that a vineyard?' she asked.

'Yes,' Liana replied. 'We're producing some good grapes, too.'

A bot, about Ophelia's height, rolled toward them. It was holding a tray which carried two glasses of water.

'Ophelia, this is our w8r,' Liana said.

'Please to meet you, Ophelia,' it said, handing her a glass of cold water.

'Thanks,' said Ophelia, sipping the water, still staring out of the window. 'How do you get the water to irrigate the vines?'

'We have a special licence to receive desalinated water from the ocean,' Liana replied, smiling.

'Incredible,' said Ophelia.

'And expensive!' Liana said. 'Let me show you to your room.'

Ophelia followed Liana down a white hallway with exposed beams the colour of over-ripe plums. A long strip of glass in the ceiling allowed the sunlight to shine upon the paintings that adorned the walls. Ophelia stopped to touch one.

'Ah! No, Ophelia!' she said. 'It's probably still wet!'

'Sorry. I was just checking to see if it was real,' Ophelia said, feeling her face flush.

'Oh, yes, it's real,' Liana replied. 'My husband Diego is an oil painter.'

'How wonderful,' Ophelia replied. 'Hardly anyone creates art.'

Walking behind Liana, Ophelia could see the woman was fabulously fit and elegant. And rich. But how that could be, when she had permitted her own daughter to be surrogate, Ophelia could not determine.

When Ophelia followed Liana into the bedroom, she felt she might weep with relief. 'Oh, wow, this is beautiful,' she said.

The windows in the walls and ceilings let the sunlight in, but not the heat. 'I can't believe how cool it is in here,' she said.

'It's our plumbing system,' Liana responded. 'There's a deep space inside the walls which is filled with ice.'

'Really?'

'Well, desalinated water, to be more precise, and electric coils running through it,' Liana replied. 'It works on the same principle as those old-fashion refrigerators that people once used to keep their food cold.'

'Oh yes, my grandmother had one of those,' Ophelia replied.

She dropped her bag on the floor beside the king-size bed then wandered into the en suite. All granite, from floor to ceiling, but with opaque windows, it was fitted with a large sonic shower that was so clean it sparkled. On the wall, where she expected the mirror to be, Ophelia saw a visual recording of orchids opening under droplets of water amidst a tropical rainforest.

'Oh, my goodness,' she whispered. 'How lovely.'

'And when you tap the screen, you get this,' Liana said.

The beautiful recording vanished and a mirror appeared in its place.

'That's far less lovely,' Ophelia said, noticing her wig and clothes were filthy.

'If you wish to launder your clothes,' Liana said. 'Just drop them on the floor of the shower and close the screen. That's all that's required.'

'Ooh,' said Ophelia. 'I look forward to trying that.'

Liana gave her a weary smile. 'You look very tried, Ophelia,' she said. 'Why don't you stay here and rest for a while? If you wish, you can join us for pre-dinner drinks in the lounge room at 17:00 hours.'

Ophelia felt a surge of relief expand throughout her body. 'Thank you, Liana,' she said. 'That sounds glorious.'

The instant Liana felt the room, Ophelia dropped every stitch of her clothing into the shower recess, closed the door and waited. A second later, the familiar hum of the sonic shower started. And through the opaque screen, she could see her clothes leaping around inside the recess.

The cool granite soothed the soles of her feet as she pattered back into the bedroom. She unzipped her bag and unpacked her few possessions. Then she spread the emerald green dress across her bed, pressed it flat with her hands and lay down.

• • • •

OPHELIA ENTERED THE dining area at precisely 17:00 hours. The mahogany dining table, large enough to seat twenty people, was highly polished and covered with about thirty bottles of wine. The w8r stood at the head of the table, ready to serve.

'Good evening, Ophelia,' it said. 'May I serve you a glass of wine?'

'Yes, please,' Ophelia replied, looking at the list on the table. 'May I have a glass of the 2110 Tempranillo?'

'That is a fine choice,' said the w8r.

While the w8r poured the wine, Ophelia gazed out of the window, enjoying the expansive view and feeling somewhat jealous of Liana's lifestyle. Wealth was not something Ophelia had ever aspired to, or even thought about, but this lovely home and property was something she wanted. Badly. Martin would love this, she mused. If this were their home, she fantasised, she would make love to him in every room. A thousand times over.

She leaned against the window and stared at the neat rows of bright green vines stretching all the way to the horizon. The colour green, she knew, was like medicine for her eyes. Eyes which were still protected by the lenses Philippe had given her. She could hardly wait to see Philippe and Emilie again. She desperately wanted to share with them the time she had spent in Tarragona.

She saw a silver drone, about the size of her head, flying low and slow over the vineyard. It watered one vine, and then the next, every bit as precisely and uniformly as the vines' growth along the trellises. It was hypnotic to watch.

'May I refresh your wine, Ophelia?' the w8r asked.

'Indeed, thank you,' Ophelia replied.

She tilted her glass toward the w8r and watched it pour more wine, her mouth-watering at the sight of the green-gold liquid filling her glass.

'Hola,' she heard a voice beside her.

She turned around to see a portly man with jet black hair, eyebrows, lashes and a neatly trimmed goatee. He wore black pants, black shoes, a crisp red shirt and the most outrageous dinner jacket Ophelia had ever seen. It was purple and bright red with gold brocade.

'I'm Diego,' he said, extending his hand.

'Oh, how lovely to meet you! I'm Ophelia,' she replied, shaking his hand. 'It's an honour to meet a real painter, I must say! I was enthralled by your paintings in the hallway.'

Diego smiled. 'Thank you,' he said, smoothing his moustache with his forefinger. 'It's a passion and an obsession, something I must do every day.'

'I know exactly what you mean,' Ophelia said. 'I feel the say way about reading ancient literature.'

'Ah yes, I have heard you are one of the world's top experts on Shakespeare,' he said, swilling a glass of red wine.

'Really?' Ophelia replied. 'I never imagined that part of my life would have preceded me all the way to Spain.'

'We know a bit about you, Ophelia,' he replied, winking.

Ophelia felt slightly unnerved by Diego's words, but not enough to retreat. 'What else do you know about me?' she asked.

Diego shook his head and smiled. 'Honestly, Ophelia, I only knew what Liana told me last night after you attended her support group meeting. She was highly impressed by you,' he said. 'And this afternoon while you were sleeping, we received a message from Philippe. He confirmed that he knows you and he promised to transmit to us a holo-recording of you speaking at one of his meetings.'

'Did Philippe say anything else?' Ophelia asked.

Diego seemed to reflect for a moment. 'Just that he and Emilie are glad you found us,' he replied. 'And they're looking forward to seeing all of us in Paris tomorrow.'

'Did he say anything else?' Ophelia asked, hoping to hear about Martin.

Diego looked blank. 'No, I don't think so,' he said. Then he took Ophelia's hand and kissed it. 'Please, excuse me, Ophelia. I must mingle.'

Ophelia watched Diego's luxurious dinner jacket trail along the floor behind him as he approached a group of men who were dressed just as flamboyantly. She scanned the room for familiar faces but there were none. But she caught the gaze of a man and woman standing in a corner. They seemed shy, or nervous, she wasn't sure which. Both were dressed in dowdy clothes. Their hair was combed flat against their heads and their eyes were sunk deep, but they smiled and nodded.

Ophelia approached. 'Good evening,' she said, extending her hand. 'I'm Ophelia.'

'Hola, Ophelia, we saw you at the meeting yesterday,' said the woman. 'I'm Marika, and this is my husband Alejandro.'

'It's lovely to meet you,' Ophelia said. 'And in such beautiful surroundings.'

'Yes, it's quite incredible here,' Alejandro said with raised eyebrows.

'Have you been going to the support group meetings for long?' Ophelia asked.

'Just two months,' Marika replied. 'Since our daughter died.'

Ophelia felt her heart sink. 'I'm truly sorry for your loss,' she said. 'I hope you're finding some comfort from the meetings.'

Marika and Alejandro nodded, then stared into their wine glasses.

'Are you travelling up to Paris tomorrow morning?' Ophelia asked.

'Yes, we want to help as much as we can,' Alejandro replied.

'That's wonderful,' Ophelia said. 'We'll need a mighty force, and a clever plan, to infiltrate that place. Having said that, I don't know what the plan is. Do you?'

They shook their heads.

Ophelia realised she could not think of a single thing to say to this couple. Their pain was so intense, it seemed to occupy the space around them, so she was relieved when another couple joined them.

'I'm Zeska,' said the woman, offering her hand.

As she shook Zeska's hand, Ophelia felt disorientated and fearful. And yet, the woman was perfectly charming. It occurred to Ophelia that she had probably drunk too much wine and it might be time to stop.

'And this is my husband Sebastian,' said Zeska.

'It's wonderful to meet you both,' Ophelia replied, placing her empty wine glass on the w8r's serving tray as it rolled past.

'We enjoyed listening to you speak at the meeting yesterday,' said Sebastian.

'I was quite concerned that I might have said too much, too soon,' Ophelia said.

'It was a bit shocking,' Zeska replied, looking at Ophelia from under her thick dark eyebrows. 'But it was important information. You've done a lot, already, to help mobilise us into action.'

Ophelia felt her face flush. 'I'm curious,' she said. 'Do you know what we'll be doing when we reach Paris?'

Zeska shrugged their shoulders. 'I'm sure we'll receive some instructions from the people in Paris,' she said.

There was a confidence in Zeska's tone that Ophelia admired, and felt rattled by, in equal measure. She wanted to ask more questions, but what, she could not yet decide.

Sebastian broke the ice. 'We're keen to help however we can,' he said. 'We want this surrogacy trade to end as soon as possible. It's causing too much harm to too many people. Our own daughter has been through hell since she returned.'

'And she's taken us with her,' Zeska added, rolling her eyes.

'Good evening, friends!' Liana called out.

Ophelia turned and saw Liana standing in the hallway, with her hands on her hips, waiting for everyone to notice her. And they did. She looked stunning. Her hair was swept up in a formal coiffure. Her make-up was heavy and dramatic. Her dress was long and flowing. And she wore several gold bracelets and rings and a diamond necklace.

'I didn't know this was a red-carpet event,' someone called out.

'We're celebrating our success in advance!' Diego shouted, applauding.

Several people joined in Diego's applause.

Liana dipped her head and smiled. 'Friends, we are thrilled to welcome you to our home,' she said. 'But most of all, we are humbled and inspired by your commitment to joining us in our journey to Paris tomorrow morning. We have no idea what to expect. We only know that we will be welcomed by Emilie and Philippe and their crowd of equally-committed friends.'

There was more applause.

Liana raised her hands, palms facing the crowd and laughed. 'So, please, enjoy the food and the wine,' she said. 'But not too much wine, as we have a long drive ahead of us and, no doubt, a lot of work to do when we get there.'

Liana signalled to the w8r with a flick of her hand and it rolled through the crowd, offering morsels of food. The frivolity resumed.

'Hola,' someone whispered in Ophelia's ear.

Ophelia turned toward the voice. The man had an earthy appeal that reminded her of Martin. She felt instantly drawn to him and felt her face flush.

'I'm Niccolò,' he said, offering his hand.

'I'm Ophelia,' she replied, shaking his hand.

'I know who you are,' he said, smiling warmly. 'I saw you at the meeting yesterday. I was there with my mother, the woman who had trouble standing up when she spoke.'

'Oh yes, I remember you,' Ophelia replied. 'You stood close to her, and then helped her back to her chair. I was very touched by that.'

Niccolò blushed, which made Ophelia like him even more.

'May we speak privately?' he asked.

'Yes, of course.'

They retreated to a corner and Niccolò leaned in close to her. 'Liana has many fine qualities,' he said. 'I've known her for a long time.'

Ophelia nodded, then smiled at Niccolò, which made him blush again. 'I believe you,' she said, aware she was staring far too deeply into his eyes. 'I am curious about one thing.'

'What's that?' Niccolò asked, raising an eyebrow.

'Why on earth would Liana allow her daughter to be a surrogate when she already has so much money?' Ophelia asked.

Niccolò smiled awkwardly for a moment. 'Ah, I see your point,' he replied. 'But that was eighteen years ago. Liana's life was very different then. She lived in a tiny apartment in El Serrallo.'

'Aha,' Ophelia replied, now aware of leaning in too close to Niccolò.

'The most important thing for you to know,' he said. 'Is that Liana and Diego are good people. You're in very safe hands travelling with them.'

'Will you also be travelling with us?' Ophelia asked.

'I would like to, but I can't,' he replied. 'I'm the sole carer for my children.'

Ophelia's eyes explored Niccolò's face, seeing a kind and honest man and she felt even more drawn to him than she had a moment before.

Niccolò leaned in even closer to her. 'There's something I wanted to say to you,' he said.

'Yes?'

'Please be careful of Zeska,' he whispered. 'She is not what she seems.'

Niccolò's words resonated with Ophelia. 'I did pick up an awkward vibe from her,' Ophelia said.

'I know, I was watching you,' Niccolò replied. 'That's why I'm telling you this.'

'Oh.'

'I want this mission to be a success,' Niccolò said. 'But I'm uncertain of Zeska's role in it.'

Ophelia's eyes roamed every part of Niccolò's face. She felt an intense moment of déjà vu; certain she had experienced this moment with him before. It was odd. She felt herself preparing to say something to him, but the words did not escape her mouth.

Suddenly, she felt as though she was looking at Niccolò through a thick glass wall that neither one of them could penetrate. She heard a high-pitched whine pierce the air then she saw Niccolò fall to the floor, blood gushing from his throat. People were screaming, and running, but she felt frozen, staring at the pool of blood around Niccolò's head.

'Curtains!' Liana shrieked. 'Ophelia, get back!'

Someone pushed Ophelia against the wall, and she fell, almost on top of Niccolò.

'It's the spiders!' someone shouted.

Ophelia looked out of the window, just in time to see three bots, shaped like gigantic spiders, running toward the house. Their bodies, made of round black armour, glistened under the sun. And their legs, higher than the trellises, ambled over the vines without effort or resistance. Ophelia tried to run, but her body would not move. She tried to scream, but the sound was trapped inside her. She tried to look away, but her eyes remained glued to the scene outside.

The bots fired again, this time smashing a vase and tearing a hole through one of Diego's fabulous paintings. Ophelia heard more screaming. The bots fired a third time, but the steel curtains had now descended, covering every window and door in the house.

'Lights!' Diego shouted.

A ring of algae lamps started to glow, offering just enough light for Ophelia to see everyone slowly emerging from their hiding places. Another round of laser fire hammered the steel curtains, this time tearing a small hole in them. A thin, but bright, beam of sunlight burst into the living room.

'They'll soon be in!' Diego called out. 'Everyone into the hallway!'

Ophelia watched everyone run from the lounge room. She wanted to run, too, but she could not move. She placed her hand on Niccolò's shoulder and shook, as though expecting him to wake up.

'All accounted for, but two,' she heard the w8r say.

'Who's missing?' Diego called out.

Ophelia wanted to alert Diego to her position, but she could not call out. She shook Niccolò's shoulder again, but he was solid. Unmoving. Another laser ripped through the steel curtain, enlarging the hole that was already there. Ophelia heard an ornament smash, then she heard the spiders' legs clattering against the curtain. She somehow managed to get back onto her feet.

'Rescue Ophelia!' Diego shouted.

The w8r rolled over to Ophelia, its large round eyes focused upon her. She reached out toward it, feeling the need to hang on to it. But before she had the chance, it scooped her into its arms and carried her into the hallway. 'More wine, Ophelia?' it asked.

Diego called out to the thing. 'W8r, come to the top of the line!'

The w8r did as it was told.

'Ophelia!' Liana cried, grabbing Ophelia's arms.

Ophelia heard Liana's voice as though she were shouting in the wind. In a wild and raging storm. But, in some strange and distant way, she could also sense what was happening around her.

'Ophelia!' Liana shouted again slapping her across the side of the face.

Ophelia felt her cheek sting.

Liana shouted again. 'Snap out of it, Ophelia!'

Ophelia gasped. 'Okay. I'm okay, Liana. I'm okay,' she said.

Shuffling down the hallway, Ophelia stepped on the heels of the person in front of her. She heard others bumping into each other and fumbling about in the dark. It seemed the w8r's shiny titanium body was the only source of light.

'Approaching the end of the hallway,' it called out. 'Please exercise caution.'

Ophelia heard more laser fire rip through the house, more ornaments being smashed and the thumping of heavy feet.

'They're inside!' she shouted.

'W8r, lead us up the stairs,' Diego commanded.

'Please count twenty steps as you ascend,' the w8r said.

When Ophelia counted twelve, she saw a sliver of mauve sky through a small window at the top of the stairs. Silhouetted were the heads of those in front of her.

'W8r, you go through the window first,' said Diego. 'And destroy those spiders!'

Ophelia saw the w8r hurl itself through the window and she heard it roll onto the rooftop. Then she heard it fire. There was a sound of something smacking the ground outside.

'He got one!' Diego shouted, excitedly. 'We can proceed now. With care.'

One by one, everyone followed the w8r's lead.

When it was Ophelia's turn to roll onto the rooftop, she heard a rattling sound on one of the external walls. 'They're climbing up here!' she shouted.

She pressed the back of her pendant, feeling the familiar vibration of the recording function, just as the second spider's fangs, glowing red with firepower, appeared above the line of the rooftop. The w8r fired directly into the centre of the fangs, blasting the thing to the ground. Everyone cheered. Ophelia turned her recording device toward Diego, who was standing behind a weapon. Fixed to the roof with a tripod, the weapon was almost as big as Diego. He kept his eyes on the aperture and his hands on the trigger.

'Be careful, darling,' said Liana softly.

Even faster than the one before, a third spider leapt onto the roof. Ophelia guessed it would have been almost two metres high. Its fangs glowed red as it prepared to fire, but Diego was faster. He swung around and blew the thing high into the sky. At the apex of its fall, it exploded, then fell to the ground in a ball of flames.

Sebastian, crouching beside Ophelia, rose to his knees. 'There's another one somewhere,' he said.

Ophelia saw Diego swivel the weapon from side to side, seeking the next opportunity to fire. But the fourth spider, so much faster than the ones before, leapt onto the roof and fired first. Diego's body vanished, instantly, leaving nothing but a splash of blood, just like one of his paintings, on the surface of the roof. Liana let out a scream so primal that rattled every bone in Ophelia's body. The w8r returned fire on the spider, ripping apart its gut and splaying it like a filleted fish before it landed on the roof.

In the silence that followed, Liana stepped over to the place that Diego had been standing, but there was nothing left of him for her to hold. Staring at the pool of blood, she started to shake. Ophelia wrapped her arms around her.

'Come on now, we can't stay here,' said Sebastian, guiding them both to the far side of the roof.

One by one, they all descended a set of external steps as the house started to burn from the inside.

The instant Liana's feet met the ground, she collapsed, sobbing. 'Leave me here,' she cried just as her house burst into flames. 'I can't go. I need to stay here.'

Sebastian and Ophelia lifted Liana to her feet and brought her to the nearest car. Ophelia helped Liana into the back seat, secured her safety belt, then slid in beside her. Clutching Liana's hand, Ophelia closed her eyes for a moment and silently prayed for help to get through the next moment. And the one after that.

When she opened her eyes, she saw Sebastian in the front seat. Zeska beside him, in the driver's seat, pounding the accelerator. The car lunged forward into the dust, following the others. When it reached the top of the driveway, Ophelia looked over her shoulder and watched the last wall of Liana's lovely home collapse under the flames. She rubbed her forehead, feeling something sticky. Then she examined her fingernails. They were caked with dried blood. Niccolò's blood.

• • • •

THE ONLY SOUND IN THE car was Liana's gentle sobbing. Sebastian stared ahead, intently, as if he was driving, but it was Zeska behind the wheel. Ophelia stared at the reflection of the woman's right eye in the rear-view mirror. 'I still can't believe what just happened,' she said.

Zeska glanced at Ophelia, as though only just noticing she was in the car. 'The police are under strict instructions to prevent any person, by any means necessary, from disrupting any of the formal trade arrangements,' she said. 'Obviously, someone tipped them off about the meeting at Liana's place.'

'Who would do that?' Ophelia asked. 'And why was the police response so vicious?'

'I intend to find out,' Zeska replied, pushing Sebastian's hand off her leg. She retrieved her disc from her pocket and handed it to him saying: 'Read this.'

Sebastian cleared his throat and read aloud. 'Police bots disrupted terrorist activity in a private home in the Montblanc area. Two arrests were made.'

'But, we're not terrorists!' Ophelia exclaimed.

'In the eyes of the law we are,' Sebastian replied.

'But no one was arrested!' Ophelia argued. 'In fact, two people were *killed*!'

Zeska flicked her long shiny hair off her shoulder and shrugged. It was a micro-expression, but it was enough for Ophelia to know that the death of two people, less than thirty minutes ago, had not made an impact on the woman.

But Ophelia persisted. 'Why are they lying?' she asked.

'It's all part of the corruption we live with,' said Sebastian. 'You're not used to it Ophelia, but it's how things work here. Everyone knows how to read between the lines.'

Incredulous, Ophelia threw herself back against the seat and stared out of the window.

'Any message from the station?' Zeska asked.

Sebastian scrolled through Zeska's disc. 'Just one, asking where you are,' he replied. 'Why do they want to know where you are? It's almost 20:00 hours! You're not supposed to be on call this evening, are you?'

'No, but they probably want me there to make a public statement,' Zeska replied.

Ophelia concluded that Zeska must have been a government official or a media liaison. That, she decided, would explain Zeska's composure in the face of the horror they had just survived.

'In that case, you'll have some explaining to do when you go back,' said Sebastian.

Zeska scoffed. 'You must be joking!' she said. 'I'm not going back there!'

Ophelia felt confused. One the one hand, it seemed that Zeska had been working with the police. But now she was fleeing with no intention of re-joining them.

'When were you going to share *that* piece of information with me?' Sebastian asked.

'Grow up,' Zeska groaned.

'But I'm your husband!' Sebastian shouted. 'You're obliged to discuss things with me!'

Liana started sobbing again.

'You know I can't discuss *everything* with you,' Zeska shouted. 'But I can tell you one thing. When they discover I was at that meeting, all hell will break loose. I'm on my own, now.'

'No, you're not, babe. You have me,' said Sebastian, returning his hand to her leg.

Ophelia had to ask. 'Exactly who are you, Zeska?'

Zeska glanced at her in the rear-view mirror. 'I'm the Tarragona Chief of Police,' she replied. 'At least, I was.'

That was not the response Ophelia had been expecting. 'Then why didn't you know the spider bot attack was about to happen?' she asked.

'I can't know everything!' Zeska snapped.

'Who does, then?' asked Ophelia.

'That's a ridiculous question,' Zeska snarled.

'But how will you find out if you don't go back there?' Ophelia asked.

Zeska looked incredulous then turned to Sebastian. 'I can't take much more of this,' she said.

Sebastian turned around to face Ophelia. 'I know this is confusing, Ophelia,' he said. 'But please understand, Zeska can't tell you everything. She can't even tell *me* everything and I'm her husband. She's in a tight spot. It's a complicated situation, so please, just trust her. Everything will work out.'

Ophelia tried, but she could not follow Sebastian's advice. She simply did not trust Zeska. Not even slightly. Niccolò had said, only moments before he died, that Zeska was not what she seemed. Already, his words had proven true.

Ophelia's heart started pounding. Her mouth became so dry, she felt her face might cave in. Her hands roamed around the inside of the car door, finding something that looked like a handle. She pulled it, but nothing happened. Then she saw something that looked like a button that might release the handle, so she pulled on that, too. It was unresponsive.

'The central locking is activated,' Zeska said, frowning. 'We're also travelling at one hundred and ten kilometres per hour. So, no, you're not getting out. Deal with it.'

But Ophelia could no longer follow a logical line of thought. She was having trouble breathing. She undid her safety belt and crawled toward her door, pushing it hard, desperate to get out, but it didn't budge. Somewhere, in the distance, she heard someone screaming then she realised it was her, inside her own mind.

Sebastian reached into the back seat and gently clasped Ophelia's leg. 'Ophelia, please, calm down,' he said. 'We're free now. It's okay.'

Ophelia heard Sebastian's words, but her mind replayed the sound of the bots' laser fire. She saw the kindness in Sebastian's face, but her mind replayed the sight of Niccolò lying on the floor in a pool of blood. She felt concern for Liana but more than that, she felt she could take no more.

• • • •

WHEN OPHELIA AND HER companions entered a roadside café, she headed straight for a coffee machine. But Sebastian intervened.

'Ophelia, please don't,' he said. 'Coffee is the last thing you need right now. Let me find you something better.'

Ophelia shuffled toward Liana, took her hand and brought her to a table.

Sebastian joined them, holding a small bottle of brandy and some clean glasses. He filled the first few centimetres of two glasses and handed them to Ophelia and Liana. 'Ladies, I recommend you knock this back fast, then wash it down with this,' he said, holding two small bottles of fruit juice.

Ophelia watched Liana do so and she did the same. Within seconds, she felt every muscle in her body start to relax. Her thoughts became vaguer and less terrifying.

Liana exhaled loudly, leaned back in her chair and stretched back her head.

Looking around at her companions, Ophelia noticed they all seemed to have been shocked into silence. Not one of them spoke. Zeska continued to scroll through her disc, furiously searching for something. Sebastian sat beside her, stroking her back. Alejandro's luscious brown toupee, which had resembled hair that Ophelia had assumed was his own, was now gone, leaving his bald head red and blistered. Marika was feeding him hot potato chips. Smoke wafted from the fibres of her coat. Liana's evening gown was damaged, several threads standing on end and other parts missing completely.

Finally, Ophelia looked at herself. The lovely green silk dress that Emilie had given her was no longer opalescent, but a deep shade of green. A sad green, Ophelia decided. The disc she had been carrying in the pocket was gone. But she took solace in the fact that her pendant was still intact.

'I'll be back in a moment,' she said.

Inside the ablution unit, Ophelia removed the wig from her head, then placed her head under the tap. The sonar started, so she massaged her scalp, face, neck and hands until all the blood and soot were gone. When she stood up and looked in the mirror again, she saw the same empty lifelessness as that of the pregnant woman on the train.

'But it *will* get better,' she said to the woman in the mirror, positioning her wig.

When she returned to the café, it was not difficult to find her entourage in the crowd. They looked like people who had just escaped a war zone.

OPHELIA FELT BETTER for having slept. 'Where are we?' she asked.

'Gare du Nord station,' Sebastian replied, parking the car.

Ophelia saw that Zeska was waking up too and that several of their entourage were parking their cars. Some were already outside, stretching under the pale light of early morning.

'How are you feeling?' Ophelia asked, stroking Liana's hand.

'Not bad, considering,' Zeska replied, getting out of the car.

As the door slammed shut, Liana shook her head. 'Zeska seems to think everything is about *her*.'

Ophelia laughed. 'She's an oddball, that's for sure,' she said. 'So, I repeat, how are *you* feeling?'

Liana shook her head. 'I can't believe it,' she replied, her eyes refilling with tears.

'I know,' Ophelia said. 'Let's get some air.'

As she stretched her arms toward the sky, Ophelia thought of Emilie and Philippe. A flurry of warm memories rushed through her mind – Philippe's coffee and chocolate delights, the sparkling conversation, Emilie's warmth, creativity and hugs, the fresh breeze flowing through the top floor of their apartment and the colour of the evening sky peeping through the vents in the bedroom ceiling – then she noticed the others looking at her.

'It's probably best if I go alone,' she said. 'I'll be back in about twenty minutes.'

'Take your time, Ophelia,' said Alejandro. 'The fresh air is most pleasant.'

Ophelia walked across the car park, through the hole in the strange fence and passed the familiar dishevelled houses. As she crossed the patch of barren dirt at the end of the cul-de-sac, she touched her flower pendant again, hoping again that it had made some useful recordings.

When she stepped toward the apartment building, she heard a loud crunch underneath her shoe. She lifted her foot and used the ragged pavement to scratch away some broken glass from the sole of her shoe. Then, as she brought her finger to the buzzer, she realised she was feeling uneasy. Something was wrong, she knew, but she had no idea what.

The weeds growing around the base of the building looked more obnoxious than usual, but they were not the cause of her discomfort. There was something else. She pressed the buzzer, but there was no answer. She waited a moment and then pressed the buzzer again but still, there was no answer. She placed her hand around one of the bars of the gate and pulled, but it was unmovable. Then she stepped back and looked up toward the top floor.

It took a moment for her mind to register what her eyes were seeing. A piece of antique furniture protruded from a broken window and a lace curtain flapping around the broken glass of another. She thought of calling out to Emilie, but her voice stayed in her throat.

Slowly, and reluctantly, Ophelia realised the apartment had been raided. Again. With a thumping heart, she imagined her worst fear – that Emilie and Philippe had been arrested and were being interrogated and possibly tortured. Furthermore, their research and intel could now be in the hands of the French Police. Someone might even be watching her now.

Without another thought, she walked, far more briskly than the heat would normally allow, back to the car park. One way or another, she told herself, she had to find refuge for her comrades. It would not be easy, given there were almost thirty of them, but there was one person she could turn to. Frederick.

• • • •

ZESKA'S VEHICLE WAS one of seven that stopped outside the Café Coquelicote. From the back seat, Ophelia watched her comrades assemble on the pavement. She felt confident they could present themselves as a party of happy diners while she found a way to speak with Frederick.

• • • •

ENTERING THE CAFÉ, she found it every bit as charming as she had remembered. Best of all, Frederick was there to greet her. While feigning a light-hearted greeting, he gave her a knowing glance, then he led her to a table. Zeska was the first to sit beside Ophelia, followed by Sebastian and a few others she still had not yet spent time with.

Ophelia noticed that everyone was starting to relax. As the food and wine flowed, they chatted like any group of happy diners. A holo-film of Coltrane and Hartman, only a few metres away from Ophelia's table, performed one of her favourite songs *Dedicated to you*. She recalled slow dancing to that song with Martin, on their first night together. His fascination with archaic music had struck her as strange at the time, but now it had a direct portal to her soul. Just like Martin.

Zeska and Sebastian were hunched over her disc, still searching, Ophelia assumed, for media reports about the attack on Liana's home.

'Anything new or interesting?' Ophelia asked.

'Not really,' Sebastian mumbled.

Ophelia excused herself for a trip to the toilette, catching Frederick's eye as she put her foot on the staircase. A moment later, she felt his presence behind her then she felt his hand on the small of her back.

He swept her aside, onto a small landing. 'Come with me,' he whispered, his eyes bulging with anticipation.

Ophelia followed him down a short hallway and then through a door. 'This is nice,' she said, looking at the brooms, mops and cleaning powders.

'Madame Ophelia!' Frederick said, his eyes still wide. 'I hoped you would come.'

Ophelia felt a wave of anxiety rising within her. 'I went to Emilie and Philippe's apartment,' she said, her eyes filling with tears. 'It was smashed up. They have been raided. Please tell me they're all right.'

'They're fine,' Frederick replied, clasping Ophelia's arms. 'They're here, in my basement, working on their materials.'

Ophelia flopped against the wall with such relief, she almost knocked her breath from her torso. 'Oh, thank God,' she said. 'I was so worried.'

Frederick smiled. 'It's okay, Ophelia.'

'But what do you mean by materials?' Ophelia asked.

'They are creating a short holo-film to release to the public,' Frederick replied. 'Through that Gaia machine thing in London, I believe.'

'Really?' Ophelia said, surprised, but not sure why.

Frederick nodded. 'Soon, I believe, they will transmit something incriminating.'

'God, I hope so,' Ophelia replied.

'Please, go back downstairs to your table,' Frederick said. 'Tell your friends to finish their meals in a casual manner. And when they are done, they should approach the basement. I will let them in.'

• • • •

THE FIRST THING OPHELIA noticed was that the basement was huge, reflecting the entire floor space of the café above. It was highly organised, like a hospital ward, with two long rows of bunk beds and an aisle down the middle. At the end of the room was a tiny desk which, Ophelia could tell, was occupied by Philippe.

'Ophelia!' Emile cried, stepping toward her.

'You have no idea how relieved I am to see you,' Ophelia said, wrapping her arms around Emilie. 'I saw your apartment. I've been worried sick!'

'Sorry you had to see that, Ophelia,' Emilie replied. 'But we were warned in time, so we collected our evidence and came here.'

'Thank goodness for informants,' Ophelia replied, smiling.

'Now, what have you got for me?' Emilie asked, removing the pendant from Ophelia's neck.

'I hope I've captured something useful,' Ophelia said. 'I must warn you though, the last twelve hours are horrific,' she added, her eyes burning.

Emilie took the pendant over to Philippe and Ophelia followed.

'Hi, Philippe,' she said.

'Madame Ophelia,' he said, not looking at her, immersed in whatever gadget he was playing with.

'He's barely slept during the past two days and I can't seem to convince him to take a break,' Emilie said. 'My darling, this is Ophelia's recording device,' she added, placing on the desk by Philipp's hand.

'Welcome,' Emilie called out to Ophelia's entourage.

In pairs, Ophelia noticed, they were slowly trickling into the basement. Ophelia watched Zeska mingle with the crowd, shuddering to think what the woman might be saying, asking or doing.

Alejandro stepped towards her. 'Hi, Ophelia,' he said.

Ophelia could not help but notice, for the second time, the terrible burns on the top of the man's head. 'Come with me,' she said, taking him by the hand. 'We're going to get your burns attended to.'

Taking Alejandro through the crowd, Ophelia finally found a familiar and caring face. 'Doctor Dubois,' she said, smiling.

The doctor's beautiful face lit up 'Ophelia! How wonderful to see you!' she replied. Then she saw Alejandro, standing awkwardly beside Ophelia. 'Oh dear. Please come with me.'

Ophelia watched Doctor Dubois take Alejandro to her bunk. She sat him down then started to work on his burns with one of her many devices.

Emilie approached. 'Isn't this wonderful, Ophelia?' she said. 'I never imagined we'd get sixty people to show up. And stay with us.'

Ophelia shrugged her shoulders. 'What can I say, Emilie? You and Philippe are deeply loved and respected,' she said. 'Not to mention the fact that your fine reputation precedes you.'

Emilie hugged Ophelia. 'You are too kind, my dear.'

Philippe approached, looking even more exhausted and sombre than before. 'Ophelia,' he said. 'I have just viewed the last recording on your pendant.'

Emilie looked at Ophelia then at Philippe. 'What it is?' she asked.

Philippe kept his eyes on Ophelia. 'My darling, I have just witnessed the nightmare departure that Ophelia and her friends have just had, from Montblanc.'

Emilie returned her gaze to Ophelia. She looked frightened, as she reached for Ophelia's arm. Ophelia felt her eyes prickle with tears then she shook her head, determined not to cry. Not again. 'What happened?' Emilie asked.

Ophelia cleared her throat, clearing away the tears. 'It seems someone tipped off the Tarragona Police about the meeting at Liana's house last night,' she said. 'Four spider bots, almost the size of the house, attacked the property, killing two people, Diego included. The house burned to the ground.'

Philippe shook his head and returned to his desk in the far corner.

Emilie, her hand over her mouth, muttered: 'Poor Liana. Where is she?'

Ophelia and Emilie wandered through the crowd until they found Liana. Sitting on one of the bunk beds, in a corner, Liana was sobbing into the end of her once-glamorous evening dress. Someone Ophelia did not know, was on their knees, in front of Liana, holding her hand. Ophelia and Emilie joined them, sitting on either side of Liana.

Emilie wrapped her arm around Liana's shoulder. 'Hi Liana,' she said. 'I'm Emilie.'

Liana looked into Emilie's kind eyes, nodded then continued crying.

'I'm so very sorry for your loss, Liana,' Emilie said. 'It's a shocking tragedy.'

Ophelia, exhausted from the emotional strain, sat back, comforted by the knowledge that Emilie was caring for Liana. Then she caught Doctor Moreau's eye and called her over with a curl of her hand.

The doctor arrived, her concerned eyes fixed upon Liana.

Ophelia surrendered her seat to the doctor, desperate to disengage from the grief. She had reached saturation point, she knew, so she wandered through the crowd. Her eyes scanned the room then rested on Zeska, chatting with Philippe. Zeska stood with her hands on her hips, her breasts thrust toward him and her forefinger twirling a strand of her hair. Philippe was barely looking at her, distracted by the disc in his hand. Zeska touched Philippe's arm, which got his attention, then she pointed at something on the wall behind him. When he turned around to look, Zeska brought her disc toward his, trying to press them together. But before their discs had made contact, Philippe had brought his disc up to his chest and slid it into his pocket. Zeska's body slumped in disappointment, like someone who had just messed up their shot on the snooker table. And that confirmed for Ophelia what already knew – Zeska was not to be trusted.

'Are you all right, Ophelia?' Emilie asked.

Ophelia looked around, seeing they were alone.

'Not really,' she replied. 'I feel we're in a bit of danger. That woman. Zeska, I'm sure, is trying to sabotage our work. I just saw ...'

'Relax,' said Emilie. 'We know that Zeska is the Tarragona Chief of Police. She's working undercover. For us. She's been in our network for almost a year.'

'Really?' Ophelia asked, incredulous. 'And do you trust her?'

'I think so,' Emilie replied.

'You think so?' Ophelia repeated. 'Is that enough?'

Emilie seemed offended.

'I'm sorry to be so blunt, Emilie,' Ophelia continued. 'But I just saw her trying to copy data from Philippe's disc. Without his consent.'

'Really?' Emilie asked. 'That's odd.'

Ophelia's gaze returned to Zeska, unsurprised to see that Zeska was already staring at her. The woman's stare was calm and confident, and it chilled her to the bone. She noticed Philippe was alone now, so she seized the opportunity and approached him.

'Ophelia,' he said, barely looking up from his disc.

'Philippe,' she whispered. 'We're in trouble!'

'Mm?'

'Philippe, do you know who Zeska is? I mean, do you *really* know?' Ophelia asked.

'Yes, Ophelia, I know,' Philippe replied. 'She's been helping us for a while.'

'Emilie told me,' Ophelia said. 'But Zeska might not be who you think she is.'

'I'm aware Zeska works in grey zones,' Philippe replied, his head down, still fiddling with his disc. 'But don't worry. I'll be careful.'

'I'm relieved to hear you say that because Emilie seems to think that Zeska is fully on our side.'

Philippe shook his head. 'Emilie has her doubts, too, but she's keeping them to herself for now,' he said. 'I suggest you do the same, Ophelia. After all, you catch more bees with honey than with vinegar.'

'I know, but I just saw Zeska trying to copy data from your disc to her own,' Ophelia insisted.

Philippe laid his disc down on the table and stretched. His grey hair and grey shirt blended into the grey wall behind him. Finally, he looked into Ophelia's eyes. 'I saw that too,' he said. 'Again, don't worry, Ophelia. I've already disabled Zeska's recording device. I've disabled everyone's devices. No one will be able to send or receive data from this location.'

'You look very tired, Philippe,' Ophelia said.

'I'm okay, Ophelia,' he replied. 'Now, please take a seat. We're about to begin.'

Philippe stood up, rolled his shoulders, then stepped into the centre of the room. 'Friends, please sit down,' he called out.

Within seconds, everyone was sitting on a bunk bed and looking at Philippe. As Ophelia gazed around the room, she realised that every bunk bed was now filled.

'Thank you,' said Philippe. 'You've all worked hard, and you've put yourselves at risk, just to be here today. I have no doubt of your commitment to unpicking the surrogacy trade. There's a lot of work to be done, in all areas of our lives, across the northern region and what's left of the southern region. We have some grave challenges ahead if we want to heal our planet and our lives.'

Applause broke out around the room, but it was quickly silenced when Philippe raised his forefinger to his pursed lips. 'We don't want the diners above us to hear us,' he said.

The basement was silent.

Philippe rubbed his forehead, clearly exhausted. 'Friends, you're aware we've been collecting recordings from the Garden of Eden,' he continued. 'Madame Ophelia has been instrumental in this.'

Several people looked at Ophelia, smiling and nodding.

'We've seen the devastation caused to the women and their families when they participate in the surrogacy trade,' Philippe continued. 'The trauma and the grief permeate every aspect of their lives, causing even more economic decay to those communities which, as we know, are already in deep poverty. This vile practice is one of many symptoms of the disgusting imbalance of power and resources between the northern region and the southern region. And the imbalance between the wealthy five percent of the human population and the remaining ninety-five percent. It is a vicious cycle inside a complex system in which we have all been locked, one way or another, for decades. But we're here tonight to plan our entry to the Garden of Eden, to rescue those women and to expose as much of that underground place as we possibly can.'

People around the room shook their fists in the air.

'From the recordings of the Garden of Eden and associated underground operations, we've made a three-minute holo-film which, we hope, portrays the full breadth of the horror of the surrogacy trade,' Philippe said. He nodded to someone at the back of the room. The lights went out, then a story unfolded through voice and images.

'DO YOU WANT TO HAVE A BABY?'

Image – a northern couple kissing.

'THE SOCIABLY RESPONSIBLE WAY.'

Image – a thin young girl, wearing raggedy clothes, wandering amidst a dry landscape, her hair unkempt and her face burnt from the sun.

'THE CLEAN WAY.'

Image – a row of unkempt young women with their knees up, being inseminated by nurse bots.

'THE NATURAL WAY.'

Image – a row of young women in the Birthing Suite, screaming, sweating, giving birth.

'THE LAWFUL WAY.'

Image – babies being taken out of the women's bodies and the women's outstretched arms being slapped down by nurses.

'IT'S ALWAYS FOR THE BEST.'
Image – surrogates laying back in bed crying.
'GAIA IS ALWAYS CARING FOR YOUR BEST INTERESTS.'

Image – Nina, exhausted, shocked, in pain, only minutes after giving birth, being stuffed into a hyperloop pod.

'ONCE YOU HAVE THAT BABY IN YOUR ARMS,'
Image – a northern couple smiling, holding their baby in their arms.
'YOU WILL KNOW IT WAS WORTH THE WAIT.'
Image – Nina, having a psychotic episode.
'YOU WILL ENJOY YOUR FAMILY FOR MANY YEARS TO COME.'

Image – a row of headstones, all with woman's names on them, and years of birth and death, showing an average life of twenty-three years. Empty water bottles litter the graveyard.

'OBEY THE RULES.'

Image of a nurse bot performing surgery on a female body.

'STAY ON THE RIGHT SIDE OF THE LAW.'

Image – a woman, being dragged, by her armpits, down a dark tunnel by two large men in white suits and masks.

'OR YOU MIGHT GET CANCER.'

Image – rows of jars filled with organs, in the Anatomy Lab.

The recording stopped, leaving the room in darkness. And silence. Ophelia was amazed by how quickly Philippe had integrated some of her recordings into the mix.

'That was incredibly powerful,' someone said as the lights flicked on again.

'Not to mention delightfully sardonic,' someone else said.

'It certainly makes an impact,' Ophelia added.

'Madame Ophelia,' said Philippe, pointing to Ophelia.

Another round of silent applause broke out.

'Friends, I'm glad you approve of the holo-film,' said Philippe. 'But we still have a long way to go, to make an impact. Before we discuss that, though, I'd like to suggest that we all take a break, resurface to the café for some lunch and a walk in the fresh air.'

• • • •

PHILIPPE STEPPED INTO the centre of the room and smiled at the crowd. 'Friends, thank you for returning. It's incredibly heartening to find that we have so many people willing and able to be here and committed to taking affirmative action. Does anyone have comments or questions about the holo-film we played before lunch?'

No one spoke.

'Okay then,' Philippe said. 'For maximum effect, we'll need to upload the recording to one of Gaia's peripheral processors in London.'

'About that, Philippe,' someone called out. 'Why can't we do that from here?'

'It will be transmitted more rapidly if we upload it from London,' Philippe replied. 'As we know, Gaia's interface is slightly different in every part of the world. From what I can gauge, it's more likely to transmit the holo-film widely, if it receives the upload from a processor close to its core.'

'But we don't know where the core is,' the same man called out. 'Do we?'

'That is true, Bertie. We don't know for sure,' Philippe replied. 'However, we're *reasonably* sure it's somewhere in London. Let me walk you through the plan I've constructed. Lights!'

The basement went dark for a second then a spotlight shone onto the wall behind Philippe. A holographic image appeared. 'This is the floorplan of the exit from the hyperloop,' Philippe said. 'For those of you who aren't aware, it's in Saint Pancras International Station, London. All traffic is scuttled *this* way, toward the security gates. We, however, will have permission to exit over *here*,' he said, pointing to a red arrow on the map.

It was a curious sensation for Ophelia to see Philippe's map. Despite the artificiality of the image, she knew it was accurate. So accurate, she almost felt sick.

'All authorised personnel go down this flight of stairs then through these security gates. To enter, we must be wearing the standard white suits and we must have our identity discs in our top pockets where the scanners can read them. We will also be wearing protective lenses in our eyes to disable the iris scanners from reading our true identities. This is especially important for Madame Ophelia who spent time underground before obtaining lenses from her rescuer.'

Martin the rescuer, Ophelia mused.

'Friends, I cannot emphasise enough,' Philippe continued. 'The surveillance down there is intense. So please, maintain a demeanour of boredom, as though you are commencing yet another day of work.'

'The suits, badges and lenses,' Emilie prompted.

'Ah yes,' said Philippe, I have enough suits, identification badges and lenses for everyone in this room,' he said. 'Emilie will show you where they are before you travel.'

Zeska stood up. 'Philippe, I understand we will leave in stages, rather than all of us leaving at once,' she said. 'May I ask, who will go first?'

'I will be the first,' Philippe replied. 'Accompanied by you and Madame Ophelia.'

Ophelia felt a cold chill creep up her spine. The thought of being so close to Zeska, on such a dangerous mission, set her on edge.

Philippe continued. 'Many of you here today are aware of Madame Zeska's police and military training,' he said. 'I will need her by my side while I negotiate Gaia's peripheral processor. And once our holo-film has been uploaded, I will need Madame Ophelia, given her familiarity with the Garden of Eden.'

Ophelia recalled the first time she had entered the Garden of Eden through the massive double doors, straight into the luscious open space. What a glorious and unexpected sight it had been. But this time, she knew, they would be entering through the service elevator that travelled down to the Garden of Eden and down to the Birthing Suite.

'Once the three of us are in the Garden of Eden,' said Philippe. 'We will blend in with the other staff. We will do whatever we're asked to do. And while we're waiting for everyone to be evacuated, we will learn what we can from their information systems.'

'What makes you so sure they will be evacuated?' someone call out.

Philippe nodded. 'I can't tell you that I'm one hundred percent sure they will be, Andre,' he said. 'There are no guarantees, but I'm very confident that's what will happen.'

'Why?' Andre asked.

'If the holo-film is transmitted as widely as I hope, there will be public outrage,' Philippe replied. 'The police and the media will have no choice but to investigate. And, given what I know of the RESS, I'm certain they will prefer to evacuate the underground than face media interrogation.'

'But, what if they don't evacuate?' Andre asked.

'If, after a twenty-four-hour period, the Sentinels and staff don't evacuate, we three will exit,' said Philippe. 'We'll travel back here and figure out what to do next.'

'So, Philippe, let's assume you're right,' said Andre. 'Let's assume those fascist filth do *foutre le camp*. What then?'

'Then, I'll send a message to Emilie, asking her and three others to travel to London and proceed to the Garden of Eden as soon as possible,' Philippe replied. 'About ten minutes after she leaves, another four of you should leave, and so on, until you all reach the Garden of Eden.'

'Will we wear the same disguise as you?' Doctor Dubois asked.

'Yes, Genevieve,' Philippe replied. 'You should all wear the suits and carry the identification discs in your top pockets. It's a sensible precaution, I believe.'

'What about the masks and the voice distortion?' the doctor asked. 'Do we need them, as well?'

'Ophelia, Zeska and I will need those things,' Philippe replied. 'However, by the time the rest of you enter, they won't be necessary. The entire security system should have collapsed by then.'

'But, how is that going to happen?' someone called out from the back of the room. It was Frederick, and he was walking toward Philippe. When he reached the end of the basement, he stood beside

Philippe and looked at him, with a seriousness and concern that made Ophelia's eyes prickle with tears. 'What if the security system does *not* collapse?' Frederick asked again.

For a moment, Philippe seemed thrown off balance, uncertain how to respond. Then he wrapped his arm around Frederick's shoulders and continued. 'Once you enter the Garden of Eden, your top priority must be the pregnant women,' he said.

Ophelia felt the sobriety around the room.

'We must attend to any woman who seems alone or vulnerable,' Philippe said. 'The surrogates will probably feel quite surprised by the sudden exit of the Sentinels and staff. So please, be calm and gentle when you speak with them. Just explain that the staff were ordered to evacuate and that you have arrived to ensure they are paid and escorted home. The lives of these women and babies are our primary concern. Do we all agree?'

Murmurs of agreement rippled around the basement.

Frederick looked at Philippe. They kissed. Then, with a sad smile, Frederick sat down.

A young man stood up. 'Philippe, I know we're probably not supposed to think like this,' he said. 'But, what if the surrogates really do not want to keep the babies? I mean, they are doing this for the money, not the love.'

'That's a very fair question, Marcus,' Philippe replied. 'We can't assume anything. Therefore, we must be prepared for any response they might have.'

'But, Philippe, what will happen to the babies?' Marcus asked.

'I confess, my friend, I don't have an answer for that,' Philippe said.

Someone else stood up. 'Philippe, I suspect the answer to that question might be related to my own question which is – what if some of those women are too heavily pregnant or unfit to travel for any other reason?'

'Thank you, Madame Sophie,' Philippe responded. 'These three ...' he said, pointing to three women sitting on the bunks near him.

The doctors stood up and smiled at the crowd.

'These three angels in human form are Doctors Dubois, Moreau and Durand,' said Philippe. 'They will examine every one of the surrogates. If they determine any woman to be unfit for travel, they will escort her to the surface and bring her to a hospital in London.'

Doctor Durand stepped forward. 'As much as possible, I will ensure that any baby born in London can remain with the surrogate, if that's what the surrogate chooses,' she said. 'However, I suspect all babies born in London hospitals will be automatically scanned and genetically matched with their biological parents. If that happens, we may have some negotiating to do.'

Suddenly, Ophelia felt they may as well have been talking about merchandise. The discussion, important as it was, was causing a crushing pain in her chest.

Doctor Durand continued. 'Conversely, any surrogate who *is* fit enough to travel will deliver her baby in her own town and then make her own decision,' she said.

'Thank you, doctor,' Philippe said. 'I should also point out, to everyone here today, that we intend to hack into the payment system in the Garden of Eden and pay the surrogates far more money than they are expecting to receive.'

Sophie stood up again. 'Are we expecting to accomplish anything else while we're down there?' she asked. 'Other than rescuing the women and babies, I mean.'

Philippe nodded. 'Yes, indeed, we will,' he replied. 'While the surrogates are being attended to, by all of you, Zeska and I will interrogate the information systems. We will download as much data, and incriminating evidence as possible, about the operations of the Garden of Eden.'

'So, is it just data then?' Sophia asked.

Philippe shook his head. 'Attached to everyone's suit will be a backpack. I suggest that everyone fills theirs with as much equipment, medication and associated supplies as possible and give it to your local hospital.'

Emilie stepped into the centre of the room. 'For those of you know your British history,' she said. 'You can think of yourselves as Robin Hood.'

Ophelia giggled, along with a few others, despite feeling awful about returning to the Garden of Eden. And, in the moments that followed, she felt a growing certainty that the plan was going to work. Because it had to.

London

NO MATTER HOW FREQUENTLY Martin looked at Kingpin's cell, he could not see the lad. All he could see was the remains of the chair, now smashed to pieces, that had been used to enable the hideous torture. He could only hope his young friend was in a dark corner, recovering, and that he had received some food and water.

Martin's mind wandered to Ophelia. Was she safe? Was she still with Emilie and Philippe? The sound of laughter and the memory of her silly facial expressions danced through his memory.

The glass door slid open.

'Jesus, what now,' Martin muttered.

A security bot placed a tray on the chair in the centre of the room.

Martin stood up, seeing there was food, and several bottles of water, on the tray.

'Will you also provide food to the man in the next cell?' he asked, motioning to the spot-lit area in Kingpin's cell.

'It has been done,' the bot replied.

'I didn't see that,' said Martin. 'Are you certain?'

'It has been done,' the bot repeated.

Martin watched, helpless, as the thing left his cell, then feasted on a cube of gelatinous substance. What it was, he had no idea. It had no discernible taste, texture or scent. It did, however, fill his belly, and for that, he was grateful.

• • • •

INSIDE THE HYPERLOOP, Philippe opened a backpack and retrieved three white suits. 'Ladies, please put these on over your clothes,' he said. 'You'll find the identification badge in the top pocket, the lenses in one side pocket and the mask in the other.

Ophelia donned the suit, keeping her eyes on Zeska the entire time. 'Are you feeling optimistic about our mission, Zeska?' she asked.

Zeska looked at Ophelia as though Ophelia had just suggested they divert to the moon.

Ophelia decided to try again. 'What I meant to ask is – are you willing and able to protect Philippe?'

For a micro-second, Zeska's eyes that said *no way*, but she was quick to recover her composure. 'Of course, Ophelia,' she replied, her voice like honey. 'Why would you ask such a thing?'

Ophelia opened her mouth, ready to ask another question, then thought better of it. There was no point winding Zeska up, and making herself look ridiculous in the process, she realised. It also occurred to her that she might learn more about Zeska's intentions by being a bit more circumspect, a notion that would not have entered her mind a week ago.

• • • •

'THIS IS IT,' PHILIPPE said, descending a narrow flight of stairs. 'Apply your masks now.'

Ophelia fixed the black mask to her face as she approached the security gates. The familiar turquoise light of Gaia's scanner zipped across her chest, reading the identification badge that rested in her top pocket.

As they walked, single file, along a dark and narrow hallway, Ophelia felt engulfed by the familiar fecundity of underground. She watched Zeska's hands hanging loosely by her sides and her arms swinging slightly to the rhythm of her confident stride.

Then a crackling sound came from Zeska's right hip.

'What was that?' Philippe whispered, turning sharply to face Zeska.

'I'm sorry, Philippe,' Zeska said. 'There must be some interference from my disc.'

'Turn it off, then,' he snapped.

Zeska placed her hand in her hip pocket. 'All done,' she said.

The hallway terminated at a steel door guarded by a security bot.

For a moment, Ophelia froze, recalling the spider bots in Spain. She forced herself to notice that the security bot emitted a soft turquoise light, unlike the red of the spider bots. She watched it grant access to Philippe and Zeska.

But it stopped her.

'Are you fit for duty?' it asked.

'Yes, of course,' Ophelia replied.

'I am reading elevated blood pressure and heart rate,' it said.

'I just drank a strong coffee,' Ophelia replied. 'It keeps my brain sharp long after my blood pressure and heart rate have returned to normal.'

The bot stepped aside.

Ophelia entered the maintenance hub, surprised by how small it was. Determined to stay out of Philippe's way and keep her eyes on Zeska, she leaned against the steel door, enjoying the sensation of the cold material against her back. The opposing wall, it seemed, was made from a large sheet of dark glass.

'I think that's the starting place,' Zeska said, pointing at it.

'Indeed it is,' Philippe replied, stepping towards it.

Then he waved his disc across its surface and it lit up, with a soft white glow.

'I didn't see that coming,' Ophelia whispered.

Philippe slid his hands over several parts of the glass, each movement causing a swirl of bright white light. He pinched at some of the swirls, causing them to rise from the surface of the glass, towards him, where he manipulated them further. Then, with a dramatic flick of his arm, he whipped the swirls of light into one large ball.

'Wow,' Zeska whispered.

For a moment the ball of light was coherent, expanding and contracting, ever so slightly, as though keeping itself floating in the air. Then suddenly, it exploded, like a collapsing star. The light disappeared completely, and the glass returned to its previous dull and lightless state.

'Oh, so what next?' Ophelia whispered.

The glass slid down into the floor, revealing a plain grey wall behind it. At its centre Ophelia could see a small steel door, about the size of Philippe's head.

'What are we supposed to do with that?' Zeska asked.

Philippe waved his disc across the door, but there was no reaction. 'There's no lock for a key,' he said. 'And no iris scanner.' He attempted to pull the steel door from the wall, but it was unmoveable. 'Hm, this is a puzzle,' he said.

But Ophelia could see the solution. 'You have to see it from this distance,' she said.

Philippe and Zeska approached her.

'See that?' Ophelia said, pointing to a thin grey circular line etched into the wall around the steel door.

'See what?' Zeska asked impatiently.

'That line,' Ophelia replied, pointing to it again.

'For God's sake, Ophelia, what are you pointing at?' said Philippe.

'Perhaps it's my imagination,' Ophelia said. 'But I can see, ever so faintly, a thin grey circle around the door.'

'It *is* your imagination,' Zeska snapped.

Ophelia approached the wall. She placed her hands on the tiny steel door, pressed it into the wall, then turned it clockwise. She spun the door a few more times, then it fell from the wall into her hands.

'Ophelia, you're a genius!' Philippe said, hugging her.

'What's that?' Ophelia asked, pointing at a white console on the wall.

At its centre was a small black hole.

'That's the data entry point,' Philippe replied, retrieving his disc from his pocket. 'This is where we upload the recording,' he said.

As Philippe brought his disc toward the data entry point, Ophelia's heart raced with excitement. She glanced at Zeska and saw that she, too, seemed excited. Or nervous. Or angry. She wasn't sure. 'It's okay, Zeska,' she said.

But, suddenly, and with lightning speed, Zeska pushed Philippe aside. He fell to the floor, releasing a heart-breaking gasp of dismay.

'What did you do?' Ophelia shouted.

Philippe scrambled up, but only made it to his knees, before Zeska pressed her disc against his throat and he collapsed, unconscious. Ophelia leapt towards Zeska, gripped her long ponytail and pulled it hard. 'I swear to God, I'll kill you,' she hissed, watching the woman's veins bulging from her throat. 'Give me that disc!'

Zeska clutched her disc and swung her arm away, out of Ophelia's reach. Then she tried elbowing Ophelia in the stomach, but Ophelia's tiny frame helped her avoid the contact. Zeska lost her balance, twisted her leg and fell. Ophelia grabbed at Zeska's hand, trying to pry the disc from it, but Zeska's grip was so fierce that Ophelia went down with her. Zeska punched Ophelia in the side of the neck, causing her to collapse on her back, gasping for air. Then Zeska leapt on top of her, knees on either side of her body and her hands gripping her throat.

'Sissy ... little ... bitch,' Zeska said through clenched teeth, shaking Ophelia's neck.

Struggling for breath, and with her arms pinned below Zeska's knees, Ophelia could do no more than lift her knee and ram it into Zeska's backside. Zeska screamed in pain and loosened her grip on Ophelia's throat. With one forceful exhalation, Ophelia pushed Zeska aside and ripped the disc from her hand.

She stood up, pointing the disc at Zeska. 'Give it up, Zeska' she said.

'You don't even know how to use it,' Zeska scoffed.

'You have me there,' Ophelia replied. 'I've never used a disc as a weapon before. Clearly, that's your thing. But I'm inventive enough to give it a go. Let's see now. What does this button do?' she said, sliding a tiny button down the length of the disc.

A white laser beam shot through the air, narrowly missing Zeska's ear and burning a small hole in the wall.

The door opened and the security bot stepped in, occupying almost the entire hub. 'Weapons are not permitted,' it said. 'Surrender your weapon.'

Ophelia knew that if she surrendered the weapon, she would lose control of Zeska. And then, anything could happen. 'This weapon belongs to her,' Ophelia said, pointing at Zeska. 'She attacked me.'

'Assault is not permitted,' said the bot. 'You must come with me.'

'I didn't assault her!' Zeska shouted. 'She attacked me. And she took my disc.'

The bot looked at Ophelia again. Then it looked at Philippe, still sprawled across the floor but awake and coughing. 'Surrender your weapon,' it said.

Ophelia kept hold of the disc, pointing it at Zeska.

'This is your final warning,' said the bot. 'Surrender the weapon or I w ...'

The bot's knees buckled then it fell to the floor. Its turquoise light dimmed, then went out completely, leaving nothing but a pile of titanium and silicone on the floor.

Philippe looked up from his position on the floor.

'How the heck did you do that?' Ophelia asked.

Philippe coughed. 'I have a few extra features on my disc, too,' he replied.

'Are you able to get up?' Ophelia asked.

'No,' he whispered.

'You will be very sorry for this, Zeska,' said Ophelia.

'Ophelia,' Philippe croaked. 'Keep the disc pointed at Zeska, but step toward me.'

Ophelia did as he asked.

'Good,' he said. 'Now slowly crouch down and hand me the disc.'

Ophelia complied.

'Okay, now take my disc,' he said, handing it to Ophelia. 'Do you see the tiny white button on the bottom of it?'

'Yes.'

'Gently flick it to the right.'

Ophelia did so, and the disc beeped.

'Good. You've just released the protection,' said Philippe. 'If you look carefully, you will see a small hole at the bottom of the disc now.'

'I see it,' said Ophelia.

'Great,' he said. 'Please point that hole at the data entry point on the wall.'

Ophelia did so. 'Nothing's happ ... Oh!' she said. 'The disc is warming up!'

'That's okay,' Philippe replied. 'The temperature should stabilise now.'

'Yes, it seems to be,' Ophelia said.

'Good,' said Philippe. 'Now, slowly move the hole in the disc towards the data entry point.'

'There's a slight vibration in the disc now,' Ophelia said.

'That's right,' Philippe reassured her. 'Keep moving the hole toward the data entry point, until ...'

'Hey! There's a stream of white light wafting out of the disc!' Ophelia said.

'That's it, Ophelia, you've done it,' Philippe said. 'Just hold your position like that until all the light leaves the disc and moves into the data entry point.'

'You two have no idea what you're doing!' Zeska snarled. 'You're into something so much bigger than your tiny minds can comprehend.'

Ophelia heard a sudden movement behind her. She was not sure which she heard first – the laser fire or Zeska screaming. 'Are you okay, Philippe?' Ophelia called out.

'Yes, thanks,' Philippe replied. 'But I had to shoot Zeska.'

'I'm not surprised.'

Still holding the warm vibrating disc to the data entry point, Ophelia was starting to feel the strain in her hands, wrists and arms. The precision required to hold the posture with exhausting her, so she was relieved when there was no more light emerging from the disc.

'I think it's finished,' she called out to Philippe.

'You can stop now, Ophelia,' Philippe replied. 'Well done.'

Ophelia released a loud sigh, rolled her shoulders and stretched. Then she stepped toward Philippe and lay beside him, her arms and legs splayed across the floor.

'You're a pair of fools,' said Zeska, standing up. 'There will be consequences that you can barely imagine.'

Ophelia lifted her head to look at Zeska, noticing blood seeping from the woman's shoulder.

Philippe returned Zeska's disc to Ophelia. 'Keep this pointed at Zeska while I try to get my body working again,' he said, rising to his knees. He stood up, took a step forward, then fell against the wall. 'What exactly did you hit me with, Zeska?' he asked.

Zeska shrugged her shoulders.

'Why did you do this, Zeska?' Ophelia asked.

Zeska scoffed and shook her head.

Ophelia stood up, reaching towards Philippe.

'I'm okay now,' he said. 'It's time to go underground.' He retrieved a small pellet from his pocket. 'The distortion chemical,' he said, placing it under his tongue. 'Open your mouth, Ophelia.'

Ophelia took the pellet under her tongue and felt the familiar tingling in the bottom of her mouth and throat as it worked its magic. 'Start walking, Zeska,' she said, feeling the power of her distorted voice.

. . . .

AS THE ELEVATOR DESCENDED, Ophelia felt the oppressive humidity of the underground. She noticed Zeska was breathing rapidly, panting almost. She pulled the mask from Zeska's face, seeing that her entire head and neck were dripping with sweat. The sight of the woman's suffering reminded Ophelia what it had felt like the first time she had descended and then it occurred to her – the last time she descended it was *she* who was held captive.

When the elevator door opened, Ophelia was surprised she could recognise her surroundings. During her last visit, the tunnels had all looked the same and the entire experience had been overwhelming. She had felt like a mouse being chased through a maze. But this time she felt like a spectator.

'This map is amazing,' said Philippe, staring at his disc.

'Please lead us to the nearest black cross,' Ophelia said. 'It will be a prison cell.'

'Right.'

Ophelia gazed at Zeska. 'Don't worry, Zeska,' she said. 'The cells down here are quite comfortable.'

'You should know,' Zeska snarled.

'You can have a long think about what you've done,' Ophelia said. 'And while you're doing that, we will be briefing your husband and friends on what you did.'

Zeska looked sour then shook her head in dismay. 'You have no idea what you're doing,' she said. 'You'll never get away with it.'

Still staring at the disc, Philippe said 'It should be here.'

'Okay,' Ophelia replied. 'Point your disc at the wall.'

Phillipe did so and a door appeared then slid open. 'Amazing!' he said.

'After you, my friend,' said Ophelia.

About one hundred metres in, the tunnel terminated at a large glass wall. On the far side of the wall, the room was completely dark, except for the one dim light that shone from the centre of the ceiling.

'This is it,' Ophelia said. 'Now press your disc against this gel pad.'

Philippe did as Ophelia instructed then a portion of the glass door separated from the rest of the wall. When it slid aside, Ophelia motioned for Zeska to enter the cell.

Zeska hesitated.

'This is not optional,' Ophelia said. 'Get in or I'll zap a hole in your other shoulder.'

Zeska stepped into the dank space.

'Make yourself at home, Zeska Hernandez, big shot Tarragona Chief of Police,' she said. 'We'll send a medibot to clean your wound, and provide you with food and water, which is more than you'd do for us if our situations were reversed.'

Ophelia watched Zeska shuffle towards the grubby bunk on the far side of the cell and, when she sat down, Ophelia returned to the door.

A deep, but soft, voice interrupted her. 'Ophelia?' it said. 'Ophelia?'

Ophelia spun around, ready to defend herself. But there was no one. 'Who said that?' she called.

Someone stepped out of the darkness. 'Ophelia,' he said.

Ophelia looked at the man. His clothes were torn and grimy and his hair was thick with dirt. He was unsteady on his feet. But it was Martin. 'Martin!' she cried. 'Oh, my God! I can't believe it! Martin!'

Kissing as many parts of his face as she could access, Ophelia felt all the worry and the yearning from the last week give way to relief and joy. She sobbed one deep heave after another.

Martin did the same. 'I was so worried about you,' he said, stroking Ophelia's arms and back.

Ophelia kissed his throat. 'Your voice, my darling. It's returned to normal,' she said.

'Yes, the distortion chemical has worn off,' Martin replied.

'It's *so* lovely to hear your voice after all these years,' Ophelia said. 'And to see your handsome face again,' she added, holding his face in her hands.

They embraced again, burying their faces in each other's necks.

'Philippe!' Ophelia called out. 'Meet my Martin!'

The two men shook hands then embraced.

'I'm so thirsty,' Martin said, taking a bottle of water from Philippe's backpack. He drank like a man who had been wandering through a desert for a year. Then he pointed to Kingpin's cell. 'There's another cell,' he said.

Ophelia noticed the spotlight in the distance. 'Yes, my love. I see,' she said.

'My friend is in there,' he said.

'I know how to get us in there,' Philippe said, staring at his disc.

Still clutching each other, Ophelia and Martin followed the Frenchman back into the tunnel and through another door. They approached another glass wall identical to the one they had just imprisoned Zeska behind.

'These cells seem to be set up like a beehive,' Ophelia said.

'Sort of,' said Martin. 'The angles optimise the live feed from the cameras.'

'Really?' said Philippe. 'I'd quite like to access those recordings.'

'You'll see some foul behaviour,' Martin said, stepping into Kingpin's cell. 'Kingpin,' he called out.

There was no response.

Ophelia's eyes scoured the cell, looking into the darkest places but seeing nothing.

'Kingpin, mate, I'm here to help you,' Martin called out. 'I'm so sorry. For everything. Please, mate, step forward. We need to get out of here.'

Still, there was no response.

Martin stepped further into the darkness. 'King ...'

A man stepped into the light and swiftly punched Martin to the floor.

Ophelia leapt to Martin's defence, but Philippe stopped her.

Martin stood up, rubbing his jaw. 'I understand why you did that, mate,' he said. 'But believe me, I'm in bad shape too. Please, come with us. We're free now.'

The young man studied Martin's face, as though unable to believe him.

Ophelia looked at the young man, seeing the hurt in his tiny eyes. Like two black holes in space, they sucked the life out of the room. Even more bruised and filthy than Martin, the mounds of flesh that hung from the lad's torso seemed to have been pinched and torn. Ophelia could barely imagine what he must have suffered at the hands of the Sentinels.

'Young man, we're here to help,' said Philippe.

'Come on, mate,' said Martin. 'I'm serious. We're free.'

'My name is Walter,' said the young man.

Martin's voice croaked with relief. 'And I'm Martin,' he said, extending his hand.

But Walter did not move. He did not even accept Martin's hand. He just stood there, almost swaying on the spot. Ophelia stepped forward, keen to get Walter moving, but Philippe stopped her again.

'Walter,' he said. 'I know what it's like to survive prison. You're having trouble believing we are here to help you. But please, believe us, we are.'

Martin took a step toward Walter. But the young man stepped back.

'Walter,' Philippe continued. 'Those bastards who hurt you are soon to be driven out into the light for the entire world to see,' he said.

Walter looked at Philippe, trying to comprehend what Philippe was saying.

'Walter, you didn't deserve any of this,' Philippe continued. 'But the nightmare ends now. Ophelia and I have uploaded some evidence to Gaia, and we expect it will soon be transmitted live to the public.'

Martin looked at Philippe. 'That's what we were trying to do when we were arrested,' he said.

Walter's fingers bent like claws and pulled at his short hair. Then he dropped his head and stepped towards the door. Martin followed him into the tunnel.

Ophelia linked her arm through Philippe's. 'How about you navigate us to the nearest shower?' she whispered.

• • • •

ONCE INSIDE THE SHOWER block, Philippe retrieved suits and identification discs for Martin and Walter.

'What about our masks?' Walter asked.

'Good point,' Philippe replied, sitting on the bench. He scratched his head, as though trying to extract a solution to the problem. 'I'm guessing you two might have to hide in a sleep pod until it's safe for you to walk around without masks,' he said.

Walter walked to the shower chamber down the far end of the room.

Martin and Ophelia stepped into another. When she removed Martin's clothes, she saw his entire torso was covered in bruises.

'Oh, my darling,' she cried, feeling her lips quiver with grief, despite the mask across her face.

'I'm fine, love,' Martin replied. 'Honestly, Ophelia, don't worry.'

Ophelia gently rubbed every millimetre of Martin's skin and hair until every dot of grime had disappeared. 'Now, *there's* the man I have known and loved for so long,' she said, holding his face in her hands again.

Martin smiled sadly. 'I feel terrible,' he whispered. 'Walter is severely traumatised and it's all my fault.'

Ophelia shook her head. 'I'm sure it's *not* your fault, Martin,' she replied. 'You can't possibly take responsibility for the monstrous system down here.' But she could see, Martin was holding himself accountable. 'You really do have an over-developed sense of responsibility, my darling,' she said.

Martin looked at her, almost ready to agree with her. But not quite. Then the shower shut off. Ophelia watched him step out, his gloriously muscular frame moving under the light. For a moment she felt a rush of lust, but that feeling soon gave way to distress when she saw him wincing as he lifted his arms. She could not take her eyes off the bruising all over his torso. Her instinct was to lean into him and fuss over him, but she restrained herself, aware it would irritate him.

Instead, she just watched him folding each of his manly limbs into his suit. And then the symmetry of their story occurred to her. 'Last time we were down here,' she said. 'It was you who rescued me.'

Martin looked her, smiled softly and then laughed. 'And I thank you for returning the favour, my love,' he whispered.

'You're exhausted, my darling, I can see it in every line of your face,' Ophelia said.

'Philippe!' she called out. 'The sleep pods are indicated on the map by ...'

'By the purple circles,' Philippe replied. 'Yes, I can see them. And, may I suggest we either find two pods close to each other, or a double pod? Is there any such thing, Martin?'

'Surprisingly, yes,' Martin replied. 'But not many. You can spot them by two purple circles interlinked. Kind of like ...'

'Found one!' Philippe replied.

'Then we have to move fast,' said Martin, detaching the backpack from his suit. He did the same for Walter's and handed it to him. 'We'll need to put these over our heads and walk between these two,' he said. 'I'm not getting arrested again!'

• • • •

WITHIN MINUTES, THEY had found a twin share sleep pod.

'Thank God!' said Walter, throwing himself onto the bunk.

'Two bottles of water,' Martin said to the sustenance bay. 'What shall we eat, mate?'

'Roast chicken, potatoes, vegetables, gravy and a litre of lager,' Walter called out.

'Make that two litres,' Martin added.

A large loaf of golden-brown substance appeared, surrounded by small parcels of a white substance and even smaller parcels of a green substance. As Walter pulled the loaf apart with his hands, Ophelia took pleasure in remembering that she had eaten a *real* chicken during her time in Spain. But now was not the time to gloat, she knew. She watched her beloved eat like a wild animal.

'Okay, we're going to leave you two now,' said Philippe. 'I suggest you stay here until 07:00 hours tomorrow. 'One of us will come back and get you.'

Ophelia kissed Martin goodbye through a puddle of gravy, then left with Philippe.

• • • •

DESPITE THEIR ENTRY into the Garden of Eden via the service elevator, Ophelia was still struck by the beauty of the place. The plants and flowers were just as vibrant as she remembered. The music, the water feature and the soft lighting were just as glorious. The six archways and the narrow cream hallways beneath them looked just as mysterious and enticing as they had last time. And the pregnant women looked just as happy and relaxed as before.

A Sentinel approached.

Ophelia handed her disc to him. 'Good morning, sir,' she said. 'We're here to do some maintenance on the sustenance bays.'

The Sentinel examined Ophelia's disc, and then Philippe's. 'It's unusual for two interns to be on a job without a fully qualified member of the maintenance team,' he said.

Ophelia nodded. 'Yes, sir. Our supervisor had to deal with an unexpected glitch in one of the maintenance hubs upstairs,' she replied. 'He asked us to get on with this job without him, but I understand he will join us soon.'

The Sentinel's disc beeped, and a yellow light flashed, visible through his pocket. He removed it and read the message. 'Fine,' he said, distracted. 'Off you go.'

Ophelia noticed the disbelief in Philippe's eyes as he took in a view of the Garden of Eden. 'It's lovely, isn't it?' she said.

'Even more lovely than your recordings suggested,' Philippe whispered.

'The sustenance bays are over here,' Ophelia said, nodding at a curved wall on the far side of the space.

Philippe ran his fingers around the inside of the bay. 'No controls here,' he whispered. 'I suspect they're behind this wall.'

Ophelia followed Philippe out of the space, under an archway and down one of the hallways until they arrived a small, but open, space. It was about the size of a single sleep pod, she mused, noticing the walls were covered in controls. Staring at the blue, yellow and green lights, randomly blinking, she was reminded of one of the walls in the cancer care centre. 'As above, so below,' she mumbled.

'Pardon?'

'Never mind,' Ophelia said. 'How do we make sense of this mess?'

'Well, I suspect w ...' Philippe started.

A Sentinel appeared at the entrance to the control room. 'Why are you two still here?' he asked.

'Sorry, sir' Ophelia replied. 'The controls behind the sustenance bay were a bit tricky today, but we m ...'

'That's not what I'm referring to,' the Sentinel interjected. 'A message was sent to all the computer engineers a few moments ago, instructing them to gather in the basement. 'Surely you received it,' he said, taking Ophelia's disc from her hand.

Terrified of what he might find on her disc, Ophelia felt her knees buckle.

'I can't believe it!' the Sentinel exclaimed, scrolling through her disc. 'Your supervisor should never have let you out of her sight without the comms system activated.' He swiped his fingers over Ophelia's device, then pinched the screen. 'There,' he said. 'Comms is activated. Now, get moving.'

'Yes, sir.'

• • • •

AS THE ELEVATOR DOOR closed, Ophelia felt she might vomit. 'I promised myself I would not go down to that Birthing Suite ever again,' she said, gripping the rail.

'I'm sorry, my friend, but it seems we have to,' Philippe replied. 'Unless, of course, there's something else in the basement. Is there?'

'I really have no idea,' Ophelia replied. 'My last journey down there was rather stressful.'

When the elevator door opened, Ophelia could see a Sentinel standing at the entrance of the Birthing Suite. 'That way,' he said, motioning to a door adjacent to the suite.

Ophelia and Philippe followed his instructions and soon found themselves entering a large room. She counted ten rows of white chairs arranged with precision, all occupied by staff dressed exactly as expected. The opposing wall seemed to be made from the same dark glass she had seen in the maintenance hub only a few hours earlier.

The door closed behind them and two security bots stepped in front of it.

'Our latecomers,' said a Super Sentinel at the front of the room. Also wearing a black mask, he appeared faceless in front of the dark glass. But the red armband, and the red stripes down the sides of the legs of his suit, were unmistakable. 'Surrender your discs to the bot behind you, then sit down,' he said.

Ophelia and Philippe did as they were instructed.

The Super Sentinel stepped behind a plinth and placed his hands upon it. 'Engineers,' he said. 'We have summoned you here to inform you of a very serious, Grade One, violation of our information systems.'

The staff shifted around in their chairs. Some mumbled words of discomfort, while others turned around, gauging the responses of their colleagues. To Ophelia's eyes, they all seemed nervous.

The Super Sentinel continued. 'Early this morning, at approximately 10:00 hours,' he said. 'Someone accessed the maintenance hub on the surface, near the primary access point for authorised personnel. They hacked through Gaia's external, and mid, layers of code and uploaded some malicious data which has been released to the public.'

Ophelia saw several staff put their head in their hands, seemingly frightened of what might happen next. Then she pressed her leg against Philippe's as if to say, 'that was us, we did that.'

The Super Sentinel stepped away from the plinth and walked, slowly and deliberately, between the rows of chairs. 'The technology used to hack through Gaia's code is not familiar to us,' he said. 'It is, however, of a similar level of sophistication to that used by the Sentinels. Therefore, all Sentinels with the computer engineering qualification have been confined to another location where they are being interrogated.'

Ophelia felt relief, sensing this new development would work in her favour.

The Super Sentinel spun around and stared into the eyes of a staff member sitting close to Ophelia. 'Whoever is found responsible for this heinous crime will be identified. And dealt with. It is therefore up to you, Engineering staff, to get Gaia's systems working again. Once the system is stable and secure, your discs will be returned to you.'

Ophelia noticed several people shift in their seats. Discs, she knew, were like DNA – no one wanted to work without them – and she was loath to imagine how the Super Sentinel would make sense of the data on hers and Philippe's discs.

'In the meantime,' the Super Sentinel continued. 'The bots will give you temporary discs containing the schematics and security access you are accustomed to. But that is all. You will make full use of them to correct any of the malfunctions you encounter today. No matter how small you think the adjustment might be, you will be helping, in some way, to get us back on track.'

Ophelia sensed the anxiety in the room.

The Super Sentinel paced between the chairs again. 'What's in it for me, you may ask?' he said. 'Well, it's simple. When the bots hand these temporary discs to you, they will scan your iris then imprint the pattern of your DNA into the disc before giving it to you.'

Ophelia panicked. And she felt Philippe do the same. What sense the bot would make of their DNA through the protective lenses, she could not imagine.

The Super Sentinel returned to the plinth at the front of the room and placed his hands upon it. 'Every action you take to restore Gaia's code, no matter how large or small, will work in your favour,' he said. 'Nothing only will you earn merit points, but you will reduce the likelihood of being taken to a private meeting with me and my friends at the back of the room,' he added, pointing to the bots.

Ophelia could not help but turn around and look at the bots guarding the exit. Both in excess of three hundred centimetres tall, and programmed to do whatever the Super Sentinel desires, were a menacing reminder of the powerlessness of people working in this underground place. They would have no choice but to comply with the instructions given to them.

'Dismissed,' said the Super Sentinel.

Standing beside Philippe, in the queue of staff exiting the meeting room, Ophelia was terrified of the impending iris scan. She had been through this before, she knew, but the last time was different. Last time, the bot had been scanning for a specific DNA pattern. This time, it was just scanning for a pattern, any pattern, to imprint on the temporary discs and store in its memory.

As the person in front of her looked into the bot's eyes, Ophelia felt her entire body spring to action, ready to run away. Then, when she stepped forward and tilted her head up, she felt her legs turn to jelly. Memories of Martin, her childhood home, the University of Oxford, her friends and the theatre raced through her mind at lightning speed. Her throat was dry and her heart was racing.

'Are you unwell?' the bot asked.

It took Ophelia a moment to process the question. 'Um, yes, I'm fine,' she replied.

The bot looked in her eyes again, its turquoise light flickering, then it looked down to its own hand. 'Here is your disc,' it said.

Ophelia took the disc and exited the meeting room, waiting for Philippe. She felt a pool of sweat under her hood and mask. When she saw Philippe exit the room, holding his new disc, the liquid poured down her neck and chest.

· · · ·

BY THE TIME THEY FOUND another maintenance hub, Ophelia felt ready to collapse. 'How the hell did we get away with that scan?' she said, sliding down to the floor as the door closed behind them.

'Simple,' Philippe replied. 'The iris scan was an empty threat. And a lie. There is no intention to award merit points to staff. Those bastards will do whatever they want to do.'

Ophelia gulped from her water bottle. 'I can't take too much more of this, Philippe,' she said.

'Not long now, my friend,' he replied.

Ophelia watched him approach the sheet of dark glass against the wall, just as he had done earlier in the day. He waved his disc across it then manipulated the stream of code just as dramatically as before.

But, this time, with the ball of white light between his hands, Philippe did something different. 'Ophelia,' he whispered. 'Please open the protection switch on my disc, as you did this morning.'

Ophelia slid button aside, revealing the familiar hole at the base of the disc. 'Done,' she said.

'Good. Now please position the hole in the disc close to this ball of light,' he said.

Ophelia's did so. To her astonishment, the ball of light morphed into one long thin stream then burrowed into the hole in the disc. 'That's incredible,' she said. 'But the disc is getting hot. Hotter than it did this morning.'

'Steady,' he said, holding what was left of the ball of light between his hands.

'The heat is awful,' Ophelia said. 'Surely we're supposed to be wearing special gloves while we do this. I don't think I .... Oh ... hang on ... it's cooling down. Yes. Oh, thank God.'

'Well done,' Philippe said, pushing the last particle of light into the disc. 'Now, seal the disc again.'

Ophelia slid the button back over the hole. The glass wall, now completely dark, slid down into the floor revealing the pale grey wall behind it and the small steel door. 'Déjà vu,' she said.

Philippe unscrewed the small steel door and placed it on the floor. Then he removed the button from the base of his disc and brought the hole at its base to the data entry point.

Ophelia had to ask. 'Philippe, why are you inserting Gaia's access codes back into it?'

Still holding the disc in front of the data entry point in the wall, Philippe replied. 'I intend to confuse Gaia so badly that, with a bit of luck, the entire system down here will fall to pieces.'

As the last particle of light disappeared into the data entry point, Ophelia could only hope Philippe was right.

'Okay,' he said, returning his disc to his pocket. 'We need to get out of here. Now.'

• • • •

OPHELIA FELT SOMETHING scratchy against her cheek. 'That's your leg beside my face,' she said. 'Go back to sleep.'

'No, Ophelia,' Philippe said, rolling off the bunk. 'We have to get up.'

Ophelia stretched out, flat on her back, enjoying the space.

'Ophelia, wake up!' Philippe repeated.

'Mm.'

'Come on, Ophelia,' he said, shaking her.

Ophelia woke enough to realise she was in a sleep pod with Philippe. Then she remembered. It was the only one they had been able to find the previous evening.

'What time is it?' she asked.

'Just after 04:00 hours.'

'Go back to sleep,' Ophelia snarled.

'We've received messages via the comms system,' Philippe said. 'They're telling us to evacuate.'

'That's interesting,' Ophelia replied, sitting up.

'Here,' said Philippe, handing her a cup of coffee.

Ophelia took the first gulp. 'Oh, that's good,' she said, feeling it rush through her body. Her disc bleeped. 'It says there's been a second security breach,' she said, smiling. Then her disc glowed again. 'Now it says the underground will be on emergency level power with limited access to systems and only the medibots will remain.'

Without warning, the door to the sleep pod slid open.

'That must be an automatic, emergency reaction,' Philippe said, lifting Ophelia off the bunk.

She jumped into her suit, threw on her mask and followed Philippe out of the sleep pod. The dim strip of light along the floor changed from its usual dull white to yellow and then red. They scuttled down the tunnel.

A Sentinel appeared, through a side door. 'Move it, sleepy heads,' he said, swinging his arm towards the elevator.

Ophelia followed the herd of staff. Just as she was about the step into the elevator, Philippe grabbed her wrist and pulled her from the crowd.

He took her around the back of the elevator and into a maintenance hub.

'God, not another one of these tiny rooms,' Ophelia groaned.

'I know,' Philippe whispered. 'Just be patient.'

'When they've all evacuated, we can make our way back up to the Garden of Eden,' Ophelia said. Then she slid down to the floor, curled onto her side and closed her eyes.

• • • •

BY THE TIME OPHELIA and Philippe entered the Garden of Eden, it was almost empty. There was no music. The water feature had stopped working, leaving a dark pool of still water in the concrete bowl. The lighting was much dimmer than usual and the once vibrant flowers were now grey and drooping.

A security bot lumbered toward them. 'You were instructed to evacuate,' it said.

Ophelia looked at Philippe, hoping he could deactivate the bot.

Philippe fiddled with his disc. 'Nope, I don't have the function,' he said.

The bot, now standing so close to them that Ophelia could only see its face by bending back and looking up, repeated itself. 'You were instructed to evacuate.'

'Hey, look at this,' said Ophelia, starting to dance the Charleston.

While the bot looked at Ophelia dancing, Philippe picked up a chair at threw it. He missed, but the bot went down anyway. A second later, it's lights expired.

Ophelia looked at Philippe. 'Could that be the final effect of the disruption you've caused to Gaia?' she asked.

'I certainly hope so,' Philippe replied. 'But the medibots should still be active,' he added, looking at his disc. Then he sat on one of the large swivel chairs and dropped his head into his hands. 'I'm so tired,' he groaned. 'And yet, there's still so much to do.'

Ophelia, just as exhausted, sat beside him, rested her head on his shoulder and closed her eyes. She felt herself relax. Deeply. So deeply, it took her a moment to understand that she could hear someone clapping. Loud and slow. She looked up.

Emerging from one of the archways was the Super Sentinel she and seen earlier that day. And one of the Sentinels. 'It truly is a pleasure to meet you both,' he said, striding towards Ophelia and Philippe with supreme confidence, and in no obvious hurry.

He sat down beside them. 'You two were the latecomers to the meeting this morning,' he said.

Ophelia could not speak. Or move. Or breathe. The second Sentinel stood beside her, staring at her.

'After you left, we had a good look at your discs,' the Super Sentinel continued. 'You may imagine our surprise when we realised they were not from this place.'

The Sentinel, standing even closer to Ophelia now, pulled the hood off her head and slid his finger down the back of her neck. Philippe watched, clenching his hands.

'Don't waste your energy defending the little slut,' said the Super Sentinel. 'You're going to need it later.' The man leaned back, crossed one leg over the other and placed his hands on his knee. 'I absolutely applaud your genius and your courage,' he said, looking at Philippe and then at Ophelia. 'So much, that it seems a shame to imprison you again, Ms. Alsop.'

Ophelia almost vomited when she heard the man speak her name. The Sentinel beside her curled his finger behind her ear.

'The clever Ms. Alsop,' said the Super Sentinel. 'You managed to escape imprisonment once. With the help of Mr. Huxley.'

Ophelia almost jumped when she heard Martin's name.

'Yes,' the Super Sentinel continued. 'We know about the romance between you and Mr. Huxley. He told us every dirty little detail. I admit he needed a bit of encouragement, be cracked in the end, and told us the story. And we rewarded him with faster death than the one we had planned for him.'

Ophelia felt rage burn through every cell in her body and her eyes filled with tears.

'Yes, I know it's very sad,' said the Super Sentinel. 'A clever girl like you should not be punished so harshly. But you have left us with no choice.' Then he looked to the Sentinel standing beside Ophelia. 'Please, dry her eyes,' he said.

The Sentinel, now stroking Ophelia's throat, curled his finger under her chin and pulled the mask from her face. Although this brought some relief, Ophelia felt naked, humiliated, as though her clothes had been removed. She wiped her tears away.

'Oh look, she's quite pretty,' said the Super Sentinel. 'Don't you think?' he asked of the Sentinel.

The Sentinel gazed at Ophelia, cocked his head to the side and then responded. 'Almost,' he said, returning his hand to Ophelia's neck.

Before she knew what she was doing, Ophelia had slapped the Sentinel's hand away and leapt out of her chair. The Sentinel lunged toward her, but tripped, on the backpack she had left on the floor. The man started to lift himself up, but Philippe slammed a chair down upon his head, rendering him unconscious. Then the Super Sentinel charged towards Philippe. Unable to watch, Ophelia crouched down, on the floor, with her eyes shut tight, clinging to the wall. But she could not block out the sickening sound of flesh pounding flesh, nor the grunts of exhaustion and hatred as Philippe and the Super Sentinel threw each other around the floor.

'Ophelia!' she heard.

She opened her eyes just in time to see Martin reach towards her.

'It's okay, Ophelia,' he said, wrapping his arms around her. 'You're safe.'

'Martin!' Walter called out.

Martin ran towards Walter and, together, they pulled the Super Sentinel off Philippe. Then Walter threw the Super Sentinel onto his back, sat on his belly, ripped the man's mask from his face and pounded it with his fists. Within seconds, the man's face became a ball of red mush.

'Okay, mate, that's enough,' Martin said, squeezing Walter's shoulder.

But Walter would not stop.

The Sentinel started to regain consciousness. Slowly, he pushed the chair off his head and started to rise. Philippe lunged towards him, grabbed him by the scruff of his neck and pulled him to his feet. Then he dragged the Sentinel to the stagnant pond and plunged the man's face into the water.

Ophelia watched, horrified, as the Sentinel's arms flayed around, trying to break free. 'Philippe, you're going to kill him!' she called out. 'Stop!'

But Philippe persisted.

'Martin, do something!' Ophelia called out.

But Martin was busy, trying to stop Walter from killing the Super Sentinel.

Ophelia pulled her disc from her pocket and opened the medical database, desperately trying to find something that would sedate the Sentinels – anything to stop her friends from murdering them – but all she managed to find was the medibot activation. A moment later, a medibot ambled into the reception lounge, its head swivelling from side-to-side, assessing the situation.

Ophelia ran towards the thing. 'Sedate the Sentinels,' she said.

The medibot lunged towards the Sentinel, whose head was still submerged in the pond, and pressed its fingertip into the side of the man's neck. A second later, the man fell to the floor, unconscious. And Philippe suddenly started to look like himself again.

'The other Sentinel,' Ophelia said, pointing to the man struggling to breathe under the weight of Walter's body.

The medibot leapt over the mound of chairs and pressed its finger into the side of the Super Sentinel's neck, ending the struggle instantly. But Walter kept punching.

'Seriously, mate, that's enough,' said Martin, pulling Walter away from the man.

But Walter refused to stop.

'Stop it, Walter!' Martin cried.

Walter pushed Martin aside and kept punching the Super Sentinel.

'Philippe! Help me!' Martin called out.

Philippe helped Martin to pull Walter away from the Super Sentinel.

In the silence that followed, Ophelia looked at the lounge, horrified by the mess. Several chairs were broken, others were upturned, the water from the pond was all over the floor and there was a splash of blood on the wall. And her friends were bloodied and dishevelled.

'Well,' Ophelia said. 'The women will be getting up soon. 'I think we can all agree that we don't want them seeing this mess.'

The men barely responded.

'Do we?' she asked.

They shook their heads.

Philippe scrambled to his feet then the other two did the same.

Ophelia looked at the medibot. 'Lift the Sentinels,' she said.

The bot lifted the men and held them, one under each arm.

Ophelia addressed the bot again. 'You are to follow three conscious men to a prison cell where you will deposit these Sentinels and remain with them and treat their injuries. Understood?'

'Understood,' the bot replied.

Then Ophelia looked at her friends. 'Agreed?' she said.

Philippe and Martin nodded.

'After that, I'd like to ...' Philippe started.

'I don't care,' Ophelia interjected. 'Just go,' she said. 'And make sure you all shower and straighten your clothing before you come back here.'

They looked at her, blinking and silent.

'Well?' she said. 'Off you go.'

• • • •

ALONE AND EXHAUSTED, Ophelia flipped the chairs back into their upright position then sat on one. In the silence that followed, she felt surreal, almost unable to believe the scene she had just witnessed. But she took comfort in the fact that the mission was almost over. Soon, she told herself, she would be free, as would her friends and the surrogates.

'Just hold on, a bit longer,' she whispered to herself.

She scrolled through the disc, exploring one menu after another, until she found the medical database. She tapped on the tiny blue cross and then it opened. Over two thousand surrogates' records. For, what seemed like a long time, Ophelia read through the records – one perfunctory entry after another – outlining the dates, times and details of each woman's insemination, pregnancy and delivery. In the entries from the Birthing Suite, were the details of all drugs administered – their dose, time of administration and effect – just as Ophelia had wondered. She had no idea how to interpret the data, but she knew that Doctor Dubois and her colleagues would. Furthermore, she knew she held in her hands, evidence of the full scope of the monstrous activity in the Garden of Eden.

• • • •

WHEN SHE HEARD THE elevator doors opening, Ophelia's instinct was to dart under one of the archways and hide. From there, she watched four women stepping into the reception lounge.

'Emilie!' she called out.

As she fell into her friend's embrace, Ophelia almost wept with relief. 'I take it you didn't have any trouble getting in?'

'None at all,' Emilie replied. 'All the gates were down. Just as Philippe said they would be. Where is he, by the way?'

'He's helping Martin and Walter scrounge for evidence,' Ophelia replied.

'Who's Walter?' Emilie asked, looking around, frowning.

'A friend of Martin's,' Ophelia replied. 'Sorry about the mess here. There was a bit of an accident.'

'Ophelia, you remember the doctors,' Emilie said, sitting down.

'Of course, doctors,' Ophelia said. 'Please join us.'

The three doctors sat down beside Ophelia and Emilie, clearly disconcerted by the mess.

'Where's Zeska?' Emilie asked.

Ophelia rolled her eyes. 'It's a bit of a story, too,' she replied. 'But, to cut it short, Zeska attacked Philippe in the maintenance hub, so we had to imprison her.'

Emilie looked upset.

'I shouldn't say *I told you so*, should I?' Ophelia said.

Emilie frowned. Again.

Ophelia looked at the doctors. 'Please,' she said. 'Permit me to transfer the medical database to your discs.'

Doctor Dubois scrolled through the new dataset on her disc. 'Oh, dear God,' she said. 'There are just over twenty thousand records in here.'

Ophelia nodded. 'I think you'll find a few more shocking details in here,' she said. 'We're going to need every bit of this data for evidence.'

'Indeed we are,' said Doctor Moreau,' reading from her disc.

Two surrogates shuffled into the lounge, sleepy and confused.

'Good morning,' said Emilie, her arms out, ready to hug them.

The young women recoiled from the hug but seemed pleasantly surprised to be looking at the women's bare, unmasked faces. 'What's going on?' one of them asked.

'We're doctors,' said Doctor Durand. 'We're here to make sure you're well enough to travel before our friends escort you home.'

The surrogates looked confused. 'Why do you want to escort us home?' another one asked.

'All Garden of Eden staff have gone,' Ophelia replied. 'There was a security problem and they were all evacuated. But we're here to help you. More of our friends are turning up soon to help escort all of you home.'

The surrogates looked uneasy.

'Please, don't be concerned,' Emilie replied. 'We'll ensure you're paid properly first.'

A few more surrogates shuffled in. 'What happened in here?' one of them asked.

Ophelia knew the woman was referring to the hideous mess. 'I'm sorry about this mess,' she said. 'There was an emergency evacuation and a bit of a kerfuffle along the way.'

'Why was there an emergency evacuation?' the woman asked. 'Is there something wrong?'

'No,' Ophelia replied.

Another dozen surrogates entered the lounge, all appearing confused. 'Where's breakfast?' one of them asked.

Ophelia's heart sank as she realised the sustenance bay probably would not work. Then she saw one of the women retrieve a meal from one. 'Ah, good,' she said. 'Part of the emergency back up.' She looked around, seeing there must have been about sixty women in the space, all looking bewildered by the disarray.

'Now might be a good time for an explanation,' Emilie whispered.

Ophelia stood on her chair, elevating herself above everyone else in the space. 'Good morning,' she said. 'Apologies again for the mess in here. There was an emergency evacuation. But you are safe. There are three doctors here who will examine you, to ensure you're fit to travel home,' she added, motioning to the doctors. 'But I will speak with you first, to confirm your family account details, and then transfer your payment to your accounts.'

The surrogates looked at each other.

'Please,' said Ophelia. 'May I have four women join me over here?'

Four of the surrogates sat in a circle with Ophelia. They stared at her, waiting.

'I'm Ophelia,' she said.

The women smiled politely and nodded.

'I know this is unexpected.'

'Um. Yeah,' one of the women responded.

'Okay,' Ophelia said, suddenly wondering where to start. 'This place, this Garden of Eden as they call it, has been making a lot of money from women like you.'

One of the women scoffed.

'I know you already know that,' Ophelia said. 'And I know you've chosen to be surrogates to bring money to your families. I also know you've been treated well in here, but what you don't know is that the surrogates are treated very badly once they reach the Birthing Suite.'

The women suddenly looked suspiciously at Ophelia.

'I was down there, only a few days ago,' Ophelia continued. 'I saw the way they treated my friend, Nina, when she was in labour, and after the baby was born. It was disgraceful. I would not wish that treatment on anyone.'

The women looked at each other.

'I remember Nina,' said the small one with the black hair.

Ophelia looked around, satisfied that more of her comrades had entered the lounge and were speaking with the surrogates. The doctors, she could tell, were especially busy.

'My friends and I are deeply concerned about the way the surrogates have been treated,' Ophelia explained. 'We've worked hard to shut this place down.'

'Well, you've done it,' one of the surrogates said, her mane of frizzy red hair enveloping her shoulders.

Ophelia felt it best to get to the part of the discussion the surrogates were most interested in. Their payment. 'You've been promised one hundred thousand euros for your service as a surrogate. Am I right?'

They all nodded.

'And a crate of water,' one of them said.

'I can't do anything about the crate of water,' Ophelia said. 'But I am going to pay you exactly what a northern couple would pay the Garden of Eden to manage the pregnancy and childbirth. One million euros.'

The women appeared doubtful.

'Please, may I start with you?' Ophelia asked the woman sitting to her left. 'What is your name?'

'Almira Anchari,' the woman replied.

Ophelia opened the woman's record and held it in front of her. 'Is this you?' she asked.

'Yes,' Almira replied softly.

'And this is your family account details?'

'Yes.'

'Fine,' said Ophelia. 'Please watch while I transfer one million euros to your account.'

Ophelia tapped on the payment system and made the transfer.

Almira blinked for a moment then gasped. 'She did it!' she said.

The other three women sat up straight.

'May I ask your name?' Ophelia asked the woman with the red hair.

'Zarina Galas,' she replied, almost giddy.

Ophelia found the woman's name in the register. 'Is this your family's account details?' she asked.

'Yes!'

Ophelia made the transfer while Zarina watched.

Zarina released a great and heaving sob of relief. 'Oh my God,' she said. 'That's so incredible. I can't believe it. Thank you, Ophelia. Thank you so much.'

'And may I ask your name?' Ophelia said to the woman with the scar on her face.

'Carla Andrez,' she replied.

'Okay, I found you,' said Ophelia. 'Can you confirm this is your family account details?'

'I don't have a family,' the woman replied.

'Well, your account details then,' Ophelia said.

'Yes, those are my account details,' Carla replied. 'And I appreciate the money. Honestly, I do. But I don't want this northern spawn. I mean, yuk! And I can barely care for myself!'

To Ophelia's ears, Carla's words seemed harsh. But she reminded herself – none of these women *had* to love the babies – the pregnancies were a matter of survival, nothing more. 'When are you due?' she asked.

'Another few weeks,' Carla replied.

'So, what do you want to do with the baby?'

'Give it to someone who cares,' Carla replied, slumping in her chair.

'That would be me,' said someone outside the circle.

'Liana!' Ophelia said. 'Please, sit with us.'

As Liana pulled a chair into the circle, Ophelia took a moment to look around the space. It was so full, she felt certain that most of her comrades had arrived, now. She could see them, in groups of two, three or four, speaking with the surrogates. And she knew some of them would be in the Birthing Suite taking whatever medication and equipment they could get their hands on.

Liana smiled at Carla. 'You can stay with me until you've had your baby,' she said. 'And then you can decide what you want to do.'

Carla appeared dumbfounded. Her eyes watered.

'But, Liana, what about your home?' Ophelia asked.

'I have a few more,' Liana replied, winking.

Ophelia looked at Carla again. 'Carla,' she said. 'Are these your account details?'

Carla nodded, a single tear rolling down her cheek.

'Okay, there it goes,' said Ophelia. 'One million euros.'

'Thank you,' said Carla, wiping the tears from her face.

'May I ask your name?' Ophelia asked the fourth woman in the group.

'Tamillia Sanchez,' she replied.

The name grabbed Ophelia's attention. 'That's a good Spanish name,' she said, smiling.

'Thanks,' said Tamillia. 'The Sanchez women have been around for a long time.'

Ophelia knew she was out of order, but she had to ask. 'Where in Spain are you from?' she asked.

'An old fishing village,' Tamillia replied softly. 'You wouldn't know it.'

'Try me,' Ophelia replied.

'El Serrallo,' said Tamillia.

'Oh yes, I've heard of it,' Ophelia replied, feeling Liana squeeze her shoulder.

'Will your parents be there to greet you when you return home?' Ophelia asked.

Tamillia seemed uncomfortable with the question, but she replied. 'I have a mother, that's all,' she replied. 'She's very busy with her work at the hospital, but I guess we'll have a nice meal together when I return. She'll be pleased to receive that money,' Tamillia added, looking at Ophelia's disc.

'Oh yes, of course,' Ophelia said. 'Are these the right account details?'

'Yes,' Tamillia replied.

With Tamillia watching, Ophelia made the transfer.

'Thanks, Ophelia,' Tamillia said.

'You're most welcome,' Ophelia replied. 'So, what kind of work does your mother do at the hospital?'

'She's a psychiatrist,' Tamillia replied. 'At Tarragona Hospital.'

And there it was – irrefutable evidence of the complexity in which Doctor Sanchez lived – and Ophelia could not help but pause to reflect. On the one hand, the doctor had seemed to be working herself into an early grave caring for the surrogates, aware of the inherent abuse in the surrogacy trade. But on the other hand, she had allowed her own daughter to become a surrogate. Nothing was what it seemed, she mused.

• • • •

OPHELIA LEANED BACK in the biggest, most comfortable chair, watching the last of the surrogates leave the Garden of Eden. Feeling satisfied, she stretched her entire torso and arms backward, enjoying the sensation of the blood and oxygen surging through her joints. Emilie sat down beside her.

'Is it my imagination or is it getting darker down here?' Ophelia asked.

'I think it is getting darker,' Emilie replied. 'We'll have to leave soon.'

'So, are all the surrogates accounted for now?' Ophelia asked.

'Yes!' Emilie replied with a loud sigh.

'That's good,' Ophelia said, leaning back in the chair again.

'It's just so bizarre, isn't it?' said Emilie. 'I mean, this part of the system is so opulent and yet the Birthing Suite is a hideous chamber of misery and disarray. I can't understand it.'

'I can,' Ophelia replied. 'It's like throwing away the shell once you have the pearl.'

'That's an awful metaphor,' said Emilie. 'But an accurate one.'

'Were any of the women too late in their pregnancy to travel home?' Ophelia asked.

'Five of them,' Emilie replied. 'Genevieve and the other doctors have escorted them to the surface, and they've been admitted to hospital.'

'I hope they didn't have any trouble getting through the security gates,' Ophelia said.

'No trouble at all,' Emilie replied. 'Genevieve has already returned once to collect someone's personal belongings then she returned to the hospital. She said the bots have all been deactivated and the human guards were overwhelmed with questions from the public, so there was no one to stop her.'

'How wonderful,' said Ophelia, swinging on the chair.

'All we have to do now is turn ourselves in,' said Emilie.

Ophelia suddenly felt she might fall off her chair. 'Turn ourselves in?' she stuttered.

'Yes,' Emilie replied. 'At least Philippe and I will do that. We don't want to run and hide anymore, Ophelia. We're getting too old for that. We'd much prefer to face the consequences of our actions and, with a bit of luck, we'll have some support from the public.'

Ophelia's heart sank. 'Where's Philippe now?' she asked.

'I believe he's still with Martin and Walter collecting as much evidence as they can get their hands on,' Emilie replied.

Ophelia looked down at her disc. 'There's still one hundred and thirteen million euros in this account,' she said. 'Do you think it would be okay if I transferred one million to Nina's family account?'

'By all means!' Emilie replied.

Ophelia found Nina's record then made the transfer. 'What shall we do with the rest of the money?' she asked.

'I think we should leave it in there,' Emilie replied. 'The government will consider it public funds, so we shouldn't go overboard.'

'The government?' Ophelia asked.

'Yes,' Emilie replied, frowning. 'Think about it, Ophelia. The Sentinels and their staff have evacuated. The recordings have gone public. The public will want answers, so the government will have no choice but to investigate. Thoroughly.'

Ophelia tried to access her pragmatism and logically predict the next steps, but her mind banged into one invisible wall after another. She had no vision of the future, not even the vaguest intuitive sense of it. The only thing she knew for sure was that she wanted to be with Martin. 'I hope our men don't do anything stupid,' she said.

Suddenly the lights went out. Completely.

. . . .

WHEN THE LIGHTS FLICKED on again, Ophelia saw the Garden of Eden's grand doors open. Martin entered first. Philippe trailed along beside him, absent-mindedly tinkering with a gadget in his hands. And then Walter entered, holding a piece of cord attached to Zeska's bound wrists.

'Oh, good heavens!' said Emilie.

Ophelia looked at Zeska's sour face. 'You're just in time Zeska,' she said. 'We're turning ourselves in.'

Zeska sat on the floor, leaving Walter no option but to sit beside her.

Martin greeted Ophelia with a kiss.

'Did you lot have something to do with the lights going out?' Ophelia asked him.

'Sorry about that,' Martin replied. 'But you'll thank us for it.'

Philippe sat beside Emilie, still tinkering with the gadget in his hands.

'Will you men please tell us what you've done?' Emilie asked, laughing.

Martin answered. 'We upload the entire recording from my lenses.'

'What?' Emilie asked.

'I've been wearing the same lenses that Ophelia wore during her time down here with me,' Martin replied. 'Over the last nine days, I've captured almost two hundred hours of recordings. So, in addition to the three-minute recording you guys uploaded earlier today, the people of Britain will see even more of the horrors of this place.'

'The people of the *entire northern hemisphere*, you mean,' Philippe interjected.

'Yes!' said Martin, slapping his leg.

Philippe cleared his throat, his eye still on the gadget. 'But our evidence is less than it should be,' she said.

'What do you mean by that?' Ophelia asked.

Philippe glanced at Martin, as though seeking permission to respond.

Martin took Ophelia's hand before speaking. 'In addition to the surrogates,' he said. 'There are places down here we wanted to investigate and, if necessary, release people from. But they're gone.'

'What people?' Ophelia asked, horrified.

Martin glanced at the floor for a moment before responding. 'There's a place called the Enhancement Suite,' he said. 'It's filled with gifted children, or perhaps children who have been given a gift. I'm not sure I could tell the difference.'

'What do you mean by gifted?' Emilie asked.

Martin' eyebrows lifted, almost to his hairline. 'They made physical objects disappear and then re-appear,' he replied.

'Are you sure that's what you saw?' Ophelia asked. 'Did they play a trick on you, perhaps?'

Martin frowned at Ophelia. 'No,' he said. 'They're breaking through the natural laws of science.'

'Why do you think they'd do that?' Emilie asked.

'They referred to those experiments as the future of humanity,' Walter replied, shifting around in his chair, loosening his grip on the rope.

'Jesus!' said Emilie.

'Are you *sure* the children weren't there?' Ophelia asked.

'Absolutely,' Martin replied. 'There was not a soul. And no sign of the equipment, the furniture or the lights they had down there. Nothing. It's as though the place never even existed,' he added, shaking his head. 'And none of the babies from the nursery were there either. Everything was gone.'

'If that's the case,' said Ophelia. 'They've probably packed away all those jars, and organs, from the Anatomy Lab. If that's at all possible.'

'It seems a logical conclusion,' Martin replied. 'Unless they know how to block off the tunnels between here and Oxford.'

Emilie let out a sigh of despair. 'Well, at least we have the video evidence of all those places,' she said. 'And thank goodness we transmitted it to the public before surrendering to the authorities.'

Philippe stood up, still holding the gadget in his hands. 'And this, my dear, will enable us to record our testimonials right here, right now, then remotely transmit them to Gaia,' he said. 'I'll speak first.'

· · · ·

AS THE ELEVATOR ASCENDED, Ophelia felt the pressure of silence. She and her four comrades and Zeska stared at the floor. It felt so awkward that Ophelia wanted to break the silence. But she could not think of anything to say.

'It's amazing how dramatically the air quality improves as we ascend,' said Emilie.

Ophelia smiled and nodded, trying to make herself feel better, but she was shaking. She clung to Martin's hand. Tight.

'You're hurting me,' he whispered, wrestling his hand free.

'Sorry, my darling.'

Ophelia looked at Zeska, still sour-faced and still tied to Walter. 'You're not happy, are you, Zeska?' she said. 'Never mind. I'm sure the prison cells on the surface are a bit more pleasant.'

· · · ·

WHEN THEY APPROACHED the security gates, Ophelia felt her gut churn, just as it had done a thousand times before. And when they reached the top of stairs, on the platform, facing the external gates, Ophelia knew something was wrong.

'Oh God,' said Emilie, pointing to the gates.

They were wide open, and the concourse was crammed full of people. There was no order, only chaos. The lines on the floor that had previously guided the public to walk in one direction or another were now invisible under hundreds of feet. And almost everyone was staring up at Gaia's holo-film.

Ophelia recognised the image immediately as the Anatomy Lab under the University of Oxford. The image scrambled for a second, then showed the inside of Martin's prison cell, then Walter's cell and

Walter being beaten by the Sentinels. The image scrambled again, then cut back to the Anatomy Lab and then to something she did not recognise. She blinked hard, trying to recognise and make sense of what she was seeing. It appeared to be eight or more tanks, filled with golden liquid and human organs.

'What's that?' she whispered. 'I don't recognise it. What's in there? Who recorded that bit?'

Martin did not respond.

'Martin, answer me,' she said, tugging at his sleeve.

Still, Martin did not respond.

'Answer me!' Ophelia demanded.

Martin pulled Ophelia in close to him, drawing her face into his shoulder. But she pulled away and returned her gaze to the image.

'I want to know what that was,' she said.

'I would also like to know what that was,' Emilie said.

'Me, too,' said Philippe. 'I haven't seen that recording before.'

Martin exhaled nervously. 'That particular recording,' he said. 'It was the inside of a room they call the Incubation Lab.'

'Wha ...'

Martin looked upset. 'Ophelia, I didn't want you to find out about it like this,' he said.

'Well, I have, so now you have to tell me,' she replied. 'You have to tell all of us because we all want to know. Except you, Walter. You already know what it is, don't you?'

Walter looked down, then nodded.

'Walter was with me when I found that place,' Martin replied. 'As I said, they call it the Incubation Lab. There were about eight tanks in there. Each one contained a human organ. A uterus. A pregnant uterus. And ...'

'Oh, God,' Ophelia said. 'I think I know what you're trying to tell me.'

Ophelia felt Emilie step beside her, placing her hand on her back, and she felt a bit stronger. Then her legs bent, and she fell. Martin grabbed her before she hit the ground and wrapped his arms around her. The others huddled around them.

'I'm so sorry, Ophelia,' Martin said. 'There's been no time to tell you.'

'They have my baby in there, don't they?' she said.

Hearing those words, even from her own mouth, Ophelia felt she was hearing them from another realm.

'Yes, my love,' he replied. 'I'm sorry, but they do.'

'God help us all,' said Emilie. 'Is there no end to this evil?'

'Is my baby alive?' Ophelia whispered.

'Yes,' Martin replied.

For a second, Ophelia felt a spark of joy. But the feeling was soon drowned by the flood of grief she'd been carrying for months, the awful sickness that came with feeling violated, and the horror of the image she had just seen. It was too much. She clung to Martin, afraid she might fall again.

'Here it is!' Philippe said.

Ophelia and her friends looked at the projection again, this time seeing their own faces, and hearing their own voices, as they freely admitted to releasing the recordings and freeing the women from the Garden of Eden. Each of them stated their own reason for their actions. Ophelia watched the recording of her own statement –

I am Ophelia Alsop. All my life I wanted to create a baby with the husband I loved, to carry it in my body and bring it into the world. It felt like the ultimate act of love. But that joy, that right, was taken from me, without my consent, by an evil and dishonest system; a system that has been lying to its people for decades. A system that has, at its core, no regard for human life and a profound lust for profit and control. Deep below the surface of Britain's land, there is a secret operation, acting outside of the laws of its own country. In that underground place, I saw thousands of human organs, all of which had been taken from innocent people for implant into the wealthy minority. I saw a place they call the Garden of Eden, where young women from the poorest southern region are inseminated with the cells of wealthy couples living in the northern region. These surrogates carry the babies until the moment of birth and then, like broken shells, they are thrown away. In pieces, they travel home to their families who have no way of understanding what their young women have endured. Many of the women develop a psychotic illness, some commit suicide and a few live on in silent hell. For their trauma, they are given a puny payment of one hundred thousand euros, even though northern couples pay one million euros for a surrogate. I believe the people of the world deserve to know the truth – the surrogacy trade is deadly, and the harvesting of human organs is an equally sick and unlawful practice. Yet both of those horrors are in progress every day, right under our noses, and they are presented to us as a normal part of life. But none of it is normal, nor is it natural. I have taken no pleasure in seeing or experiencing any of these things, but I take every responsibility for sharing them with the world. Please join me in putting an end to this vile and abusive system.

As she watched her face disappear from the projection and the other images return, Ophelia felt vindicated. She had spoken her truth for everyone to hear and now they were hearing it. She watched the reaction of the crowd. People were looking at each other, anxious and unsettled. She hoped that, in time, as the recordings had been digested by the people, they would bring about a change for the better.

A young woman broke free from the crowd and pointed at her. 'It's them!' she called out.

'Penny, come back,' a young man called out after her. 'They could be armed.'

Ophelia saw Philippe raise his hands, demonstrating that he was not armed.

A few other people scuttled over to them. 'Have you just surfaced now?' an elderly man asked.

Zeska tried to take advantage of the rising chaos by attempting to break free from Walter. But he remained steadfast, holding her rope even more tightly than before. 'Give it up, lady,' he said.

The crowd around Ophelia and her friends continued to grow.

A woman with glasses and frizzy hair stepped closer. 'You people are so brave,' she said.

Ophelia and her friends were soon surrounded by paparazzi, asking questions, their tiny recording devices strapped to their foreheads. 'An extraordinary breakthrough in the story ...' one of them started. Then she heard another. 'Here, live from Saint Pancras International, we meet the five people responsible for the astonishing recordings that ...' Then another. 'Only moments after the confessions were released, the five ...' And another. 'Witnesses report there is a sixth member of the group, but she seems to be restrained ... Can you tell us ...'

Ophelia and her friends were surrounded by the crowd. There was no room to move. Everyone was talking at once. There were so many questions, so many tiny lights flickering from Ophelia's face to her friend's faces and back again and a live holo-feed played in the air above them. Ophelia buried her face in Martin's chest, feeling his hands upon her back. Then she heard a loud crack. A cloud of white smoke descended upon them. After that, she knew nothing.

• • • •

WHEN OPHELIA WOKE, the first thing she realised was that she was lying on thick grey carpet. In a room with windows from floor to ceiling. Martin, Walter, Emilie and Philippe lay nearby, sleeping.

'Where are we?' she whispered.

She gazed out of the window. She could see the River Thames, full to overflowing. And she could see over the top of Lambeth

Palace, into its vibrant gardens. Beyond that, she could see the Imperial War Memorial upon which a holo-film played, acknowledging the lost southern hemisphere. Lambeth Bridge, tightly packed with people, seemed to be the starting place for a protest march, which continued all the way to the Palace of Westminster. Never had Ophelia seen so many people compressed into one place.

All the way to the horizon line, Ophelia could see that the entire city was covered by the great dome. Transparent, it revealed the soft pink sky of early evening. Then, from the corner of her eye, she saw movement.

Philippe had sat up. 'I suspect we might be in custody,' he said.

'Zeska's not here,' Ophelia said.

Philippe looked around then nodded.

Ophelia studied the room, noticing how comfortable it was. The carpet was clean and fresh. The windows were clean and new. There was a table and several chairs. Against one of the walls, there was a long bench covered with neat rows of cups, glasses, fresh sparkling water, fresh fruit and pastries. The smell of coffee brewing grabbed her attention.

As she filled a cup with coffee, she examined the wall behind the bench. 'I guess that's a one-way window,' she said. 'Whoever is on the other side can see us and I'm sure they can hear us, too. HELLOOOO!'

The door opened and a woman stepped into the room. 'Hello, Ms. Alsop,' she said.

Dressed in the kind of suit Ophelia had always wanted to own, the woman strode over to the table and sat down, resting her hands on her knees. 'I hope the coffee is to your liking?' she asked in a crisp, charming accent.

'It's lovely. Thank you,' Ophelia replied.

Emilie, Walter and Martin were waking, looking as confused as Ophelia had felt a few minutes earlier.

Four more well-dressed people entered the room. 'Please,' said one of the men. 'Join us.'

Ophelia and Martin sat together, holding hands. Walter, Emilie and Philippe sat on the opposite side of the table and the five strangers sat amongst them. As Ophelia looked at those five, she realised there were two women and three men, reflecting the genders of Ophelia and her group – a detail she did not know how to interpret.

The woman who had first entered the room spoke first. 'I'm Agent Sparks,' she said. 'You're in the INTERPOL building.'

Philippe nodded sagely.

'Please don't be concerned,' said Agent Sparks. 'We needed to get you out of the crowd so we could speak with you in private.'

'You dropped the bomb on the crowd,' said Emilie, as though waking from a dream.

'No, it wasn't a bomb,' Agent Sparks replied. 'It was sleeping gas. And, yes, we did do that. We've had agents all over the city since your first recording went live. I have to say, to all five of you, that was an extraordinary achievement.'

Ophelia and her friends remained silent.

'Please understand,' said the agent. 'We're deeply concerned by your allegations and by the evidence you seem to have produced to date.'

Ophelia fumbled around for her disc.

'My Alsop, we have confiscated your discs,' said Agent Sparks. 'And the discs of your comrades.'

Ophelia and her friends looked at each other.

But the agent continued. 'In a moment,' she said. 'We'll take each one of you aside, to interview you privately, then we'll all reconvene back here at 19:00 hours.' She nodded at her four colleagues who, in turn, motioned for one of Ophelia's friends to leave the room with them.

'Ms. Alsop,' said Agent Sparks. 'Please stay in here with me.'

Ophelia watched, sadly, as Martin left.

'May I get you anything else?' asked the agent.

Ophelia shook her head. 'No, thank you. I'm fine,' she replied.

Agent Sparks nodded at a camera on the far side of the room then looked at Ophelia. 'Please, Ms. Alsop, start at the beginning.'

• • • •

OPHELIA TOLD AGENT Sparks her entire story, from the moment she realised she was pregnant to the present moment. She remembered everything with perfect clarity. To her surprise, she felt no fear in telling it and no remorse over a single action she had taken.

• • • •

'THAT'S A TRULY REMARKABLE story,' said Agent Sparks. 'And it all happened in a very short time period.'

'Yes,' Ophelia sighed. 'I conceived on the third of February and it's now ... Um ... I guess it must be the twenty-fifth of May. Is that correct?'

The Agent nodded. 'And what year is it, Ms. Alsop?'

'2120,' Ophelia replied.

Agent Sparks nodded. 'Your baby must be sixteen weeks' gestation by now,' she said.

Ophelia felt her eyes fill with tears.

The agent brought a box of tissues to the table and placed them in front of Ophelia. 'I truly am very sorry for what you have suffered, Ms. Alsop,' she said. 'I can barely imagine how awful it must have been to endure that loss, and to then discover your baby is alive but still out of your reach.'

The agent's words poked through Ophelia's pain like a needle lancing a boil. But at least, Ophelia mused, she saw the pain for what it was and did not attempt to diminish it.

Then Agent Sparks leaned back. 'What action, if any, do you wish to take, Ms. Alsop?' she asked.

Ophelia blew her nose and blinked hard, trying to answer the question. 'I have no idea,' she said. 'Martin and I need time to recover. We all do.'

'Of course,' the agent replied.

Ophelia inhaled deeply, feeling this should be when her sense of her future would be strongest. But no. She was only aware of feeling exhausted by the bizarre experience of the underground and her travels through two southern countries. There was only one thing she could think of – a pragmatic and necessary task – and she voiced it immediately. 'I should probably divorce Peter Green,' she said.

Agent Sparks bit her bottom lip. 'I'm afraid that won't be necessary,' she said. 'I'm sorry to inform you that, after you were abducted, Mr. Green was found dead in his apartment.'

'Oh no,' said Ophelia, burying her head in her hands.

'From the police report, it was obvious that there was no struggle,' said the agent. 'It seems he was shot dead whilst sleeping.'

'Who would do such a thing?' Ophelia asked.

'We're almost certain the culprit would have been associated with your abductors,' the agent replied. 'They probably wanted to ensure that no one would start looking for you.'

Ophelia had to ask. 'If INTERPOL is confident in drawing that conclusion then surely you've had some knowledge of that underground place. Am I right?'

Agent Sparks exhaled long and loud. 'We've had our suspicions for several years,' she replied. 'But we've never been able to collect any evidence, I'm afraid.'

'That's not surprising,' said Ophelia. 'By the time we got inside the Garden of Eden, only the women remained. And a few chairs and plants and a medibot. Everything else was gone. I simply can't imagine how they, whoever they are that control that place, could have possibly removed all their equipment and research materials so quickly. It just doesn't make any sense.'

'Are you referring to the Anatomy Laboratory, the Birthing Suite and the Garden of Eden?' the agent asked, looking at her notes.

'Yes, that's right,' Ophelia replied, suddenly feeling cold. 'Those three places I have seen, but I'm aware Martin and Walter have seen much more.'

Ophelia reflected, silently, on her unborn baby, once more. 'Do you think it's possible I might one day see my baby?' she asked.

Agent Sparks looked genuinely bereaved on Ophelia's behalf. 'Ms. Alsop, I'm in no position to make any promises to you,' she said. 'But I will say, we've committed significant resources to investigate that underground network. We have to, given the evidence you and your friends seem to have produced.'

Ophelia exhaled heavily. 'About that evidence,' she said. 'You've removed all of it, from out persons while we slept on your floor. Is that correct?'

Agent Sparks nodded.

'I feel a bit violated by that,' Ophelia said.

The agent took a moment to respond. 'Please understand, Ms. Alsop, the evidence your captured is in the public interest and therefore in INTERPOL's interest. It is most definitely our property now.'

For a moment, Ophelia was not exactly certain why she felt disturbed by the notion that INTERPOL had taken her evidence. 'Forgive me,' she said. 'I seem to have developed a few trust issues.'

Agent Sparks laughed gently. 'That's perfectly understandable after the things you've been through, Ms. Alsop,' she said. 'I do, however, need to inform you that our analysts are inspecting every bit of that evidence and, if they find anything to suggest it's been falsified, you and your friends will be in serious trouble.'

'What!' Ophelia shouted, getting to her feet.

'Please, Ms. Alsop, sit down,' said the agent. 'I'm not accusing you. I'm simply exercising my duty by informing you of the consequence of producing false or misleading evidence,' she added. 'Especially as you have released it to the public.'

'I understand,' Ophelia replied, smoothing the legs of her filthy white suit.

'On that basis, Ms. Alsop, I need to ask you to look into the camera and confirm that everything you have told me is true to the best of your knowledge and recollection.'

Ophelia looked at the camera. 'I absolutely confirmed my statement,' she said.

'All right, then,' said Agent Sparks, tapping the glass wall behind her.

The other agents returned to the room. Martin, Walter, Emilie and Philippe followed.

'Please, everyone, make yourselves comfortable,' said Agent Sparks. 'Just give me a moment with my colleagues.'

Ophelia watched the five agents leave the room then she looked at her friends. 'Is everyone okay?' she asked.

'Yes,' said Emilie and Philippe looking pleasantly surprised.

'Walter?' Ophelia asked.

The young man was looking at his hands, apparently deep in thought.

'We're all free to live normal lives now,' said Martin, massaging Ophelia's shoulders.

'Maybe,' said Philippe.

Everyone looked at him.

'I'm simply suggesting that we don't get too excited,' Philippe said. 'Our actions will not be without consequences. We're not completely free yet.'

The five agents entered the room again.

'Okay, everyone,' said Agent Sparks. 'We're aware you've been here for a while.'

Ophelia noticed, for the first time, that the sky was now dark. The light shining through the clock face on Elizabeth Tower looked like a celestial orb, the surrounding lights from London city paling in comparison.

'Just to wrap up,' said Agent Sparks. 'We've taken statements from each of you, and you've each confirmed your statements. Over the next few weeks, our analysts will review your statements, in conjunction with the evidence you've presented to us. That evidence, by your own words, is several visual recordings of activities underground including, but not limited to, the Garden of Eden, the Birthing Suite, the Anatomy Lab, the Incubation Lab, the Insemination Suite and the Enhancement Suite. You have also given us a database of over twenty thousand surrogates' medical records. Is all of this correct?'

Ophelia and her friends nodded.

'Have I missed anything?' Agent Sparks asked.

Ophelia and her friends glanced at each other and then shook their heads.

Agent Sparks leaned forward. 'Okay, so we'll get on with our analysis and we'll meet with each of you again in a few weeks,' said Agent Sparks. 'Do you have any questions?'

'I have one,' said Philippe.

'Yes, Mr. Trudeau.'

Philippe looked as if he was carefully framing his question. 'How much knowledge did INTERPOL have about the RESS before the evidence we have provided?'

The agent's face flushed. 'We've always known about the RESS,' she replied. 'They're an intrinsic component of the Ruling Elite and they have access to information that we don't have access to. However, we are not necessarily jumping to the conclusion that the RESS is responsible for the underground network we have been discussing here this evening.'

Philippe leaned back in his chair, processing the agent's response. 'You must be joking.'

'No, Mr. Trudeau,' I am not joking.' The agent replied. 'Nor am I joking when I tell you that there will be multiple trials in the Supreme Court, reviewing the evidence you have presented, so please be prepared to be subpoenaed, perhaps many times, during the next two years.'

'Interesting,' said Philippe. 'And may I ask what will happen to Zeska?'

Agent Sparks cleared her throat. 'Detective Hernandez has been charged with a range of crimes unrelated to her involvement with you. However, she will be subpoenaed to court, when you are, to give evidence about your upload of the recording to Gaia,' Agent Sparks replied.

Philippe and Emilie exchanged glances.

'So, we need you to remain in London for the next two years,' she said.

'But we have no home in London,' said Emilie.

'I understand, Ms. Trudeau,' replied Agent Sparks. 'I also understand, from your statement, that your home in Paris was destroyed, so you will be pleased to know that we have secured a home for all five of you. It's a very comfortable ten-bedroom house, with a beautiful garden, on the outskirts of the city. I promise you will be well cared for, but you will be under continuous surveillance. Visual and auditory.'

'So, we're under house arrest,' said Philippe. 'Is that what you're saying?'

'We prefer not to use that term,' the agent replied. 'But, yes. You'll be under house arrest for the next two years while we process the evidence through the formal justice system.'

'What about Gaia?' Ophelia asked. 'Does it still work?'

'Gaia's functionality was temporarily compromised by the volume of data you uploaded, and the way you executed the upload,' Agent Sparks replied. 'But it's still able to perform the basic tasks of navigation and food production.'

Ophelia breathed exhaled. 'We're okay for now, then,' she said.

The agent glanced at Martin and Walter. 'Mr. Huxley and Mr. Jones,' she said. 'You both signed the Official Secrets Act when you commenced your work underground.'

Martin and Walter nodded.

'Your actions would, ordinarily, be considered treason and you'd be imprisoned without bail while awaiting trial. However, given the insidious nature of that underground operation, the fact that it's been carried out without our knowledge, and the obvious torment that you've both suffered down there, we will not recognise your signature as binding.'

Ophelia squeezed Martin's hand.

'All right, then,' said Agent Sparks, standing up. 'It's almost 23:00 hours. We're all tired and it's time for you to settle into your new home.'

Ophelia stared at the five security guards entering the room. They seemed serious, but not menacing like the underground Sentinels had been.

She turned to Martin and wrapped her arms around him. 'We're in for a hell of a ride over the next two years,' she said.

Martin slid his hands around her waist. 'Perhaps,' he replied. 'But whatever the future holds my love, let's take comfort in the knowledge that we've done the right thing.'

Ophelia sighed. 'That *is* the silver lining around this cloud, isn't it?'

'I'm fairly sure there's another silver lining,' Martin replied, raising an eyebrow. 'And it starts when we enter our new bedroom tonight.'

'You're on!' said Ophelia.

About the Author

V.M. Andrews is an author of science fiction. She is also a visual artist and author of several books about creativity. Although fascinated by space exploration, she is constantly inspired by the wondrous life on our home planet, Earth.

Read more at vmandrews.com.